BOOKS BY JIM HAMMOND

THE PHOENIX SOCIETY

WINES OF ENCHANTMENT:
A GUIDE TO FINDING AND ENJOYING
THE WINES OF NEW MEXICO

THE BURREN WEEPS

JIM HAMMOND

GALWAY PUBLISHING CO.
Corrales, NM

Galway Publishing Co.
Copyright © 2020 by Jim Hammond

southwesternwineguy.com
jimhammondauthor.net

Library of Congress Cataloging-in-Publication Data
Names: Hammond, Jim
Title: The Burren Weeps / Jim Hammond
Description: Ireland, Bantry Bay, IRA, Inspector O'Neill,
romance, murder mystery, 20th century

ISBN: 9781507582077

Book design by Carolyn Flynn/The Story Catalyst

Printed in the United States of America

To Barbara, my rock, my support
And to Ireland and its people,
always welcoming, always close to my heart.

PROLOGUE

Detective Chief Inspector Brendan O'Neill disliked funerals. He'd seen too many die during the The Troubles and knew that each death lead to retribution and more killing. Then again, an Irish wake was a big production that required a large cast of friends and relatives. In Brendan's mind it went on for too long. Surely this was agony for a spouse, offspring or sibling? But this was his time to mourn. He was back in Belfast to lay his mother to rest. Once again, as with every visit before, painful memories assailed him.

When he had lived in the north, he had served in the Royal Ulster Constabulary. As a minority Catholic he had put up with the abuse from some of his Protestant RUC mates. However, he fought hard against the mindless violence that had swirled around Northern Ireland and spilled out into England and the Republic of Ireland. After the Good Friday Agreement in '98, violence had only gone to a simmer. The Troubles, as that time was euphemistically called, had been closer to horror at times.

The city certainly looked a lot cleaner and friendlier now. Looking down from his upper floor suite of the Fitzwilliam Hotel on Great Victoria Street he could watch all the activity down at street level. The Belfast Central District was alive with pedestrians and vehicles swarming from place to place. From his room, the sounds of traffic were almost nonexistent, as if someone had punched the mute button.

The luxury hotel was living up to its billing. His room was large and inviting. Contrasting shades of gold and pale green on the king bed and sofas were paired with an ebony vanity and large oval mirror. He turned from the window and stood in front of the mirror to check his appearance.

His dark blue three-piece suit stretched a bit tighter over his large frame, but the pale blue shirt and navy blue tie and matching handkerchief looked properly distinguished. Whenever he had the option of not wearing a white shirt he did, which was one of the reasons he did not wear his uniform. The other was just common-sense for a Detective Chief Superintendent of the Garda Síochána.

The Garda Síochána, or "guardians of the peace" in the Gaelic translation often had to work very hard to maintain that peace. This was even truer in Belfast when he'd finally left in 1980. Taking a friend's advice he moved to Cork, in the south of Ireland. There he made a new home, made lasting friendships, finally found a woman to share his life, and now headed the Cork Garda.

Knowing he could postpone the moment no longer, he sighed deeply before going out the door.

The funeral went better than he'd hoped, but meeting some of his old RUC buddies had unearthed memories he'd thought had moved far into the background. Now that he was back in his mother's home to deal with the paperwork and decide on what things to bring back to Cork, a deep melancholy overtook him. He regretted that his wife, Mary had not been able to come along.

The living room of the flat had quite a chill for April and he laid bricks of peat into the fireplace. The winking flame and rich smell of the peat teased his brain and in a rush he was back in the winter of '92, reliving the events of his greatest case in Cork and meeting the enigmatic Beth O'Hara.

CHAPTER 1

The living room had not changed except now it looked actively cared for and he could hear his mother clanging pots in the kitchen. He remembered that his mood on that long ago evening had been as dark as a Belfast night. The peat fire glowed feebly in the old stone fireplace and whiffs of smoke drifted up lazily. He conjured phantoms of the past in its swirling depths and knew of a sudden that he *was* back in that winter of '92.

He forced his gaze up. The light reflected dully off the unpolished copper pans hung in the fireplace's cavernous interior. In the center was a cast iron pot, once used to hold the delicious stews his Mum cooked. "With all me brood spread across God's earth, I have little need of it now." He remembered that she'd said that earlier in the evening when he'd looked down into its barren bottom. He felt his back relax as he sank lower into the rocker, his sigh deep. The chair's backrest slats stretched with him, providing a muted timpani accompaniment to the deep rumble of his chest.

"Did ya' hear what I said, son?"

He turned to his mother. She stood with her arms folded across her ample bosom, and seemed undressed without the wooden spoon she usually brandished in one large rawboned hand.

"What was that again, Mum?"

She unhitched her arms and pressed firmly on the bun twirled at the back of her head, as if to push the thought out again. "I said your old cronies over at the barracks were asking after you."

"Right."

"Important, they said. Dangerous business, I suspect."

He looked intently into her soft face. Her eyes, a steel blue, were unwavering, and seemed to see everything. Her lanky frame looked appropriate beside the huge fireplace. He might have inherited his barrel-chest and broad shoulders from his Da, but his long frame was her bit of the stew. As if acknowledging his unspoken thought, she stood up straighter, the pain of unbending visible in telltale twitches.

"That's what I thought. They couldn't give me one bloody day till they put out the word." He rose slowly from the rocker, rubbing his shoulders.

"Brendan!"

"Yes, Mum."

"Don't let 'em upset you so. They don't have any hold on ya now."

"It's not them that are callin' to me, love. It's a mother and child sufferin' a fiery death in a bombed-out car. It's a bunch of maniacs cloakin' death and destruction behind a patriot's flag. I can never rest while that's still going on."

"Yer soundin' like one of them now. I know where all that hate came from, but don't try that pious stuff on me. Yer not so big I can't box yer ears good still."

"I'm sorry, Mum." His voice dropped and he sheepishly stroked the stubble on his face and felt the heat of shame. "You, being in the middle of it here, have a lot more to rant about than us in the Republic." He dropped his hands to his sides and sighed. "It's just that every face that I see masked in death looks like the face of one of my own." He looked at her intently, aware of the catch in his throat. "Maybe they've become part of my family."

"Just so ye remember, 'tis you took on the job of being a policeman." She brandished a finger at him, but there was love for him in her flashing eyes. "And you not stopping yer own niece from joinin', for Mary's sake.

"I'll not fight with you, Mum." Even though he towered over her, he never felt less his six foot four. "I'll be looking out for her."

"You'd better. And her just a wee slip of a thing."

"We both want the same thing, love," he said in a conciliatory tone. "To see an end to it."

"An end to it." Her voice was a whisper now. The sorrow of a lost son and husband softened the steel in her jaw. Brendan knew she was trying to remember better times. Her sidelong glance seemed to be revisiting the past. Still she held back even the glisten of a tear. He knew she was the strongest of them all, and it made him proud and sad all at the same time.

Over the top of her head, he glanced out the barred window that fronted on Mill Street, and beyond it, Shankill Road. The smear of yellow street lights did little to soften the sight of shuttered houses and barricades. Two dirty-faced children were throwing rocks in the far alley. The clatter of stones on brick and the bark of a hungry dog marred the stillness.

"So yer going?"

He lowered his eyes to her again. "As you say, Mum, it's my job."

He snatched his cap off the table, while she handed him his overcoat. The warm embrace they exchanged would have to carry him through the rest of the night.

The old warehouse seemed to lean into the alleyway. Brendan wondered if the rusted fire escape was the only thing that kept it from tumbling down. A few scraps of paper stirred and circled in the chilly breeze. The scene was illumined by large incandescent bulbs that sent heat vapors into the cold air, probing every dank spot between the old brick buildings. It brought back memories the inspector would rather have kept buried.

"Brendan! Good of you to come." The outstretched hand was

harder and rougher than the last time they shook, but it was Johnny's hand, nonetheless. His friend's eyes had the same tired look as his; eyes that had seen too much pain. But Johnny's whole face looked pulled down, with eyelids drooping, and jowls heavy. His welcoming smile crept halfway up his cheeks before falling.

"Johnny, what have you got here, then?"

The area was cordoned off, but a sizable crowd, many standing on tiptoe, tried to peer into the alley. Most kept a respectable distance away. The clatter of countless Belfast tongues hummed in the background, and the scraping of Brendan's shoes seemed unnaturally loud to him. A bunker of sandbags had been raised to waist height in a semicircle over which the inspector could see two bent backs. The street noises were punctuated by the sounds of TV camera crews setting up their equipment, and reporters shouting questions across police tape.

He walked slowly over to the sandbagged area and looked in. Two men worked soundlessly inside. One was sweating in spite of the cold. Their breath obscured the focus of their attention, but Brendan knew what it was without being told. He tipped a finger to his temple and returned to Johnny's side.

"How long ago did they find the bomb?"

"Little over an hour."

"Timers?"

"None detected. A kid was chasing his dog down the alley. Saw a man run off and came to have a look. Lucky he had the presence of mind to call us in. If he'd played with it..." Johnny left the rest unsaid. "Must have got an eyeful, just the same." He paused in his recitation to peer back at the media people and frowned. "Bet they'd like to see it too." He jerked his head in the direction of two light-mounted video cameras panning the scene.

"Couldn't move it to a blow-out box?"

"They think it's got a gravity switch. They slid it carefully out of the side entrance, but feared lifting it up would set it off. Didn't want to take the chance."

"Why here?"

"It's what we found in the warehouse when we went in to clear it out." Johnny's face was tinged with fear, but he straightened and leaned over, speaking softly. "There was no one in sight, but it looked like somebody left in a bit of haste. Didn't get all their munitions either."

"How much?"

"Ten automatic rifles, six Uzis, grenades, assorted pistols." He paused for a second. "And a laser-sighted portable missile launcher. God only knows what they took with 'em."

That was when they both heard the sound. It cut across their words like a dagger, reminding Brendan of oil being dropped into a hot skillet. He rapidly leafed through his memory for the association. "Christ! A wire shorting," he said, swallowing hard.

"Jesus, Mary, what was that!" A raspy voice, tinged with disbelief, rose from within the bunker and echoed its warning off the alley's too-close walls. The nervous cry caused all eyes to turn to the men in the bunker.

"I think the wire just shorted!" The other man's voice was high-pitched. His head appeared over the top sandbags, his dirt-streaked face a mask of fear. He looked imploringly over to where Brendan and Johnny stood, and then ducked down out of sight.

"Fook sake! That bloody well cuts it." The raspy voice said again.

"They're not the best at this, Brendan." Johnny was clutching his notebook, bending it in two.

Brendan nodded to him, and then moved in fast. The bunker was six paces from him. Long paces it seemed as he approached it. Checking for room, he took a breath then leaped over the bags at the far end. Moving closer to the men, he rested on his haunches between them, directly facing the bomb. They stared at him, eyes wide and mouths open.

"What the hell are you doing?" The shorter man with the raspy voice spoke. He was straddling the bomb on Brendan's right, but slowly pulling away, as if, any minute, it would clamp down on his privates.

"Easy. Name's O'Neill. I've worked ones a lot like this. Which wire was shorted?"

The other man squinted at him for a moment in confusion, and then realization played across his face. "O'Neill? From Cork?"

Brendan nodded as he looked over the bomb. "You're lucky. That wire was for the timer. The fellow that left it never had the chance to arm it."

"Then why is it vibrating?"

Brendan looked down at the shorter man and could see the play of muscles in his lean face. "Let me feel it." His long fingers stroked the side of the bomb, feeling delicately around it, and stopping at a vertical slot midway around the back. His heart seized in his chest and he had to remind himself to breathe. *No fear. Stay calm. Think before you move.* He silently repeated the litany that had brought him safely out of many such spots before. *Breathe out. Calm.* "Should have guessed. A secondary timer. He must have manually armed it."

"How long?" The shorter man continued edging away from the black box.

"No idea. Usually less than ten minutes."

"But we've been here an hour." The taller man also was moving away. A burn mark covered his left cheek. He rubbed it as he continued backing up.

"Maybe it wasn't fully armed until you shorted the wire. Common armed circuit ground. Don't have much time. Give me your tools."

Brendan began unscrewing the side away from the mechanical timer. He cursed as he stripped off the head of a screw. "Give me some pliers." Both men looked at him, unblinking fear in their eyes. "Look, only one of you has to stay. Just hand me what I ask for."

Licking his lips, the shorter man nodded. "I'm your man,

then."

"How're you called?"

"Michael Blake."

"Well, Michael. It's you and me, then." Brendan took the pliers while the other man scrambled over the bunker. The torn head of the screw gleamed brightly, refracting shards of light off its irregular surface. Applying the pliers around the shaft, he began slowly moving the obstinate screw. It made a metallic tearing sound that tied Brendan's stomach into even tighter knots. Michael's gulp sounded like he'd swallowed a fish. "Just one more turn, I think..." Brendan slowly pulled the screw out, praying there was no hold-down contact behind it. His balls tightened in a prayer of their own. "Got it!"

Opening the plate, the sound grew louder. "Sounds like an angry bee. Let's see, this should do it. No! Another false wire. Bastard must have had great crack putting this one together."

"Can you stop it?" Michael's voice was very small. He cleared his throat and began again. "D'ya know which wire to cut?"

Brendan's eyes were on the mechanical timer's indicator plate. The metal glowed in the torch light as though alive. The time gradations swam before his eyes and he blinked before looking again. "I'd better know. Looks like we've only got a minute left." Brendan barely registered the man's muttered oath as he concentrated on the bomb's innards.

Brendan thought he knew the workings of the bomb now as he looked at the maze of wires spilling like entrails into his hands. And he could guess whose hand had guided and trained the bomber. There were three variations in the wiring of the detonator and he had to trace each possibility. He poked through the mass of wires warily, as though dealing with live snakes. All the time the timer's cylindrical indicator moved closer to the zero mark.

It wasn't the first variation; too obvious, he thought grimly. Did he have enough time? *Block it out. Concentrate.* It wasn't the second variation. Now he could only trust his intuition that it was the third. He had run out of time. "Wire cutters!" He grabbed the tool from a shaking hand. "Steady on, Michael."

The snap of the wire cutter seemed preternaturally loud within the bunker. Then all was quiet. Brendan looked at Michael who was staring at the bomb in disbelief. "It stopped?"

"If it hasn't, we're in for a big surprise in a second," Brendan said. His smile was picked up by Michael who grinned broadly before slumping back against the sandbags in relief.

Beth O'Hara jumped out of her dream and sat bolt upright, disoriented and edgy. She was in her own bed, and the barest glimmer of a new day was sending light through her window. She wasn't on the cliffs, with the wind ripping at her clothing. Thank God! The bed linen clung to her naked body, a chill working its way up her shoulders. One long, shapely leg was still entwined in the green sheets, her freckled, glistening skin standing out in bold contrast. But this was her own bed; she was safe here. Stripping off the damp sheet, she pulled up the comforter, thrown off during the night, and pressed it to her breasts. "It's just a dream, O'Hara. Just a dream." Somewhat reassured, she began to slowly gather her thoughts.

The dream had seemed so real to her. She knew that the setting was the Cliffs of Moher, but the winds had never made that fierce a sound, nor felt like icy hands pulling at her, clutching at her dress, whirling around her like a violation. And she would never have let her son go so close to the edge. Not with winds like that.

Still feeling the chilling effects of the dream, she went up to Julian's room in the loft. Softly opening the door, she saw him still sleeping peacefully, his red curly hair matted to the side of his head as though he had been sweating. An image of him rising out of dark waters flashed though her mind. Quietly moving to his bedside, she felt his warm, moist face. A touch of the flu was more like it, she decided.

Julian mumbled something in his sleep and turned over. Assured that he was all right, Beth went back downstairs and made some tea. The large kitchen, dominated by an ancient stove, never failed to warm her spirits on the many cool mornings above the bays of southern Ireland. But the dream's ominous warning played darkly in the back of her mind.

While the kettle slowly came to a boil, she parted the lace curtains next to the breakfast nook table and sat down to gaze out the window. Sunlight was just beginning to glint off the pond at the north end of her property. This place had been home to her and Julian for many years now, and it never failed to warm her heart or reassure her that life could still be good. Even without Eamonn. Even in spite of Eamonn.

She cleared the unpleasant thoughts from her mind and watched the ducks splashing about in the water. The soft bleat of a newborn lamb echoed across the pond. The familiar sounds began to dispel the gloom which had pervaded her sleep.

As was her custom on Saturday mornings, she took her tea and freshly-buttered scone out to her wicker chair on the broad rear porch. This was her favorite spot for viewing the activity around the pond. She looked up at the blunted top of Coomhola Mountain and then turned west toward the Caha Mountains sloping towards the sea. This view was her anchor, pulling her safely back to the shores of reality.

The soft burr of the telephone broke into her reverie and she reluctantly went into the small study to answer it. The modern phone looked out of place on her ancient roll-top desk. She heard Julian coming down the stairs as she lifted the handset.

"Yes? Hello, John, how are you? Are you calling from England?"

"Why wouldn't I be?"

Beth heard the static on the long-distance line and the thinning of her father-in-law's usually powerful voice. "It's just that I wasn't expecting your call. I thought you might actually be in Ireland. Is everything all right?" Beth glanced around her to see if Julian had joined her. She caught herself chewing her lip and willed herself to stop.

"Everything's fine here," he said, "excepting the weather. Here it is mid-April and more bloody rain. Is Eamonn there?"

"No, he's still in Belfast. Keeping busy. You know him."

"In Belfast, you say...hmm. Well, I'll try again. I'm having trouble reaching him, and I need some information on a potential client in Cork. By the way, what are you doing this Wednesday?"

She took a deep breath before answering, trying to absorb the significance of this request. "This Wednesday? Oh, I'm going to the annual faculty party at the Fitzsimmons's home. I'm looking forward to meeting the new professors the dean brought in from Dublin. Why did you ask?"

"Ian's flying out to Cork to discuss our patronage of your university. We may need to reduce the level somewhat. The unions have been hitting us hard, of late, and the contract negotiations have been rather drawn out this time. Perhaps he can drop by and see you and Julian. You know how fond he is of your son."

"Yes, that would be nice. Just have him call me when he arrives." After a few more pleasantries, Beth hung up. She looked forward to Ian's visit about as much as she would to that of an undertaker. His reed-thin body and somber mien flashed through her mind. His dead fish eyes; that was what had always bothered her about him. They made his false smile all the colder. She considered whether she was being fair, but immediately pondered the more important question her father-in-law had raised. Where was Eamonn? It was a question she could not answer.

While deciding how to treat this news, she turned to see Julian staring at her. Sleep was still in his eyes, and he had a puzzled look on his face.

"Good morning, Julian. How are you this morning?"

"Morn, Mum. Okay, I guess."

"What is it, Julian? Is something wrong?"

"Well..." He seemed hesitant to discuss it, but something was clearly troubling him. Beth took him by the hand and led him into the living room at the rear of the cottage and sat him on the couch.

"Now tell me. What is the matter, dear?"

At first, Julian's lips trembled as he grasped for words, and then they came tumbling out.

"I had a ... a bad dream. We were p-playing by some cliffs, like the ones by Grandda, and a man came and pushed you off." Beth looked sharply at his face; the barely withheld tears witness to the dream's effect. Her heart froze for an instant, and it took her another moment to recover. They had both had similar dreams. Beth was not one to take stock in premonitions or other occult nonsense like her friend Katherine, but this was beginning to seem very eerie. Perhaps if she got more details, and the dreams were different, her feeling of dread would go away.

"Julian, what did the man look like?"

"His face was black"

"You mean he was a black man?"

"No, I couldn't see his face, it was all dark."

She grasped his shoulders and gently massaged them while she continued questioning him. "Did you recognize anything about him or where you were?"

"No, but...he did say something."

"What was that, Julian? Can you remember?" She held her breath while watching her son swallow hard and form the next words.

"He said...he said he would take care of me, now that you were gone for good."

Something in the back of Beth's mind set off an alarm, but its tone was muted and the thought fleeting. She thought first it could be Julian's father, but Eamonn had seldom expressed much interest in their son and taking care of Julian? Ridiculous, she thought.

"It's all right now, Julian. It was only a dream. We're here together, and we always will be." She hugged him close to her, but not all of the trembling was his.

CHAPTER 3

Peter Deagan yawned into his closed fist as he careened into the bathroom. Last night's ale lingered on his tongue, but the taste wasn't to his liking now. He stared at his reflection in the mirror and decided he must be feeling better than he looked. His heavily-muscled body still reflected power, but his face looked as if it had been folded in a dozen places and then unfolded again. He rubbed his hand from forehead to chin to iron out the creases, but it didn't help. Sleep still crowded his eyes and resisted every attempt at banishment.

He aimed the toothpaste at his brush, his hand shaking, and watched it topple off the bristles and drop into the sink. "Shite! What next?" Casting his eyes heavenwards, he set his mouth in a grim line and concentrated on not missing on his second attempt. This time, the phone defeated him, its insistent ringing destroying his concentration. He dropped the brush and toothpaste into the sink and stalked into the bedroom, swearing under his breath.

He yanked the phone off its cradle, which almost slid off his bedside table before he grabbed it. "Yeah?"

"Well, you're in a good mood this morning, me boyo."

Peter recognized the voice instantly from this unexpected call. "Mike! What are you calling this early for?"

"Peadar," Mike said, "I've got some news for you from Derry."

"Wait a minute. Let me get a pencil." He rummaged through

the end table, pulled out a pencil and some scrap paper and began writing down the information.

"One had been in the RUC. Brendan O'Neill is his name. The other one was in Para 1 and probably changed his name, but it was Bill Ealey."

"The inquiry only indicted the British Army Parachute Regiment, Mike. Bill Ealey is the most likely bastard. You're certain about this?" Peter gripped the phone until his knuckles whitened. His pencil pressed heavily; printing in large block letters.

"Pretty certain," Mike said. "Do the names mean anything to you?"

"Yeah, I know O'Neill. He's an inspector here in Cork, but what about the other one?"

"Sorry. The information on him is very sketchy," Mike said.

"Damn! Well, do you have any description?"

"Tall, black hair, thin and quietly spoken, is what I've been told."

Peter tried to imagine who this might be from the threadbare description. "Where did he head off for? Any idea what he might be calling himself?"

"Don't have any information on the name," Mike said. "He left in '74 in the midst of The Troubles and relocated somewhere in England."

"Just England? You can't narrow it down more than that?" Peter tapped the pencil impatiently on his knee, sighing as he looked at what he had written.

"Maybe near London was all my contact would speculate."

"Thanks, Mike. I'll make the bloody whore pay, whoever it is. I might get more information this Wednesday. A local contact."

"Who?"

"Patrick McElheny," Peter said. "He's a professor of Irish literature here in Cork, and a Sinn Fein member. Some of his people may know about this Ealey."

"If he's well connected, he can fill you in on your inspector, but this other fellow..." There was silence on the line for a moment. "He seems the most likely to have done it and you'll have trouble getting anything on him. So you're meeting McElheny Wednesday, Peadar?"

"Actually, it's a faculty party. Time to get my contract renewed, so I have to put in an appearance. Rubbing elbows with the university crowd isn't my idea of fun, but there's plenty to eat and drink." After a few more exchanges, he hung up.

There was something about the call that bothered him. The thought played disturbingly in the back of his mind, until it hit him. There was no noise on the line! It sounded more like a local call. But what was Mike doing here, and what was the real reason for the call, considering how thin the information was? His eyes narrowed as his suspicions grew. Looking once more at the list, his hand began to shake with anger and he took deep breaths to cool down.

Peter's machine shop and home sat on the slopes of the town of Bantry. The second story living quarters were spare, but spotless, with the west-facing windows looking out on Bantry Bay. Through the open window sea scents mingled with the spring air and the perfume coming from a flowers box just outside the bedroom window.

Abruptly he got up and headed down stairs where his offices were located, across the four bay garage and down the final stairs into his basement. It had been part of the original house before it became his shop and home.

The musty smell of the basement brought back memories that Peter was unable to suppress. He moved quickly to the northwest corner where he'd built a small room to house his personal things. Unlocking the door, he moved to the far corner and unlocked the lid of an old steamer trunk. His hand shook again as he took out the upper tray. Close to the bottom, he located the metal box, unlocked it, and extracted an object wrapped in an oil-soaked rag. When he held the gun up to the light, it gleamed, looking as new as when his division commander had placed it in his hand.

He ejected the magazine and checked the load and then worked the slide of the Beretta. Once the slide returned, he dry-fired it to test the trigger pull. Finally he snapped in the magazine and chambered a round, watching how the extractor held the bullet in position. Satisfied, he put on the safety catch and replaced it.

When he straightened up, he saw his face reflected by the mirror set into the steamer's lid. The eyes staring back were remorseless; the muscles along the jaw quivering in anticipation.

CHAPTER 4

John Conor leaned back in his desk chair and inhaled the rich scent of leather. The musty tang distracted him, and he swiveled the chair to face the huge garden behind the main house. The large bay window revealed most of the expansive sweep of intricately-formed flowerbeds. His eyes picked out the graceful arch of a footbridge rising above a meandering brook that emptied into a dark pond beyond the formal gardens.

His architect had done a good job of replicating Monet's gardens in Giverny and John could almost imagine a lonely painter at his easel, tirelessly bringing the garden to life.

Returning grudgingly to the business at hand, John cleared his throat and continued with the dictation. "I don't want this matter to get out of hand, Edward. Be firm with the union; let them know who's boss. I know they think they are, but don't let them discover it from you. They can have the extra holiday and the 5 percent raise across the board, but I'm standing firm on the other issues. Oh, and you don't have to copy Eamonn on this." Sighing heavily, John swiveled back to face his secretary.

"That should do it for now, Glynnis. Thank you." He noted that she was still trying to wipe the surprised look from her face. She wore a white blouse, unbuttoned enough to display fine cleavage, and her blue skirt had moved to mid-thigh, legs slightly open.

Glynnis was a good secretary so he considered her stimulating out-fits a bonus; even if he hadn't taken advantage of the situation.

While he was still gazing fondly on her form, there was a knock on the door.

"Answer that, would you, Glynnis, and put the paperwork on my desk for signing when you have all the documents."

"I'll get right on it, Mr. Conor."

She leaned forward slowly before getting up from the chair and John drank in the lush curve of her revealed breasts before she stood. Bless you, Glynnis, he said to himself as she swished toward the door.

A heavy-set man with a florid complexion under bushy white brows entered the room carrying a black bag. He was followed by Ian, John's solicitor, dressed in his usual dark suit, a trace of gray on his cheeks hinting at the futility of a close shave. Glynnis brushed lightly against Ian as she left, eliciting a raised eyebrow from John.

John looked curiously at the shorter man, who walked as if he was on the swaying deck of a ship. By contrast, Ian moved like a cat, gliding into the room.

"John, this is Doctor Mansfield, for your scheduled physical."

John stood up to shake hands, amused at the contrast be-tween the two men. For that matter, he thought, his dapper figure served as an odd counterpoint to the doctor's portly one. His Fred Astaire to the doctor's Peter Lorrie. John noted the doctor even had the same large soft eyes as Lorrie. But there he hoped the similarity ended.

"Right, the physical. I'm afraid I had completely forgotten. We might as well do it now, but I'd like you to stay, Ian. We have things to discuss, when, eh, Manfred has finished. How long will this take doctor?"

"About half an hour for the preliminary work and the name is Mansfield, but you can call me Tommy. All my patients do."

John raised an eyebrow at this, watching in morbid fascina-tion as the doctor took instruments out of his case. After a moment, he realized that the doctor was looking at him expectantly. "Sorry, eh, Tommy." He was sure he'd never get used to calling a doctor Tommy. "Well, go ahead then."

The exam triggered buried memories of his last hospital visit. He had not set foot in one since his wife, Florence, had died during childbirth. Their second child had been delivered stillborn. He had blamed the doctors, but he knew his own neglect had been the primary cause. He had failed to heed the first doctor's warning that it would be a difficult birth.

To make matters worse, he'd seen his wife only briefly in the final month of pregnancy. He was closing the biggest deal of his life and couldn't be bothered with details; the details that would cost Florence her life. He pushed the thoughts far back in his mind, just as he had with countless unpleasant memories, but that process was interrupted by the prick of a needle.

He glanced down to see yet another vial being prepared. He was convinced the doctor had drawn enough blood to run a battery of tests. To make matters worse, the doctor was humming and it was getting on his nerves. He turned to Ian for relief. "Ian, were you able to reach Beth today and follow up on the call I placed earlier?"

"No, the sitter mentioned she was taking her car in for repairs. The repair shop telephone was engaged when I tried to call there."

"Ring Dean Fitzsimmons at the university. Tell him you need her to contact you as soon as she gets back. Ow! What the hell are you doing?" He looked down at his arm, reddening where the needle had been inserted.

"Sorry, just getting the last vial filled. It's hard to draw blood from your veins when you keep moving about."

"Christ! Be more careful, would you." John didn't think the doctor empathized with the pain he was experiencing. Perhaps it was professional detachment, perhaps not. The sound of the doctor rummaging in his bag was followed by the cold touch of a stethoscope on his chest. This, at least, did not surprise him, as he was now convinced he'd become the doctor's latest lab specimen. At least Tommy had stopped humming as he listened through the scope.

"Breathe in deeply, Mr. Conor, if you please." After a moment the doctor exclaimed, "Oh dear!"

The words were more chilling then the stethoscope. "What is it?" He did not like the look of concern that spread across the doctor's features as he removed the instrument.

"How long ago did you first get pneumonia, Mr. Conor?"

"Why, about a year ago. Isn't that right, Ian?"

"Yes, sir. A year and a month, to be exact."

John was becoming very uneasy and his heart rate was accelerating as the doctor probed and tapped.

"I'm hearing a lot of fluid in your lungs. You may be having a relapse. What medication did Doctor Strauss have you on?"

"He hasn't been on any since the doctor's visit last winter," Ian interjected.

"Hm, and what level of physical activity have you been engaged in, of late?"

"Oh, the usual, just working out of the office here mostly. I only go into London a couple of times a month," John said.

"Haven't been caught out in the rain though, eh?" Tommy was looking at him very closely now.

"Well..." John looked over to Ian for help, but decided to be honest. "Well, yes, I was out in the rain last week. But I had a raincoat on."

"So you didn't get wet then, and it wasn't cold out?"

"I suppose I did get a chill." He sank back in his chair, feeling like a child caught red-handed. The doctor's tut-tut didn't help.

"I'm going to give you a shot now, and then I recommend that you have a nurse check on you regularly. In fact, since you can easily afford it, you should have her full time." Doctor Mansfield gave him a severe look as if daring John to contradict him. "Yes, a nurse," he repeated.

John sighed deeply, resigned to the disruption of a meddle-some nurse. He realized he had been too careless with his health of late; perhaps as far back as when his very young wife died with a curse on her lips. While his mind drifted free of its moorings, the memory of Florence's final hours arose unbidden.

She had lost a lot of blood, and her energy, already depleted from the delivery, was almost gone. He had left ten-year-old Eamonn home with his grandmother, fearing the worst. When he entered the room, she weakly lifted herself up from her pillow. "Where's my baby?"

"I'm sorry dear." He could not bear to tell Florence her still-born son never took a breath of life. She sank back into her pillow, her head moving from side to side as tears spilled down her cheeks.

"So it's just you and Eamonn now, is it?' Her eyes were sharply on him now. "If he turns out anything like you, I hope you both rot in hell."

Then a look of fear replaced the anger and her hand dug at her throat as if it had clamped shut. She twisted in the bed in pain, her other hand lost in the tangled sheet, her eyes widening. He watched the indicators of her vital signs sink slowly on the moni-tor. She coughed once, a bubble of blood on her lips, and then only lifeless eyes stared accusingly at him. Eighteen years later, her eyes still stared back at him in his very bad dreams.

"John? John, are you listening?"

John looked up, startled, not recognizing Ian for a moment. What was the matter with him lately? "Yes, yes, of course, Ian."

"I'll make all the arrangements for the nurse, John. Thank you very much, doctor."

When the doctor had gone, John watched Ian staring out the window while nervously pulling on an ear. There was a frightened look on Ian's face when he turned back to face him. John sensed how frail he must look, his suits hanging loosely, the skin pulled back from face and hands. He looked at the veins on the backs of his hands, and imagined that the blue cords were filled with corrupted blood. He shuddered. "Well, let's have it, Ian."

"John, are you all right? You do want me to secure a nurse for you, don't you?"

"Yes, I'm fine. I suppose we'll need one on staff from now on." Suddenly another thought occurred to him; one that had troubled him a lot lately. "What word do you have on Eamonn and his strange behavior? When I called Beth this morning, she didn't know where he was either." Then he added, almost to himself, "Mind you, she didn't admit to it."

"As you suspected, he seems to have had different women up to his apartment in Dublin. I haven't been able to check on his routine in Belfast yet, but my contact in Cork reports that Eamonn is seldom there. It appears that he and Beth have separated; even if not technically so."

"Blast him! What in hell is the matter with him? I secure him a good position in Belfast, my first shipping office mind you, and he botches it. Then, to make matters worse, he starts whoring around. Do you know he hasn't advanced in over two years? He's just marking time, waiting for me to rescue him again, no doubt; or die."

"John, don't..."

John got up abruptly and paced the room, his hands clasped tightly behind his back. His breathing grew raspy with agitation. "Now he's set himself up a little love pad for every strumpet that walks the street, paying no heed to his wife and son." He turned back to Ian. "My grandson!" This started a fit of coughing that John had difficulty controlling.

When he got his breathing back to normal he wheeled on Ian with hand raised in a fist. "I need to keep him under tighter rein. I won't let this happen to our family." He finally returned to his chair and sat down, out of breath and very tired.

"Please, John, calm down." Ian moved towards him, his downturned palms fluttering, as if he could still John's rapidly-beating heart. "How did he react to your threats to write him out of the will?"

"Hmph! He knew I was bluffing. Who else would I leave the company to?" He watched Ian move over to his desk and balance on the edge, then move in closer, talking calmly and softly.

"What if you really did change your will, John?"

"What?" John looked up, his eyes tightening at the corners. Ian was one of the few solicitors he trusted, but talk of wills always made him uneasy, as though one false step on his part would lead to eternal damnation when all his acts were tallied.

"What if you gave a controlling interest in Conor Shipping to Beth? I know you want her and Julian to have a share in it. When Eamonn learned about the changes, he would have them to answer to. He'd have to become the loving husband and father he has always pretended to be if he was to win her confidence and cooperation in all his business deals. You've only threatened him with being written out of the will. Now you can let him know how serious you are."

John pondered the idea, looking at it from all angles. It was a good idea and it just might work. "You're right. Beth has a good head on her shoulders. Better than Eamonn's, quite frankly. She'd know better than him what was sound business or not. He wouldn't be able to bully her around, either, as you say he has in the past."

"The beatings are public record, Sir, I'm sad to say."

The look on Ian's face, as always, betrayed nothing, but John was sure there was no love lost between Eamonn and him. Or between Eamonn and me, he thought ruefully. "Yes, I think you may be right. Call in Joshua and tell him to bring all his instruments. I'll want to see a rough draft when the two of you are through with it."

"Certainly. Anything else?"

"Yes. Make sure you contact Beth after you arrive in Cork next Tuesday. You can meet her at the Fitzsimmons party, if not before at the university." John rubbed his chin as he considered his next words. "I'd like you to get a feeling for her frame of mind. I'm not sure how you should go about this, but I need to be sure this won't make matters worse for her."

"You want me to ascertain her current relationship with Eamonn; how far apart they are, how she thinks he would react to her being in charge." Ian smiled thinly. "And use discretion, above all. Yes?"

John nodded. "Yes, above all, use discretion." He tried to keep the strain out of his voice as he added, "Do you think there's still time for them?"

"It's hard to say, but with the leverage the changes in the will would give her, knowing she and Julian would be free of physical harm from him, there is a very good chance they could be reconciled."

"And she is a fighter. We have that to count on," John said with a touch of pride. "Thank you, Ian. I know I can depend on you."

Ian left the room and went into his own office, closing the door behind him. Closing the drapes the maid had left open, he ran his hands along the polished mahogany finish of his desk, reflecting for a moment. He loved this office and the substantial desk that faced his diplomas and the photos taken with political leaders in Northern Ireland. He had little use for the gardens behind the closed drapes that Conor spent so much time admiring. But working for Conor was not all bad.

Then he took a worn business card out of his breast pocket and dialed a number. The phone was picked up after the first ring.

"It's Ian. I have some more work for you around Cork."

"You want me to meet you?"

"Yes, I'll give you a schedule. I'll hire the car."

"Good, I don't think you want 'em to see my driver's license."

"Precisely. While I'm inspecting our warehouses in Cork I want you to keep an eye on Beth Conor. I need to meet her later. And find out what the hell Eamonn Conor is doing there, too."

"The son?"

"Yes," Ian said. "He's been very sloppy lately. I don't want him meddling in this."

"I got more photographs of his latest bird. Real handsome, this one. How does a bloody whore like him rate, anyway?" The voice was faint, with static momentarily filling the ear piece.

"Money. I'll want a full report when I get there. I have some other things for you to look into."

"Right. What am I looking for?"

Ian gave him a checklist, writing an occasional note on his pad. After hanging up, he turned and opened the drapes and tried to see beyond the gardens, resting his chin on templed fingers. "Idiot!" He said it softly, to no one in particular.

It had been a grim ordeal for Inspector O'Neill to return to Belfast while the investigation into the attempted bombing played out. He had shifted through reports of the possible suspects and the technical data on the bomb itself, but was no closer to identifying a prime suspect. He was again frustrated by the politics and hidden agendas that seemingly every official brought to the investigation. He tried to avoid the media that constantly put a mic in his face anytime he returned to the abandoned warehouse site. He was beyond tired of the no-comment replies he had to make.

Now that the investigation was stalled and he was no longer needed, he was allowed to return home to the relative peace and quiet of Cork.

He entered his office in old Cork, relishing the familiar smells he had complained about not too long ago. His desk was uncharacteristically clear of all paperwork. He had barely settled into his swivel rocker when there was a sharp knock on the door.

"If that's you, Regis, I'm not interested."

The door opened and his sergeant's ruddy face appeared. "How'd you know it was me?"

"No one else bangs so loudly on my door. You must think my

hearing is shot."

Nonetheless he invited Muldoon into his office, knowing they would not be going out looking for a bomb around Cork. The less about bombs the better, he thought.

"So how is the bomb investigation going on up in Belfast, Inspector?"

"Not now, Regis," he groaned. "I think a nice murder would be a better topic. Do we have any?"

Amused, Regis replied, "I'm terribly sorry, but it's been a very slow month, April has. The best I can offer is Billy Clancy was caught shoplifting again."

Brendan sadly shook his head. "Jesus, the least his criminal family should do is teach him how to do it proper so we don't have to drag him in again."

Getting out of his chair, Brendan went over to the open window and breathed in as much of Cork's air as his chest could hold, breathed out and finally relaxed.

"I think a little boredom now and then is a good thing, Regis. No sense looking for trouble." Then added, "Or IRA chaps for that matter."

"Oh that reminds me, we do have a list suspects in that railway car fire. Maybe arson will be your cup of tea this week."

Home at last, Brendan thought, as he leaned back in his chair.

CHAPTER 5
CLONAKITTY
WEDNESDAY

Beth O'Hara pressed the doorbell, enjoying the musical notes of the Fitzsimmons's sonorous chimes. The sounds of muted conversation seeped out from within. The large carved door opened, and a servant bowed her in.

In the hallway she saw Katherine Fitzsimmons coming to her in a gold chiffon dress that served as a dramatic counterpoint to her auburn hair. They hugged briefly, and Katherine led her through the long, formal hall into the ballroom at the rear of the house. The sounds of conversation, punctuated by the notes of a Debussy Etude on the grand piano, grew steadily louder as they approached.

Beth drank in the scene as she entered the cavernous room. Most of the light came from two chandeliers, their multi-tiered crystals scattering gold on the walls. She swept past a fireplace large enough to walk into, its ornately-carved mantle just above her head. There were over sixty people in the room and another hundred would still not have filled it.

"Welcome to my ancestral home," Katherine said. "How do you like it?"

"It's wonderful. And everything looks authentic. Did you say it had been in the family for centuries?"

"Yes, although we only opened it up last year," Katherine said.

"I personally saw to the renovation, hand-picking many of the accoutrements." She leaned over and in a conspiratorial voice said, "There is someone I want you to meet."

Katherine led her over to two men engaged in earnest conversation. The taller of the two was smartly dressed and moved like a dancer. His dark hair was fashionably cut and framed a face that took her breath away. Sharp features, an aquiline nose and tanned skin below deep blue eyes that saw much. He had just finished making a point.

"...and he didn't wait for a confirmation before proceeding. Can you believe it?"

"Excuse me, gentlemen. Could I borrow Sean for a moment, Patrick?"

"Indeed you can. I'm off for another Guinness myself. See you later, Sean." Patrick wandered off to join another group.

"I want you to meet a good friend who works over at the university. Now you will be on your best behavior, won't you, Sean?"

"Aren't I always, Katie?"

Beth loved his mischievous smile and immediately thought of Cary Grant. Katherine gave her a he's-not-to-be-trusted look, before turning back to Sean.

"Beth, this is Sean Carey. He's a visiting professor from Dublin, here to set us all straight on mesons and protons and such stuff. And Sean, this is Beth O'Hara, our best lab technician and sometime-poet." Beth felt her face flush from the effusive introduction.

"I'm very pleased to meet you, Sean. I have, in fact, already read your treatise on particle physics. I was very impressed." Beth's breath quickened at the warm smile of gratitude he gave her.

"I'm impressed that anyone actually went to the trouble of reading it." Sean nodded towards Katherine as she touched his sleeve before moving on, and then he continued, "What exactly do you do at the university, Beth?"

"Oh, I set up the physics and chemistry labs, run new tests, try out some new experiments when I get bored. Lately, I've been lending a lot of assistance to Professor Dunoon."

"Really? You know Seamus Dunoon? I haven't seen him since he left Edinburgh. Frankly, he was one of the reasons I accepted this post. How do you like him?"

"He's a wonderful bear of a man, brilliant, and not as intimidating as I would have thought. How do you know him?"

"Oh, Seamus and I go way back. He got me started on my own exploration of meson activity. Before that, I was working as a paleontologist."

"That's quite a jump, from dinosaurs to subatomic particles."

"Yes, I know. It mystified all my other professors, but I wanted to work in a field that was making an immediate impact."

"Why did you first choose paleontology, then, Sean?"

"It was a safe, well-established science, without a lot of competition. I thought I needed that safety then, but not now."

"No, not judging from your article. I'd say you made the right choice."

Beth detected a slight blush before he answered. "Well, thank you. And what about you, a poet mixing meter with mesons? How did you get into physics?"

"Oh, poetry is just what I do for pleasure. I've only had a few published. You can't make a living at that."

"No, sadly, you can't."

Even though the ballroom was expansive, Beth found herself standing very close to him. She sensed that he was finding her just as fascinating. He certainly had trouble keeping his eyes off her; they dropped more than once to the bodice of her emerald green dress. Did men think their subtly wandering glances went unnoticed, she wondered? Or that women didn't work at it; exposing more cleavage?

"Oh, where are my manners? Would you care for a drink, Beth? The Meursault is quite excellent."

"Yes, I'd love a glass. Katherine loves the white Burgundies of the Cote De Beaune."

Sean plucked a glass of wine off a tray as a waiter trudged by, and held it to the light. "And herself knows something about French wines, I see," Sean said in an exaggerated brogue. The amber liquid scattered light through the multi-faceted glass he held for her, bathing her bodice in a shower of golden, ever turning light.

They softly chinked glasses and gazed at each other over the rims. Beth felt a coquettish grin steal across her face, which Sean responded to with a warm flush. The moment seemed to hold for a long time before Patrick returned.

"Excuse me, Beth. Is it all right if I take Sean away for a moment? We're in hot debate over here about whether O'Carolan penned four or five airs for Bridget Cruise." Beth smiled at the look of eager anticipation on Patrick's face.

"Turlough O'Carolan, the blind harpist? How do you know so much about his music?"

"Sean hasn't told you about his passion for the Irish harp, Beth? He plays it quite well, in fact, and could be called upon to deliver all four or five airs if prodded sufficiently. What do you say, Sean?"

"All right Patrick, I'll settle your bet since that's what it has probably come to." Sean appeared amused by the request as he turned to Beth and bowed. "I'll be back." It was a promise Beth hoped would be filled soon.

Patrick pulled anxiously on his arm. "Yes, but come quick! I don't want this one to slip away." Sean shrugged helplessly at Beth before turning to follow him.

As she watched him walk over to a group of men clustered by the open French doors, Beth admired the way he moved. Her cousin had always told her that if a man looked good advancing and retreating from view, she should grab him. She blushed at the memory, but never took her eyes off him.

He was well over six feet, lean, and clearly athletic, judging from the way he moved. His presence was noted by the many women clustered in small groups along the path he navigated on his way to the back of the ballroom. Beth was surprised to find herself feeling a twinge of jealousy. She tried to suppress it, but it flared anew when one of the women clutched at Sean's sleeve as he passed by. Beth stiffened while he answered her question, but relaxed when he continued on his way.

Peter decided he could wait no longer, and yanked Patrick by the arm when no one else in their group was looking. They were all too busy listening to prattle about blind musicians, anyway. "We need to talk. Now."

"All right," Patrick said. "Just let me collect my winnings."

Peter dug his hands into his pockets and breathed heavily through his mouth. His patience was at an end. He turned and headed for the door as soon as he saw Patrick stash his money. He walked slowly but purposely to the end of the formal gardens, and rested against a gnarled oak that provided shade from the afternoon sun. In the shadows of its overhanging branches, he began to relax. When Patrick arrived, Peter spoke in harsh whispers. "What can you tell me?"

"Impatient, aren't we, Peter? I did spend a few hours getting what you wanted. At considerable risk, I might add."

Peter tried to look appreciative, but quickly reminded himself of the risk he himself was taking. He had spent years covering his tracks, and staying away from any contact with the IRA or Sinn Fein. And now this. "I do thank you for your help. But this is the closest I've come to finding my Mum's murderer, and I need that information."

"My contacts in Derry, Belfast, and London all contributed on this. You picked a very slippery one. The information I got back is thin."

"Anything you've got." Peter looked at the man closely. His brown tweed jacket sported leather patches at mid-arm that probably never cushioned elbows against a desk's surface. The face was thin, with sunken gray cheeks accentuating the look of a man just out of prison. But, as far as Peter knew, he had never spent a day there; unlike some of his brethren.

"I'd like to be compensated for my trouble first," Patrick said.

Peter had expected this. He knew McElheny well enough to guess he'd line his own pockets with money. Peter's own reserves were getting low, however. "Why don't we work out a little trade, then? I'll take care of your car, no charge. What do you say to that?"

"For life?"

"Your life?" Peter paused for effect. "Or the car's?" Seeing the look of uncertainty on Patrick's face, Peter quickly changed course. "Never mind," he said, backing further into the shadows. "But tell me something."

Patrick glanced over his shoulder before moving closer to the tree, joining Peter in the shadows. Peter listened for footsteps. Hearing none he spoke in a low, urgent voice. "What d'ya have on Ealey?"

Patrick kept his voice low as well. "Bill Ealey worked as a law clerk for Conor Shipping in Belfast after the riots in Derry. He disappeared after four months. No one at the shipyard knew where he was heading, but a couple of my mates thought he had help from high up in the company to leave as quietly and swiftly as he did."

"No idea what his name or address might be?"

"As far as we can work out, he's using a new name and living around Portsmouth, or some other port city in the UK. Probably still working for Conor, if they had him moved."

"That could prove useful," Peter said. "Conor's son often comes to Cork on business. Maybe I could ask him."

"I'd be really careful with him," Patrick said. "He isn't exactly sympathetic to our cause. If he even guessed at your intentions and knows this fellow, he might warn him. Let me probe a little more."

A little surprised that Patrick was suddenly being so helpful,

Peter said, "You can reach me at my shop in Bantry if you find out anything."

"It's been a long time since the Derry massacre, Peter. Why are you still pursuing this?"

"I promised my Da at her funeral." He looked at Patrick intensely. "Told him I wouldn't give up until I had the bastard's throat here." Peter lifted up his hands, claw-like, as if squeezing an invisible neck, and watched Patrick swallow hard. "Of course, by then he'll be beggin' me to finish him off."

After a few moments of feeling at odds, Beth began to scan the room looking for other colleagues. She spotted Patrick coming through the French doors and started to walk towards him when she noticed Peter Deagan behind him. She stopped. Unconsciously, she looked for Sean but he was not in the ballroom. Surely he had not left? She turned her back on Peter, hoping he would not notice her.

She recalled their last meeting at his garage. He had been working on her cranky Rover, which, once again, was back in for repair. When he asked her about the car he stayed uncomfortably close, the warmth of his body engulfing her. The scent he gave off reminded her of a tomcat in pursuit. She felt as though she had been violated, even though he had only touched her arm. Her skin crawled at the very memory of it.

Still, he had made friends with her son, entertaining Julian for hours while working on the Rover. Beth didn't trust him, but couldn't say why. It was only a vague, uneasy feeling that came over her whenever he was around. She turned back slowly, hoping he had gone, but he was in front of her, grinning.

"Well, what a pleasant surprise. How are you, Beth?"

"I'm just fine Peter, and you?"

"Nice of you to ask Beth. I'm fine."

He appeared to be looking for an opening gambit but was not having much luck. Keeping her neutral expression, Beth was not about to relieve his discomfort.

"So, tell me," he continued, "what brings you here? The university crowd? The food and drink? Or maybe it was me you wanted to see."

Beth rolled her eyes at the ego of the man, but she refused to be drawn in. "I came for the conversation, which we obviously aren't having." Then she sensed someone approaching from behind. It was Sean holding out a small plate.

"I'm finally back," Sean said. "I brought some starters for you."

She watched him size up the situation; certain that he must be wondering what was going on. "Thank you, Sean. Have you met Peter Deagan?" Beth's voice held little enthusiasm.

Sean frowned in thought for a moment. "Why yes, he tuned up my Jaguar right after I arrived. It's humming contentedly for the first time in years. How are you, Peter?"

"Sean," Peter said, nodding slightly, but ignoring Sean's outstretched hand.

With Sean standing beside her, Beth felt protected and decided she liked the feeling. She watched Peter move between them and the hallway, as though to cut off their escape.

"How long have you known Beth?"

Even though Peter's inquiry sounded casual, one look at his eyes told Beth his question was anything but. She answered before Sean could reply. "Oh, we're great friends. We were just discussing particle physics when you arrived. What do you know about mesons, Peter?" Beth glanced obliquely at Sean to see how he was reacting to her ploy. She almost felt guilty when she saw Peter's confused look.

"Masons? That's one of those secret societies, isn't it?"

Sean smiled indulgently. "Mesons are subatomic particles, Peter. Although they have been hidden from us for many years." Sean turned to Beth, puzzled by the turn of the conversation.

Just then Beth noticed Katherine approaching with a worried

look on her face.

"Beth, Margaret just called," Katherine said, out of breath. Then she whispered in her ear, "Julian was throwing up and she wants to know what to do."

Beth felt a twinge of guilt. She had debated staying home with her feverish son, but hoped her housekeeper could deal with the situation.

"Oh dear, I must get back. Please excuse me, Sean...Peter."

"I can drive you home, Beth." Peter's smile was not inviting. "It'd be no problem."

"No, thank you, Peter. I'll just call Duncan. He dropped me off here; he can drive me back as well."

Sean said, "I can drive you home, Beth." He dropped his voice to a whisper. "It will give me an excuse to leave early."

Was he picking up the growing tension between her and Peter? At first Beth was going to reject his offer - she was used to doing things for herself - but she was becoming increasingly fearful of Peter's foreboding presence.

"If you really don't mind, Sean." She gave him a grateful look, and avoided glancing in Peter's direction.

"No, not at all. We can leave right away, if you want."

The sound of glass shattering stopped the conversation. Beth turned to gape at Peter and then down at the broken glass in his hand. She watched in horror as he slowly opened his hand, and pieces of glass dropped to the floor. The expression on his face was one of barely-checked rage, his color was high, and his mouth clamped shut as though sealed against an unrelenting pressure. She bit her lip as he pulled a shard out of his palm and dropped it on the floor.

Katherine Fitzsimmons hurried over at the sound, but stopped and gasped when she saw the blood. "Oh, dear me, Peter, you should have that looked after," she said while handing Peter a linen cloth from the banquet table

Peter held the cloth tightly in his hand and Beth felt the heat of his focus. Katherine glanced from Beth to Peter, unsure what else to add while Sean moved protectively closer to Beth. She felt his firm hand on her arm and was reassured.

"I'm sorry you cut yourself, but I must go."

"Yes, do go, Beth. We'll carry on here," Katherine said as she ushered them towards the hallway.

Beth looked away from Peter as she followed Katherine with Sean in her wake. She felt his strong hand on her shoulder as he steered her down the long hallway. She still could sense Peter's menacing glare, and still picture his hands tightly clenched around the blood-soaked linen, his eyes murderous. At the door, she turned to Sean, not sure how much she could trust him either, but now firmly committed. "Let's go, Sean. I'm worried about Julian." He held the door as they went out to his car.

CHAPTER 6
ABOVE BANTRY BAY

Beth enjoyed the car's surge of power as the acceleration pressed her back into her seat. The Jaguar XKE, as sure-footed as its namesake, clung to the twisting road on the climb up Coomhola Mountain as the last rays of the sun bled color on low-hanging clouds. Her mind ricocheted off conflicting emotions as she vaguely registered her surroundings. She followed Sean's gaze south to the Beara Peninsula stretching out into the sea, the spine of the Caha Mountains fading into mist. The scent of flowers mingled with the chilly wind whistling through the car's open window vents.

"How long have you known Peter?"

Beth started from her reverie as she replied, "Since he took over maintenance of the university's fleet of vehicles two years ago. I first spoke to him when he worked on my car about a year ago."

"I guess you don't like him very much. Has he been bothering you?"

"No, well..."

"Yes?"

"Oh it's just a feeling of danger I had about him. It's probably nothing."

"Are you sure? His reaction was most extreme."

"I know," Beth sighed, and then pointed to direct Sean at the next turning.

Soon, they were off the main road following the Curramore River to its source, Curramore Lake. Above the lake, she had him slow down and gestured to the right as her cottage came into view, in the shallow upland valley. She directed Sean to park near a low fence.

They walked along a narrow path beside the reed-edged pond, while a dying sunset reflected on the water. Beth watched their figures floating over its smooth surface, turning curiously when Sean's image disappeared. He was glancing up at the cottage, then around at the countryside, as though trying to orient himself. He stroked his jaw, a look of concern on his face. "Sean, what is it?"

"Eh, nothing. Just...nothing."

"I'm going up to look in on Julian. Why don't you make yourself comfortable in the living room when you come in?"

"Yes, fine."

Beth entered the cottage, hastily greeted her housekeeper and headed for the stairs leading up to the loft. Julian sat up in bed, reaching out his arms as she came to him, his eyes squinting in the light.

"Mum, I don't feel well."

"I'm sorry, my darling, let me feel your forehead." Beth placed her hand on his head, but he wasn't feverish. "Where does it hurt?"

"My stomach hurts, and I threw up all over the bathroom rug. I'm sorry."

It was typical of him to be concerned about other people, other things; that was one of his endearing traits. She gently laid him back down on the bed. His feet protruded from the covers and she gave each big toe a squeeze before covering them again. It was time to get him a full-sized bed.

He was normally a very active child, so any sickness was an immediate concern. She gently rubbed his stomach, and was rewarded with a smile. "Does that feel better, Jules?"

"Yes. I'm glad you're back."

"Well, I'm glad you're feeling better, but I have to go downstairs. A nice gentleman from the party brought me back." Julian held her hand on his stomach. He was reluctant to see her go, and she waited for the inevitable question.

"Who is he, Mum?"

"Sean's a visiting professor from Dublin, Julian. He was at Katherine's party, and we've been having a nice talk about particle physics and whatnot."

"Oh," was all Julian replied, as he relinquished her hand. Beth kissed him on the forehead before going downstairs.

"I'll look in on you later, okay?" She heard his muffled reply as she slowly closed the door.

Heading downstairs, she heard Sean and her housekeeper conversing, and decided to wait for a moment in the alcove. Margaret moved past carrying a tray, laden with scones and steaming tea that she set down on the coffee table. She looked tired, and why shouldn't she, after a full day of cleaning and caring for Beth's son.

"This is a lovely cottage," Sean said. "How long have you worked for Beth, ah, Mrs...?"

"Margaret Fitzgerald. The mister is long since gone. And what might your name be?" She tilted her head and gazed at him curiously.

"Oh, I'm sorry. Where are my manners? My name is Sean Carey."

"And where might ya be coming from, Sean Carey?"

"Well, I was living in Dublin, but I just transferred down to Cork. I'll be looking for a permanent place to live soon. The area down here around Bantry Bay looks good to me."

"Yes indeed. I've lived here all my life, and I can tell you I haven't regretted a minute. We take in more rain than some areas, but we're not complaining. Even though my hip does act up on these cold evenings."

Beth came into the living room, and took a seat opposite Sean in front of the fire. Margaret handed her a mug of hot tea. "Thank you, dear. I think Julian will be all right. He doesn't seem to have a fever, probably just an upset stomach."

"Ah, that's good news indeed. He looked so sick earlier, but he was on the mend after I called."

She knew Margaret was watching them intently as they sat together by the fire. Her housekeeper's sense of propriety was shaken by the scene, in spite of Sean's gallant assistance.

"So if you won't be need'n me any longer, Miss?" After a significant pause, she continued. "I'll be getting on home with the last of the light, then."

Beth ignored her raised eyebrow, and tried to pretend everything was normal; a lie her rapidly-beating heart demolished. "No, thank you. We'll be just fine."

Sean half rose from his seat. "Can I drop you off, Margaret?"

"No, thank you, sir, the walk will do me good. It isn't far, only a kilometer or so." Margaret wrapped herself in a red shawl with a flourish and headed for the door.

Sean whispered to Beth, "Is she all right to go? I mean, with the limp and all."

"Oh, she's a tough old bird. Fell while riding many years ago and broke her hip, but it hasn't stopped her at all. Just takes her a little longer. I asked her once about it. She said, 'I have more time to gaze upon all the wonders here, so where's the harm in that?' And off she went."

After the door had softly closed, Beth took a deep breath, but found she was at a loss for words. She looked at Sean for a cue, but he appeared lost in thought. After an uncomfortable silence, he began working his mouth, as though not sure what words to form.

"And how long have you had this cottage, Beth?"

"Oh, a few years now...well...longer actually," her voice trailed off, unable to grasp the next thought.

"Your son, Julian, is he from a previous marriage? Or are you..."

Beth watched his hand gestures. They tried to fill in the void he was uncomfortable breaching with words. She pondered how best to answer him. She was torn between wanting to see him again, and telling a wee lie. Besides, would he still be interested if he knew about Eamonn? She finally settled for a partial answer. "My husband abandoned us. He left us this house and the lands surrounding it." Her heart seemed to beat hard around each word, while her tongue lumbered over each syllable.

"What was your husband's name, Beth?"

"Eamonn Conor."

His eyes opened wider at the mention of her husband's name. The thought that Sean might know him struck hard against her lurching stomach. "Why do you ask?"

"I knew someone at school who had a wife somewhere in these parts," he stammered. "Maybe her name was Beth." He shrugged. "I was just curious."

Beth watched his averted eyes as he spoke. Was he hiding something, she wondered. "In any case, he called me Liz. I hate that name." Beth thought he squirmed a little in his chair as she spoke. Now she was making him even more uncomfortable. She decided to change the subject.

She moved over to the fireplace, hoping some distance would relieve the tightness in her chest. She stroked the side of the use-worn mantle and stared fixedly at the painting above it. The depiction of a stormy sea blasting the Aran Islands mirrored her emotions perfectly. She felt as lost as the wave-tossed ship at its center. Beth picked up a figurine to busy her hands and dismissed the topic of her husband. "Well, it's all in the past now. And you, Sean, did you grow up in Dublin?"

"Born and raised there. I went to Trinity for a while, then to Cambridge and finally graduate work at Stanford. That's in California."

Sean once again was animated, and it was as though they were resuming their conversation from the party. "Yes, I've heard of their excellent science programs. I've wanted to go there for some time."

"You would enjoy it there, but you've obviously made a life for yourself here. Dean Fitzsimmons tells me you've made quite an impression on the professors at Kerry University; and me, I might add."

Beth gave him her warmest smile. Turning to set the figurine down, she saw her image in the painting's tinted glass. It provided an imperfect reflection of her curly red hair, her oval face floating in it like a pale ghost. As she faced Sean, she scrutinized herself in the large hall mirror behind him. He had assayed her figure at the party, but the firelight was revealing curves only his imagination could have filled in before. The effect it was having was obvious, and she liked it. "And just what sort of impression have I made on you, Sean?" She had caught him off-guard and barely suppressed a smile as he blurted out a reply.

"A very favorable and lasting one. I...I would very much like to call on you again, Beth."

Beth watched his expression change from surprise to a smile. He came towards her, as if pushed by unseen hands. She was not sure if the gathering heat was from the fire or a response to his approach. "I would like that very much too, if..." Beth was interrupted by a loud noise outside.

"What was that?" Sean said.

"I don't know." She forced down the tremble in her throat. Who, or what, could it be, she wondered. Her nearest neighbor was some distance away, and the animals were all in their pens. She had no idea who, or what, was prowling out there.

"I'll check it out. It may be nothing at all," Sean said, as he moved to the hallway.

"Sean, be careful." Beth held her hands tightly to her chest; her alarm mounting as Sean opened the door and went out into the garden. She prayed it wasn't her unwelcome ghost.

The moonlit landscape yielded more shadows than distinct

images. Sean adjusted his eyes to the darkening night before stepping off the threshold. Only the rustle of wind through the trees broke the silence. He went to the car, took a torch out of the glove compartment, and pointed it over to the left side of the house. The beam picked up a pail lying on its side, its rocking motion gradually slowing to stillness. Off to his right, he heard a rustling sound in the low-lying bushes by the fence and walked slowly over to the spot, shining the beam in the direction of the sound.

The noises stopped, and at first he saw nothing. Then his torch picked up twin eyes flashing malevolently back at him. They seemed to draw in the light and turn it back on him in waves of hate. As Sean stepped back, the movement in the bushes became more violent. Suddenly, a large cat leapt out of the bush, brushed by his leg, and jumped over the fence.

He was sure his heart had leapt from his chest, and was thudding heavily in his ears. "Damned cat!" He lowered the torch, put his hands on his hips, and shook his head. When his breathing returned to normal, he chuckled at his reaction. Some hero.

After the cat's scramble through the bushes, all was quiet. Even the wind had suddenly died down. "So, was it you knocked over the pail then?" The cat hesitated for a moment, as if pondering a reply. He saw its eyes, luminous still in the distance. Then it turned and disappeared, leaving only the sound of the gentle breeze filling the silence. Sean looked around but could detect no movement or odd noises. Listening intently, he only heard the soft whisper of grass thrumming to the wind's tune.

The area around the side of the house looked undisturbed except for the pail. As he set it upright, he thought he caught sight of movement by the road in the distance, but he was hesitant to venture into unfamiliar territory. His torch grew dimmer, and he rapped it against the palm of his hand. It sputtered back to life, then went out. "Damn thing!" The night swiftly closed in, and Sean felt exposed on all sides. He backed up, keeping his eyes on the road until he was close to the porch, then turned his back on the night.

Beth was waiting in the doorway for him. "Did you see anything?"

"It was probably just a pail being knocked over; I spotted a gray cat running away."

"Oh, that would be Felix, looking for a mouse, no doubt." Beth began to relax a little.

"Well, that certainly added some excitement to the evening. I have an early day tomorrow, but I'd like to take you out to dinner after my classes on Friday. We'd have the evening to talk. What do you say?"

"I'd love to, Sean. I can be ready by seven, and I know just the place."

"Grand! 'Til then."

Beth sensed hesitation as his face hovered above hers. She raised her lips, encouraging him to close the remaining distance. What she thought would be a short kiss lengthened and deepened. Intense desire spread through her in hot waves; the kind of sexual desire she thought Eamonn had all but extinguished. Her lips fed hungrily on his; her arms around his neck became her anchor. She drifted momentarily, borne on a dark inland sea, and was startled by her soft moan, signaling sensual abandon. She pressed her hands against his chest while she sought to control her unchecked emotions. "No, Sean." He yielded to the pressure and released her grudgingly. She stepped back inside the doorway, using it as a barrier between them.

"Sorry. Hadn't meant to take advantage like that. You...I'm sorry," Flustered and off-balance, he backed off the porch.

"I like you, Sean, but please, let's take this slow. I...I need time." Beth refused to catalogue the thoughts crowding her brain as she began to close the door.

"Friday? Dinner?"

"Yes." She closed the door firmly.

Close by, another pair of eyes observed them. The dim shape kept close to the ground by the old storage shed, obtaining an unobstructed view of the front of the house. The figure rose slightly to get a better view.

"Well, well, Sean, what are you and Beth up to?" The words softly spoken, the man retreated to the safety of the shed while Sean got into the car and drove back down the mountain. When the last whine of the Jaguar's engine dissolved into the night, he emerged from his hiding place and quickly scuttled towards the north side of the cottage.

When Beth's bedroom light went on, he moved in closer. He could see her figure projected onto the translucent shade, in the act of removing her dress. Then slim arms reached behind to unhook the bra. He held his breath and cautiously moved closer, reassured by the muted sound of her humming. At the window, he looked up to see that it was firmly closed, and swore under his breath.

He froze at the sound of a cat's angry hiss, moving again only when Beth's shadow grew, filling the window. The shade made a jarring, ratchet-like whir as she opened it, covering his sounds as he jumped out of the light's path. He pressed flat against the side of the house, near the window.

Into the rectangle of light thrown out by the drawn shade he saw her silhouette appear, filling the space. He leaned forward, chancing a look, sliding closer as she turned away from the window. Glancing in, he caught a glimpse of her naked back.

Taking a deep breath, he scanned the illumined scene, looking for the cat. Felix hissed again, and he spotted it where the moonlight held sway outside the penumbra of the window's light. The cat was stalking him, moving diagonally back and forth. It came closer with each pass.

The moonlight abruptly disappeared, swallowed by low-hanging clouds streaking across the sky. The cat did not betray itself with sound, no matter how intently he listened. How he hated that cat. He tried to discern shapes from shadow. Then the uncovered moon once more painted ghostly signatures upon the ground. The cat, poised in mid-step, looked up at him with its teeth bared, but came no closer.

The sound of tapping at the window jolted him. She was unlocking the window! He felt dread mixed with dark urgings as he heard the window slowly open. He feared what he might do next, and held his breath.

"Felix! You've caused enough trouble tonight. Off with you!"

He watched the cat calmly walk away as if nothing had happened, its tail curling then flicking, as if at some insignificant pest. The slamming of the window brought his attention back to Beth. Once again pressed against the wall, he watched the light from the window go opaque as she pulled the shade down again. Keeping his eye on the cat, he moved back away from the side of the house, then over to the shed and down a path to his car. His figure seemed to leave no retreating shadow, his boots no depression in the earth. Even the click of his car door opening was muffled in the night.

CHAPTER 7

Peter Deagan was greeted by the same faces he saw every lunch time at the Bay Mist pub, but he was intent on getting his first drink. He took his glass to an empty table away from the high traffic areas and sat with his back to the west-facing wall. He hunched forward in his chair as he sipped his ale, the scowl on his face suggesting dark thoughts. One of his drinking mates came over and Peter fed monosyllabic replies to his queries until, shrugging in defeat, the man returned to his table. Peter overheard his first comment to his drinking companions.

"He's in a bit of a mood. Not a word out of him."

The rest of their conversation came to him in soft murmurs accompanied by glances in his direction. He tried not to think about last night; certainly not later that night. Instead he focused his attention on activity elsewhere in the pub.

As the door swung open, he squinted against the mid-day light streaming through from outside. A man's shadow passed over Peter's face as he stepped up to the bar. It was another fisherman bringing the smell of the sea with him. The salty tang mingled with the ripe scent of beer and whiskey that permeated the bar. Peter's hand rubbed the table top, feeling the film left by spilled drinks and moist sea air. The barman's rag did little more than blend it all together.

From the other side of the pub, the clatter of flatware announced another diner feasting on lamb stew. Peter looked over in that direction, moving his chair to see around a beam. He looked intently at the man's face, sure that he should be able to place it, but he was interrupted by footsteps approaching his table. Shannon was staring down at him, her lower lip jutting out as though she had already been slighted.

"Well then, Peter, aren't you going to invite me to sit down?"

"Sure, plenty of chairs. Take one."

"Is that any way to greet an old friend, now?"

Shannon sat down next to him, an injured look on her face. Peter noted that her lush figure was doing a credible job of filling out one of the flowery off-the-shoulder blouses she favored. She leaned towards Peter, revealing more cleavage, and he finally raised his eyes toward the ceiling hoping to regain his previous train of thought.

"Peter, you were going to tell me when I could come up to your place. You didn't forget, now, did you? You've promised for a week."

He had forgotten, but he wasn't about to admit it to her. "No, of course not. I've just been lost in thought, that's all." He took another pull on his beer and wiped the dregs off with his sleeve.

"Lost in thought, is it? I didn't think you had any to get lost in."

"Oh, you're a fine one to talk. When was...," he abruptly cut off his sarcastic reply and, in a quieter voice asked, "D'ya know that fella over there in the corner?"

She turned and, after some scrutiny of the area, said, "What man? I don't see anyone."

Peter leaned over, again looking beyond the beam, but saw only an unfinished plate of food at the corner table. "He was there. Something about him looked very familiar. Hmm."

Shannon got up abruptly and leaned over to stare in his face. "Well, I can see you aren't in the mood for having any company now. Try to be a little more with it later, will you? I've got the rest of the day off, so expect me at seven."

She swept regally by him and out the door. Peter made a lewd gesture at her departing figure, which brought appreciative snickers from his drinking mates. Then, with one last draught, he set the glass down heavily, slapped coins beside it, and walked out into the afternoon sunshine.

The pub was huddled beside other shops around the quay. The town of Bantry exuded a quiet charm that was often lost on Peter. It provided a meager livelihood through his garage, and company at his favorite pub. Beyond that, only the grand sweep of its majestic bay piqued his interest.

He shaded his eyes as he faced west, looking across the bay. Much of the Beara Peninsula was obscured by Whiddy Island, site of the infamous Betelgeuse Incident, which helped end the island's usefulness as an oil platform for large tankers. He and his Uncle Jack had seen the fireball from Dursey Head where he used to play.

"Damn the past," he chided himself as he stretched and flexed his massive arms. His Uncle Jack would have been proud of the way he had turned out after spending many nights in his uncle's basement working with his barbells and weights. That was long before he found work in Belfast. Some of it very dangerous work indeed.

He headed up Aston Street, which swung steeply away from the bay. A line of stunted trees protected one side of the street. The other side was a string of tired shops that tilted back towards the bay, as though gravity was drawing them inexorably down to the sea. His shop was only two streets away on the fringes of the commercial end of Bantry.

This afternoon, though, he was content to exercise his legs with short, steep climbs up the interconnected roads from the bay. Soon the sounds of activity around the dock dropped off, and he was aware of another presence following close behind. Turning into the sun, he spotted the hazy outline of a back-lit figure across the street.

"Hello, who is it goes there?" he said, hailing the wraith-like figure.

"Hello, Peter. Surely you remember me?"

The face, still backlit from the sun, was not recognizable. Peter squinted into its dark folds, seeing glimpses of light against cheekbone, deep hollows by the eyes, and a flash of auburn in the hair. Then the man turned fully into the light and Peter caught his breath and hissed it out slowly. "Eamonn Conor!"

"The very same," Eamonn said.

Peter noted that his smile was mirthless. "What are you doing here in Bantry?"

"Just visiting old haunts and getting away from my Cork office." Eamonn, the much taller of the two, came to stand just below Peter on the sloping street. Both now looked eye to eye.

Peter had worked on Conor's Audi whenever Conor was in Cork, but the last time was several months ago. And now he was accosting Peter in his home town. "This wasn't a chance meeting, was it?

Eamonn's smile was sly as he confided to Peter. "It seems I have need of your services, Peter, and not as a mechanic. What do you say? Would you be interested in earning a lot of money, now?"

Peter sensed nervousness in the man's darting eyes. "A lot of money, you say? Just how do I go about earning it, then? Is it illegal? No, of course it is, considering that you're the one making the proposition." Peter crossed his arms and gazed imperiously at Eamonn.

"Well, now, this requires a man with nerves of steel and a firm resolve. How much would you want to help me arrange an accident for someone?" His smile reminded Peter of a wolf's sly, tongue-lolling grin.

"What did you say? What kind of an accident did you have in mind?"

"One of a permanent nature."

Peter looked around them to make sure they were alone. "Are

you talking about murder, then? Are you crazy?"

"You heard me right enough, Peter. Members of the IRA, I'm told, are not averse to killing."

A stab of anger and disbelief shot through Peter. All his secrecy and the careful rebuilding of his life could be compromised by one weasel of a Prot. Almost before he realized it, he had Eamonn's jacket in his grasp and was lifting the man off his feet. He watched Conor's eyes grow large in his face. Peter enjoyed having the man completely in his power. He wouldn't so easily regain his composure while his feet dangled uselessly, either, Peter decided.

"Calm down, Peter," he croaked, "I'm not going to bandy that about."

"Damn right, you aren't." Peter set him back down, still holding his jacket. "You'd be long dead before your first word. How did you know?"

As Eamonn got his breath and composure back he said, "Money buys a lot of confidences if you know who to ask. I just wanted to be sure I had the right man for the job, that's all." Eamonn was breathing hard as he straightened the folds of his jacket before he continued. "Look, I'm talking about a lot of money here. What would you say to a hundred thousand pounds sterling?"

"What! A hundred thousand, you say? Who d'ya want dead, the Pope?" Peter placed hands on hips and waited while Eamonn nervously loosened his tie.

"No, but someone just as important to me."

"Who?"

"I'm not ready to say, just yet. I just wanted to be sure, in principle, that I had your interest."

"Aye, you can be sure you have my interest. But why would I do such a thing?"

"Money. I've heard you are in need of some, last time I talked to my contact."

Peter looked at him curiously. Everything he remembered about Eamonn told him not to trust the man. "You seem to know a lot about me. Who is this contact?"

"Now, Peter, you wouldn't expect me to reveal that, would you? What I hear is you lost a lucrative contract with the university." When Peter didn't respond, he added, "Thought they were too good for you at their bloody well-to-do university, did they? Chucking you out after how many years of faithful service?"

The sting of Eamonn's words caused him to recall the Dean's curt dismissal at the party. The scene that Peter made at the party didn't help his cause any. His hand still ached from the cuts he suffered. The following day he was informed that his contract had been terminated. That final insult caused his face to redden again.

"That may be, but why would I want to kill someone? This is dangerous talk now, Eamonn. How do I know you're not puttin' me on?"

"Oh, you can be sure I'm deadly serious. Besides, you might enjoy killing this one anyway. But don't worry; I've already got a plan worked out."

"If you already have a plan, why don't you do it?"

"I could, but I'd be the first one the police would suspect." Eamonn paused and looked around before continuing. "I need someone else to carry out the plan. But don't worry, its foolproof."

"Yeah, and I'm your fool if I do it." Peter turned to walk away but then another thought struck him. "Wait. If you're the first they'd suspect, it must be someone you know well." Peter stroked his chin as he considered the possibilities. "I don't think I like this." As he started to move away, Eamonn caught hold of his sleeve.

"Please, hear me out."

"Well, all right then. Let's hear it."

The two men went down the street towards the quay, and then turned off toward Peter's garage. The soft mumble of their conversation was swallowed up in the sounds of the water lapping at the shore, and the staccato resonance of a joiner's hammer striking wood.

CHAPTER 8

CORK
FRIDAY

Sean Carey gazed up to the top row of the auditorium, searching for the questioner. He spotted the student trying to balance his book and notepad on his knees, while simultaneously straightening his glasses and flipping to the page that had sparked his question.

"I believe that was on page forty-two, Jack. Yes, that anomaly has been commented on by our own Seamus Dunoon. I concur with him that more work needs to be done before we have truly established a complete cycle of events."

Seeing no more hands raised, Sean closed the textbook and straightened his notes as he dismissed the class. He shaded his eyes against the sun streaming down from the high windows onto the first row of darkened wood seats. Only one student was still seated. The rest had exited, with the usual buzz of conversation.

He felt at home here, the large podium providing a comfortable resting place for his long arms. He preferred to slouch slightly so that his height did not make him appear too intimidating to his students. He knew his subject and how to present it, seldom worrying about the attention of his students. However, the dark-haired willowy student in the front row was spending more time concentrating on him than on her books. She was squirming in her seat now, and he braced himself for the inevitable request. A moment later, she looked up expectantly at Sean.

"Professor Carey, I'm really lost on that last point you made. Could you go over that again... maybe over lunch?" She had a look of unquenchable thirst on her face, but her suggestive movements made him doubt that physics was the source.

"Sorry, Sally, but I'm meeting Professor Dunoon. Perhaps before your next class?"

"Oh, we wouldn't have enough time then." She had the good grace to blush before adding, "Maybe after classes."

"Sorry, I don't have any free time until next week. Why don't you re-read the chapter? That may resolve your confusion."

Sean was not sure re-reading the chapter would help, but it gave him a reprieve as she hugged the books to her chest and turned to leave. He gave her an encouraging smile anyway, as she strolled out the door.

Crossing the grassy commons, Sean gazed up at the newer glass-and-concrete campus buildings, noting how out of place they seemed beside the older ones. The old Ballinure School buildings that had become Kerry University were inadequate to contain the university's growing population. The stimulus of having Apple headquartered here being one factor.

Even now, new buildings were sprouting up around them. The urgency of meeting immediate needs had made architectural compatibility a low priority. Sean wasn't sure they had their priorities straight.

While the heart of old Cork still held the history of centuries in its darkened stones, the many industrial parks suggested a commitment to technology. Sean reflected on the many contrasts. Old Cork, on the River Lee, had its claustrophobic streets, ancient buildings, and narrow bridges. Below it, here in southern Cork, the wider streets were filled with row upon row of warehouses, punctuated by schools, depots, and hospitals. He was torn between preserving the old traditions and supporting Ireland's commitment to joining the new Europe. In this newer world, he longed even more intensely for views of the old Ireland.

He found a table in the nearly-empty faculty lounge next to a tall, mullioned window. His stomach growled angrily at the lateness of his lunch hour. While he sat waiting for Seamus, he looked out across the eastern tip of Cork. Here the Glashaboy River crept under Dunkettle Bridge to join the River Lee before emptying into the lake that served as a buffer to the outer harbor.

He was lost in thought, mesmerized by the swirling of the waters, when the scrape of a chair intruded. He looked up to find a man sitting across from him, a cryptic smile playing across his face. It took Sean only a moment to place him.

"Eamonn! What are you doing here?"

"Sean, how nice to see you again, too. I come here on business every so often. Surely you remember our fishing down south by Bantry Bay, drinking ourselves into a stupor in my little cottage on Coomhola Mountain? But that was before you met Liz, wasn't it?"

Sean was confused. "Liz?" Slowly he realized it was Beth, Conor was talking about. Sean wondered how Conor knew he was seeing Beth. He hated that gloating face. So self-assured, happily spending his father's money, and believing everyone else had been put on the planet to serve him. He willed himself to stay calm, refusing to let Eamonn see what fear those memories dredged up. He would wait him out. Let him play his hand first.

"Not talking, hmm? You know, I really haven't seen very much of you since the accident. Why is that? You weren't ashamed of me, were you?"

"Look Eamonn, we've been over that before. You know how I felt about what you did. I don't see any good reason to go over it now."

"What I did? Ah yes, but you didn't do anything, did you, Sean?"

Sean winced, as he experienced the stab of pain that memory invoked. Once again, he had let Eamonn slip the knife in.

"Yes," Eamonn continued, "I'd say we both had too much to

drink. And the fog, the fog was so thick that night. Maybe we really didn't run over that drunk. Maybe we just imagined it. What do you think?"

"Look! Is there some reason you wanted to parade our past sins, because I'm getting very angry." Sean squeezed the arms of his chair, suppressing his building rage.

"Sean, me boy, you mustn't get so upset over this. But I do hear you've been seeing Liz, hmm? No, it would be Beth. She never seemed to like Liz."

"Since you left her what do you care?"

Eamonn paused, stroking his cheek with his forefinger as if to absorb this bit of information before replying. "Er...actually, I wanted to make sure you didn't mention this to any of our mutual friends."

"Like your father, for instance?" Sean saw that his remark had hit home. Now Eamonn was starting to look uncomfortable.

"Just remember, you're as guilty as me. You don't want Beth to know about our past history any more than I want my father to know." Eamonn leaned over the table. "And he doesn't need to know Beth and I are not together, does he?"

"No. If that's what you came here to find out, you have. Now get out of my sight." Sean stood at his last remark, glaring down at Eamonn who shrugged his shoulders, as though unable to understand Sean's hostility. Glancing to his right, Sean noted the remaining diners were looking in their direction. Following his gaze, Eamonn got up nervously and walked off.

Seamus Dunoon came over to the table just as Eamonn left. He raised his eyebrows, looking at Sean for clarification. Sean knew from past experience that when Seamus' bushy eyebrows were raised, they spoke as loudly as a question. The eyebrows completed a theme that included a full beard well suited to his large frame. Sean seldom looked up at anyone, but Seamus was inches taller and twice his size.

Seamus settled down in the chair, and it groaned in protest.

He looked over at Sean while stroking his beard, then laid his huge forearms on the table. "So, what was that all about, then? D' ya know him now, laddie?"

Sean smiled in spite of himself. It always tickled him when Seamus called him laddie, just the way he'd always hoped his Da would say it. In truth, Seamus was closer to him than his own father, who avoided all discussions of a personal nature. But this was something he'd told no one else.

"That was Eamonn Conor, an old classmate of mine." Sean thought hard on an appropriate answer. "We fought over the same woman once, and he-" Sean hesitated. "He was bringing it up again."

"Ah, an old wound, was it? What does he want with you now?"

"I'm not sure, Seamus." More to himself, Sean added, "Partly to keep quiet, and partly something else he has cooking in that devious brain of his."

"So there's bad blood between you?"

Sean considered his answer. "Let's just say I wasn't thrilled to see him again."

"Um hm, and what's the rest of it? This is not why you invited me to a late lunch, is it?"

Sean felt the last of the tension flow from him. He always felt safe with Seamus, who included him in the warm circle of his affection with his eyes as easily as his bear hug gave it physical substance. "No. A much...more pleasant topic, I promise you."

"So who is she, laddie?"

"I met this... is it that obvious?" They both laughed before Sean resumed. "I met this stunning woman two nights ago at the Fitzsimmons' party. Beth O'Hara. I believe you know her."

"Oh yes, a stunning woman indeed. You've set your sights very high, my boy. Very beautiful and very smart. A dangerous combination, if you're thinking of staying unhitched."

Sean's face lit up hearing this unalloyed praise, but then quickly darkened again. "Not nearly as dangerous as this fellow I met at the Fitzsimmons party along with Beth."

"Sorry I couldn't make it, too many papers to grade. Who was it?"

Sean looked behind him nervously, as if the diners several tables away were listening to his every word. "Peter Deagan."

"Aye, a bad choice to run afoul of, no doubt about it. What did he say, or do?" Seamus's expression had turned from playful to serious at the mention of Peter's name.

"He was upset enough to disintegrate a glass when Beth refused to leave with him, and instead drove home with me." When Seamus only nodded, he added. "His hand was bleeding like a stuck pig, and he didn't care. Didn't even seem to know he was bleeding. He just kept staring at Beth like only murder would satisfy him. I can tell you it was very unnerving."

"His reputation with the women is not good, Sean.

"How's that?"

"He's attracts a lot of 'em. My secretary said his devilishly handsome face and rough manners excite women that like danger. And I don't think he takes rejection well."

"Count on it."

"But you intend to see her again, anyway."

It sounded like an irrefutable statement rather than a question to Sean, and he realized it was true. But it wasn't just Deagan that bothered him. "What in the hell is his problem, anyway?"

"I don't know, Sean, but I've heard he knows more than a little about the IRA."

"Christ, what else do I have to watch out for?"

They were interrupted by another visitor. "Professor Carey? I'm open for the rest of the day now if you have some free time later," a student breathlessly intoned as she walked past him.

"Eh? Oh, fine, Sally. I think I have some time after four."

They both watched in admiration as she walked away. Talk at the other tables stopped as well. Sean turned at Seamus's delighted chuckle.

"So much change has been going on lately. What is it you'd like to talk to me about, Sean? Beth, or that salivating student?"

"The curse of being a charismatic teacher. They won't leave me alone." Sean chuckled while leaning back in his chair. "It's so good to see you again, Seamus. I missed you while I was in America. I couldn't believe my good fortune to find you had come here from Scotland."

"And also find out that Beth lived here, no doubt?"

Sean easily returned to the subject of Beth. "Yes, we managed to catch lunch yesterday. We talked for over two hours, mostly about ourselves and..." Sean realized the gnawing in his stomach was a signal to bring up the reason for this meeting.

"What is it, laddie?"

"How much do you know about Beth and her son?"

"It's not something she talks about other than mentioning her love and pride in her son. He's a fine lad."

"So her um, ex-husband left them? Is he still alive?"

Seamus looked at Sean oddly. "I don't know. She never said his name that I recall. She never mentioned divorce, which isn't possible in the Republic anyway, so I think he just abandoned them. Fool that he was."

Sean tore bits of his napkin as he pondered his friend's reply.

"Are you worried he might come back into her life?"

Sean looked up, startled by the thought. "Well, if they weren't divorced, and he isn't dead." Sean hesitated. "I suppose he could come back into the picture."

"I never got the impression she'd welcome that."

Sean, still puzzling over their conversation gave a noncommittal nod.

Seamus asked, "Do you think it could be serious between you two?"

Sean, at last, reacted. "Serious, did you say? Yes, I think so." He leaned back in his chair; pressed fingers to his forehead and sighed. "I'd have to eventually tell her about my less-than-illustrious past, though."

Seamus looked intently at him and then smiled. "Sean, d' ya think it's possible that Beth's own past is less than glowing?"

"You're right, of course. If I've learned one thing from you, it's to look objectively at life." Sean sat up, his voice charged with energy again. "Yes, I think possibly we've both had bad times in the past."

"I'm pleased to see the lessons took," Seamus said.

"Lord, why are relationships so bloody complicated? Yet we just want them to be simple, to the point and uncluttered with human cant and dissembling. Like us. We meet after how many years, and it's like we never were apart. That still seems uncanny to me, yet its part of our relationship."

"It is indeed. But it's your relationship with Beth that interests me now. How d'ya see that?"

Sean talked at some length about what he had always wanted in a woman, and had nearly given any hope of finding. He reeled off all of Beth's good points, real and imagined, which matched that list so well. Seamus drew him out, and gradually Sean's fears and doubts abated. "Yes, I already care about her, and think about her, and worry about her. And I've only just met her! I might as well admit it; I'm already in pretty deep." He looked up at Seamus, amazement animating his features. "How do you see to the heart of things so easily, though? That's what I'd like to know."

"It's simple, Sean. I just listen to you and feed it back. You already have all the answers, laddie. You just need someone to remind you what they are from time to time."

They laughed again and went on to reminisce over old times and how good it was to get back together again. Then they ordered a lunch of smoked salmon with stacks of brown bread and strong tea. They ate in companionable silence, enjoying the flavors of the food and each other's quiet company. Finally, Seamus touched the napkin to his lips and shook the remaining crumbs from his beard.

"One last thing, Sean. Be careful around Peter. I'm told he

can be right nasty and if he's set his sights on her, there's no telling what he might do."

And that gave Sean more to worry about than even Seamus realized.

CHAPTER 9
GOUGANE BARRA
FRIDAY

Beth's time-ravaged Rover usually stayed in the garage on Friday. She enjoyed her three-day weekends after driving the seventy kilometers to and from Cork each day, and avoided getting back in the car whenever possible. Not that the drive to Kerry University wasn't pleasant enough; at least she didn't have to deal with the traffic jams in Dublin. She'd been told it sometimes took Dubliners an hour to drive ten miles. Sean had mentioned that it was even worse on California's expressways. She found that hard to imagine, since there were few dual carriageways outside Dublin in Ireland.

But now she felt a sense of urgency to get to Gougane Barra, and it wasn't just to see Sean. Over lunch, Thursday, she had suggested they meet there for dinner at a cozy roadhouse hotel. She had described the lovely dining room overlooking the lake, and he had readily agreed.

The road elbowed into a steep ascent and the Rover's engine whined from the exertion. When the road opened into upland pastures, the green Honda was still following her. It had pulled in behind her as she passed Kitty Doyle's bed and breakfast, and was still there, keeping just within sight. Few people lived high up on Coomhola, so she was a little surprised to have company. As she turned left off the main road for the last couple of miles to the lake, the Honda also turned.

Why was she worried about that car? After all, it wasn't that unusual for another car to be tagging along; particularly at the speed her aged Rover managed. But for the last week she had the distinct sensation of being followed. In her car, on her bike, and walking around the campus of Kerry University, a tingling in her neck kept sending warning messages to her brain; warnings that she was having difficulty ignoring the longer they persisted.

She sighed with relief when she spotted Sean's Jaguar in the hotel's parking lot. Getting out, she glanced once behind her and saw the Honda drive slowly past. The driver was hidden behind tinted windows, only the hands visible through the windscreen. Suddenly, an image of death arose in her mind. In horror, she watched as the hands grasping the wheel turned white as bone. Then the driver's window descended soundlessly, and a skeletal face grinned at her from inside a black cowl. Squeezing her eyes shut and opening them again, Beth saw the sun glinting off the still-closed window, reflecting the hotel's gothic tower as the car completed its circuit and turned off the road. The image had evaporated, but not the chill left in its wake.

Sean was at the restaurant entrance and warmly grasped her hand, waiting to take her inside. The smile on his face quickly faded.

"Beth, are you all right? You look as though you've seen a ghost."

"Maybe I did. Or maybe I need to get my eyes examined. Did you see a green Honda follow me in?"

"I don't believe so."

"Never mind." She didn't want her over-active imagination to spoil the evening, and quickly changed the subject. "What do you think of this place?"

"You've made an excellent choice, Beth. I'd always wanted to come here. The lake, these mountains." He smiled as he turned to her. "It's breathtaking. Do you come here often?"

"Oh, yes. I bring all my gentlemen callers here for the first date." Seeing his disappointed look, she quickly relented. "I come

74

here at least once a year with Julian. We have a grand time playing in the forest park and walking about the lake front, but I haven't been to the restaurant. We always bring a picnic." She smiled at his expression of relief.

They were promptly led to a corner table with views of the lake from both sides. They were lost in conversation the moment they were seated. The starters came but were barely touched, so intent were they on each other.

"You mentioned that you do a lot of cycling. Where do you go around here?"

"Oh, everywhere. The roads around here are perfect for it. Very few cars, compared to Dublin, and the scenery is so varied. I never get bored. Tomorrow I'm going on the Beara Peninsula and crossing over Healy Pass."

"Healy Pass, that's the one that crosses the peninsula and drops down to Bantry Bay, isn't it?"

"Right. Duncan and Julian usually meet me in Glengariff for tea and scones afterwards. That way, I don't have to do the last climb home."

"It still sounds like a lot of cycling to me. I'm ready to get off after a few miles, myself."

"Well, I'm a very strong cyclist and I'm used to riding around here. I know almost every road. That's the wonderful thing about cycling." Beth's hands described arcs and swirls as she tried to communicate her passion to Sean. "You own the road, much more than someone driving on it. I'm in intimate contact with everything around me. I greet all the sheep grazing along the road, enjoy the lush smell of the earth, and hear the softest bird trill."

"Ah, the poet in you comes out at last. Does the cycling serve as inspiration?"

"Yes, indeed, it does." Beth was flattered by Sean's incisive comment.

"Well, maybe I should trade in my Jaguar for a Raleigh and join you, then."

"Oh, I'd love the company, Sean, but don't turn in the Jaguar just yet." Beth flushed as she remembered how sensual the drive up to her cottage had seemed. The throbbing engine had vibrated her seat, making her squirm. She prayed her smile was not too revealing.

The time passed swiftly as the avocado and prawn salad gave way to the main course, a wonderful steak flambéed in an Irish whiskey sauce, followed by a walnut-and-orange gateau. Beth felt very much at ease with Sean. It seemed like they had known each other for a long time; her friend Katherine would have said it was from a past life. They had shared many intimate details, although she knew there was more in their past to discuss. Sooner or later, she would have to mention her 'arrangement' with Eamonn. But not this evening. She didn't want any ripples to spoil the atmosphere. Then she remembered her drive and shivered.

"What is it, Beth? You're wearin' the same look you had when you arrived."

She looked into his alert, caring eyes and hoped she could confide in him. She took a deep breath. "Sean, I think I was followed here this evening."

"What? Do you know who it might be?"

"No, the car passed by here, but I didn't get a good look at the driver." Suppressing another shiver, she continued. "I've had this feeling of being followed for almost a week now."

Sean leaned in closer as they continued talking. "Do you know why someone would be following you? Is it Peter, do you think?"

"I don't think so, it looked like one of those generic cars they have at the airport, not a local." She shivered before continuing. "But he'd certainly be a logical choice. It's not just a feeling, though. You remember the ruckus Felix caused the other night?"

"How could I forget? I went out to investigate and..." He looked at her intently. "What is it, Beth?"

"I don't think it was Felix that caused the commotion." Beth saw the concern in his expression, and almost wished she hadn't destroyed the romantic mood, but her instincts screamed at her to tell him. "I'm almost sure there was someone out there. After you left, I heard more noises; sounds like someone moving fast across the garden and up to the house. I was in my bedroom."

"Christ, are you sure you're safe there?"

"Why?"

"I'd volunteer to watch over you. If you thought..."

Beth watched him swallow an embarrassed smile, before she replied. "You'd take on that little job, would you?"

"I can think of worse chores."

The words downplayed what she sensed was a yearning as strong as her own. "So can I." Then she turned serious again. "But I'm not used to feeling danger in my home. Not since . . . not for a long time."

"No, of course not. It worries me, too."

"I know. Well... I pulled up the shade and didn't see anything. Just sensed that something was amiss. The moon going in and out of the clouds may have influenced my mood. I did see Felix out in the garden, but he wouldn't have made those sounds or frightened me enough to make me close the window."

Beth looked down to find that her hand, which had been flailing over the table in agitation, was now tightly wrapped in his. Oh, hell! The imprecation rang in her head. She knew what it meant. A pressing need to have someone caring for her, even if just for a little while. Just until the dread waned and she felt in control again. Was it so much to ask? To let him hold her and tell her everything would be all right, if only for a little while? Then she could once again wear the tough outer shell that was her salvation.

She looked up, startled, afraid the thoughts and emotions they produced were visible, but she saw only concern and... and what? She looked intently at his face. She wanted to name that look love. It had the same intensity, the same softness, but it had been misnamed by her before, and she was afraid to trust her instincts. Confused, she dropped the narrative as though its previous importance was lost on her.

"What is it, Beth?"

"Where was I?"

"About being followed?"

"Oh, yes. I spotted that car on the drive up. It's the first time I've actually seen anyone. It made it all seem more real. But who would be following me? And why?"

They discussed it over coffee and, after exhausting the possibilities, were restless to go. To work off the meal, they took a stroll by the lake, stopping by a small grove. She felt his hand tighten in hers and turned toward him. She looked up into his earnest face and noted the look of expectation and she smiled.

When Sean took her in his arms, there was no hesitation. Her mouth opened eagerly and she tasted his tongue against hers. Her arms swept across his broad back, pressing him to her. She felt her nipples harden as they brushed against the weave of his sweater, and a delicious shiver roamed her body. He moved his hands down her body, traversing the flare of her hips, his fingers probing the firm flesh of her buttocks. Beth felt him hard against her and reveled in the sensation. She felt the heat spread outwards from that point of pressure, until every particle of her body vibrated to a primitive beat. This time it was Sean who pulled away.

"Sean?"

"Sorry. I guess I need to take it slow, too." He was still breathing heavily, but there was also pain in his eyes that she did not understand.

"Is something wrong?" She watched him slowly regain control of his emotions and the pain left his face. "It was just so abrupt, I wasn't expecting it." She leaned back from his slackening embrace. "You really are troubled, aren't you?"

"It's just that a lot is happening all at once. My new position. Meeting you. Someone following you. Strange noises in the night..."

"All right, I get the picture. Enough."

"Beth, I...I think there's much we need to talk about."

"What, Sean?"

"Well, not here. I think I need the bright sun on me to think straight. You have my brain all a-whirl just now."

Beth smiled into his sincere, troubled face. He was having the same problem with control as she. "You're right. We couldn't hold a serious conversation now, could we?"

"No, indeed. We can talk about it this weekend...if you're free."

"I have all Sunday open. Where should we meet?"

"You name it. You're good at that."

"Then it's the Bantry House at eleven. You know where it is?"

"No, but why don't I pick up you and Julian? I still haven't met him."

"Wonderful. Julian will enjoy meeting you." Beth thought to herself, he wants to meet my son. We are getting serious no matter what we have both said. Her smile broadened.

They walked back to Beth's car and kissed again before Sean opened the door for her. He watched her drive off before getting into his own car. He thought he spotted a dark figure by the park and a reflection of light off glass. He thought of binoculars and then chided himself for an overactive imagination. But was it his imagination that someone was observing them?

He started the engine and, glancing in his rearview mirror, saw a green Honda depart, trailing a fine cloud of smoke. Had it started at the same time as his car? He decided to keep one eye on his mirror, as he drove off toward Cork.

CHAPTER 10

COOMHOLA
SATURDAY

Beth O'Hara watched the sun redden her chintz drapes. The bite of a crisp early Saturday morning breeze prompted her to finish the preparations for her ride. Mentally ticking off the check list, she packed some food to take along and loaded it on the bike. After giving her bicycle a thorough check, she snapped a tool kit under the seat. The bike was Beth's one extravagance, an American-made mountain bike in bright green with yellow accents, ideally suited to the rough, pot-holed roads.

Contemplating the ride ahead, she felt the familiar stirring in her stomach. As she started off, Beth tightened the straps of her toe clips, locking foot to pedal, and was ready for the first downhill stretch. The wind became a physical force as she gathered speed, leaning expertly into each turn, and feeling the pull of gravity pressing her more heavily into the seat. The road, like the maw of a giant snake, swallowed her in its many coils.

Her concentration was on the bank of each turn, her eyes ceaselessly searching for debris. Taking one corner too high, she fought to bring the bike back in line, the tires hissing from the intense lateral pressures. Pumping the brakes lightly, the bike corrected its track, just missing the pebble-strewn shoulder as she came out of the turn. Her heart dropped from her throat back to her chest and she whooshed air out between pursed lips. "Nice recovery, Ritchey," she said, patting the bike. It amused her to give the bike a name, and the one painted on the down tube was perfect.

Chastising herself for her lapse in concentration, she again focused on what lay around the next bend, over the next rise. The lush, encroaching foliage was a green blur. In this insular world of woman and machine, her creative mind was free to roam over topics her logical mind found insoluble. She remembered once asking Katherine how she solved problems through meditation. "Well," she said, "it's a way of switching gears. Let the brain make its own connections, unfettered by logic's nagging and limiting messages."

Beth realized that these long rides were her way of meditating, and she put all the conflicting problems into a stew and let it simmer. What could she do about Eamonn? How would Sean accept the information? How would all this affect Julian? Perhaps, by the end of the ride, she would have some answers to replace the agony of confusion.

The scent of a huge flower garden finally brought her back to her surroundings. She was coming to the Doyle's farmhouse on her right, its stark white front relieved by crisscrossing scarlet vines. She slowed to better take in the sight. It had taken Beth years to train her own vines to come close to looking like Kitty's. They encircled the house in a lace of red leaves and gnarled vine.

The window boxes were filled to overflowing with pansies and flowering herbs, and row upon row of heavily-scented roses drew her nearer. The gaily-painted sign beside the door proclaimed 'Coomhola Roost,' a name she'd heard Kitty and Sandy argue over endlessly. Beth imagined the view of Bantry Bay as glimpsed from the guest rooms, and remembered Kitty mentioning that all four rooms were taken.

That was when she noticed that one of the cars parked by the old barn was a green Honda. "Jesus, Mary, and all the saints! No, it can't be the same one."

She glanced up at the second story. A lace curtain in one of the guest rooms briefly parted, then slowly closed, and a now-familiar chill coursed through her body. She was sure the hand on the curtain had been human; this time. And didn't she notice a green Honda following her just after she had passed Coomhola Roost yesterday? Unable to tear her eyes away, she unwittingly let her bike drift towards the right side of the road as she was about to crest the hill.

The truck driver was near his last stop, tired and bleary-eyed. It had been a long night and morning and he was knackered. As his lorry crested the hill, his attention was on the map resting on the passenger seat, marking the location of his final delivery. Something in his peripheral vision caused him to look up just as a bicycle swung into his path. He punched his horn and then swung over to his left as far as the road's margin would permit. Oh lord, he was going to hit her.

The blare of the lorry's horn brought Beth back to the present and saw a truck bearing down upon her. On full alert, she quickly swerved to her left, eyes wide. The lorry driver's eyes also looked big in his face. He was moving partly onto the margin as she narrowly missed the front bumper. She felt the heat of the exhaust as she past the vehicle, which slowed as the brakes were applied. "Mind the road," the frightened driver shouted after her.

"I am now," she said under her breath, and put her focus back on the ride as her heart stopped fluttering. Being careless on her bike was not like her, but then Beth realized she wasn't like herself anymore. Pulling over on the road she took several deep breaths to let the adrenaline subside and her breathing return to normal.

She was only halfway down the hill and a mile past Coomhola Roost. Beth turned in that direction and considered what she should do. Kitty was always full of stories about her guests, and would probably be happy to tell her all about the owner of the green Honda.

Not that Kitty was a gossip. The high art to which Kitty had brought it called for a more prestigious title. Maybe 'chief-dispenser-of-what-nobody-knows-about-anyone-else' would do. The title was a bit wordy but, considering its subject, probably appropriate, Beth thought to herself, in amusement.

Deciding on a course of action, she pushed off and continued her descent which took her to Bantry Bay and the N71, which took her past Glengariff where her handyman Duncan and Julian would wait for her on her return loop. The N71 would take her to a lowland valley, near the delta of the Kenmare River. The mouth of the Kenmare was actually a narrow bay separating two peninsulas. She would then take the R571 along Kenmare Bay between the Beara and Iveragh Peninsulas to the R574, which would take her to Healy Pass.

It was late morning when she reached the summit of Healy Pass. The sun was bright and warm on her face, and the day clear with few clouds. The large-flowered butterwort was in bloom, sprinkling color through a sea of grass. Behind her were Kenmare and the Ring of Kerry, and ahead a breathtaking view of Bantry Bay. The tip of Sheep's Head peninsula was clearly visible at the mouth of Bantry Bay, but Mizen Head beyond it was lost in the mist of the Atlantic's gray domain.

She paused for a rest by the bone-white statue of the crucifixion; a sharp contrast to the lush, green valley below her. Her hand stroked the foot of the statue as she gazed across the broad valley. The road below corkscrewed as though unsure of which direction to take to reach the bay. She pushed off on her final descent and began picking up speed again as she leaned left, then right, then left again, around each hairpin turn.

She was a third of the way down, when a large, black sedan passed her on the right, going up the hill. It set off a warning bell, which became an icicle of fear dancing down her back. She didn't dare turn around - her attention had to be on the road - but she listened for any hint of danger, and prayed that her instincts were wrong.

Then she heard the sound of a car downshifting and then the staccato ping of gravel striking metal that signaled it was turning around. Her alarm bells were more strident now, as she glanced back to see the car heading back towards her. Normally, drivers were very courteous; giving cyclists a wide berth, but this one was staying close to the edge of the road, almost on the margin. She stayed far over to the left and, with quick glances behind, saw the sedan approaching.

The driver drew abreast of her, staying uncomfortably close. She could feel the heat from the engine only inches from her leg. The roadside shrubs gave her no room on her left and he was closing in on her right. What was he doing? Didn't he have anything better to do than pester her? She snapped her head back for a quick look at the driver but the heavily-tinted windows made it hard to see inside the car. She could only see his hands tightly wrapped over the steering wheel, twisting slowly.

Abruptly, the car swerved over towards her. Half expecting it, she'd already decided on a course of action. Wheel-hopping over the rock-strewn margin, she slid and churned through loose earth, then rode the drop off beyond where the car could follow. The knobby tires dug in and held as she made quick corrections with her handlebars and body.

Adrenaline surged through her, sharpening her senses. Part of her mind clinically observed its effect as she tried to control every motion, every shift of the bike, but she knew she would only survive if she let her instincts take over. Beth wasn't aware of her fear. It played in the background, while she busied herself with reactions.

The car tried to follow, but the irregular surface and steep drop caused it to fishtail, and it remounted the road. Beth knew she couldn't evade the car indefinitely. Soon the road would level off, and then the driver could run her over, if that was his plan. Perhaps he was only trying to scare her. Well, if so, he had succeeded.

She was plenty frightened.

Even though the car was an expensive sedan, and not the green Honda she had spotted before, she wondered if there was a connection. Later, she decided, would be time to ponder it further. Now she had to escape alive.

Although she wasn't an experienced off-road cyclist, her only course of action was to get away from the road. Soon, all she could do was concentrate on staying on the bike, avoiding large rocks and making rapid corrections over tufts of hardy grass and loose earth along the way. This was becoming one hell of a Saturday ride.

Looking ahead, she noticed that the course she tracked was coming to a ravine. Could she make it across? It looked very wide as she came up on it; perhaps too wide? She timed her jump at the apex of the rise, pushing up with her body. She was airborne! She thought everything would move in slow motion - it always did in the movies - but, instead, time sped up. She felt the bike dropping fast; too fast.

But the surge of adrenaline had added enough power to allow the bike to sail over the deep trench to safe terrain again. Thoughts flashed through her mind as she determined how to land properly, her decision coming a split second before the tires bit into the soft earth.

The impact was more violent than she had expected. Her left hand momentarily broke free of the handlebar, and the bike swerved crazily. She was losing control, the ground a brown-and-green blur, and the ceaseless vibrations from the front wheel numbing her hands. Then a darkly-shaded area warned of yet another yawning precipice ahead.

She pulled her left foot out of the pedal grip to brace herself, grabbing the brakes hard and leaning over to set the bike down, just before she reached the edge. She slid in the earth, kicking up a spray of soil and stones and the bike hurtled forwards like a dropped anchor. The ground dipped down sharply, her momentum carrying her to the edge. "No!" One last downward twist of the front wheel digging in the earth, and the bike finally came to rest.

At first, she was too dazed to do more than hold tightly onto the handlebars and stare at the still revolving rear wheel. Gradually, she noted the smell of moist earth in her nostrils and a stinging sensation along her calf. Hesitantly, she explored her leg for bleeding, and then slowly moved first one leg and then the other. Her left side had struck a jagged rock that had opened a gash along her leg. A sob arched her body before she could recall it, but she was glad to be alive and mobile.

Turning towards the road, she spotted the car. Unable to follow her, it had stopped on the roadside. Abruptly, it sped off down the mountain, tires squealing. Getting up, Beth checked the damage to her bike and decided it was in a lot better shape than she was. She pulled her water bottle out of its down tube rack and poured water onto the wound.

Clenching her teeth against the pain, Beth removed her jacket and T-shirt. Tearing the shirt into strips she wrapped one strip around her left leg to stem the flow of blood. The other strip she wound over her left forearm, which was also badly scraped.

A coastal wind caressed her naked chest, raising goose flesh. Shivering, she quickly put her jacket back on and zipped it up to her chin. She slowly walked around, checking for other damage. She was sore, but nothing else major appeared to be wrong. Beth thought how lucky she was to have escaped serious injury, until she became light-headed and had to sit down. She didn't want shock to settle in. Not when that car could still be out there. Finally, the dizziness went away and she walked the bike back up to the road.

Looking left and right, she considered her options. This was the only road down to the bay. Would it be better to go the other way? She quickly rejected that possibility. She didn't have the energy for any more hill climbs. If she went down towards the bay, would more cars reduce the chance of another attempt? What if the car was waiting up ahead for her? She replayed the rest of her ride down. Where below her could it hide? Or would the driver come back up the road and meet her, head on?

She was tired, cold, and hurt and desperately wanted to see Julian again, but she had to be careful. "Come on, Beth girl, time to get going." The sound of her own voice helped bring her back to reality.

The road above and below her was deserted, the last vestiges of dust had settled on the ground. Only the sounds of her labored breathing broke the silence. It was time to go. She looked intently down to the next bend in the road, wondering what might appear there, and when.

CHAPTER 11
BANTRY
SATURDAY

Eamonn Conor had always disliked the Irish phone system. Each coinbox seemed to have its own personality quirks, accepting different coinage and requiring special handling. The one he chose away from the shops in Bantry used the large twenty pence pieces. Cursing, he stomped off to a curio shop for the right coins.

When he returned, he impatiently jammed the coins onto the track which fed them into the machine. The first large coins rolled down the ramp into the open slot. As the coinbox impassively gulped one down, the rest moved along the track.

He switched the phone to his other ear and looked out over the glistening bay to the distant mountains. His gaze was unfocused, and sweat poured down his face even though a cool breeze was blowing. He was shaking with fear, the tension causing his muscles to spasm.

He heard the phone being picked up and then a pause, followed by "Yes?"

"Peter, I need to talk to you." He watched the descent of the coins, hoping to get what he needed from Peter before they ran out.

"What do you want?"

"The, eh, job we talked about last Friday. I'll make it--"

"Where are you calling from?"

"A coinbox in Bantry," said Eamonn, confused by the question.

"Fine, wait a minute."

Eamonn heard a shrill tone, followed by a hiss, and then Peter was back.

"Go ahead."

Eamonn held the receiver away from his ear, startled. "What was that?"

"Protection," Peter said.

Eamonn put the phone back to his ear, looking around him as he spoke. "I was saying, about that job. I'll make it two hundred thousand. But I need you to get right on it."

"Oh, the price is going up, is it? And how much do you think it'll take to turn me?"

"Look, I can't spend a lot more time here. If you don't do it... well, people could find out things."

There was silence at the other end. When Peter replied, his voice was cold. "Eamonn, have you ever heard of knee-capping?"

Eamonn had lived long enough in Belfast to have heard many of the gruesome stories. His cousin Kieran delighted in telling him about how so-and-so had come by his limp. "Not from a skiing accident, I can tell you, me bucko," he would say with a wink.

He would then describe the procedure in detail, no doubt relishing Eamonn's green complexion. "Well, it's like this, now," he would say, warming to his subject. "Depending on the type of offense, the bugger might have one or both kneecaps blown out by a bullet. How messy it is would depend on how good the gunman and how far from the knee when he pulls the trigger."

Once, when Eamonn had steeled himself against the vivid descriptions, he had added, "And did I tell ya what they're doing now to save bullets, or perhaps to prolong the agony? An electric drill. Can you fancy that, now?" The mere memory of it produced a chill that shot up Eamonn's spine, causing his body to quiver even more.

"You wouldn't dare, Peter. I'm a high-placed businessman in the North, and they'd toss you in jail in a minute."

"Well, I'm not saying I'd be the one. I only have to pass the word along and, well... I might supply the drill. You do know what they use it for, don't you?" Peter waited while Eamonn swallowed hard. "Maybe a nice variable speed model to slow the process down even more. How would that sound to you?"

Eamonn closed his eyes and ran a tongue over his drying lips before replying, "All right. But can you at least recommend some-one who would help me? I'll pay you a finder's fee, of course."

"A finder's fee, is it? That's what I like about you, Eamonn. You'll throw money at anything to get what you want. If you think I'd name any of my fellow republicans just to make you happy, you're sadly mistaken. Besides, we aren't criminals, no matter what you Prots think."

"No, no, think of it as a donation. Surely you can always use that?"

"To kill someone? Not bloody likely. You're on your own, Ea-monn. And I'd tread very lightly, if I were you. Very lightly."

The sharp click at the other end of the line set Eamonn's pulse racing, and he swallowed the anger constricting his throat. He knew he had done a very stupid thing, and had compounded it with this call. In his frustration, he looked for something on which to vent his rage, finally attempted to rip the coin rack off the phone but only succeeded in tearing a fingernail. A woman approaching the phone box blinked in surprise at his antics.

"Put out over losing the coins, are we, sir?"

Eamonn looked at her vacantly, and then stalked off down the street, swearing loudly at her over his shoulder. As he walked away the thought that he had met her before played at the edges of his memory.

"To hell with it. Who cares, anyway," he said to himself, to quell his growing unease.

Julian and Duncan were waiting impatiently for Beth in Glengariff, a picturesque, well-kept town set above a harbor at the west end of Bantry Bay. On his second tea, Duncan found the liquid cloying on his tongue, a bitter mix for his growing fear. He silently wondered where Beth was, knowing she should have called by now if she had had any trouble. He could no longer ignore Julian's silent request, his eyes urging Duncan to do something. Finally getting up, he pushed his thinning blonde hair off his forehead and announced his decision.

"Well, son, here's what I think we need to do. I want you to stay here." Seeing Julian begin to rise, he signaled him back into his chair. "No, I mean it. If I miss her on the road, I want you here to wait for her. Martha will watch over you 'til I get back. I know the road she'll take, so I'll just trace my way backwards. She'll show up." Seeing the concern still on Julian's face, he added, "Now I'm sure she just had a problem with the bike and was too far from a phone or help. Probably wondering why I haven't come by to pick her up."

Julian sat back unhappily in his chair and pushed his cold scone across the plate before looking up. "All right, I suppose," he mumbled.

Duncan got into his truck after talking to Martha in the shop. He headed west along Glengariff Harbor, which abruptly opened into Bantry Bay. Turning left onto the R572, he followed the road heading south.

He had only gone a few miles before he spotted a lone cyclist coming the other way. He knew instinctively it was Beth, although she was riding slower than usual. He quickly swung over to her side of the road and stopped, before noticing that she had an arm up defensively, as if expecting a blow.

Beth held her breath and then relaxed when she saw it was

a lorry and not the black sedan. As the driver came closer, she recognized her handyman, his lanky frame and bowlegged gait unmistakable. He was staring at her blood-soaked leg.

"Christ, what happened, Beth? Are you all right?"

Duncan had always been more of an uncle than a handyman to Beth, and she never appreciated his affection more than now. When he reached her, she didn't hesitate to avail herself of his support. He held her steady with one hand and moved the bike onto his shoulder with the other.

"Duncan, thank God you're here! Someone tried to run me off the road up on Healy Pass! I had to wait to make sure he wasn't waiting for me down the road." When she glanced inside his vehicle and saw it was empty, she added, "Where's Julian?"

"He's fine. I had him wait back at the tea shop in case I missed you on the road."

She waited for him to load her bike into the bed of his lorry while she stood at the open door. Then, grasping his hand, she climbed into the high seat, wincing in pain as she swung her sore leg in. Her head spun with the truck as Duncan headed back to Glengariff.

Now safely inside, Beth felt her anger uncoil as her fear subsided. "Blast him! Damn that cowardly bastard to hell!"

She realized Duncan had moved away from her after her very unlady-like outburst. It had probably unsettled him. Yet she could feel the rage still building inside her and could not restrain another curse.

"I'll be damned if I let that bastard scare me off the road!"

"Who? Do you know who did this? We'll go to see Dennis after picking up Julian."

Beth exhaled shakily, her anger giving way to fatigue, and pondered what she should do next. "I'll report it, but I don't know who it was, or why he would have done that. I just feel violated, Duncan. You know how much I enjoy riding. And now, until we find the bast... assailant, I won't feel safe. That makes me really mad!"

As they came close to the teashop, Beth began to calm down, not wanting to upset Julian. She took the blood-soaked bandage off her leg and inspected the wound. "It doesn't look deep, just nasty. I think we should pick up some medical supplies, though."

"I've got a first aid kit behind the seat."

Beth looked behind her and saw the white box with its red cross, a universal symbol, and grabbed it.

"Would you pull over for a moment so I can clean the wound? I don't want Julian to see me like this."

When Beth had finished, she took inventory. Her left side was sore where she had landed, and she knew there would be bruises and strained muscles to tend to later, but she hoped she would look fine to Julian. Satisfied she's done her best, she settled back in the seat as Duncan pulled back on the road.

When they pulled into the parking lot, they didn't see Julian at the table. Beth's heart stopped for a second.

"Where is he, Duncan?"

"Well, he was right over there." He pointed to a vacant table, where Julian's cup sat unattended.

They quickly hurried towards the shop, and Beth urgently called out for the shopkeeper. Martha came out drying her hands on a towel. "Good afternoon to you, Beth. You look a sight. Did you take a spill?"

Beth stole a glance at herself in the shop window, confirming the telltale marks of the crash, the bandaged leg, the torn jacket covering her damaged arm, with dirt and dust covering the rest. But her growing anxiety about Julian would not be deflected. "Where's Julian? Duncan said you were looking after him."

"Well, there's no need to shout, now. He was just here a second ago."

Beth touched her hand in apology, and Martha grasped it in shared concern. With her other hand, Beth clutched Duncan's arm so tightly he grunted in surprise. Then they all turned as they heard a commotion in the shrubbery.

To their relief, Julian came racing through the hedge at the side of the patio, his clothes covered with grass stains and twigs. Beth picked him up and hugged him tightly, oblivious to the sharp pain in her side. A few tears of relief escaped down her cheeks.

"Where were you?" Putting him down and keeping him at arm's length, she said sternly, "Didn't Duncan tell you to stay right here?"

"I did, Mum. I was only in Martha's garden playing with Boxer."

"And letting him slobber all over you too, from the looks of it." She couldn't keep the laughter out of her voice, as she acknowledged the innocence of his world.

"You all right, Mum?"

"I'm fine, just took a little fall, that's all."

"You sure? You look messier than me, and I got yelled at."

"I'm fine, Jules." While he pointed and peered at her leg, she brushed the tears away and looked gratefully over at Duncan. "Thanks."

"No bother."

"Well, how about those scones? Martha, three scones and tea please. My treat."

Beth accepted the chair Duncan pulled out for her, cautiously sitting on its unyielding surface. Out in the warm sun, she was oblivious to all but the softly-buzzing insects and the whoosh of air that accompanied each passing car. Beth reveled in the sun's touch on her face and tried to brush the dark thoughts of horror away. They departed reluctantly, like dry leaves in a slackening wind.

CHAPTER 12

Inspector Brendan O'Neill opened his third-story flat's street-facing windows, letting the sounds of Cork rush in. He breathed a sigh of relief as the noise filled the room, bringing the dead space back to life. Welcome aromas from the downstairs bakery mingled with Mrs. Dougherty's heavily-scented flowers, replacing the stale air with the life of a bustling Cork morning. He sat on the old mahogany ledge of the center bay window, idly swinging the latch up and down.

The emergency trip to Belfast to look after his ailing mother ended on a positive note. She was much better now and he'd promised to help with the bills that accumulated during her long illness. The danger level in that city was still high, but two of his RUC mates had committed to check up on her since nothing short of a nuclear explosion would convince his Mum to leave.

He leaned out the window to his left when he heard water dripping. It was Mrs. Dougherty watering her flowers; a daily ritual that went off like clockwork. Sure enough, it was half past eight in the morning. She had been after him for years, convinced he should remain a bachelor no longer, nor she a widow. The potted flowers on her balcony announced her availability every time he unlatched a window. He wondered to himself if his commitment to police work wasn't unhealthy. Too much time alone. Too much time to think.

Leaning down, he rummaged in the open top of his leather briefcase and took out his favorite pipe. Next he unzipped his tobacco pouch and tapped in his special Cavendish 105 blend. Before striking a match he glanced over to his favorite tobacconist shop across the street. Residing in the corner of a brown flat iron building, it had a wide green band bordering the top of the first floor and a large display window.

His eyes fell on the uppermost rack of Meerschaum pipes in the center of the window, catching the morning sun. He longed to wrap his hand around the pipe's broad, creamy bowl, but the money to buy one would go instead to his mother. She needed it more than him, anyway.

"Are ye back then, Inspector?"

He poked his head out the window and smiled dutifully at Mrs. Dougherty, tipping an imaginary hat. "That I am, Rosie. A fine mornin' it 'tis."

"Your dear mother, how is she doing? You haven't been disarmin' more bombs, have ye?"

Brendan had hoped that the news of the attempted bombing last winter would not reach Cork, but by the time he had returned, everyone in Cork knew. He even had to endure TV interviews. Now, with the warmth of a late April morning, it seemed more like a dim nightmare. "Mum's grand, thanks."

"Why don't you bring the dear woman down here, away from all that? Instead of making these six-month pilgrimages to Belfast."

"She's determined no one is going to run her out of her own house, even if she has to barricade it against a rampaging horde. Now, how d'ya convince yer own flesh to leave that?" Brendan was thinking this wasn't the first time they'd had this conversation.

"Well, ye need a good woman of yer own that can look after her, is what! Now, how long have I been tellin' ye that?"

"Every chance . . . er . . . very often, if I remember right, Rosie." He showed more teeth in his grin than usual; part embarrassment, part forced smile.

"I've tea brewing and scones cooling on the stove. Why don't ye come in and have some with me? We can talk about it some more."

Brendan didn't miss the wink that followed her invitation. He was sure it was automatic now; she hardly knew she was doing it. "A lovely suggestion, but I just ate, my dear. Maybe later." He quickly cleared his throat to cover the rumbling of his stomach, threatening to expose his lie.

Seeing her obvious disappointment, he almost relented, but he remembered the last time he had been trapped in her kitchen. On that occasion, he had been ready to jump out the window when his sergeant rapped on his door, calling him to a crime scene. His sergeant's booming voice reverberating down the hall to Rosie Dougherty's place was like a reprieve from purgatory. He never did tell Regis why he had been so glad to see him.

"Ah, well, perhaps you'll take a scone in for your sergeant, then. Surely he still has an appetite." Her voice had lost a bit of its enthusiasm, and he couldn't bear to turn her down again; even though it was tempting fate to get so close to the lair of her kitchen.

"That's very kind, Rosie. Regis will appreciate the thought."

"He'll appreciate the scone, if I know your sergeant."

"There's no doubt you do." With a wave and one last smile, he ducked his head back into the room. Just as he turned, the phone rang. "Oh, sure, now you decide to ring," he mumbled under his breath, as he went over to the sideboard.

"O'Neill."

"Inspector, Muldoon here. I just got a strange request from a Duncan Cowell. Claims to be a friend of yours."

Brendan paused a moment, the name tickling his memory. It finally surfaced from far back in his past. In Belfast. "Yes, Regis, he is. What did he want?"

"Didn't go into detail. Something about needing advice for a friend in jeopardy. Said he could only discuss it with you."

Brendan suspected his sergeant hungered for the details. But why would Duncan call him now? And himself not long back from Belfast, with his past closing in on him. He didn't like it, but he did owe the man. "Did he leave a number?"

He was about to hang up after taking down the number, when Regis added, "D'ya think you could talk that neighbor of yours into a scone for me, Inspector?"

Brendan rolled his eyes towards the ceiling, "I'll try, Regis. I'll try."

Sean's thoughts were of Beth as he drove up to her cottage, barely noting the lush, green pastures on the gently-sloping hills. It was a bright Sunday morning, full of promise. The sun's warm embrace was drawing the moisture from the ground and setting a fine mist over the low-lying valleys. The morning light, refracted by the mist, gave the land a mystical glow. If he had been an artist, this was the kind of day that would tempt him to snatch up a palette. Instead, a familiar melody, lyrically recalling the dance of light in a wooded glen, played through his mind.

Why hadn't he thought to bring his harp? A perfect day, a picnic by the bay; what better setting? Perhaps it was something he'd detected in Beth's voice when last he'd called. Or maybe that he was preparing to tell her more about his past. But not about the drunken ride to hell. Yet, could he keep that secret from her, because they were fast becoming close. So fast, that Sean's intimacy alarm was loudly clanging. Really, what was he getting into?

He parked the car near the house and knocked on the door. A slim boy with Beth's curly, red hair and mischievous green eyes opened the door, looking up at him with obvious interest.

"Gosh, you almost hit the top of the door. My name is Julian, and you must be Sean."

"Indeed I am, and pleased to finally meet you, Julian." He

shook the boy's hand. It was warm and reassuring somehow. "Is your Mum about?"

"She'll be down in a minute. She's still fixing herself up." Julian made a face. "Did you hear about her bike accident?" Julian led Sean to an overstuffed chair facing the fireplace. No sooner had he sat down, than the boy rushed to tell him all about it.

"When she came back, she had this bandage on her leg, and she—"

"Julian! I'll explain it to Sean. You go check that everything is turned off." Beth's warning preceded her into the room. She paused at the doorway for effect, dressed in a floral print skirt and peasant blouse. The blouse showed off her well-toned and broad shoulders honed on countless mountain climbs.

Dark-brown boots climbed her calves and disappeared under the flare of her skirt, and she carried a wide-brimmed straw hat, bedecked with dried flowers and a scarlet bow.

Sean leaned back in his chair in admiration, enjoying what the blouse revealed and hid, and flashed a lustful smile. "Oh, you look good enough to eat, Beth."

Beth smiled through an admonitory finger raised to her lips. "Julian," was all she said.

As she moved into the room, he detected her slight limp and his smile vanished. "What was that about a bicycle accident?"

"I'll tell you about it later when I can send Julian off for a bit, but I'm fine." Sean saw other things behind her cheery greeting, and barely restrained himself from asking anyway. When Julian returned, they all went out to the car, Beth carrying a picnic basket that matched her hat.

A bright sun reflected off the Jaguar's bonnet as they headed down to Bantry Bay. A glance in the rearview mirror showed Beth that Julian was happy in the 2 + 2 coupe's smallish rear seat. He leaned forward between the front seats and peeked into the car's center console. Pulling out a tire gauge he asked, "Sean, what is this?"

Smiling at Beth before replying Sean said, "That's for checking my tire pressure, Julian." Then he added, "That was one of the last things my Dad gave me."

"Oh", Julian said, placing the tool carefully back into the console.

As they drove past the Doyle's place, Beth looked for the green Honda. When she couldn't see it, she looked out the back window to see if they were being followed. Nothing there.

"What is it, Beth?"

"The car is gone! The car that..." She stopped for a moment and looked back at Julian again. Then, more softly, she said, "The one I told you about, following me."

"It came from here?"

"I'm not sure." She had meant to ask Kitty about her guest, but it had slipped her mind after the accident. It hadn't been an accident, but she tried desperately to believe that it had been. She felt Sean's eyes upon her and worked up a smile to reassure him. In the back seat, she saw Julian also looking at her curiously. "It's a perfect day for a picnic, isn't it, Julian?"

They soon arrived on the outskirts of the town, and came upon Bantry House, imposing even from a distance. The addition of two side wings the previous century had given the building a total of fourteen bays. The park surrounding the house was built on the slopes of a hill in Italian-styled terraces, interspersed with statues and benches. The gardens went down to the bay, with Bantry Pier off to the right.

It had been a long time since Beth had been inside the house, and she was eager to show it off to Sean. As they walked up the marble steps, she enthused, "They have an art collection gathered from all over Europe that you'll just love, Sean. Paintings, icons, tapestries, and the furniture in each room are authentic seventeenth and eighteenth century." She was sure even Julian would enjoy it now. The last time, he had glumly trudged after her through seemingly endless rooms, constantly asking when they were going to eat.

They entered the house and set the old, highly polished floorboards groaning. Heads turned in the cavernous living room, and Beth quickly ushered them into the spacious library. Its thick carpets quickly swallowed their hushed conversation, and their whispery footfalls no longer disturbed the mood of contemplation, or the drowsing of an elderly guest, balanced over his cane.

They were in their third room, looking at a faded tapestry in a sunny, west-facing room, when Julian tugged on Beth's sleeve. She leaned down, and he whispered in her ear.

"When do we eat?"

Beth couldn't hide a smile. "Soon, Julian, soon."

Finished with their tour, they went outside to select a place for lunch. Julian found a perfect spot under an ancient tree, its heavy branches close to the ground, as if resigned to losing its battle with gravity.

They ate hungrily, with only passing comments, until the end of the meal. Beth poured tea for everyone as they finished the Irish soda bread she had baked the night before. The soda bread was Julian's favorite, particularly when she added raisins.

After a contented burp, Julian rose and looked out on the bay. "Sean, would you like to watch the sailboats with me?"

"Well, it de..."

Beth interrupted Sean's reply, "Not just yet, Julian. Sean and I have things to discuss. We'll join you down there later." Julian looked disappointed, but he picked up the binoculars Beth had brought along and headed off towards the windswept bay.

When her son was out of earshot, Beth turned to Sean and gave his hand a squeeze. Then, taking a deep breath, she related the details of her narrow escape from the mystery car. Sean became more agitated as she continued, holding her hand tightly.

"Who do you think it was, Beth? My God, why would anyone do this unless they were trying to kill you?"

"I'm not sure. It could be Peter, but I don't think so."

"Why not? He certainly seemed dangerous at the party. That glass didn't shatter by itself."

"I know, and he does frighten me, but it just doesn't seem to be his style."

"His style?"

"I think he'd be more confrontational, don't you?"

"I don't think confrontational begins to describe his attitude, Beth." Sean's face was full of concern now, "But who, then?"

Beth felt the tension build until she was sure she was shaking. She took a deep breath and then plunged ahead. "I... I think I should tell you more about Eamonn, Sean."

His face bore an apprehensive look. Beth took his hand again and held tight while she related how their marriage had become impossible. She also told him, hesitantly, how Eamonn had brutally assaulted her, and how she had fought back when he started beating Julian.

Painfully, she mentioned the calls to the police, the looks exchanged by their neighbors as the officers stepped in to stop the fighting; the impassive stares when she tried to explain her side, and Eamonn affecting a look of ridicule and amazement that anyone would accuse him of this kind of thing. Worse still, the police looked at her suspiciously before nodding sympathetically at him. Gradually, she came to see that life with him would always be a living hell.

"Did this all happen here?"

No, in Belfast. I was a secretary at Conor Shipping when I met him.

"But you didn't get a divorce? It is legal there."

"We had moved to Dublin by then. Besides, Eamonn was afraid his father would disown him if he'd learned the truth." Beth paused and took a shaky breath. This was harder than she thought. "We made an arrangement."

"An arrangement?" Sean appeared more fearful then she and

that made it harder to continue.

"He moved Julian and me to the cottage from our home in Dublin. That way, no one would know when he was home, or even if he was home. Since he always had business in Dublin and Belfast, he set up apartments there. If his father ever called at the cottage I was to say he was away on business, or he was out and then contact Eamonn so he knew which lie to tell."

"And in return he stayed away from you?"

Beth tried to stifle a sob, but it broke free. She managed to say, "for the most part."

She couldn't tell him the ugly truth. That Eamonn would show up at night, unexpectedly, when Julian was asleep and abuse her sexually. He seemed to take delight in her attempts to suppress any cries of pain to avoid awakening Julian. His rough hands on her were a violation with never a caress or word of endearment. Only rude curses if she didn't do what he asked.

After she had the locks changed a month ago he seemed to lose interest, but she always feared there'd be a knock on the door late at night.

She released his hand when she had finished and hugged herself, waiting for and fearing Sean's reaction; hoping all the while that he would understand, forgive her, and still consent to be her friend. Beyond that, she dared not think.

At first, Sean was too stunned to reply. The words, for the most part, still hung heavy in the air. He almost didn't want to know what that meant. But if she trusted him enough to tell him this, perhaps she could understand his past relationship with her husband. Suddenly, Sean realized the identity of the hit-and-run driver. It was Eamonn who had asked him about his relationship with Beth, and tried to ensure his silence through threats. Eamonn who always had to appear respectable to appease his father.

"It was Eamonn, driving the car."

"What?" Beth looked up at him, her mouth agape.

"He's here. I saw him in Cork last Friday."

"Eamonn is here," she whispered. Sean watched her eyes dart fearfully around, then back to him. "What makes you think it was him?"

Sean stood up and looked across the bay, the road Beth bicycled dimly seen in the distance. He imagined Beth riding down that hill, pursued by Eamonn, a maniacal look on his face, the veins in his hands bulging and bluish as he tightly gripped the wheel, swinging the car like a weapon into Beth's path.

He shook his fist at the apparition he had created and cried out, "Damn you, Eamonn. I'll see you in hell, if I have to put you there myself!" He barely noticed that some people walking past had stopped to stare at him and then retreat the way they had come. He was visibly shaking.

"Sean, for God's sake, what're you doing?"

Sean looked around, startled by the vista of trees and strollers. Momentarily disoriented, he came back, searching for her hands, unsure if it was to comfort her or calm him. "It's what he said to me . . . and other things." He ran his fingers nervously through his hair. "He - give me a second to gather my thoughts again."

"Talk to me, Sean. What do you know about this?"

He took a deep breath before continuing. "I also have something to admit. I was trying to find the right time to tell you, and now you've given me a reason to tell you about Eamonn and me."

"Eamonn and you? What is this, Sean?"

Her eyes were wide and he took solace in their dark-green stillness. This was a woman he could safely bare his soul to, and not be burned. Not like the last time. "I've known Eamonn ever since college. We used to come down here to get away from our studies. I even slept in your cottage a couple of times. It was a real shock to see it again when I took you home that first time. He wrote to me about you after we went our separate ways. He called you Liz in the letters, so, at first, I didn't make the connection."

"Letters?"

"We wrote for a year after the... after I was at Stanford. I never saw his face again, until this week, but I couldn't stop writing. I think because he had just met you and his letters were filled with descriptions of you and what you were like. I was fascinated with that first glimpse of you his letters provided."

"But why didn't you tell me about this sooner?"

"It - it was because of my own past with Eamonn. I wanted it to stay buried, but I don't think it ever will now." Sean got up and paced back and forth while he continued talking.

"We were regular party animals back then. Drinking and raising hell. For a while I even neglected my studies. Eamonn showed me the good life. I finally tasted good food and wine." Sean stopped for a minute before continuing. "And there were lots of women that came to the parties. One accused me of getting her pregnant, but Eamonn said he'd take care of it."

Beth looked shocked and put a hand to her mouth. "Did you, Sean?"

"I don't know. I tried to find out later, but Eamonn said she'd moved away." Sean gave her an imploring look. "Eamonn could make it easy to forget."

Beth reflected on her own life with him. He could make it easy to forget, up to a point. A point she'd reached that last hellish night with her husband in the cottage. "Yes, he could make it easy."

"Anyway, I thought I'd heard the last of him after his letters stopped. I only regretted that I would get no more news about Liz. Never realizing it was you all along."

"And it all came back when I took you to my cottage."

"Yes, but I didn't know that it was you he married. I thought he'd discarded Liz and was looking for a new victim." He saw the hurt look and stopped. "I'm sorry, that was uncalled for. This is still a shock, I guess."

Beth smiled ruefully. "And herself a married woman taking up with Professor Sean Carey."

"I'll admit, I was confused," Sean said. "But I wouldn't leave you. Even if we were living in sin." Sean sank to his knees next to her, now able to look into her eyes. "I realized that not even Eamonn, not even the Pope, would keep me from you."

"Nor I you, Sean. I think he has abused us both long enough."

He felt the pain and guilt of what he'd left unsaid. Momentarily, he flashed on the events of that dark night as though it had just happened. The sickening thud of a body hitting the speeding car and the acrid smell of death. When would he confess that?

Then she came closer, their knees almost touching. "Beth, I just want the past to stay in the past and to build a new life here." A tear trickled down his face, and he tried to wipe it away, but she stayed his hand. Her long fingers stroked his cheek, and then caressed his neck. The tension he carried seemed to flow into her hands. His head, now too heavy, lowered until his cheek nestled in the crown of her bright curls.

"Sean, you're the gentlest, kindest man I've ever known. God, how much pain has Eamonn caused us both?"

He straightened again and saw in her face more love and compassion than he would have dared hope was his for the asking. "I love you, Beth."

"I know."

They embraced tightly, while a freshening breeze brought the scent of roses from the garden. Unseen, Julian stood behind a bench, watching. A mixture of love and jealousy, like two warring factions, played across his face.

CHAPTER 13
BANTRY BAY
MONDAY

Patrick McElheny's senses were still acute after his clandestine love-making. But what he'd done was stupid. Stupid! He felt exposed, even on this dark, twisting road, and coming this close to tenure at the university, it wouldn't do to be caught in an adulterous affair. He didn't expect to find anyone on this stretch of road so early in the morning, but his eyes were in constant motion, flicking between the waters of the curving bay illumined by his headlights, and the distant town of Bantry in his rearview mirror. It was while his eyes restlessly probed the lonely shoreline that he saw a car abruptly pull out beyond the next curve and drive off in haste.

Patrick slowed as he came to the primitive lay-by, glancing at the still-settling dust, then the dim shape of the retreating car. The vehicle was somehow familiar and it was a strange place to stop. Impelled by an instinct he barely acknowledged, he stopped to see what had caused the car to leave so suddenly. What had it seen? Or done?

Patrick listened for any telltale sounds, but the rustle of a soft wind through the reeds and the gentle lapping of the bay's waters were the only sounds he heard. No approaching headlights, nor the growl of a slow-moving lorry, disturbed the quiet of the night. Reassured that he was alone once again, he took his torch out of the boot and went to the water's edge, scanning the ground to avoid rocks he might stumble over.

Once there, he breathed in the chilly morning air, mesmerized by the mystical glow of moonlight cavorting over the bay's rocky shore. Then he sensed that something was amiss. There was a dark shape floating close to shore, and he swung the beam of his torch over to it. The light caught on an object holding fast against the tide. At first, he thought it was a log, but a chill along his spine was sending a different message. It was human!

The body rolled gently with the waves, anchored somehow to a rusted pipe jutting up from the seabed. His light reflected brightly off the bloated face, the mouth agape in a rictus of surprise while the eyes stared into oblivion. Patrick dropped the torch in shock, its beam spinning wildly before extinguishing as it struck the ground. He knew that face!

As darkness closed in, panic seized him. Dropping to his hands and knees, he groped for the torch, but never took his eyes off the body floating only a few feet away. When his fingers grasped the barrel's ribbed surface, he snatched it up and raced back to his car. He barely drew breath as he gunned the engine, raking dirt behind him as he accelerated up the road.

Inspector Brendan O'Neill had not been to Bantry Bay since his last holiday and couldn't remember when that was. His gaze took in the bay's wide curving instep as old memories returned. This was a sparsely-populated but well-travelled area of gently-sloping hills. The grazing cows above him looked out onto the shimmering bay with scant company to share the view.

He fixed the geography in his mind; the western end bounded by Glengariff, the eastern end by Bantry. The connecting road between the towns was a popular throughway for tourists and the light commercial traffic that fed the area. The wide two-lane road courted the shore at various points. It was at one of these that the body had been discovered.

The local Garda related to Brendan how the body had been found. It was just after dawn when a lone stroller noticed the incongruity, a black shape floating gently at anchor; a shape that took on human form as he drew closer. The frightened man put out an alarm to the police. By the time the inspector arrived, there was a small crowd around the crime scene, looking, pointing, and whispering excitedly.

The corpse had been covered with a sheet before it went into the body bag so that Brendan could examine it. He squatted near the body and lifted up the cover. Lifeless blue eyes stared up at him. He moved the head from side to side, examining the bruised face and broken nose. When he drew on his pipe, it deposited a nasty residue on his tongue and he spat it out before putting the pipe in his jacket pocket. He wondered if the bad taste was only coming from his pipe, or the unpleasant task still before him.

After examining the chest for other wounds, he turned the corpse over, immediately spotting the wound high on the back. He gingerly separated the folds of cloth covering it. It was puckered a dull red around the skin, leached of color by the bay's salty water. It appeared to be an entry wound from a sharp object, but the flesh was torn, not the clean wound of a stiletto, but something sharp.

Turning the corpse back over he checked the fingernails but, as he feared, the watery resting place had eradicated much of the evidence. Still, cracked finger nails suggested a struggle and indicated he had not died easily.

Getting up slowly, his cramped muscles protested. He signaled for the waiting aides to take the body to the morgue. Scratching his neck, he turned to the policeman who had taken the call. "Now, tell me again, if you'd be so kind, Constable Dennis O'Reilly, who was it identified the body?"

The constable scanned the crowd until he spotted the man who had introduced himself as Patrick McElheny, now in earnest conversation with a shorter, burly man. They both looked anxiously over at Brendan and then returned to their discussion. The shorter man appeared to be very upset about something, and moved off as the inspector approached. Brendan opened his worn tweed jacket and placed his hands in his pockets as he came up to Patrick.

"And do I have the pleasure of addressing Patrick McElheny, then, sir?"

"Yes, that's right, Inspector. What can I do for you?"

"Much. I have a number of questions touching on the unfortunate circumstances that have brought us all here." The buzz of conversation grew louder at the inspector's approach. "Can we go off to the side a bit? It's too noisy here."

The man shrugged, "Certainly."

They both walked over to the water's edge, the lapping sounds gradually blending with the conversations that continued unabated behind them. Brendan sat on a smooth rock and began filling his pipe while he talked. He noticed that McElheny could scarce keep his eyes off the rusted pipe that had anchored the body.

"Now, as I understand it, you came over to the constable and identified the body as that of one Eamonn Conor. Is that right, Mr. McElheny?"

"Yes, I did, Inspector. I'd known Eamonn for a number of years, but I hadn't seen him around here much lately, so I was doubly shocked to come upon him like this."

"Yes, I'm sure you were. Um, were you the first on the scene as well?" Brendan was aware of a measured beat before the witness replied.

"Uh, no." Patrick looked away for a moment before continuing. "I was driving to Glengariff, and saw a number of people gathering around here. It looked quite peculiar, so I stopped to have a closer look. And then I saw the body . . ." Patrick paused a moment and swallowed hard before resuming, "drifting slowly in the bay."

As if speaking in a trance, Patrick shook his head and turned to the inspector. "When the constable had the body on a tarp I went over to have a look."

He took out a handkerchief to blot beads of sweat. "Then I looked at his face." He grimaced again at the thought. "All bloated and bruised like," he made a face. "Well, I couldn't believe it was Eamonn. But I let Constable O'Reilly know straight away."

"And glad we are that you did." Brendan touched flame to his pipe and spent a few moments puffing on the glowing bowl, absorbing what the man had related. His sharp eye did not miss the facial tics that told him something was wrong. He felt the story was contrived. He observed the man more closely while it appeared he was only concentrating on his pipe. "Would you have any idea what he might have been doing around here, then, seeing as how you'd considered it unusual for him to be here?"

"He works for a shipping business based out of Belfast. I think he also has an office in Dublin, and I guess Cork. He has made a few trips to Bantry, and I think he has a cottage just above the bay. He might have just been here for pleasure."

"And what would he do for pleasure?"

"Well . . . he's well-to-do, money's no object." At the inspector's questioning look, he quickly added. "His father is John Conor, of Conor Shipping, so he has unlimited resources. He used to fish and hunt around here, so he could have taken a few days off to relax."

"His father is *the* John Conor? Does he have any relatives around here?"

"None that I know about. But I didn't know him that well."

"Well, I shall have to notify Mr. Conor, then. Do you know what kind of car Eamonn Conor drove? It is possible robbery was the motive; a fancy car that someone would notice, perhaps?"

"I'm sorry, Inspector, he does drive luxury cars, but I wouldn't know what he was driving on this trip."

Brendan looked at him intently. The man kept looking off, unable to meet his penetrating gaze. His instincts screamed at him that this man was lying, but he didn't have enough facts to probe more deeply; yet. "Is there anything else you can think of that would be useful to us?" The man was beginning to look uncomfortable under Brendan's constant stare. He finally shrugged his shoulders and spread his hands out, indicating he could think of nothing. "I have one more question. Was he a citizen of Northern Ireland, or the Republic?"

"Northern Ireland, Inspector."

"Well, thank you very much for your help, Mr. McElheny. We will probably be contacting you later." Definitely.

Brendan watched him walk back to the shorter man who was intent on asking a question, but McElheny drew him further away from the crowd. Brendan wished he knew what they were discussing. When he walked back to the constable, he felt their eyes on his back. Dennis O'Reilly was still talking to the other onlookers, trying to get them to stay back.

"Dennis, who is that man talking to McElheny?"

"Oh, that's Peter Deagan, a local mechanic and handyman in these parts."

"What can you tell me about him?"

"Well, he used to live around here, but moved to Cork about a year ago. He still runs a small garage in Bantry. Quite a successful mechanic, he's fair-minded in his business. On the other hand, he also has a reputation as a brawler. He doesn't pick fights, you understand, but it doesn't take much to get him riled. Some folks tread very carefully around him."

"I don't think I've run into this fellow in Cork. But somewhere . . ." Brendan drew on his pipe while he watched Peter slowly move away, then get into a sleek black sedan and speed off.

"You don't suppose he's ever been to Belfast, do you?"

"Belfast? I don't know, Inspector. He lived around here for some time, but I don't know about before then. Why? Oh, you mean when you were in the RUC?"

"Maybe, perhaps not." Dennis looked at him quizzically, but remained silent.

Brendan continued to scan the crowd while he talked, positioning himself so that he could observe inconspicuously, when Dennis extended his hand.

"I certainly appreciate your taking over this investigation. We've been understaffed here for some time and can barely handle the occasional domestic argument, let alone a murder. It is a murder, is it not?"

"Unless the victim self-inflicted a knife wound in his back and then threw himself into the bay, I would say so, yes."

Dennis only smiled as he walked off.

Brendan wandered back to the water's edge, his mind drifting with the swirling currents. Belfast! A lifetime ago, but still always with him. When he joined the Royal Ulster Constabulary; one of the minorities of Catholics who did, he thought he could make a difference. That was before the Special Bs were mustered in, making it uncomfortable for anyone sympathetic to the Republicans or critical of the Loyalists. He had tried for a long time to convince himself that nothing had changed, but that was before the Derry massacre and the violence in Belfast; before things were scrawled on crumbling walls in words of hate.

He remembered too many details from those years. One was attending his first interrogation. The man, Peadar-something, was being questioned about a car bombing on the outskirts of Belfast. Deagan had a similar build and the same hard look in his eyes. If it was the same man, was he an agent of the IRA? And, if so, what was his connection to the dead man, if any? He glanced down at the notes the constable had taken, and waved Dennis over. He gave him back his notebook, not sure he was correctly deciphering the constable's uncertain hand.

"Yes, Inspector?"

"So, we have only one person here that could reliably ID the body. Is that correct?"

"That's right, sir. There were a couple of others said he looked familiar but didn't know the name. His wallet was missing, of course, but we found some papers on him that I'll dry out and turn in to you."

"Any idea what they might contain?"

"No," Dennis said, "I didn't want to chance tearing them."

"Probably just as well. There was no weapon found, that might have caused the wound in the back? No one picked anything up, as far as you know?"

"No, sir. I was here bright 'n early and cordoned off the area, best I could."

"And how many cars were here when you arrived?

"About six, I would say. You know how these things attract a crowd."

"Don't I though. So you've indicated that there were no signs of a struggle around the area and no car left behind. Furthermore, there was no blood on the ground, except close to where the body was pushed or fell into the water. Is that correct?"

"Yes, Inspector, someone was very careful about this one."

"Rigor mortis had set in by the time you got here and pulled the body out. At what time?"

"The body was discovered at about 7:05 this morning," Dennis said, consulting his notes. "I had a local help me pull him out and cover him just like you found him."

"How did McElheny ID the body, then?"

"After the area was secure, I invited anyone that thought they might know him to come forward. After a bit Mr. McElheny took a look and immediately ID'd the body."

"Not when it was still in the water?"

"No, sir. By the way, we'll need your coroner to fix the exact time and cause of death."

"Weren't you using that fellow from Macroom?"

"He's had an autopsy done on himself since we used him last."

"Too bad. He was a good man. But until we have a coroner's report, my guess is that he was most likely killed in the early morning hours when no cars would have been travelling this road. But why would two or more people agree to meet here at that time of night?"

"Doesn't make sense, does it, sir? Do you think the body was dumped here?"

"Yes, I think it's very likely the man was beaten and stabbed somewhere else and dropped into the bay. The tides didn't take him out. Why was that?"

"Oh, I'm sorry, Inspector. I didn't mention that the belt of his coat was wrapped around a rusty old pipe stuck out in the bay."

"Really? And how was the belt attached?"

"I'm not sure I know what you mean, sir."

"Is it possible that it was wrapped around the pipe deliberately?"

"Well . . . yes. It did seem odd, now that you mention it. What do you think that means, Inspector?"

Brendan flashed his first genuine smile. "It could mean much, Dennis, me lad. Much." But that led to many other questions he wasn't prepared to answer just yet.

CHAPTER 14
THE BURREN
MONDAY

Beth opened the desk drawer once again, looking for the report she had done for Professor Dunoon. He was going to need it when she returned on Friday. If she didn't have it, he would go into his growling bear routine while she tried to keep a straight face; a difficult task at best. When the report didn't magically appear on the fourth try, she gave up.

"Julian, did you move anything on this desk?"

"Not me, Mum. Why?"

"Nothing seems to be where it should be." When Beth glanced down she spotted the report on the floor near the desk. She looked once more at Julian who simply shrugged his shoulders. "Oh, well, I'll ask Margaret later in the week. Are you almost ready, Jules? I only have one more call to make, so why don't you put the rucksack in the car."

Beth waited until Julian was out of earshot and then rang up her friend.

"Hello, Kitty?"

"Is that you, Beth?"

"Yes, do you have a moment? I'd like to ask you about one of your guests."

"Who would that be, dear?"

"I don't know his name," Beth said. "He was driving a green

Honda. I think he was tall and thin."

"The green Honda? No, he's a short, squarish sort of fellow. Very serious. Doesn't talk much either."

Beth frowned into the phone as though it were defective and putting out bad information. "Well, maybe it isn't who I thought it was." She paused a moment then asked, "Is he still there?"

"Oh no, he left this morning. Strange fellow, that one," said Kitty.

"He checked out today? Why did you think him strange?"

"It's just that he didn't use the room Sunday. He came by in the morning to get his things, and he was gone. Peculiar."

"Hmmm, well thanks, Kitty, I'll see you when I return." She set the phone down, thinking that perhaps the image of death following her in a green Honda Friday night had merely been her overwrought imagination.

However, the mysterious call she received from Ian Williams earlier, hinting at will changes and requesting a meeting had put her on edge. What did Williams or her father-in-law know about her and Eamonn?

She knew Williams had arrived in Cork the previous week since she had received a memo from the Science administrator Thursday. In it, Williams had requested a meeting with her, but did not say why. She assumed it was about Conor Shipping's patronage of her university, but now she wasn't so sure. They knew!

And here she was being courted by Sean Carey as if she hadn't a care in the world. What if it was John Conor and Williams having her followed? That could mean they knew about her and Sean, too. As if she didn't already have way too much to think about. She was glad now that she was leaving Cork for a couple of days. Maybe her life would make more sense once she was with her parents.

She finished her morning tea, staring at the dregs in the bottom of her bone china cup, half expecting an image to form out of the tea leaves. Gathering up the remaining bags, she reproached herself aloud, "Get a grip on yourself, O'Hara, this is no time to be letting your imagination run wild." She turned as Julian came back inside. He looked around for the person she was speaking to, then to the phone.

"Did you say something to me, Mum?"

"No, Julian, let's be off."

"Can't we stay all week with Granny and Granddad?"

"I only have two days now, but in another two months we'll have all summer to play, Jules. Come on!"

They clambered into the car, and Beth prayed it would start again. It had just come out of the garage, but it had a long history of motorist abuse, and her level of trust was not very high. It groaned and shook as she engaged the starter, then caught and began to run, only to quickly die again. "You banjaxed heap," she said under her breath

At the sound of snickering she darted a look at Julian, who was trying unsuccessfully to suppress more sounds by clamping a hand over his mouth. The innocent look didn't fool her, either. Her second attempt succeeded, and she revved the engine, not wanting to give it the opportunity to backslide into slumber again.

The ride was uneventful until they made the turn onto the main road heading towards Bantry. There, around a sharp curve, they saw a number of people milling about, and the blue flasher of a Garda car. "Gosh, did someone go off the road, Mum?" Julian's head swiveled around to get a better look.

Beth peered in the rearview mirror, trying to make out the details. "I don't know, Julian, but we don't have time to stop." She shuddered, but pretended not to notice. Julian looked at her, and then returned his attention to the rear window.

The tension in her neck and shoulders eased by the time they had taken the main road north at Ballylicky. But it wasn't until they were past Gougane Barra that she finally relaxed, enjoying the ride through upland hills. They picked up the N20 out of Charleyville that would take them to Limerick, and then on to the Burren.

She regretted that Sean could not join her, but with exams

coming up he was unable, and considering her latest revelations it was just as well. That they both had hidden things about her husband had stunned her. And Sean reading letters about her from Eamonn felt creepy, somehow. She needed the moral support of her mother more than ever, and her wise counsel. If things went well, perhaps she'd call him later.

"Mum, are we going to have a picnic on the Burren today?"

"Not today, darling, tomorrow. First we'll see Casey and Mairin."

"Will Mairin tell me more old stories about the high kings?"

"I'm sure she will, and with little prodding from you." She ruffled his hair, smiling at his mock long-suffering face, and eyes cast heavenward. The link with her parents had become doubly important since Eamonn had left, with Casey, her father, providing the vital male link that Julian so desperately craved. Each visit seemed to strengthen the bond between all four of them and, after her relationship with Sean had blossomed, she needed to confide her doubts to Mairin. Her stomach knotted at the thought.

She told Julian to count the planes taking off from the airport once they had left Limerick behind. They entered an outcropping of land, bordered by the Shannon River below and Galway Bay above. Her excitement and apprehension began to build as the last few miles rolled rapidly by, and they touched the outskirts of Ennis. "We're almost there, Julian."

Beth shot expertly through the roundabouts ringing Ennis. "Like sand traps to the unwary," said one tourist staying at her father's house. The distraught man made the comment after spending two hours trying to get out of Ennis. He then added, "Did they plan it that way to keep you from leaving until you'd spent all your bucks?" The frustration was plain on his face, and Beth and her father had rolled their eyes at each other.

Just past a lay-by, she found the road leading to her parents' home. After spotting the faded Raleigh Bicycle sign, she took a hard left onto a dirt road. Next to her, Julian said, "Mom, how come they call it 'the all steel bicycle' on the sign?"

"I think they should call it the solid steel bike as heavy as they are. Not like my Ritchey."

She headed up the hill, past thickets and stunted trees, and out to a sweeping vista. Beth pulled off the road and stopped the car so she and Julian could enjoy the view. The large hill in the foreground sprouted trees on its broad slopes, below which limestone jutted out, ready to catch the leaning trees.

"It's Uncle Dick," Julian said, and they both laughed at their private joke.

Beth easily remembered her Uncle Dick, with his bald pate and prominent ears, kept company by what was left of his hair. The hill mimicked his face so well she could almost see his enigmatic smile spreading across the lower plain. On the top of the hill, set like a jaunty cap, was the O'Hara ancestral home. It probed the sky for three stories and boasted four large gables, one on each side.

Beth put the car back in gear and took the winding road up to Caislean O'Hara. Castle O'Hara to the tourists. The house seemed to grow in size as they continued up the hill, sunlight flashing off the bay windows. The Lincoln-green siding and red shutters gleamed. Her father must have given it a facelift. Casey no longer rented out rooms, and the place seemed deserted with only a car and the old battered van in the driveway. As she drew closer the glass-enclosed entry way beckoned. A row of potted ferns pressed against its tall windows, vainly trying to reach the light. By the time Beth had turned off the ignition, Mairin had burst out of the door.

"And where is my fine young lad, now? You haven't forgotten him, have you, girl?"

"Here I am!" Julian said, laughing all the way into her arms.

Beth came around the motorcar, and gazed up at her mother. Mairin stood tall and erect and, Beth was pleased to see, still the beauty. She was all smiles and teeth when she first caught sight of them, but now she was inspecting Beth more carefully.

"Julian is grand, but you look a little worn, love. What is it?"

"I've much to tell, dear."

"Aye, I can see that. Well, come in, come in. Tea's await'n."

Mairin shepherded them both into the main part of the house, and into the large living room, dominated by a broad stone fireplace. Beth envied her ability to make even this room cozy and intimate. Overstuffed chairs were separated by small tables laden with flowers and books. The walls were covered with Casey's photographs and Mairin's paintings, while the grandfather clock intoned the hour in its best Big Ben fashion. When they sat, Julian chose the arm of Mairin's chair.

"So, and how have things been?"

Beth seldom could hide things from her mother for long, and thought Mairin was already reading her mind. Where should she begin? Then she remembered that Julian was in the room, and bit her lip as she debated how to get her mother alone.

"Mum fell off her bike on Saturday." Julian blurted out.

Beth faced her and nodded towards Julian, hoping her mother would intuit her meaning. She didn't want to explore the events of last week with Julian present. Mairin returned the nod.

"Did I hear my grandson's voice in here?" Casey came into the room, the smell of sea and fish following in his wake. He took off his cap to rub his curly hair with weather-beaten hands. He looked down to make sure his boots were clean before proceeding into the room. Beth smiled, remembering how many times her mother had yelled at him to take them off before coming inside.

"Julian, what do you say we have you help Granddad get ready for an afternoon of fishing?"

Beth was always fascinated by the silent interplay between her parents. Mairin stared significantly at Casey, and he returned it with a look that said, "What is it you want, woman?" Mairin gestured emphatically and swiftly when Julian's attention was elsewhere, and Casey pantomimed his reply.

Julian's eyes lit up at the prospect of going out with his granddad. Beth watched him grasp Casey's hand before going out the front door, the look of admiration strong on his face.

Beth's gaze wandered over the porcelain Madonna in the adjoining library, and the Pope looking down from his own corner. What kind of lecture would he deliver on the sanctity of marriage, she wondered, imagining that his gaze betrayed just a wee bit of curiosity.

"I see Eamonn chose not to come, once again. Not that I'm surprised."

Beth jumped as if her mother had poked her in the ribs.

"I'm sorry, child. I know how distressed you were when he and I fought so."

Beth remembered. Eamonn cared little for his Protestant background and, at first, appeared to view his child's Catholic upbringing with disinterest. Her mother, on the other hand, devout Catholic that she was, took in every aspect of Julian's religious development. They almost came to blows when Eamonn announced that the child should be given a Protestant baptism as well. He finally backed down, Mairin giving him little quarter. He had resented her ever since, refusing to ever set foot in her house.

"Of course, I can't say I miss him not showing up. Now..."

"Mum!"

"I'm sorry, just running on aren't I?"

"I have to...I have to tell you about Eamonn and me."

Beth watched the look of concern in her mother's eyes turn to sadness as she related her situation with Eamonn. She tried to gloss over the beatings she had endured at his hands, but Mairin would know how humiliated she felt. Beth feared her mother's stern injunction about their permanent separation. Her hope was that, when she laid out her suspicions about who had tried to run her off the road, her mother would relent.

"I'm so sorry I didn't tell you sooner, Mum, but I was so ashamed. I... I've failed as a wife. But he was so brutal."

"Aye, child, and I, the good Catholic that I am, would have

sent you back to him."

Beth looked up sharply, to find her mother sadly shaking her head.

"Maybe, once, I'd have been foolish enough to do that, but I've learned a lot since then."

Beth saw the sadness creasing Mairin's face melt away, and almost cried out at what remained. It was the look a mother reserved for a beloved child, and it shone brightly. "Mum?"

"Child, I only care what happens to you now."

Beth hesitated only a moment, and then ran into her mother's waiting arms, feeling the healing warmth of them the moment they surrounded her. Her tears felt warm, too, as they coursed down her cheeks. Finally, she felt safe and at peace. Mairin added a few tears of her own, knowing how much pain her daughter had suffered. Her gentle rocking was for both of them.

CHAPTER 15
CORK
MONDAY

Ian Williams had everything correctly organized on the table. One last turn of the teapot, to properly align the handle, and he was satisfied. He had just settled down to begin lunch when a waiter approached; holding a card in the silver tray as though it might ignite at any moment. Ian paused to look at the name embossed on the white card, then quickly snatched it off the plate, and waved the waiter off. When the man was out of sight, he turned the card over and read the message scribbled there. His eyebrows rose ever so slightly. A sigh of frustration escaped his lips as he tossed his napkin on the table and left the unfinished meal.

The waiter came over as he was leaving the table. "Does Sir wish us to hold his lunch?"

"Certainly not!" Here he had so carefully organized his meal, and now this fool wanted to toss it all in a warmer, until all the food had the same smell and taste. He wrinkled his nose in disdain, then turned and went out to the cavernous main hall, glancing in both directions before crossing to the central stairway. Climbing the stairs, he barely noticed the dramatic scenery afforded by the upper balcony windows. Scenery was superfluous, in Ian's opinion.

The Nevermore House, a sprawling Georgian residence overlooking the River Lee, suited his need for privacy and economy. He wondered if the name related to Edgar Allan Poe's famous poem. If so, he liked the lugubrious accent that it gave the hotel.

On the second floor, he looked up the hall to where one of the maids was watching him curiously, before he entered his room. A man dressed in gray slacks and sweater was sprawled on the bed, smoking a cigarette, a half-filled glass of whiskey in his other hand.

"So, what news?"

"What the hell are you doing on the bed, McAfee? Get off!"

"Hey, take it easy. I've had a long day." Mike McAfee got slowly off the bed, his short, stocky body, balding head, and bulbous nose all advertising determination and belligerence. Stubbing out the fag, he drained the tumbler of whiskey. His face was filled with secret merriment as he turned towards Ian. "Just got back from Bantry. Seems to be some excitement down there."

"Really? And what might that be?"

"It seems your friend Eamonn is food for the fishes now."

"What?"

"Yeah, they just pulled him out of the bay early this morning."

Knowing he was being closely watched, Ian worked at keeping a blank face. Mike had said he'd missed his calling as an undertaker. But Ian knew the cost of maintaining the same emotionless face, the same somber appearance, the same reaction to momentous events. It served him well in his job, but caused all his social contacts to dry up.

Well, almost all. Dear Glynnis seemed to look beyond it. More likely, she enjoyed the power he wielded. Or perhaps something else he wielded with some authority. He smiled at that before turning back stone-faced to Mike. All he said was, "And?"

"I take it you don't want me to tail him anymore," Mike smirked.

Ian peered at him like a bug on a dissecting board. He considered his reply as Mike went over to a window and stared fixedly out. Finally, Ian said, "One less worry."

"Is it? This whole thing is getting pretty messy," Mike said. "You going to tell your boss?"

Ian sat down in a chair facing him, his fine brow wrinkled in thought. He tapped his lips with a finely manicured finger before replying. "I haven't been notified through the proper channels. He'd wonder how I had heard of it. I'll wait for the police to notify Conor, but I want all the details. Do the police know his identity?"

"Yeah, some guy named Patrick McElheny ID'd the body."

Ian looked up sharply. "How did you find that out?"

"He knows my friend, Peadar...er, Peter. I met Patrick at a local pub to compare notes on another investigation I'm doing."

"What investigation?"

"It's personal. Oh, and guess who the inspector is?"

Ian looked at him expectantly; sure that Mike would tell him long before he would have to guess the man's name. He waited while the burly man shook another cigarette out of a crumpled pack and lit it with a match, inhaling deeply before continuing. Ian was determined there was no way this piece of scum was going to unsettle him.

"None other than Brendan O'Neill," Mike said, through swirling smoke. He leaned back as though pleased with his revelation.

"O'Neill. Who is he?"

"He's the cop from Belfast I told you about," Mike said, exasperated.

Ian sifted through the stories Mike had told him of his life in Belfast. Ian knew his continued contact with members of the IRA was more than social, and thought himself generous in believing a fraction of what he was told. Yet he did remember that name from somewhere. "So what is he doing down here?"

"He left Belfast years ago. He was one of the RUCs handling the investigation that nabbed my friend Peadar. Maybe he just wanted an easier job. Things are a lot quieter around here." Mike took another pull on his cigarette and smiled. "Or they were, anyway."

"Would this inspector know you by sight?"

"I don't think so. Peadar was the only one pulled in on the

Faulkner bombing, and he didn't talk."

"Like you do, now? I don't want this inspector thinking you're in the IRA, and snooping around while I'm closing a business deal."

"No one suspects me of being in the Ra, even if my sympathies were with 'em. I was in once - a long time ago - but after that bombing fuck-up, I broke all my ties. So quit your worryin'."

"It's my job to worry." Ian's voice rose, taking on a biting tone that caused the man to straighten up. When Ian was certain he had his full attention, he continued. "There's a lot at stake here so keep a low profile. I don't need any notoriety screwing things up. If you want to stay on the company books as a detective, think first."

"Okay, I read you." Mike rubbed his jaw thoughtfully before looking into Ian's eyes. What he saw there caused his mouth to gape open and his voice to disappear. "Make sure you do," was all Ian said.

After a moment McAfee once again found his voice. "Eh, do you think this news will cause you problems with Conor?"

"I'm more worried about his health, and how this might effect it. He may even want to come here to claim the body if I can't convince him to stay in England. That will complicate things." Ian tapped his silver appointment book on the end table. "But if he does come here, he better not find out the man keeping tabs on his son was in the IRA."

"Shouldn't be a problem," Mike said. "I'm a licensed investigator, now."

"Your credentials won't mean a thing if you're implicated with members of the IRA. Even the suspicion of it will compromise me." He watched Mike's eyes shifting, never stopping. What has he been up to? Ian worried about that too. He didn't like surprises.

"Fine. D'ya want me to check with my contacts to see what they know about this? You know, snoop around."

"Yes, but do it quietly." Then, after a pause, he added, "Do you think the IRA might be involved?"

"I don't know. Eamonn is far down on their hit list. But he

didn't treat the Catholics well at the yards in Belfast, and there has been talk. It's sure that no one will light a candle for him there. Want me to check up on that too?"

Ian got up and joined Mike at the window. He looked first out the window, and then at him. "No. There isn't time. We have more important things to focus on. Get on it."

Mike grinned. "That's what I thought you'd say." He walked past Ian and stubbed out his cigarette in a Waterford cut glass dish on the dresser before he went out the door.

Ian looked at the still-smoldering cigarette and wrinkled his nose. "Fucking barbarian!" He cleaned out the dish and put the whiskey tumbler on the sink. He was almost certain that his detective was still in the IRA. "Once in, never out" was their motto and he didn't think Mike was the exception.

Only then did he turn his attention to the next task at hand – what to do after John Conor received the news.

Brendan sat in his office, moodily gazing out at Cork harbor. In front of him was a list of questions to pose to John Conor after he was notified of his son's death. He thought of his own father, a leg blown out from under him on foreign soil fighting for the British. His father's friends had begged him not to go. "The enemy of my enemy is my friend," they had intoned. "But it's bloody Hitler," he had replied. "We can worry about the Brits after the war."

After the war, he had come back to scant thanks from his country. He had lived long enough to see his youngest son become a constable, in part, a legacy of his own sacrifice for England. But after Brendan's father had died one cold, gray January, what little pride he felt in wearing the RUC uniform evaporated.

He was a policeman and always would be, but it was too hard a job to do in Belfast. Too little respect, too much bloodshed, too many calls like the one he was about to make.

Looking at the list again, he crumpled it and threw it into the corner. "Time enough for that later. There's pain enough in knowing your son is gone without pouring salt in his wounds." His words echoed bleakly off the walls. Taking a deep breath, he reached for the phone.

John was listening to the inspector recite the sketchy details of his son's death. The hand holding the phone trembled, while his other hand pressed over his eyes, brimming with tears. He nodded wordlessly as Brendan described what had happened and then, mercifully, he was finished. He managed a quiet thank you, and then dropped the phone into its cradle.

"My son. My son." The words crawled out of his throat as though from a great depth. He lay back in his chair, and lifted a trembling hand to his throat, only to have it drop back at his side. What was he to do, now that his son was gone? His last link to Florence. How was he to redeem himself in her eyes, now? What new curses would fill his dreams?

Finally, he dropped his head into his hands and wept bitterly for the first time in his adult life. The sobs came from deep within him, in places that he never dared explore. Places that were now open wounds, oozing bitterness which he lacked the understanding to heal.

CHAPTER 16

Brendan O'Neill's uncertain fingers stumbled over the keyboard, and he was again rewarded with the computerized equivalent of the raspberries when the baleful tone of striking the incorrect key sounded. "Don't give me any more of your banshee screams, you useless piece of scrap!"

"Inspector, would you like me to do that for you?"

"You might as well, Regis. All I seem to be getting is shrieks and beeps out of this thing."

Brendan got up and turned his swivel chair around before bestriding it and rested his beefy forearms on its back while he watched Regis key in the data he requested. He knew the value of computers in catching criminals, but was usually at a loss using one. His sergeant, Regis Muldoon, thought that computers could do anything; a notion which Brendan constantly questioned.

"So, Inspector, I've keyed in what we have on file about Conor. Then we can make associations based on what we learn from that. I also requested a search of sectarian activity, and a profile on violent crimes in County Cork for the past two years. Will that do it?"

"Yes. How long will this take?"

"Shouldn't take long to get prelim info back."

Brendan watched his sergeant rub the bridge of his stubby nose with a fat paw. Although in other ways a typical Irishman, he had an English bulldog's face. But the smile that usually inhabited it revealed a jovial nature, not a belligerent one. Now, as Regis sorted through menus and entered data, Brendan recalled the tenacity and determination of that breed.

"Ah, here we go," Regis said. "Hello, what's this?"

Brendan stood behind Regis, who moved closer to the monitor, as though more information would be revealed behind the amber words playing across the screen. The clicking of keys filled the air while the inspector watched menus and text flash across it faster than he could read. He gasped, however, when he saw images of the deceased. Then a female, identified as Beth Conor, appeared on the screen, bracketed with personal data that he barely acknowledged before the next block of text replaced it.

"Regis, can you slow that thing down? It's making me dizzy."

"Oh, sorry, Inspector, I'll adjust the scroll index."

"Yes, do that, whatever it is, will you?" He leaned towards the monitor again and began to make some sense of what he saw. He was about to comment on the latest information when Regis let out a low whistle.

"Well, this is interesting. It seems our Eamonn Conor has been a naughty boy with the ladies, Brendan. I have four reports of assaults filed. The first three were complaints filed by his wife, Beth Conor. Her last known address is only a few miles from where we found the body. What do you make of that?"

"When were these reports made?"

"The oldest reports were from four years ago. The most recent is from this year, but that was in Belfast, and the woman wasn't his wife."

"Well, well, that's interesting. And certainly suggests a strong motive. Were there any other reports filed regarding his wife; notice of separation or divorce, that sort of thing?"

Regis shook his head and keyed in some more background data before replying. "No, she's originally from County Clare and retained her citizenship when she married. They moved to Belfast in '81, but were back here in '83, just before her son was born. That would be during the worst of The Troubles. Smart move, that. It looks like Conor had residences in Dublin and Belfast."

"So she lives around here, but he didn't. She wouldn't apply for a divorce then, would she?"

"Not unless the Pope does an about-face and we change our laws."

"What's her present phone number?"

"I've got a residence phone and a business number at Kerry University. By the way, the listing has her as Beth O'Hara."

"You say she goes by Beth O'Hara, then? That's unusual. Oh, it could be her maiden name. Run that too, would you m 'lad? I wonder what else is unconventional about her."

Regis typed in a new search and paused the main screen for Brendan to read and commented on it. "Her parents live near Ennis. Do you want her work records as well?"

On the inspector's nod, Regis brought up another screen. "Well, well, she worked at Conor Shipping in Belfast. Must have been where she met the deceased." Regis turned to Brendan. "What d'ya make of that?"

The inspector rubbed his chin as he thought it through. "She had to know he was rich from the start. I'm afraid this makes her a prime suspect."

Brendan pointed to a few more items on the screen that he wanted more information on. After asking Regis to print out the results, he went over to the printer and watched the pages pile up.

"How do we have so much data on this fellow and his wife, anyway?"

"Oh, it's not just our computer here. We're linked in to several others here as well as in England and Interpol. Like I said, you can do a hell of a lot of legwork right here."

"But not all the legwork, Regis. Most of what we need will come in from the field."

Brendan shuffled though the pages, marking here, adding notations there, requesting additional searches; until he was satisfied he had enough data. He settled back in his chair, pondering what was in front of him, and began making a list of possible suspects.

Brendan had been at this task for hours when he heard Regis's stomach rumble, followed by the scrape of the sergeant's chair. When he came over to the inspector's desk, he had a look of desperation about him.

"Inspector, I'm knackered. D'ya think we could go to the local for a bunburger, or some stew?"

Brendan was amused to hear him lapse back into his Dublin jargon, now that he wasn't in front of the computer. "What time is it?"

"It's already half-six."

"Half-six! I've lost all track. We'll go straight away." Brendan pushed the stack of papers aside, and got up, stretching his tired muscles. He clapped Regis on the back as they headed out the door.

They had only a short walk to O'Toole's pub. Brendan noticed that the usual civil service crowd was in attendance, surrounding the dart board, sipping pints of ale and stout, and complaining about the long dull hours behind a desk. Many were forestalling the inevitable press of cars crossing the bridges, fighting to get home. They found a table near the stained-glass front window.

"Well, now, we're in luck. You'll be able to see the glass at its best, with the evening sun on it. Take a gander at that."

Brendan turned to the hunting scene above their table. The retiring sun's light brought it to vibrant life, and the rich red-and -brown glass fragments glowed. Regis had been after him to visit his pub for some time now, constantly bragging about the stained glass that filled it. And he had been right; it was worth the visit.

He let Regis go to the bar to place their orders, so he could soak up the atmosphere. Stretching out his legs, he closed his eyes and took in the noise of clattering dishware, clinking glasses, sliding chairs, and talk. It was a constant wall of sound that he found somehow soothing. When he opened his eyes again, Regis was returning with a tray piled with food and ale.

"Jesus, is that for us, then?"

"It won't seem like a lot once you have a taste of this stew, Inspector."

"I'm surprised you didn't get a pint for me."

"It's coming."

"What!"

"I was only saying..." Regis held up his hand to arrest Brendan's reaction. Then, with a gentle hand on Brendan's shoulder he added, "but you do look like you could use one."

Brendan gave the idea some thought, until he remembered that that was how he had got by in Belfast. Two pints for lunch, a few whiskeys after five. Soon, most of the horror of the day receded behind an alcoholic mist. The lively sounds around him pulled him away from those dark thoughts and he tucked into the food with relish. The hot stew and warm atmosphere revived his spirits, and he was soon competing with Regis for the last scraps.

"You know, maybe we should order me a pint, Regis. I'm not sure we'll make much headway tonight, anyway."

"Done," Regis said, as he headed for the bar.

Within minutes, a pint of stout was set in front of him, its creamy white head beckoning. "Wearing a grand Roman collar," his Da used to say before getting most of the stout's head on his mustache. Brendan smiled at the thought, and then hungrily gulped down half the pint before drawing breath. "You're right, I must have needed that." He winked at Regis and started on the second half.

It tasted better than he remembered. Had it been a year since he'd sworn off the stuff? Well, maybe just one more, he promised himself, as he felt the tension in his shoulders dissolve. Slowing down on his second pint, his mind switched back to the current investigation. He was putting the disparate pieces of the case together when Regis broke into his thoughts.

"Inspector, did you see the stained glass over the bar? The barman just switched on the lights."

He noticed that Regis was grabbing the last of the brown bread as he turned to the bar. "Yes, very impressive." Brendan remembered that Regis worked in stained glass, and, even if he couldn't match his enthusiasm, Brendan could at least feign some interest.

"Which panel do you like best?"

But then again, Brendan considered, pretending to be interested could be a damned nuisance. He looked at the mounted soldier on a rearing horse and the ship under full sail. Both were impressively wrought. But what was it about the mounted soldier that was teasing old memories to the surface? "Regis, what is it they call the mounted soldier? The name escapes me."

"A dragoon?"

"Dragoon. That's it!"

"What is?" Regis replied, confusion wrinkled his normally placid face.

"Finish up. I'll get the bill. I know where I need to look now. Dragoon! Thank you, Regis"

Regis groaned. "Oh, but Brendan, I haven't had my dessert. The thought of all that lovely pastry going to waste, and myself going back to a cold computer. It's almost too much to bear."

"You'll bear up when you see what we find," Brendan said, encouragingly as he threw some money on the table, and gave a half wave at the barman. On the walk back, he turned to see Regis dragging his feet, his eyes rolling in disbelief. "Come on lad, pick it up."

Brendan squirmed in his chair as he went over the computer print-outs, occasionally pursing his lips as he read something of particular interest, then rummaging through the discarded sheets until he found what he was looking for. Finally, he laid them out on a large, heavily-scarred table under the solitary window, and beckoned Regis to come over, tapping his finger at the place where he wanted him to read.

"What is this, then, Inspector? Who is this Peadar O' Barry?"

"None other than our fine friend, Peter Deagan."

"Really? Well Peadar is Gaelic for Peter, but the last name?"

Brendan straightened up, the naked bulb suspended from the ceiling forming harsh lines on his face. He walked over to his worn oak chair and sat down heavily, sighing before he continued.

"The 'dragoon' was the code name for a man who made a number of bombs for the Provos in the early '80s, but was never caught. This O' Barry was the only suspect interrogated. There was a lot of flack after the Faulkner bombing, and he was the prime suspect. When he was brought in, I only got a glimpse of him, mind you, so I wasn't sure until now."

"The Faulkner bombing," Regis said. "I remember that one. Pretty bad, wasn't it?"

"It was for me."

"You mean you investigated it?"

Brendan could only nod his head. The long-suppressed memories rushed in, as if sucked into a vacuum; which was what he had felt like inside, ever since that day. But the memories weren't staying down now, and he needed to talk about what had happened.

Regis pulled another chair over and sat next to him. "Was that the bombing of the MP's car, then?"

Brendan drew on some inner reserve and began his narration. "Right. He was a high-ranking minister in the Ulster government. The car bomb took out the minister, all right, but his family was in the car with him."

"Jesus, Mary, that must have been horrible to see."

"And smell. I almost gagged on the stench. Christ! My handkerchief did precious little to cut it. But I recorded every grim detail. My training, you know." He waited until Regis nodded his understanding before continuing. "Even though my brain screamed at me to get the hell out."

"And you had to sift through that mess?"

"Aye and a bloody business it was too. The car was a smoking ruin. They thought he was the only one in the car, but he wasn't. I opened the rear door with a pick-axe; the front doors were buckled in. I saw the…I saw them… his wife and child. The blast had blown them all over the back of the car. I couldn't tell who it was, at first. Then I saw the blackened remains of a child's top, the small hand still clinging to the handle." Brendan abruptly stopped, drawing air sharply into his chest, hand to mouth as if to stifle a cry of anguish. Then, after regaining his composure, he continued. "I still see it in my dreams, the very bad ones."

"A thing like that can sure change a man," Regis said.

"It had a chilling effect on me, right enough. For weeks afterwards, my hand would shake just before putting the keys into the ignition. It's at times like that when you curse your imagination for playing cruel tricks on you. Yes, I'd say it changed me."

"They never proved it was the IRA though, did they?"

"No, never did." His voice trailed off as Regis moved his chair closer.

"And Peter? You think he did it?"

"Made the bomb, yes. We couldn't prove it," Brendan said, "though God knows the inspector tried every trick in the book." His voice lowered. "And many that weren't."

He recalled averting his eyes when the interrogation room door opened and he saw the beaten face. He visualized Peter's image on that defiant, proud face. It had to be the same man. "I was glad I didn't have to be in there. I don't hold with torturing a confession out of someone."

Regis nodded in agreement.

"No one could place him at the scene, and he probably only made the bomb. A different team often set them off. They did find materials in his basement that could have been used to make a bomb, but no detonators or timers."

"And did he have the skill to make it?"

"He was a demolitions expert in the army, and he was seen talking to suspected Provos. He also had a motive. His mother had been killed in the Derry riots, allegedly by a member of the Constabulary, no less. He could have made the bomb, and had someone else deliver it."

"But couldn't they just hold him indefinitely until they had the evidence? What if he went back and made another one?"

"He could have made several, but this was just before the Emergency Special order went through, and they had to let him go." Brendan took a sip of tea before continuing. "They tell me he was a cool one under interrogation. The inspector kept him up for a day-and-a-half, trying every psychological trick. But they couldn't break him down; much less get him to incriminate the other suspects."

"Did anyone ever take credit for the bombing?"

"No one stepped forward to claim they did it, but everyone was more than eager to point the finger. The Provos said it was the Ulster Defense Regiment or even MI5 trying to make them look bad. Some said it was a radical splinter group. It became a real media circus."

"So, d'ya really think the Provos had a hand in this killing?"

"It isn't their style, and officially they don't promote violence in the Republic. But as long as the possibility exists, I mean to explore it. I won't have Cork made into a battle ground for sectarian hit squads." He signaled the end of their discussion by slapping Regis on the knee and slowly standing up.

"Well, I think it is time to plan some calls for tomorrow morning. Care to help out and see what legwork is all about, again, Regis?"

Brendan watched Regis shift uncomfortably in his chair. When he massaged his over-sized belly, Brendan imagined him being pulled down farther into the seat by the ungainly bulk.

"You know, Brendan, I think I could use the exercise. Besides I've been staring at these screens so long I've forgotten what real

Irish green looks like. I believe I will go with you."

"Excellent! We can stop off at the coroner's first and see what they can add to our information pile." He noted Regis' face had lost its color. "Tomorrow, I want to talk to Conor's wife. She may be the key to this whole thing."

Peter slipped in the back door to his house after scanning his surroundings. In the windowless laundry room he pulled his clothing out of the dryer, scrutinizing his shirt and pants for traces of blood. His bruised knuckles were still somewhat swollen and raw, but otherwise no one would suspect he'd recently been in a fight.

Moving into the living room, he went through his desk near the entrance hall and pulled out the last coded messages he had received from his contact, and tore them up before tossing them into the ashtray. He lit a cigarette and set the match to the paper, watching it blacken and curl. He had anticipated that the thought of Eamonn dead would be a time to rejoice, but, instead, it was a time of concern.

There was a knock at the door of a cadence he remembered from long ago. "Who is it?" The muffled reply confirmed his suspicions, and he went cautiously to the peephole and glanced out. Satisfied, he opened the door and stepped back to let his visitor in.

"What are you doing here, McAfee? This is no time for us to be seen together."

"Came to warn you about a little murder. Did you hear about it?"

"Conor? Yeah, I was there with McElheny. He came by to fill me in on the contacts in the UK that might help me."

"Good, I hope you catch the bastard," Mike said, then noticed his hands for the first time. "Say, where'd ye get them big knuckles, Peadar, me boyo?"

Too late, Peter tried to shield his hands. "I bashed 'em on a car I was repairing. Dropped a spanner on them."

"Strange-looking wrench, I'd say," Mike said.

Peter ignored the comment. "Did you find out any more about this ex-RUC fellow?"

"No luck. Elusive bastard, I can tell you. You wouldn't happen to know anything about how this Conor was killed, would you?"

Peter tried to hide his surprise at the question. He considered what Mike might know about it, and why. "No. Why?"

"Just checking for a friend," Mike said. "He wondered if there was an IRA connection. That possibility worries me too."

"If it's an IRA connection, you'd be the one to know."

"Yeah, but my friend doesn't know that," Mike said. "He thinks I'm just a PI. But I'm more worried that someone is taking on a little work on the side, and not toeing the line like a good Provo. Know what I mean?"

Peter was sure Mike was on a digging expedition. "There's too much IRA talk around here. Someone told Conor about my own connections. Then the bastard contacts me to make a hit for him." Fearing he might reveal too much, Peter decided to ask a question of his own. "What do you know about this Conor, anyway?"

"From what I know, he's a poor excuse for a businessman. So what was this job he wanted you to do?"

"None of your business. And the less you know about it, the better. Things may get dicey soon. D'ya know who's got this case?"

"Yes, our old friend, Inspector Brendan O'Neill," Mike said. "Just like old times."

"Sure, and maybe we can find another car to bomb in Cork. They'd love us here."

"You know what they say, Peadar. You never leave the IRA."

"I know. And you never forget what you've done, either."

Mike only shrugged as he walked around the room. "You've done all right," he said over his shoulder.

Peter remained silent, regarding him cautiously as he completed his circuit of the living room and came back to face him.

"You don't sound very enthusiastic about helping your old friends out, Peadar. Why is that, now?"

"Did you stick around to see what the bomb did to the car? To the people in it?"

"Hell, I was just supposed to block traffic on the way in. How would I know?"

"Exactly, how would you know? His wife and a wee child. D'ya think I was proud of that!"

Mike ignored the comment and looked intently at Peter. "We still need those skills, Peadar. There's still a lot of work to be done."

Peter noticed the holstered gun under Mike's coat, and was sure he had deliberately exposed it. "You're not trying to recruit me again, are you? I'm fed up with it. You can carry on without me," Peter replied angrily.

"I hope that's not your final word."

"It had better be your final word," Peter retorted. He grabbed the man's jacket and lifted him into the air, tossing him on the sofa. Mike went for his weapon, yanking hard to free the pistol. Before he could Peter was on him, a wicked blade at his throat. Peter let the light reflect off the combat knife he was holding, its ugly blade breaking the light into twisted and scattered shapes on the wall.

"Have a care, McAfee." He watched the man freeze, then blink when Peter brought the blade up to his widening eyes. Slowly, Mike brought his hand out of his jacket, empty. There was dead silence in the room. Only a gusting wind, urgently working its way down the chimney, disturbed the stillness.

Finally, Mike said, "Okay then, what're we going to do now? I've got work in Cork still, and I don't want the IRA dragged into this killing. You know Brendan; he'll sniff out every fart we drop around here."

"Well, for one thing, we can't be seen together. You should get the hell out of here before someone spots you. Brendan may remember you as a suspect in Belfast. It won't take him long to put two and two together."

Peter walked him to the door, still holding the knife, and looked left and right before motioning Mike to step out. Looking after his rapidly-retreating form, Peter tried to assess what he had learned. Precious little, if anything, he decided. After locking the door, he went back to the blackened remains in the ashtray.

He tried not to think about what memories the charred paper invoked before tossing them into the fireplace.

CHAPTER 17

CORK
TUESDAY

The autopsy room was cold and sterile, and all too familiar to the inspector from countless visits. Two stainless steel tables, both empty, gleamed from the bright overhead lights. Carts on wheels loaded with scalpels, saws, clamps and other surgical instruments also sent shards of reflected light, obscuring their dark purpose. The entire room seemed bled of color, but that would change very soon.

Inspector O'Neill looked over at Regis. His sergeant was already having difficulty and the body had yet to be wheeled out.

"Regis, are you OK with this?"

"It's my first time, inspector."

"I know." He handed Regis a jar of VapoRub. "Here smear some Vicks on your upper lip."

"What's this for?"

"The smell. The body had been in the water for several hours. That always makes things worse."

"Wonderful. Do I have to be right at the table?"

"No, just take notes. Unless your curiosity gets the better of you."

Regis shuddered. "Not bloody likely."

On cue, the body was brought out and the gurney raised and locked into place so the corpse could be slid onto the operating table. Brendan nodded to the forensic specialist called in from Dublin. She was tall, mid-fifties and looked able to lift the body with one hand.

"Top of the morning to you, inspector. I'm Doctor Bridget Winchell. You can call me Bridget." She dunned her surgical mask and snapped into her gloves. "And a delightful morning it would be if we didn't have to see what's inside this body." Her eyes danced merrily over the mask. "Sergeant you won't be able to see from over there."

Regis huddled further over his notepad, if that was possible and half-turned away.

Bridget turned to Brendan. "Keeps to himself, does he?"

"It's his first autopsy," he whispered.

Bridget mouthed a silent "oh" under her mask and returned to her work.

She began with the body face-up, checking the facial bruising and looking for signs of a struggle. Taking the bags off the corpse's hands she examined the cracked nails and found something. "Andy, get me the magnifying glass," she said to an orderly leaning against the wall.

When he placed it in her hand she looked closely at something embedded in the nails of the right hand. Taking a small scalpel she removed a sample and placed it in a Petri dish. "This could be human tissue. We can do a DNA workup on it later." The doctor looked up at the inspector. "Unless you already have a suspect?"

When the inspector shook his head no, she returned to the autopsy. She spoke the results into an overhead mike. Regis would occasionally peer over to the table and then clamp a hand over his mouth and look away again. Turning the body over, the doctor examined the knife wound.

"Twas a wicked blade used on the man. A left-handed thrust, but I suspect he was unconscious at the time."

"Why do you say that, Bridget?"

"The pounding he took, the facial marks? Someone beat him

viciously first, which could have kept him out for hours. But the blows would appear to come from a right-handed assailant."

"So either two assailants, or two different attacks? Only one being permanent," Brendan said. Bridget nodded then returned to the body.

Examining the cut with her magnifying glass from every angle, she looked up again. "I don't think it was a conventional knife. The spacing is too wide and the wound is a bit ragged. It might be scissors we're looking for." She peered into the wound again. "Or it could have been a combat knife with a serrated edge."

"Would that account for the raggedness of the cut?"

Bridget nodded. "I'll have more detail on the weapon once I do some cross-sectional slices and see the X-rays. I'll have a full report later for you."

Glancing over at Muldoon, she said, "I'm thinking a nice juicy steak for lunch. How about you, Sergeant?"

Regis covered his mouth and shook his head no before heading out the door.

"You've got a wicked sense of humor, Bridget." Brendan said before thanking her and following after his sergeant.

Brendan waited outside the classroom, looking once more at his watch. The hallway was filling up with students, either milling about or intent on reaching their next class. The scent of formaldehyde and death was replaced with those of waxed floors, body odors and the perfumes and aftershaves designed to hide them.

As the last of the students exited from the classroom, he wandered in, looking for Professor Dunoon. He had no trouble picking him out. The inspector was a large man himself, but Dunoon still towered over him. They shook hands after Brendan introduced himself, and he looked down, startled to find his hand swallowed in both of Dunoon's. "Why would you, of all people, use a two-handed shake, Professor?"

The professor slowly raised his eyebrows over a benevolent

smile as he replied, "Aye, it isn't often a civilian gets the upper hand on the Garda, now is it, Inspector." Into Brendan's look of consternation he added, "Well, what can I do for you?"

Brendan quickly recovered his hand and his composure. "I was looking for Beth O'Hara, and Dean Fitzsimmons mentioned that she often worked for you."

"That's right, but she took a few days off. She'll be back to work on Thursday."

"Where? And how can I reach her, then?"

"I suppose she'd be at home with her son. What is this about, Inspector?"

"It's about an investigation I'm conducting. I can't say more just yet."

"I was wondering, Inspector. There was a news bulletin about an unidentified body found yesterday morning in Bantry Bay. This wouldn't be related to that, would it?"

"It might be. What do you know about an Eamonn Conor?" The inspector watched the man for any sign of recognition. There it was, a slight uptick of one eyebrow.

Dunoon ran his fingers through his beard while pondering the question. "Well, I've heard the name." Then he looked up. "He's not related to John Conor, one of our benefactors, is he?"

His response came too late and Brendan suspected he was holding back.

"We don't have a positive ID from the family yet, but it appears so."

"Interesting."

"And why do you say that?"

"Oh, just interesting."

"If you have any information directly relating to this investigation, I'd appreciate your giving it to me."

"If I'd thought it was directly related, Inspector, I would have told you."

Brendan suspected that the man's crafty way of defining the

scope of the investigation hid many things, but he had neither the time nor the requisite facts to pursue it further. What was this man hiding, he wondered, and who was he protecting?

"I don't believe Beth is mixed up in this."

There it was again in the form of an unsolicited recommendation. If this woman worked with him, he could be protecting her. Father figure? Later, he would have to probe this man's real agenda. For now, only the next step was important.

"Right. Now then, could you direct me to the Dean's office?"

While the inspector was at the university, Sergeant Muldoon was knocking on an ornately-carved door, the rich mahogany reflecting the early sun's rays. A large, matronly woman smiled a welcome and held open the door for him to enter.

"Good morning, Sir. Are you the gentleman that called inquiring about a room?"

"Ah, no. My name is Sergeant Regis Muldoon, from the Cork police station. I'm investigating a suspicious death. A body's been found in the bay. Might I ask you a few questions?"

"Ah, Jesus and the saints preserve us. A body in the bay, you say? Oh dear, oh dear." Kitty clutched her generous bosom and ushered Regis into a small alcove off the main hallway.

"My guests are just finishing their breakfast. If you'd be so kind as to step into my office..." She indicated with a sweep of her hand an office tucked in behind the alcove, one small window feebly illuminating the far corner. She snapped on a light and motioned Regis to a chair in the corner. "Would you like some tea, Inspector Muldoon?"

"Oh, that'd be lovely, if it's no trouble."

"No bother. And a biscuit, perhaps?"

"Tea is fine, and it's Sergeant Muldoon. I'm helping out Inspector O'Neill."

"O'Neill? I think I know that name," she said as she went out for the tea.

Regis looked around the office. It was business-like, but cozy. The desk under the window was a worn roll-top that, nonetheless, housed a small computer. This pleased him enormously. His first impression of Kitty Doyle as a sharp businesswoman, as well as a gracious hostess, was confirmed.

"Here we are, then," she said, as she set down a tray laden with biscuits and steaming tea. Regis pretended he had asked for the biscuits all along and snared a chocolate-covered rectangle with one hand as he accepted the tea with the other. After washing down the biscuit with some tea, he picked up his pad.

"O'Neill," she said, before he'd opened his mouth. "Isn't he the inspector who disarmed that bomb in Belfast, last winter?"

"Ah, yes. Brendan's the best there is, to my way of thinking." She seemed pleased as she took a seat at her desk.

"Now, then, we have reason to believe the deceased is one Eamonn Conor. Have you heard – " He stopped in mid-sentence at the look of horror on her face. "Mrs. Doyle, are you all right?"

"It's Eamonn Conor! Oh dear, this is terrible. Are you sure then?"

"We are, but we can't make it official until we have an ID from the next of kin. I presume, from your reaction, that you knew Eamonn Conor. Is that true?"

She nodded her head sadly as she set her own cup down.

"And how long have you known the, er, deceased?"

"I'd say about seven years."

"Really? What sort of dealings did you have with him?"

"Oh, very few. It was his wife, Beth, who I became good friends with. I didn't much care for him, if the truth be known."

"And why was that, Mrs. Doyle?"

"Well, now I'm not one to gossip, you understand," she said, leaning forward conspiratorially. Regis leaned in as well, praying for an earful.

"He was just a beast when he lived here. I remember going over for tea once and there she was with her eye swollen shut and a split lip. She was even limping a few times. God knows what he did to her. And her, the sweetest thing you'd ever want to see. It's fortunate he finally left her. I think she would have done him in, otherwise. And I would have helped." Kitty's eyes got quite large. "Oh, I don't mean she really would have, you know, just in a manner of speaking."

Regis noticed her glancing sideways at him writing in his pad. She reminded him of a school child stealing a look at someone else's test paper. "Er, right. So he left her, then?"

"Oh, no, I don't think so. I did see him, but less frequently"

"Well, were they separated, then?"

"I don't know. She never said."

"I see. She never said, but you saw him less frequently. How often was that, Mrs. Doyle?"

"Well, I didn't count, you know." She began toying with her cup and tried to smile helpfully.

"How many times have you seen Eamonn, say, in the last six months?"

"Oh, I don't know." She began walking the fingers of one hand over the other, mentally counting. Finally, flushed, she stated uncertainly, "Twice?"

"You think you saw him twice? But you don't think they were separated?"

"Well, he was on the road a lot," she sniffed.

Regis chuckled and shook his head. "Did you see Eamonn here on his last visit?"

"When was that? Oh, you mean... his last visit?" She patted her cheek as though reviving herself. "It's quite a shock to know he's..."

"Do you know anyone here who might have wanted him dead, Mrs. Doyle? Mrs. Doyle?" Regis looked at her strained face, her mouth forming inarticulate sounds and her head shaking mechanically from side to side. Finally, she closed her eyes and heaved her large bosom. Regis found himself breathing deeply along with her.

When she opened her eyes again, she spoke.

"Now, I'm not one to speak ill of the dead, mind you."

Regis encouraged her with a rapt expression, his body balanced precariously on the edge of the chair. He had the feeling she could hold his attention for hours, gossiping about what went on in her B&B.

"You might already have discovered the fact that no one liked the man," she said.

"Who is no one, Mrs. Doyle?"

"Everyone except himself. Sandy likes everybody, just his nature."

"That'd be your husband, then? Is he about?"

"He's gone into town for supplies. Now, where was I?"

"People who wanted Eamonn Conor dead?"

"No, no, not dead. I can't imagine anyone killing even Mr. Conor," she said, a look of shock on her face.

"Just the same. Can you recall any incident involving the deceased?"

"Well, he and Duncan had quite a row once or twice."

"Duncan?"

"Duncan Cowell, Beth's handyman. Once was right after her husband had beaten her up. Duncan is very protective, you know. As I heard it, he tossed Mr. Conor around some, warning him never to hurt her again."

"And Conor didn't sack him over that?"

"Actually, he did. But she hired him right back. Beth always stood up to him, Sergeant." Kitty sat up straighter, obviously proud of her friend.

"Were there other incidents with this Duncan Cowell?"

"They did almost come to blows over politics. Duncan is an outspoken Republican, and Mr. Conor, being contrary as he is, took the Loyalist position. I could hear them all the way over here."

"And did he get into political debates with anyone else?"

"Everyone at the Bay Mist Pub, from what I gather."

"Did Beth Conor ever fight back?" Regis noted her slow look of appraisal, as if deciding how much he could be trusted before replying.

"She always fought back. He never got out of it clean. He might have been bigger and stronger, but she never gave in. That's why he finally left, if you ask me."

She sat back in her chair, arms across her chest as if challenging him to contradict her. "He couldn't defeat her. No one can." There was more than a touch of pride in her voice. Regis was looking forward to meeting this woman, the more he heard about her.

CHAPTER 18

GARDA HQ
TUESDAY

Inspector O'Neill jammed the phone back on its cradle and eyed Regis significantly. "Well, it seems our prime suspect has disappeared. Constable Dennis O'Reilly just returned from the cottage. It was deserted. He also checked with her housekeeper, Margaret Fitzgerald." Then he glanced at his notes and made a further entry. "She said Miss O'Hara was off to see her parents." He and Regis exchanged significant looks before he moved over to the window and looked moodily out at the river swirling past.

The headquarters were located at the low end of Old Cork. Old Cork was actually an island, shaped like a battleship, which split the waters into two streams. Brendan recalled Edmund Spenser's description of the river as "enclosing Cork with its divided flood." That was when most of Cork fit on the island, he amended. Like a ship jammed in its harbor, moored by her many bridges.

Finally, with a sigh, Brendan returned to thoughts more immediate. "Well, we need to track her down, Regis. It is somewhat suspicious, her leaving like that. Get me her parents' number, would you? Meanwhile, I'll call Kerry University."

He paced nervously across wooden floors; polished and stained so many times the patina seemed ageless. The boards groaned under his weight, and he automatically avoided a loose board that made a frightening squeal. Brendan rummaged in his pockets, always stuffed with papers and detritus, coming up with a pipe cleaner he tossed in the waste basket.

"I've got another suspect for you, Inspector."

Brendan stopped his pacing. "Do you now? And who would that be?"

"Duncan Cowell, O'Hara's handyman."

Brendan stopped his pacing, and startled, turned to Regis. "Duncan? Are you sure? What makes you think so?"

"You know this fellow, don't you, Inspector?"

"Yes, I do. We were in the RUC together, but he left under a cloud and I didn't expect to hear from him again until that phone call you received. Truth be known, I wasn't eager to find out what he wanted."

Brendan sighed, drew up a chair, and sat down facing Regis across his desk. "What can you tell me?"

They discussed the results of the sergeant's interrogation of Kitty Doyle, which brought Conor's relationship with his wife into sharp focus. Finally, Regis spoke.

"And I also learned from Dennis that Beth O'Hara filed a report of a hit-and-run when I asked him what he knew about her."

"What?" Brendan leaned forward eagerly. "And what was that about?"

"Her statement only included details of the car, no license plate, but Dennis thought it might be more than an accident. She was riding her bike up on Healy's Pass and a car swerved and ran her off the road. She also claimed someone was following her."

Brendan's eyes narrowed. "Why are we just hearing this?"

"She was late filing the report and Dennis already had his hands full with the murder."

"Was there any physical evidence of her accident?"

Regis massaged his nose while he glanced at the report. "She had multiple contusions, severe cuts on her left leg. Could have been consistent with a bike crash."

Brendan nodded and then said, "Or a fight with her husband. Using the excuse of an accident to cover up physical evidence. The late filing of the report is a bit suspicious in any case."

Pointing to the report Regis said, "What about the green Honda trailing her? Could it be someone her husband hired to keep tabs on her?"

"But why tip his hand by attacking her?"

"In the report she said that car was a big, black sedan, a luxury car, not the Honda."

Brendan pondered this new information. "Has anyone else corroborated her story?"

"Yes, Duncan Cowell."

"How convenient. They could be covering for each other, Regis."

"Or she might be in as much danger as her husband."

"You're right; thank you, Regis."

Regis beamed at this last before adding, "In any case this killer may not be done with his bloody work."

Brendan nodded before dropping another report on Regis' table. "We don't have all the forensic evidence of the murder, but Dr. Winchell thought the wound was most likely made by common scissors, although she could not rule out a combat knife." He looked significantly at his sergeant. "Someone drove it in with considerable force, she added."

Peter Deagan stood over his steamer trunk. The lid was open, the contents barely visible in the weak light streaming from a casement window. He looked again at his hands and noticed that most of the swelling had gone down. Once again he had lost his temper, but this time it might cost him. Then he carefully sheathed the combat knife he had used to threaten McAfee and dropped it in the trunk. Sooner or later O'Neill would come looking for him and he would need to ditch it. He couldn't afford any incriminating evidence.

When he got back into the bedroom, Shannon was still in bed; the covers down around her waist and a wicked smile on her face. He thought about ordering her out, but then realized she might provide him with a much needed alibi and went to the bed.

Cupping one full breast and stroking the nipple with his thumb he said, "Are you ready for another go then, darling?"

She grabbed his crotch. Satisfied with his hardness she replied, "This will be a record for you, Peter dear. Maybe you do love me after all."

Peter saw the pleading in her eyes and knew a lie now would cost him later, but not his life. Putting all his effort into it he said, "I do love you, Shannon. I-I finally realized it."

He was rewarded with the most grateful look he'd ever seen on a woman and he finally felt like the bastard he was.

CHAPTER 19

CORK
TUESDAY EVENING

O'Neill and Muldoon returned to work after another dinner at the pub. Brendan was pleased he was able to stop at just one Guinness. He moved over to the table stacked with documents. "We need more background on the victim's father. He's flying in to view his son's body tomorrow. I think he's going to be difficult to deal with, but he may be able to fill us in on his son's enemies. From what we've learned, Eamonn Conor wasn't popular with anyone. What have you got on the company?"

Regis joined him at the table and extracted a large file. "Conor Shipping, as you probably know, is big. They have ships berthed in Dublin and Belfast, as well as here and Portsmouth, England." Regis referred to the voluminous research materials they had amassed. Then he looked up and added, "Dennis told me one of the witnesses at the bay later recognized Conor by the clothes he was wearing. He said Eamonn was wandering the streets of Bantry and looked totally lost."

"What was the time and date?"

"According to our report on Beth O'Hara's accident, right after it."

Brendan straightened up at that. "So we can place him near the hit and run. Interesting. That provides another motive for his wife."

Brendan moved away from the table while shaking his head, his mind following another path. "I need to verify her whereabouts. Is her parents' number handy?"

Regis shuffled some papers around, separating some sheets glued together with jam. Brendan made a face and turned back to his view of Cork harbor while his sergeant continued, red-faced. "Ah, here we are," Regis said. "Shall I ring the number?"

Brendan nodded, sat at his desk and then took the phone from Regis when he got an answer.

"Hello. Hello. Who is this, please?"

"This is Mairin O'Hara. What can I do for you?"

"This is Inspector O'Neill in Cork. I'm calling for your daughter, Beth."

"You want my daughter? Is it important? She and her son are picnicking on the Burren."

"Yes, it is important. I'd like her to call me straight away."

The voice on the other end of the line seemed wary. "What is this about, Inspector? The bicycle accident?"

"Eh...yes. Please have her call me. Thank you." Brendan swore quietly under his breath as he handed the phone back to Regis.

"Not there?"

"On the Burren picnicking with her son, or so her mother said. Doesn't sound like the kind of action a murderess would engage in, though, does it? I think we should plan to search her cottage, anyway." Then Brendan had another thought.

"And while you get that search warrant, see what the judge needs for probable cause to search Peter Deagan's garages and home. The battering our victim sustained would more likely be from a big man."

"You think he's involved in more than making bombs?"

Brendan looked up at Regis. "Yes, I do and I don't want our focus only on the O'Hara woman. She either had an accomplice or someone else wanted Conor dead."

Brendan was getting that bad taste in his mouth again. He

rose and guided his sergeant to a room at the end of the hall. The door opened onto a dreary room containing a single, long scarred table, scattered, mis-matched chairs, and one small desk along the south wall.

Satisfied it would meet his needs the inspector turned to his sergeant. "Ah, well. I want to spend a little more time with Patrick McElheny, now that we have the preliminary autopsy report. I think we should bring him here, since a more official setting is called for now."

Regis watched as Brendan positioned a chair and adjusted the light coming in through the window over the door. "D'ya need someone else to assist you, then?"

Brendan turned around, a question forming on his lips, and then understanding brightened his face. "You mean like the 'good cop, bad cop' scenario? Not this time, Regis. I prefer to do this interrogation alone, with minimal light, in a bare room like this. And no one for him to turn to for relief." He permitted himself a satisfied smile. "Then we'll see how much Patrick will suddenly remember."

Mairin put the phone down carefully, as though it might leap out of the cradle at the slightest provocation. She tried to read into what little the inspector had told her. Whatever the news, it was not good, she knew that. Somehow it was tied in with what Beth had related about someone trying to kill her. This was after she had gushed about Sean. Her daughter's revelations were a mixture of joyous and frightening news that still had her reeling.

She could not avoid a glance at the picture of the Pope. Was his stern look meant for her, now? Shuddering, she went down the hall and out into the garden. Shielding her eyes, she looked past the sheets flapping in the wind. Somewhere across the Burren, her daughter was trying to put her life back together, and back in Cork something evil was lurking, waiting to pounce. She could sense it. Then the phone rang again.

Beth relaxed against a stone chair, and wiped the crumbs off her dress. She was content now to simply watch Julian caper over the rocky outcroppings. They'd had a wonderful morning climbing over the ruins of Gragan's Castle, searching for artifacts they imagined buried amongst the rubble. Julian's intelligent conversation conveyed the wisdom he had acquired, largely due to Beth's role as his part-time teacher, assisting and encouraging him in every area he showed interest. Now archeology claimed him as he listened in rapt attention to Beth's descriptions of the significance of each structure they came upon.

"Why do they call it the Burren, Mum?"

"It's derived from a Gaelic word meaning a stony place."

"Boy, it sure is that."

She tried to see the landscape through his eyes. What shapes did he see in stark mountains and limestone uplands and plateau? Did he see mythical snakes instead of dry stone walls coiling up the sides of the mountains? It brought back sweet memories of her excursions here, wandering through tumbledown houses, and clambering over crumbling dry-stone walls. As a child she made a game of leaping from one ruined gap to another without ever setting foot on the ground. Now her impression was of a land scraped to the bone.

"Why is it so bare? Did a meteor crash here?"

Beth appreciated his incessant desire to learn. She hoped the truth would be more startling than a story of intergalactic devastation.

"No, most archaeologists believe this was the work of man."

"Huh?"

"This area once had forests of pine and yew protecting rich topsoil, but men came and cleared the forests for ships and farming. The soil was swept away by the rain and constant wind, exposing the rock you see now.

"Gosh, how long did that take?"

"Centuries, Julian. At least, back then it did. Now we can denude a forest in much less time. It takes so long to heal. So long." Beth's gaze was distant, far beyond the rocks and hills in the middle distance.

"Mum?"

"Sorry, I was thinking about something else. Where would you like to have lunch?"

"How about on the cliffs?"

"The Cliffs of Moher?" Beth asked in surprise. When Julian enthusiastically nodded his head, she shrugged her shoulders. "Well, why not. Perhaps I'll exorcise some demons."

"Demons?" Julian seemed worried as he looked behind him. "Where, Mum?"

"It's just a metaphor, dear. Not real demons." Then her smile vanished and under her breath whispered, "At least I hope they aren't real." Changing her mood again, she faced Julian. "I'll race you to the car."

They both were laughing too hard to make a real race of it. Leaping small boulders and skirting larger ones, they followed a zigzag path back to the car. Beth picked him up when they were almost there. "No you don't," she said between laughs. "I'll get there first."

"No way! We tie if you're carrying me."

"Well maybe I should drop you then."

He squirmed around in her arms, regarding her carefully. "You wouldn't, would you Mum?"

"No, never." Beth replied as she hugged him tight to her. "Never, Julian."

The drive down to the cliffs was short and uneventful. Beth parked the car in a designated parking area. Scanning the other cars already there, she noticed a number of rental car stickers, even two green Hondas. Reminding herself that it was a popular car, she tried to reassure herself that her suspicions were unfounded. However, she had a feeling that she would always be wary of green Hondas. And black luxury cars.

Pulling the picnic basket out of the boot, she followed Julian to a grassy spot, away from a group of tourists huddled around their guide. As she spread a blanket, the young guide's voice travelled clearly across the plateau.

"The Cliffs of Moher, or Cliffs of Ruin, rise vertically to well over 600 feet here. The generally flat plateau extends for five miles down to Hags Head from where we're standing. The tow... eh, Madam, please don't go so close to the edge. The ground is unstable at points and the wind is very strong here."

Beth and Julian watched as the guide tried to herd his charges away from the steep drop.

"Mum, let's go up the tower, before they do."

"Okay, why not." She followed him to O'Brien's Tower, and watched while Julian read the historical marker.

"It says it was built as a teahouse in 1835. It sure is a strange-looking teahouse."

"I know, it looks more like a castle battlement that was left when the rest of the castle was carried off." Beth took his hand and they went inside. They followed the arrows and climbed the stairs. Their shoes scraped on the stone steps, dislodging scraps of paper and candy wrappers left by less tidy visitors.

Coming to the top they were rewarded with a breathtaking view of Galway Bay. Beth pointed out the Aran Islands, nestled in the shimmer of the West Atlantic. Julian followed her hand as it swept up the coast of Galway Bay to identify the Connemara Mountains in the distance.

When they saw the tourists making their way towards the tower, they quickly descended and went outside again. Beth, impelled forward almost against her will, walked near the edge while holding Julian's hand tightly. She watched the gulls, stationary in the wind. They looked like kites pulled by invisible strings. As a wing dipped slightly, a bird would shear off to left or right. Occasionally one would dive, dropping at breathtaking speed down the cliff's steep sides.

She wondered what it would be like to plummet from this spot, diving like a sea bird, and pulling up at the last instant. A freshening breeze formed a moist mask on her face, and she leaned forward to receive its clammy touch. She gazed out at the waves below her, no more than ripples from her perch. They looked coolly inviting.

A tug of Julian's hand alerted her to danger. Shaking her head violently, as though waking up behind the wheel of a car, she was once more aware of her surroundings. She was so close to the edge. What was she doing? She turned to Julian. He looked cold and frightened.

"Should we head back?"

Julian's response was to pull her back to the blanket, holding her hand tightly. The sun was dropping lower in the sky, giving his face a pink glow. After they had settled down, a solitary figure appeared from around the far side of the tower. Light radiated behind him. Beth concentrated on him as he drew closer, trying to guess who it might be. Suddenly, Julian began tugging on her skirt, a look of anguish on his face. "It's the dark man, Mummy. He's coming for you. Run!"

Beth looked at the hazy outline, willing herself to fill in the details still obliterated by the sun. He was almost upon them now and her heart raced, threatening to burst out of her chest. She held her hand under her breast, pressing inwards to still its rampant beat. Slowly her eyes registered details as he approached and became recognizable.

"Dad, you gave us a start!" Beth let out a long-held breath, but now saw worry on her father's face. "What is it? Is something wrong?"

Julian was pressed close to her side as his grandfather knelt on the blanket's edge. She felt him finally relax when Casey ruffled his hair and the sun exposed his gentle features.

"There was a call for you, girl. The police in Cork. Your mother is worried sick about it, so I came here to fetch you. She bade me not to tell you of her worry, understand, but I think you really should get back."

Beth held Julian close, the concern and fear on her face mirrored in her father's eyes.

CHAPTER 20

Patrick McElheny waited an eternity outside the inspector's office. Light illuminated the frosted glass set high on the door, behind which vague shapes passed. To Patrick, they were shadows of sinister import. The unyielding chair pressed against every sore point in his body, and he was sure all the air had been evacuated from the room. The walls seemed to close in on him the longer he waited.

Finally the door opened and the inspector stood looming over him. Patrick hadn't realized how big the man was until now. His face no longer appeared friendly. In fact, it had the stormy aspect he always equated with the bust of Beethoven that occupied a side table in his music room. He wished he was there now, listening to the Pastoral Symphony in quiet repose in his favorite chair, not in this dingy office with Inspector O'Neill glaring down at him.

"Well, Mr. McElheny, good of you to come. I have a number of points I'd like to go over with you. Would you be so kind as to step this way?"

The invitation was not in the least attractive, but Patrick saw no way to refuse. He followed Brendan down the hall into a dark office and his heart sank. The room was as bare and intimidating as any he could remember. An image of the confession scene in some movie, with Vincent Price playing the grand inquisitor, rose unbidden in his mind. Try as he might, he couldn't shake the image. His heart raced as he sat in the chair Brendan pointed to, and rubbed his hands together, surprised at how moist they felt.

He watched the inspector go over to a scarred table and consult some papers, then look significantly back at him. He cleared his throat and Patrick leaned forward in anticipation of the first question.

"Mr. McElheny, would you relate to me again the substance of your discovery Monday morning?"

"Eh, yes, Inspector. Well, let me see..." Patrick recited the events of the previous morning, wondering, at first, why the inspector needed this information. Half way through, he realized the reason and his speech, flowing at first, became halting. The last vestiges of confidence had evaporated, and he dreaded the next question.

The inspector was looking down at some documents. "Hmm, I'm afraid there are a couple of things that don't quite fit, here. Today, you mentioned that you arrived after the body was pulled ashore, and went forward at the constable's invitation to ID the body. Yet, yesterday, you said you saw Conor while his body was still in the water. When did you actually get there?"

"I can't remember exactly, there was a crowd around it and maybe I imagined it was still floating in the water."

"Imagined it, did you?" Brendan smiled as he pointed to his documents. "There wouldn't have been a crowd around it, as the constable had by then cordoned off the area and covered the body. His notes confirm that point."

McElheny wondered if the inspector could hear his thudding heart as he tried to compose himself.

The silence lengthened until the inspector began another line of questions. "Where were you coming from when you stopped? I don't recall your home address of... let me see, Cobh Way in Cork, as being on the way to work?"

"Oh, I was visiting friends in the Bantry area. It was more

convenient to stay around there."

"And where was that?"

"It's a B&B run by the Doyles. I forget the name of the place."

"Right, that would be Coomhola Roost?"

"Eh, yes." Patrick became even more uneasy at the inspector's knowledge of his weekend retreat. What else did he know? He took a deep breath and tried to ignore the gnawing sensation in his stomach. Why, today of all days, had he forgotten his lozenges?

"And when did you leave there in the morning?"

"Oh, I'd say about 7am."

"Was that the only time you left that morning?"

"I don't know what you mean."

The sound of boards creaking resounded in Patrick's ears as the inspector walked over to his stack of papers and lifted the top sheet.

"You left twice, according to Kitty Doyle. She was up getting breakfast ready when she saw you come in at 4am. Later, at seven, after you came down to breakfast, she saw you leave for the second time. Very curious behavior for a teacher, don't you think? Where did you go that first time?"

Patrick hesitated, a thousand possibilities crowding his mind, but none staying long enough to register or indicate where he should go next. "I was going to meet some...friends."

"Friends? At that hour? Who? Where?"

"Well, eh... S-Shannon Ryan. She works at the Bay Mist Pub."

"Shannon Ryan? You're a married man, aren't you Mr. McElheny?"

"Yes... I'd rather not let that get out."

"Of course not. So you saw Shannon where? At the pub?"

"Em, yes, she has a room there over the pub."

The inspector considered this and then said, "Then you went back to your lodging to make it seem you hadn't been dallying. Is that right?"

Patrick could only nod his head, his throat too dry to form

words.

"When did you actually arrive on the scene? Mind you, I can call Miss Ryan now to corroborate your story. Well?"

"Look, I just didn't want to get involved in this whole business."

"I think you are now, Mr. McElheny. You saw the body long before your official ID. When did you get there?"

Patrick let out a sigh as he slid the chair back, as though to remove himself from the inspector's scrutiny. He felt the room closing in on him, the light from the single high window uncomfortably warm on his face. He moved his chair out of its range, and looked around the room one last time before answering.

"I got there a little after three. I saw the body floating in the bay and pulled over. I didn't have to look very long to know who it was. You see, I was supposed to meet him in Bantry that morning. You have to understand, it was really shattering to come upon him."

"What made you suspect there was even a body in the water?"

"Oh, I had stopped to relieve myself and saw a dark shape in the water. I was curious, so I got out my torch to see what was up. When I saw that face, dead, staring..." Patrick paused for a second as his mouth again went dry. The inspector handed him a glass of water and he drank greedily. "I dropped the torch and couldn't get away fast enough."

Patrick had decided to keep the information about the car that sped away from the scene to himself. He thought he knew who might have driven it away after dumping the body and the leverage that information would give him could prove useful. The inspector was looking at him suspiciously as he continued sipping the water.

"What happened after you found the body? Why didn't you notify the police?"

"I panicked. It didn't look like the kind of thing I wanted to be involved in. At least, not being the first on the scene."

"Why is that?"

"How would it look? Me knowing him, and here I was finding his body... and having to explain why I was there. I didn't like the implications."

"So what did you do, then?"

"I drove back to the Doyle house, got cleaned up for work and drove off. I started to go to work . . . and then I realized I couldn't do that. So I went back. There was a crowd by then, and I just had to confirm that the nightmare was real. When the constable lifted up the sheet, there was no mistaking who it was. Then I told the constable."

"So you got involved, anyway."

"Yes, I guess more than I wanted."

"You realize I'll need a full accounting of your whereabouts Sunday night."

"Why, I was at the Doyle place."

"Who saw you there?"

"Kitty and I chatted over glasses of port until about ten o'clock and then I went to my room. I left to see Shannon at about midnight."

"When did you leave her?"

"About three in the morning, I imagine."

Brendan consulted another document from his desk. "According to the coroner's preliminary report, Eamonn died between one and two in the morning. How long did it take you to get to the bay from the pub?"

Patrick gripped the seat of his chair as though the next word would knock him off his uncomfortable perch. He pondered the question and its consequences before answering, "Eh, about 15 minutes, I suspect."

Brendan only nodded and made another entry in his notebook. Then, moving deliberately around to the other side of the table, he dropped the stack of papers and said, "That's all for now. Thank you for your help. I will be calling you again, so don't leave the Cork area."

Patrick felt as though his dentist had just told him his root canal treatment had been postponed. Accepting the reprieve, he got up quickly, and was out the door before Brendan could open it for him. In his haste, he missed the satisfied smile on the inspector's face.

Ian Williams watched the planes coming in to land at Cork airport as he parked the car. He had questioned John's decision to come to Ireland since his son had been positively identified, but it was obvious he would not be deterred from seeing his son one last time. Ian's business dealings were almost complete, so he could serve as John's right-hand man through this ugly matter, and then send him home.

He threw a blue trench coat over his pale gray three-piece suit as more rain was promised, but he kept it unbelted in the stuffy airport terminal. He scowled as he recalled how much he hated airports and jostling travelers. He used his elbows to press through the crowds.

He swiftly made his way to the reception area, glancing disdainfully at the limousine drivers holding up their hastily-scribbled placards. His heart jumped when he saw John come out in a wheelchair, but then he realized it was probably just a precaution. Then he spotted Dr. Mansfield behind Conor, merrily pushing him along. His groan was swallowed up in the din of cries, greetings, and indecipherable metallic-sounding flight announcements.

"Ian! Over here! Tommy, he's over there." John pointed his cane towards the tall figure waiting patiently at the back of the crowd in the arrivals area. John used his cane like the prow of an icebreaker, as Tommy pushed him towards Ian. In his wake, he separated a son from his mother's hasty embrace, then a young girl and her bearded sailor, and finally almost impaled a passenger wandering in a daze under the arrival monitors. "Out of the way!

Make way there! Don't shush me, Tommy. Why do all these bloody people have to cluster around here? Don't they know people are trying to get the hell out of this terminal?"

"Really, sir," Tommy said. "I'm sure you don't have to perform like Moses. They will part for you without flourishing your cane. It's supposed to be used for walking, you know."

John, somewhat chastened, pulled his cardigan more tightly to his chest. "Ian, get us out of here, will you. I've only been here ten minutes and already I hate this abominable country. Stop patting me, Tommy, I'm not a child." The doctor's look as he straightened up suggested he thought otherwise.

"No, of course you aren't. It's just that the techniques I use on my son seem to work admirably on you as well. Now, please calm down. I'm sure Ian will get us out of here very efficiently and quickly."

"Yes, I suppose so. Well, Ian, how do you like my new babysitter? He insisted on coming along. Says it's for my health. And, do you know, he even likes this country!"

"You do too, you're just being difficult," Tommy said. "No airport is a place by which to judge a country, anyway. Or its inhabitants, for that matter," he added as someone jostled him, and then muttered a curse as the wheelchair ran over his foot. John noticed that the good doctor could not suppress a smile.

At the car, Tommy made sure John was comfortable in the back seat, but when Tommy tried to adjust his cardigan he slapped his hand away. "Oh do stop fussing over me, Tommy." John didn't miss his doctor's eye roll before joining Williams in loading the luggage into the boot.

John turned to look out the rear window. He listened in as Ian asked Tommy incisive questions about the state of his health, the concern never leaving Ian's face. Now I have two busybodies fretting over me, he thought, and sighed heavily.

Finally, luggage stowed, they drove back towards the Imperial Hotel, exchanging pleasantries on the way. John had signaled his attorney not to discuss the pending business deal until they were alone. If only he could so easily forbid his mind from confronting the reality of his son's death; at least until the moment he saw his face in the morgue.

CHAPTER 21
THE BURREN

Beth O'Hara shakily put the phone down, using both hands. She looked up to find her parents eagerly searching her face. "He wants to see me in Cork. He said it was most urgent that I return to answer questions. I told him I was just taking a few days off, and couldn't I just show up Wednesday to fill them in on the bicycle incident." Bicycle incident was how Beth was describing it to her parents. It sounded much less terrifying than "attempted murder."

Her father moved in closer and placed a hand on her arm, a concerned look on his face. "What did he say?"

"He repeated that it was most urgent, and that there were related developments," she shrugged before adding, "but he said he couldn't tell me more just yet. Doesn't that sound strange, Da?" Her father exchanged looks with Mairin before replying.

"Aye. Are you sure he's really the chief inspector?"

"Yes, he was calling from Michael's office. Michael himself said I had to come back."

Her mother also moved closer, an eyebrow raised. "Michael . . . that would be the Dean of your university?"

"Yes, maybe it has something to do with the university. They were both adamant about my returning."

Her mother was thoughtful for a moment and then came to a decision after glancing at Casey. "Since it's getting late, perhaps you should leave Julian here. He doesn't have school and you planned to return this weekend. Maybe you could bring Sean up, too. We have plenty of room here."

"Sean?" Casey said a confused look on his face.

"I'll fill you in later, Casey," Mairin said.

Beth observed their silent communication and knew her mother would do just that. She gave her a grateful look. They had become much closer again in the past couple of days and Mairin's acknowledgment of Sean's importance to Beth spoke volumes of her understanding.

"We can certainly look after Julian, and if there is some unpleasant police business, you won't be worryin' about him," Mairin said.

Beth resigned herself to the drive back to Cork. If she drove non-stop, she could be there by late evening. Her mother packed some sandwiches, which Beth eyed hungrily, and a thermos of coffee which she would not drink. Knowing it would make her mother feel better, she accepted both gratefully.

Inspector O'Neill and his sergeant entered the Bay Mist Pub just as the evening regulars began crowding into seats. Brendan thought Patrick's description didn't do justice to the barmaid deftly spinning pints on the tables around her. She was of medium height, buxom, with wide shoulders. Some of her black hair was plastered to her forehead, and she blew a stream of loose strands out of her face as she deposited another load of ales. Rubbing her turned-up nose, she frowned at Brendan as though she already knew the reason for his visit.

When the inspector was closer, he noted her narrowly-spaced black eyes, downy white skin and, most particularly, the beads of perspiration on her half-exposed breasts. She reminded him of a seductive gypsy, spent after dancing to the animated strains of a fiddle. She gave him a saucy smile before turning back to the bar. Brendan and Regis looked at each other and nodded. There couldn't be two women like this in all of Cork.

"Excuse me. Miss Ryan?"

"Right, that's me. What would you like?"

Brendan could have sworn there was suggestion in her question. "I'd like some time alone with you, Miss."

"There's a long line, deary." Her smile turned into a frown when she saw his credentials. "Oh. Wait right here."

After some whispered conversation with the barman, she motioned them to the back of the pub. Off-color comments followed them all the way across the pub. As they passed the barman, he said, "Don't keep her long." This aroused further comments that colored Regis' face a fresh red.

When they reached the back room, Shannon was waiting, arms folded, jaw set. Evening light came in through the three dirty windows on the back wall, throwing a pale light onto benches stacked on tables and empty kegs along one wall. The 'St. Patrick room,' the sign on the door had said.

"Well?"

"We'd like to ask you a few questions regarding an investigation."

"It's Conor's son, I'm betting." She glanced over at Regis, catching him staring at her breasts and smirked.

"You'd be right." Brendan replied. "How did you know?"

Shannon placed hands on her well-formed hips, elbows akimbo. "Come, now. What d'ye think the town's been buzzin' about today?"

"Fine." Brendan moved in closer and gestured to Regis to begin taking notes. "Can you tell me where you were Sunday night between midnight and 4am?"

She took her hands off her hips and leaned forward. Her breasts swelled, filling her blouse. Brendan noted that Regis's pen had frozen in the middle of note-taking.

"Are you accusing me of doin' him in?" she said incredulously.

"We're just gathering facts." Brendan waited patiently while Shannon turned her head from side to side, as if calling on witnesses to this insult. Finally, she sat on a table backed against the rear wall, her arms behind her and exposed shapely legs as her dress rose up her thighs. Out of the corner of his eye, Brendan noticed Regis' rapt attention and suppressed a smile.

"I was with a gentleman." She emphasized gentleman as if those were the only ones she associated with.

"Name?"

"I don't think he'd like it if I told you." She looked indignantly at both of them.

"You could be right, Miss Ryan," the inspector said. "But it's your neck."

She rubbed her neck unconsciously before replying. "I was with Patrick McElheny." She immediately added, "Don't you go tellin' his wife, now."

"That's not our job. When and where was this?"

She stabbed a thumb above her. "My apartment. He was there until close to two in the morning."

Brendan and Regis exchanged looks of surprise. "You said it was two o'clock, Miss Ryan?"

After she nodded yes she added, "I do need me beauty sleep after all."

Shannon eyed them both suspiciously while blotting droplets across her breasts and down her cleavage. Regis sucked in his breath.

"You're not thinking he had anything to do with it, are you?"

"We're checking all possibilities. Do you have any idea who might have had reason to kill Eamonn Conor."

"Sure. That O'Hara bitch; his wife."

Brendan and Regis exchanged startled looks before Brendan asked, "You know her?"

Shannon was enjoying throwing them off their routine. "Not to talk to, but Eamonn used to be a regular here before she drove him off." Her voice rose and her eyes took on a predatory look as she continued. "Too good for the town and too good for him, is what it looked like to me. She wouldn't even use his name. Now what does that tell you?"

"What about the reports that he beat her up?"

"Hmph! Most likely she deserved it. Eamonn said she'd pick a fight just to get him all riled up, and then pretend she was the innocent." There was a self-satisfied look on her face as she swayed from side to side on the table, which now seemed more like her throne.

Instinct told Brendan what the next question should be. "Were you romantically involved with Eamonn Conor?"

She waved the idea away as though insignificant, but not before he caught the widened eyes and tightened mouth that told him his remark had hit home.

"We just had a few drinks and a few laughs." She leaned forward for emphasis, "That's all."

They were interrupted by angry shouts and the sound of broken glass. Shannon jumped off the table. "Shite! I've got to help out Stan."

They all went into the pub. Brendan and Regis ducked as a mug smashed on the door above them. "Friendly town, this," Regis said.

Before they could do anything else, Shannon had got between the two combatants and was separating them. One of them made the mistake of pawing her breast and she swung a hard right to his jaw. Startled, the man's eyes glazed over and he dropped like a stone.

Everyone cheered Shannon, who stood over him shaking her fist. "Why don't ye have a grab of yer own wife, Clancy? Put a smile on her face, fer Christ's sake!"

She stepped over the dazed man and walked back to Brendan and Regis, triumphant. The pub slowly quieted down to its normal buzz. When she was almost touching Brendan, she looked up at him, a proud smile on her face. "So, Inspector, was there anything else ye needed to know?"

Patrick McElheny was expecting the call but he still jumped when the phone rang. He went to the window to draw the curtains, and then slowly lifted the phone, holding it as though it contained explosives.

"Yes?" The speech coming from the receiver was sibilant, some of the hissing coming from the connection, some from the speaker's insistent tone.

"What were you doing in Inspector O'Neill's office?"

"How did you know I went there?" A satisfied chuckle was the only reply. Patrick grew increasingly nervous and filled the silence with denials. "Well, he didn't get anything out of me. He tried, but I was too smart for him."

"Of course you were, Patrick. That's why O'Neill had his constable follow you home, I suppose."

"What do you mean, followed? No one followed me, I checked."

"You didn't check your bloody rearview mirror, did you? Eyes glued to the rev counter instead, eh?"

"Well, I don't care if you don't believe me."

"You'd better, if you don't want your wife to find out certain things."

The warning caused Patrick to press the receiver more tightly against his ear, trying to suppress the threats knifing down the wire from escaping into the room. Finally, he responded, "I said I'd keep quiet, but don't you dare threaten me again!" He slammed the phone down, fear and revulsion, like twin demons, tearing at him. He looked pleadingly at the phone, hoping it would not ring again before his pulse returned to normal.

"Who was that, dear?"

Patrick froze and swallowed heavily before turning to his wife. She looked at him expectantly as she wiped her hands on a dish towel.

"Umm, business. Just a persistent caller."

"Did I hear you say he was threatening you?"

"Oh no, he was just saying if we didn't have his insurance, we'd be sorry." Patrick was uneasy with how close to the truth he'd come, while assuring her that everything was fine. Everything was not fine, and his plans would have to be modified yet again if he was to stay out of trouble.

The overcoat John Conor wore did nothing to relieve the chill invading his bones as he descended to the morgue. His doctor, perhaps sensing his state, placed a protective hand on his arm. This time, John did not discourage it. Inspector O'Neill had also been most solicitous, concern marking his every move from the time he had opened the car door. In spite of himself, John found he liked the man.

The lift was cranky and slow. Just like me, John thought. Cold metal in cold colors did little to banish his darkening mood. "Christ, they could have chosen a more cheerful scheme for this blasted place, Inspector."

"The fella who painted it thought he had. But I agree, it gives me the creeps, as well."

"Most of these places are cheerless," Tommy said. "Almost as if brighter colors would be disrespectful."

"Why is it your solicitor isn't here, Mr. Conor?"

"He had business to conduct," John said.

"Business?"

"Yes. He is also my director of operations."

They were interrupted by the elevator doors slowly opening, adding its own soft moan to the somber mood of its inhabitants.

"I see," Brendan said. "Mind your step when you get out, sir."

Conor peered deep into the bowels of St Briget's hospital. There was only a dimly lit corridor in front of him. Nondescript doors flanked either side, closed and dark. In the distance, a light seeped out from under one door. He followed the others, almost mechanically, towards the slash of light. Disinfectants and a repulsively-scented cleanser hit John's nostrils like a slap in the face. The scents triggered old memories, and transported him back to another hospital and another time; the one in which his wife had spent her last days.

Then, as a more mobile man, he had rushed up to Intensive Care. As he had walked down that other corridor to his wife's room, he had noted the disapproving stares and heard snatches of comments behind cupped hands. The doctor in attendance had blinked recognition when John entered her room, and had moved away from her bedside, slowly shaking his head. He had put a hand on John's shoulder, steering him to her bedside, before departing.

Staring at Florence for what had seemed an eternity, he had tried to find a semblance of his wife within the ravaged body in front of him. He had looked into her eyes. They had blazed with a cruelty he had never associated with her. Her mouth, open and distended, had intoned foul curses, the smell of the grave ripe on her breath. Her curses echoed in his mind still, flung out anew in countless dreams.

The doctor had returned as she expelled her last breath. It had hissed through lips powerless to hold life in her body. John had never heard such a disquieting sound. The doctor had checked her pulse one last time, as if the monitor would lie to steal her to an early grave, then had given John a hollow look of sympathy. John hadn't been prepared for what he said.

"It was a girl, a daughter. Your wife said you would want to know."

John had shaken his head sadly as he sat in the bedside chair. He had so wanted a daughter. Bright, lively, someone to cheer him up when the black moods struck him, as they were striking him now, surrounding him in tight coils.

The sound of a slab sliding out on poorly-oiled rollers brought him back to the present. A loud clank indicated the table had come to the end of its travel. Conor was in the grips of a mood even blacker than on that other blasted day. The attendant lifted the shroud to expose his son's face and stepped back from the steel door as John approached his son's remains. He could not restrain himself from touching the corpse. Eamonn's arm was cold and stiff; unresponsive to his touch. He stroked Eamonn's hair; his hand shook as he touched a cold cheek. All the pain he carried inside him spilled out, no longer under his iron control.

"My boy! My son. Oh, God, who put you here, Eamonn? Who?"

The inspector put firm hand on his arm. "Steady on, sir. This is your son?"

"Yes."

The inspector nodded to the attendant. "Thank you, Billy. We're through here."

John felt the inspector's hand still on his arm as he guided him away from the body. He heard the slab sliding back into its slot and the finality of its muffled click struck him hard. He wanted to reach out to stay that final closing, but instead his hands closed into fists, and he felt clean, cold anger surge through him. He turned to Tommy, who mirrored his pained look, then over to the inspector, who reached out a hand to him sympathetically.

"I'm sorry you had to see this, sir. We only just located your daughter-in-law. She'll be coming in tomorrow morning."

"Beth? Where is she? She's all right, isn't she?"

"She should be on her way back from Ennis," said Brendan. "As far as we know, she's fine, but we do have a number of questions to ask her."

John detected the emphasis in the inspector's voice and knew he was being watched for any reaction, any hint of Beth's complicity in the... what? The murder? "Questions? But you don't suspect her, do you?"

"I have no firm suspect as yet, Mr. Conor, so I'll need all the information I can get. I'd like to ask you for more background information on your son, but I can get that tomorrow."

John nodded his head, weighing the possibilities, then came

to a firm resolve.

"I want that killer found. I'll spare no expense. I'll post a reward for any information, any..."

"Steady, John," Tommy said as he wrapped firm hands around John's shoulders. "I think we should get out of here."

"You're right," John said. "I need some fresh air." To the inspector he added, "Can we leave now? This is as cold as I ever want to be."

CHAPTER 22
IMPERIAL HOTEL, CORK

Dr. Mansfield turned at the sound of John Conor tapping impatiently with his cane while the porter was summoned. He threw a discouraging look at his doctor, who was ready to pour soothing words over his foul mood. This wasn't the first time Tommy had experienced John's intolerance for poor service, particularly at high-end establishments like the Imperial Hotel, and decided an explanation might calm him. Nonetheless, he knew John would welcome the chance to berate the incompetent hotel clerk.

The man behind the counter appeared shocked at the difficulty in finding a porter. Tommy leaned over to whisper in Conor's ear.

"I overheard a row between this fellow and the bell captain. The upshot was the bell captain stalked off with his three on-duty men, challenging him to get along without them. This he seems to be doing very badly, John."

As if overhearing their conversation, the clerk volunteered, "Eh, perhaps I should take these up for you? We don't want to inconvenience you, Mr. Conor."

"Fine, fine. Let's get going. I'm tired from all this wretched travel. Come on, Tommy."

Doctor Mansfield looked at his patient with some concern. He had insisted on coming along, and Conor had finally relented. When Tommy thought about it, it was mostly because he was forming quite an attachment for his sometimes irritable, but troubled patient. He remained eternally good humored, even when Conor was crotchety, mean-spirited and condescending, which was often.

When Conor had asked him why he stayed, he had flashed a benevolent smile and said, "You may think you're all grit and grimace, but there's an inner core of goodness fighting its way to the surface, John. One of these days, you'll see it, too."

Conor glanced up at him now as if reading his thoughts. Conor noted his amusement and scowled in return. As they preceded the heavily-laden clerk to the lift, Tommy said quietly, "Have patience, John. We'll be there soon enough."

"Hmph! Not soon enough."

With shoulders stooped and arms stretched to the limit, the clerk-turned-porter finally reached the lift. He dropped one heavy case and Tommy had to nimbly step aside. Then they heard muffled laughter from down the hallway, and spotted the bell captain, hand to mouth, suppressing laughter. When the man was back in control, he commented to the figure next to him. Whatever he said, it generated more laughter.

"If I had anything to say about it," the clerk lamented, "that fellow would be sacked tonight."

Tommy said, "Can't get good help anywhere, I suppose."

"Oh, sir, it has been just dreadful since a guest was murdered. The police were here, asking questions and poking around. You know, just generally disrupting things. We haven't had any peace since they began questioning everyone." The clerk looked over at the bell captain again. "I just wish the police had interrogated that man. For hours."

Tommy and John stared at him incredulously, and then exchanged looks as if to confirm what they had just heard.

"Idiot, it was my son who was murdered."

The man had no response to this beyond an open mouth. Tommy sadly shook his head, and made no attempt to help the red-faced clerk.

"See if you can at least punch the right button," John said as they entered the lift.

Once again trying to invoke a positive spin, Tommy said, "Well, John, at least your color is improving, and you aren't wheezing as heavily,".

"You think I should make a practice of this to improve my health?"

"You are the most persistent man at refusing to see the positive side of things I've ever met."

"I'll let you in on a little secret, Tommy." John allowed a smile to light his face. "It takes all my concentration when I'm around you."

Both men laughed heartily at this, contributing to the confused look on the clerk's face. It seemed he couldn't get away fast enough after he had dropped off the bags. He didn't even wait for the tip that he knew he had slim chance of getting.

Patrick was tiring of pretending to be amused by the bell captain. After listening to the tediously drawn-out depiction of what had occurred on Sunday night in the lobby, Patrick extracted the one gem of information. Pulled from out of the dark, it sparkled with a radiant light all its own.

"You said a burly, dark-haired man followed Conor after he left the hotel?"

"Right, powerfully built." He tugged on his ear while he pondered another thought. "I think I've seen him around Cork, come to think of it."

"Oh, and then another gent left right after. I mean it was a nice night, but we don't hardly get any of our guests venturing out at night." He tapped the side of his nose. "That's why I thought it was suspicious. Seems like they all were heading to the same place."

Would you describe the last gentleman again, please?"

"Well I only saw the back of him. He were tall and slim, but I didn't get a clear look at him. Did you, Tom?" The man standing next to him shook his head, his face devoid of thought or expression.

"Did you see where he went?"

"Nah, he just went the same way as Mr. Conor and the other bloke, headin' east on Lapp's Quay. Likely crossing one of the bridges if they was going downtown."

Patrick looked down South Mall, towards the bridges below it off Lapp's Quay, and decided he was right.

"And when did you say this happened?"

"About half past twelve, I'd say, wouldn't you, Tom?" Tom again dutifully nodded his head in support of his boss's assertion.

Patrick was visibly excited now. He knew from a previous conversation that the police had not questioned the bell captain as he had only just now come back on duty. That made this information golden to Patrick. He pressed some money into the outstretched hand and went down the street, glancing left and right and doing an occasional turn as if looking for a sign.

The pair stood outside the hotel lobby watching Patrick go down the street. The bell captain weighed the sum in his hand then leaned over to whisper to his companion. "What do you think that was all about?"

Tom, confused at not having a question he could move his head to, merely shrugged his shoulders as they headed back inside.

Beth felt the tension in her neck and shoulders. Ordinarily she would not have minded the trip back, but she had many questions and no answers to what was happening. When she opened the door of her cottage she sensed immediately that something was amiss. Then she spotted the open rear door. Someone had broken in! Oh, God, don't let it be Eamonn.

A loud noise in the kitchen startled her and she dropped her keys. Beth kept her eyes on the entrance to the kitchen while she felt around for her keys. Where were they? She heard something being dragged across the kitchen floor, the scrapping unnerved her as she finally found the keys. She held her breath.

The padding of little feet preceded Felix as he emerged from the kitchen; his empty food dish pushed in front of him. He cried out to her. It was his hungry cry and she realized she'd forgotten to put out more food. The cat came up to her and rubbed against her leg, looking for reassurance. Beth picked him up and they touched noses before she set him down.

"Oh, Felix, what has happened here?"

He only blinked at her, but satisfied that she was back, padded off to his corner. She quickly locked the back door and took a fast look around. She didn't notice anything obvious that was stolen, but someone had violated her space and she was upset. Too upset to stay in her cottage, alone. Perhaps Kitty could put her up for the night?

When Beth walked into Coomhola Roost, she spotted Kitty just leaving the dining room, a warm buzz of conversation behind her. She had a plate of steaming food in her hand, and looked pre-occupied with serving her hungry guests. She didn't notice Beth until she was at her side. Kitty's face brightened for a moment, then darkened as her brows dipped together. Beth knew the signs; something was definitely amiss.

"Beth, you came back early. Sorry I'm in such a rush. My niece is out sick, and the other help is barely managing the swell of diners tonight."

"Do you have a spare room?" Beth had noticed many cars outside and wasn't sure one was available.

Kitty looked surprised. "A room for you?" She pondered the request a moment and then said, "Well, you could use our sitting room I suppose."

Beth had known Kitty a long time, they were best friends, but there was something troubling her. "I received a call from Inspector O'Neill, requesting me to return as soon as possible. Do you know what's going on?"

Kitty put a finger to her lips and set it to tapping, her brows still turned down. Beth felt her premonition getting stronger, and she held her breath. With a deep sigh, Kitty signaled her overworked waitress to take the order, and ushered Beth into her office.

"Dear me," Kitty said, "and this is the second time today I've shut this door."

"What is it?"

Beth tried to rush her, but Kitty was not to be hurried.

"Sit down, dear, please." Kitty waited until Beth was seated, and then took the chair next to her. "The police were here earlier asking questions. They told me that Eamonn was..." Kitty came up short at the end of her sentence, not wanting to go on.

"Eamonn was what?" Beth said, impatiently.

"They found him dead, love," Kitty said it as softly as she could, and then bit her lower lip.

Beth wasn't sure she had heard right. "Dead? Eamonn? B-but how, why?"

"As to that, they didn't say." In hushed tones she added, "I only know they say he was murdered."

Beth felt the room sway about her. She used the arms of the chair for support, while Kitty, leaving her chair, hovered nervously beside her, ready to grab her before she slipped to the floor. Beth's normally healthy glow turned deathly pale. Her hands went to her face, her nails digging into her cheeks, as if the physical pain would offset her mental anguish.

She remembered Sean's anger when he realized it was Eamonn trying to kill her. Would he do this to protect her? There was so much she still did not know about him. Please, God, don't let it be him!

At first she was unaware of Kitty shaking her and saying her name over and over. She looked in the direction of the sound, unable to identify what it meant. Her eyes were glazed, the pupils, black spots. Her head slowly turned, her lips moved, but at first no words formed. Then, as though rising from deep in her gut, the sound bubbled out.

"Noooo! Oh, God!"

"Beth! Beth, dear. Look at me."

Blindly Beth stretched out her arms towards her friend. She felt strong hands grip her shoulders and was reassured by the physical contact. Her eyes focused on Kitty's concerned and gentle face guiding her back to some semblance of sanity and comfort.

"Oh, my God, Kitty. What is happening? Why?"

"I wish I knew. I talked to a constable from Cork working for the inspector, but he was precious little help.

After Beth had a moment to recover, she asked, "Did they say how he was . . .?"

"How he was killed? No, as I said, they didn't mention how. I don't think they do give out that kind of information, do they?"

"No, perhaps not. Do you know where he was found?"

"The sergeant did say he was found in Bantry Bay early Monday morning."

Beth made the connection instantaneously, her mind taking her back to that morning, Julian pointing at the gathering crowd, her shivering unnaturally and driving off. Now she knew the source of that chill and the warning it held. "My God, I drove right by there on my way to Ennis."

"Right by it? What did you see?"

"Nothing, really, I thought it was a car wreck." Beth was lost in thought until the realization hit her. She turned to Kitty. "Why was the policeman questioning you, Kitty?"

"Well, he wanted to know where you were and he was very interested in your past history," Kitty paused for a moment and then added, "I think my tongue wagged a wee bit more than it should have, though."

"Why do you say that?"

"Well, I told him about the beatings, I'm afraid. But I didn't see the connection with a motive for murder until after I'd said it. I'm sorry."

"Oh, Kitty." Distressed at first, she said, resignedly, "Well, they probably knew about them from the reports I filed. It was bound to come out." It was only as she said it that the full import struck her. "I might be the prime suspect, then! That explains why the cottage looked like it had been searched." She laughed bitterly, "And here I thought it was Eamonn had done it."

"Oh, dear me."

Beth slumped down in her chair with Kitty looking on anxiously. Blankly, Beth watched her friend worry a hole in the doily she was twisting in restless hands, and waited for Kitty's inevitable response when at a loss for what to do next.

"Would you like some tea and biscuits, dear?"

CHAPTER 23

Inspector O'Neill took a deep breath before entering the shop, steeling himself for this encounter. His nose wrinkled at the acrid tang of petrol and grease. He noted the lack of cars, and the three idle mechanics sitting on stacks of tires. They were exchanging stories when he entered, but soon grew quiet and stared at him as if he were a trespasser. No one hailed him as he walked along a pegboard-covered wall, laden with tools. At the far end of the shop, he saw his quarry.

Peter Deagan was sighting down the waxed fender of a black limousine, before taking a buffing cloth to the spots he missed. Brendan saw his reflection come into sharp relief on the vehicle's wing as Peter buffed the hazy polish to a glass-like finish. Peter's hand paused in mid-stroke and he whirled around, just as Brendan was about to tap him on the shoulder.

"A little jumpy, aren't we, Mr. Deagan?"

"You! What the hell do you want here?"

"Oh, I thought we'd have a little chat, you and me. It being a nice sunny day, I thought I'd come here instead of having you come down to the station. Wasn't that generous of me?"

"Generous? You? Don't make me laugh. You wouldn't piss on me if I was on fire."

"Really? Actually, I rather like the thought. I'm sure I could provide that service for you, Deagan. Free of charge." Peter's only answer was a scowl. They stood close together, their breath in each other's face. Peter's fists were clenched, making the muscles in his forearms stand out in sinewy cords. His stance reminded Brendan of some wild animal, standing its ground to protect its cubs. Only the bared teeth were missing. He turned from Peter to look down the car's long flanks. On the periphery of his vision, he saw Peter nervously fidgeting

"Looks like a good job, Peter. Been fixing some dents in your car, have you?"

"What if I have?"

"Well, we have a report from a Beth O'Hara, claiming to have been forced off the road by a car that fits this description. She thought the left wing would have been rather messed up from riding the margin on Healy's Pass. What happened to yours?"

"Nothing, just some minor scratches."

"If my eyes don't deceive me, those tools are used for something other than 'minor repairs,' as you put it." Brendan noted the hooks, cups, and power polisher spread around the car. Peter looked down at them, as if for the first time, and merely shrugged.

"You accusing me of that little escapade, Inspector?"

"What escapade would that be, Peter?"

Peter almost replied, but realized the trap and chose to clamp his mouth shut and turn away from the inspector.

"No, actually, I had something bigger in mind than the escapade. How well did you know Eamonn Conor?"

Brendan's sudden change in direction seemed to throw Peter momentarily off balance. He looked over at his mechanics, and then motioned Brendan to follow him to his office in the front of the garage and to the right. Brendan was taken aback when he entered. The place did not look anything like he expected.

There were two wide windows facing out towards the River Lee. The streets on the north side of the Lee climbed a steep embankment, and then slashed diagonally up the slopes, one road almost tumbling into the next. There was a vacant lot in front of Deagan's Cork garage, so the view was unimpaired. The curtains on the windows were another unexpected touch. All the furniture was of good quality and well matched, and even the ledgers were neatly shelved. Everything had the feel of order, and was pleasing to the eye.

Brendan stroked his chin as he tried to correlate this with everything else he knew about Deagan. He sat in the chair offered while Peter sat behind his desk. The only hint of the work carried out in the garage was a scale model of a '63 Jaguar on the desk. Peter slumped casually into the high-backed leather rocker and jutted his chin. The challenging pose suggested to Brendan that it would not be easy to rattle him, unless he could continue to throw him off balance.

Brendan repeated his question as he scanned the room. Peter seemed to treat the question as insignificant, and drew long on the time Brendan was giving him to answer. They made eye contact, but Brendan's icy look guaranteed that Peter was not to win a stare down.

"I've heard about the killing, of course," Peter said. "Really shocking. Not what you expect from around here. I'd met Conor before, you know. Did some work on his car. That sort of thing."

Brendan smiled at that. "You more than heard about it; you were there when I arrived. Checking up on your work?"

Deagan gave him a cold look before replying. "No, I came because Patrick McElheny told me about it. I joined him at the bay. That's where I saw you."

"And when did Patrick let you know?" The inspector watched Peter mentally calculating how much to tell.

"About half past seven or so."

Brendan did his own calculations. The constable had arrived about that time, so if Patrick already knew about the killing he was not a late arrival at the scene as he had stated. But why did Patrick tell Peter about it? Were they working together? He recalled that

Patrick was left-handed, and Sinn Fein. Not much of a stretch to think they'd work together, despite Peter's insistence he no longer did work for the IRA. Could Patrick have stabbed Eamonn after Peter beat him up?

"So when did you last have contact with Conor?"

Peter paused before answering. "A month ago, when he picked up his car at my shop."

This gave Brendan a new path to follow. "What kind of a car would that be?

He noted the trapped look on Peter's face. "Come on, you're a mechanic. Surely you remember."

"A black Audi, um . . . let me check." He pulled out a ledger and fingered an entry. "It was a 1990 V8 Quattro."

Brendan leaned over to check the entry himself. "The license number if you please."

If this was the same car Eamonn was driving during his last visit and it had been abandoned after his body was dumped into the bay it might provide a treasure trove of forensic details. The entry had not been modified so there was a chance this was the car that drove Beth off the road. He turned to Peter. "I noticed a nasty cut on your right hand. How did you do that?"

"Oh, just some broken glass."

"Not very forthcoming, Peter. You shattered a wine glass is what I heard from the Fitzsimmons. That's the other thing you have in common with Conor."

"And what would that be?"

"His wife."

"His wife? Who was that?"

The inspector studied Deagan carefully. Was he lying about knowing her relationship to Conor? "You knew Beth O'Hara was his wife. But that didn't stop you from going after her, did it?"

Peter stared at the cut while he considered the question. "I didn't know she was married to Conor. She didn't act like a married woman, going after that Carey fella at the party."

The inspector considered that perhaps Deagan was deceived by the woman, which brought her further under suspicion.

"So why would I want him dead?" Smiling, Peter rested back in his chair. "You don't have a motive, do you?"

"Oh, did I say that was your only motive for wanting Conor out of the way? How about fear of having your IRA association exposed?

Peter jerked up in his chair. "Exposed? Jesus, I think everyone around Cork must know I was in the IRA."

"Who else knows?" Brendan watched Peter smile thinly, and then spin the wheels on the Jaguar. When no response came, he changed tack. "Or maybe you are desperate for money now after losing a lucrative contract with the university?"

Deagan's eyes narrowed. "I do all right around here."

"I understand you have a garage in Bantry. Business good there, too?"

"Yeah, that's right. Do some work for the locals, but most of the stuff that pays is around here."

"I know you lost your contract with Kerry University. That's a lot of money going to someone else. That must have severely cramped your style. And all because Eamonn Conor asked Dean Fitzsimmons to cancel the contract."

Brennan knew it wasn't Eamonn Conor that made the request, but he wanted to goad Peter into a mistake. The inspector watched him turn a dark red, his mouth contorting to form curses that never sounded.

When Peter kept silent, he took out his notebook and made a detailed entry in it while he continued talking. "Not saying, hmm? I also discovered that Conor was on the IRA hit list. Any ideas why that might be?"

"Christ, d'ye still think I'm an IRA flunky, for pity's sake? Still sore because you never found out who set off that bomb? Really gets to ye, doesn't it?"

"We knew who made it, just never found out who set it. Or

why. Why someone would take the chance of slaughtering an innocent wife and child just to get one man." The inspector's anger kicked in and he was having difficulty controlling it. Now he stood in front of Peter's desk, his fists pressed down on the desktop.

"Why that someone didn't have the balls to just go up to him and shoot him, instead of taking the coward's way and blowing up every bloody thing in his path. That's what I would like to know, Peter, since you asked. You have any answers to that?"

Peter, in turn, rose from his chair and faced Brendan across the desk. "The same ones your RUC boys got last time. But here you bastards don't use torture. That's just too bad, isn't it? You'd have really enjoyed being the one to turn the screws, wouldn't you?"

Brendan forced himself to become calm while studying Peter's reactions. He was not about to get sidetracked into a slanging match. "This isn't about Belfast, Peter. This is about what you were doing last Sunday night. Be very precise. I'll be checking every thread of your story." He noted that Peter was desperately trying to check his anger before responding.

"I had dinner at Spike's Place, and went home about ten. I was at my place all night."

"Who saw you?"

"I suppose you might say Shannon Ryan saw a lot of me that night."

"You're saying she spent the night with you?"

"That's right."

"Busy girl. She must really get around."

"What?"

"It just seems like everyone wants her as an alibi."

"What do you mean!"

Brendan gave Peter his 'Cheshire cat' smile, as Regis had once described it. He continued writing, hoping Peter would sweat a little first. "It seems Patrick McElheny was with her until around two in the morning. That leaves you out in the cold, me bucko."

"That little…"

"What was that? I didn't catch what you said. We aren't so articulate now, are we? I still need to know where you were Sunday night. And I hope you have a better alibi this time."

"I was home," Peter said. "By myself. I knew you'd latch onto that, so I thought I'd save myself some grief."

"Grief is what you just bought yourself." Brendan watched his suspect intently. Peter sat forward in his chair, and began playing with the tin of pencils on his desk. "When did you get home?"

"Ten o'clock, like I said."

"So you were home, alone, the rest of the night."

Peter nodded his head. Brendan watched him roll a pencil between his thumb and forefinger of his right hand. Then he noticed Peter's skinned knuckles. As soon as he revealed his interest, Peter hid them behind the desk. "What did you do to your hands, Peter? Looks like you were in a fight."

"Nah, did it in the garage a couple of days ago."

"Let me see." He gestured for Peter to place his hands flat on the desk. He looked carefully at both hands while Peter glared at him with open hostility. "Do you generally skin the knuckles on both hands? Being right-handed, that should be the one with the damage, not both."

"I just switched hands and caught it again. Very careless of me, wasn't it?"

"Yes, it was careless, Peter. You are aware how Conor died, are you not?"

Peter was about to speak and then realized it was a trap. He relaxed a little and smiled before replying.

"He was drowned, wasn't he?"

"He was beaten . . . and then stabbed before being tossed into the bay." Brendan was watching the man intently and thought Peter registered surprise at the word stabbed. That was interesting.

"I'll have to ask you to come in for some tests. Blood and tissue samples. What do you think the odds are they match the tissue samples taken from Conor's body, Peter? Did you beat him to death and then stab him to make it look like someone else had killed him? Those marks on your hands are from a fight. The fight you had with Conor, Sunday night."

"No! I didn't do it. You can't stick me with that one." Peter recoiled in his chair, rolling it back away from the inspector.

"Well, we'll see about that after the doctor looks you over. I expect you there today. That is a direct summons."

Peter muttered obscenities for a long time after Brendan had left the premises. He continued to rub his hands, and then looked down to see that the telltale marks were now raw, and clearly visible. He reached for the phone, and angrily punched the numbers. "I may need a barrister soon. You know any good ones?"

"In Cork?"

"No, in bloody England, you sod! Of course, here. How much money you think I've got to spend on one?"

"Oh, it's money you need, Peter? And a lawyer?" There was a self-satisfied chuckle. "You've come to the right place."

Somehow he thought he had come to a very bad place, but his options were shrinking fast. He tried to keep the desperation out of his voice as he asked what he would have to do for it.

Inspector O'Neill entered a pharmacy across from Deagan's garage to use a phone. He rummaged in his jacket pockets for the correct change, extracting crumpled notes and a sticky candy wrapper before finding the correct coinage. After giving Muldoon the missing car's description he interviewed the shop keepers around Deagan's garage, but learned little. He then reentered the pharmacy and found a seat at the counter behind a window piled high with boxes of assorted plasters. He ordered a soda while he watched Deagan's place unobtrusively.

Brendan's vigil was rewarded later when he saw the black sedan back out onto the street, heading north. He was certain Peter was behind the wheel. He dropped some coins on the counter and then raced back to his car to follow Peter.

Peter waited until he saw the inspector's car follow Tom, his burly mechanic, and then drove off in an old Rover. He'd let the inspector rattle him, but now took satisfaction in giving O'Neill the slip. The man he was going to meet had the money and support he needed to keep out of trouble, but what he would want in return worried Peter a lot.

It didn't take Brendan long to figure out he'd been had. He slapped his hands on the steering wheel. "Shite!" He was doubly annoyed because Peter would only have employed this deception if he was going to meet someone. Possibly a partner in the killing. The opportunity to bag them both was lost. He drove on past the black sedan, giving the driver a nasty look before heading back to Deagan's garage on the slim chance he could pick up the trail.

The garage was closed up tight when he returned. With a heavy sigh he headed back to headquarters. He was impatient to hear what luck his sergeant had had in locating Conor's car and ran up the stairs to his office. He also wanted to know if a search warrant was issued on Deagan, He was upset with himself for not getting one earlier. But that was before Deagan replaced O'Hara as his prime suspect.

Muldoon turned when Brendan opened the door, a phone in his hand.

"Sergeant, what luck on the car?"

"Inspector, I was just going to contact you. We found it! Someone had called in to report an abandoned car earlier today and the plates matched."

"Excellent! What evidence did you find?"

Muldoon looked down at the report on his desk. "Looks like the body was transported in the boot, and they found traces of blood. Also what appears to be a cyclist glove under the driver's seat."

Turning the page he added, "When they pulled out the spare tire, they found a dark gray belt in the tire well. Garda Jenny Magruder recognized it as one used on Billingsley trench coats. She said those coats are expensive and few are sold here."

His sergeant looked up at him. "Are you putting Magruder on our case, too?"

The inspector had sensed competition between them and knew Magruder was very ambitious. Since she had come off rotation and was chaffing for a bigger case to work he thought they'd work well together.

"Right, we need another officer on this and now she's free to help us." Ignoring his sergeant's disappointed look he asked, "How long did they think the belt was in the well?"

"Not long. Magruder said it wasn't soiled or badly creased, and there were blood spatters on it."

This was better forensic data that Brendan could have hoped for and his excitement kicked in. "And we know where Conor's belt was, so this most likely belonged to our murderer. Could she tell if it was a man's or woman's belt?"

"Hard to say, Inspector. The style was popular with both, Jenny told me when she called it in. She said trench coat belts were similar for either. Oh and we got the warrant to search both of Deagan's places."

"Good, I'm going to have Garda Magruder check out the Bantry garage and home."

"Jenny? You think she's up for it?"

Brendan smiled at Regis' poor attempt at hiding his displeasure at having another officer on the case, and a woman to boot. However, Brendan knew much more about her and she was definitely up for it. Best to put Regis to work.

"Check local shops to see if any trench coats were sold here recently. If there was blood on the belt, the coat was probably stained too. There's a slim chance the murderer may have got another one."

After Sergeant Muldoon nodded and made a note, Brendan asked, "Any news from forensics about blood type?"

"Last I heard nothing conclusive. The tissue sample was only skin from his assailant, no blood. It's likely the only blood was from Conor."

If the killers were careful there probably wouldn't be, Brendan thought.

"I told Peter Deagan to come in so the lab boys could get a blood match, just in case he left a trace in the car, or something to prove he fought with Conor. I'm wondering now if he will ever show up."

Muldoon was instantly on the alert, "Why do you say that, inspector?"

Brendan mentioned the slip Peter gave him. "In any case he's our prime suspect. Treat him that way if he does come in." Brendan stroked his jaw while he considered his next step. "I want you to search Deagan's garage in Cork. Coordinate the search with Jenny. We may still catch him at one of his businesses."

"You didn't want to arrest him on the spot, then, Inspector?"

"I don't have enough on the man, Regis. And the O'Hara woman could have paid him to do it." Or offered him something else he couldn't resist, Brendan thought. "We may sweat it out of him, but if past history means anything, he'll keep his mouth tightly shut. When we find where Conor was killed, I'm hoping we'll gather enough evidence to lock him up for good."

"D'ya still plan to have him followed?"

Brendan had a sheepish look on his face."You mean after I botched it? We don't have the men to do it properly, but you're right, if we get him nervous enough, he may lead us to the scene of the crime, or his confederates. Hmm."

"What is it, Inspector?"

"We've cleared Duncan Cowell in this, right?"

"He had an alibi. And you did attest to his character. What

did you have in mind?"

"Duncan was the best tracker we ever had in the RUC. He's not a constable any longer, but maybe he'd help us. He was also very protective of the O'Hara woman and I'd bet he doesn't like Deagan either, so I think he'll do it." Brendan paused and smiled at a distant memory. "For old time's sake," he added.

Brendan recalled earlier back at Deagan's shop, he had spied Deagan placing a call. Not a pleasant one either, particularly when he drew the blinds closed. He wanted someone to keep close tabs on the elusive dragoon.

"Inspector?"

"I'll call him up. I think he'd relish a chance to catch a rogue IRA chap."

CHAPTER 24

Garda Jenny Magruder was steeping her first cup of tea when Inspector O'Neill came into the room with a stack of papers under his arm. With a look of concern, he set the folders down on her desk.

"Jenny, girl, would you be so good as to join Regis and me while we interrogate the O'Hara woman?"

"Certainly. What is it she's alleged to have done?"

"Suspected of killing her husband. That was his body we discovered Monday."

"Ah, the trench coat murderer is it?"

"Trench coat? Oh, the belt you found in the abandoned car. Yes, it is"

"Sounds interesting. What have you got?" O'Neill opened the folder and placed a copy of the case notes in front of her.

"Why don't you take a few minutes to review this before she arrives."

Jenny was on her second cup when O'Neill returned.

"Jenny, be a love and take this carafe of water upstairs. This could be a long session."

She hooked a finger around the bottle's handle as she scooped up her notepad and background sheets, and followed the inspector up the stairs to the main interrogation room.

Climbing the stairs, Jenny looked out the tall stairwell window at the activity in the harbor. She watched a ship move slowly behind the pilot, out onto the lake that fed Cork Harbor. As they covered the last step to the second floor, they were greeted by Regis. She stood balancing the carafe in one hand and the stack of papers in the other while waiting for him to give voice to the thought behind his mischievous grin.

"Isn't it nice to know you could always get a job as a waitress with skills like that, Jenny," Regis said.

"I was a bloody waitress, paying my way through college to get this job. I don't intend to fall back on it again, and I'll thank you to remember it the next time you wish to make a helpful suggestion."

"Regis, how can you get on her bad side so quickly, now? Most people here have to really work at it to get her riled up."

"Beats me, Inspector. Maybe she just takes a shine to me and doesn't know how to show it."

Jenny pretended to ignore his sly wink, but she was not going to let his comment pass uncontested. "Oh, you're a good one, you are. Why don't you try your wiles on the O'Hara woman? Maybe she'll confess and save us a lot of grief."

"Grief, that's all you give me, woman. When will you admit your search is over, and you've found your mate?"

"Oooh, that man," she said, turning to the inspector. "I swear he'll drive me crazy yet. Isn't this what they call sexual harassment then, Brendan?"

"Sexual harassment!" Regis fairly screamed at her. "Here, what kind of books have you been reading?"

"I think it's that New York paper she always has her face in," O'Neill said.

The inspector usually stayed out of their weekly argument, but she was far from finished. "Well, it just may interest you two heathens to know that there are places in the world where a women's input is encouraged and respected."

Yes, I believe you, Jenny," O'Neill said. "That's why I asked you to come along with us,"

"Oh, right." Jenny turned to Brendan and gave him a deferential bow of thanks. She lifted her nose skyward before preceding Regis into the office, but once inside waited respectfully for the inspector's instructions.

"All right, let's get serious now, you two. Jenny, why don't you sit here, and Regis, over here by the window while I fetch her."

Jenny was pleased to note that the inspector raised an admonitory finger to Regis on his way out. She watched him out of the corner of her eye for a moment, and then engrossed herself in the case notes.

Beth was focused on a calendar on the wall, which still displayed the month of March. Her first impulse was to flip the calendar to April, but then she found herself drawn into the garden scene above the numbered columns of gray days and red Sundays. Everything else merged into the background. She still felt Sean's hand on hers, and gave it another squeeze as the inspector came into the room. He nodded to Sean and then directed his attention to her.

"We're ready for you now, Mrs. O'Hara. I'd like to talk to you later as well, Mr. Carey."

Beth looked back for reassurance, and caught the look of alarm that momentarily crossed Sean's face. Straightening her shoulders, she followed the inspector down the hall and up the stairs, concentrating on the way the brown tweed jacket bunched up around his thick neck. He rubbed the spot she was focused on with the tip of his pipe, and shrugged his shoulders.

While being shown to her seat, she noticed a stenographer and two other officers with IDs hanging from their pockets. The female was strikingly beautiful, with dark hair and porcelain-like skin. Her features were delicate, soft eyes and high cheekbones, the kind a model would kill for, and she had a model's trim figure. Almost too delicate for police work, Beth thought, until the woman pulled up the sleeves of her jumper, revealing well-muscled forearms.

The other policeman looked too soft, with a round belly and smiling florid face. He was almost the caricature of the friendly Irish cop. But the eyes stopped her; they held intelligence and saw much. His tie hung loosely from a white shirt, stained with droppings from a previous meal. She guessed that this was Regis, the one Kitty had described to her the previous night.

She only half heard the inspector's introductions, followed by the formalities of self-disclosure and the option of having a lawyer in attendance. Instead, her attention was on his dominating presence as he stood in front of the long table. His tweed jacket was casual and his knitted tie loose, but not a hair was out of place on his head, and his carriage suggested a military background.

She imagined a barrister's double-breasted suit on his large frame. She could easily see him in court, cross-examining a witness. His eyes were large, the irises steel gray, and she felt their scrutiny as though they were physically probing her. She should have been chilled by that look, but her own self-assurance permitted her the choice of admiration.

"So, Mrs. O'Hara, or is it Miss? Or perhaps it's Mrs. Conor? I wasn't sure what to call you. Could you help us out, here?" O'Neill asked as he leaned back on his desk.

Beth replied to the sarcasm with her own. "You can call me Mrs. Conor to avoid your obvious confusion. I used my maiden name when I applied for a job at the university. It was my husband's idea."

"Your husband's idea?"

"When I told him I wanted to make use of my degree, he said no wife of his would be working. I insisted. He replied that I'd have to use my maiden name, so it wouldn't get around that his wife was taking a job."

"And this arrangement worked?"

"To a point. He never quite reconciled himself to it. It served as a final barrier to our living together. We agreed to separate by mutual consent a year ago. Of course, we could not have obtained a divorce, anyway."

"Anyway? Were there other reasons to seek a divorce, then?"

"Well, I'm Catholic, so a divorce would have been morally out of the question. My husband had his own reasons."

"Which were?"

"His father would have disinherited him if his marriage had failed. Eamonn would have done anything to stay in his father's good graces.

"I see, so you both lied to make sure you got the old man's money?"

Beth could think of no useful reply to the inspector's rhetorical question, and remained silent. She watched him rock back and forth on the table's edge, lips pursed, eyes watchful. She was aware of men looking boldly, intently at her enough times that her face no longer flushed when she sensed them undressing her. But O'Neill's scrutiny was different, cold and clinical. His eyes did not stop at her skin, but plunged into her soul.

After a pause, he continued. "You spent some time in Northern Ireland. Had you considered emigrating there?"

"No, I didn't find much to like up there, Inspector. They aren't too keen on mixed marriages, you know. And Belfast was insane. Eamonn got along up there, but he had a lot of ties with those people. As well as being a Protestant."

"So you resented his ease of fitting in. Probably very angry at having to adjust to such a different life. And no way out of it. That must have been very hard on you."

She suspected false sympathy, and blinked for a second before continuing. "Well, yes. It was horrible. We left there when Julian was born. I was not going to have him growing up in a place that only knew war."

"Only knew war, yes." O'Neill's voice trailed off.

She sensed that he knew just what she meant. How many

young men grew up with that hate and violence all around them? How many knew more about building a bomb or setting fires than the rudiments of education required to get on in the world? How many started by throwing rocks and swearing at the British troops, and ended by throwing jars of petrol and setting up ambushes? It was hard for her to believe the same island could hold two such different worlds. Beth waited for the next question, but O'Neill was writing in his notebook.

The female officer broke the silence. "But weren't you and your husband at war as well?"

She was looking down at some forms that looked vaguely familiar to Beth. It took her a moment to realize what they were, the complaint forms she had made out against her husband. Staring now at the forms, she replied. "Oh. Well, yes, the fights." She sighed wearily and wondered how many more times she would have to relive that period of her life.

"How many times did he beat you? When did you finally decide you'd had enough?" O'Neill said as he leaned over her.

"I don't know how many times, but...What do you mean, had enough?"

"It seems that you had a number of reasons to want to be free of him." The inspector extended his right hand, and pulled back a finger as he ticked off each reason. "He constantly beat you. You could not obtain a divorce to be free of him. He wanted you to live in a place not suitable for your son. And that gentleman out there has become a very good friend, I understand. Now you couldn't very well live with him while married to Conor. Did you ask for his help in this?"

"In what?"

"The murder of your husband."

She didn't think he could have made it sound more chilling than if accompanied by a bucket of cold water. "Preposterous! I wouldn't kill anyone. It's not in me."

"I beg to differ," O'Neill said. "I've seen people that you'd never suspect commit the most heinous crimes. It happens. Then, of course, there is the matter of his trying to kill you on Healy Pass."

Beth felt her chest burn with this newest shock. How did he know? "I... I told the Garda I didn't know who tried to kill me."

"But it was your husband, wasn't it?"

"I don't know," she said quietly. "I don't know."

"So what do you think of this, now?"

Beth watched spellbound as he lifted a newspaper-wrapped bundle out of his desk, and held it over the table in front of her. Grasping one end of the paper, he let it unroll as it descended onto the table. A large pair of blood-streaked scissors clattered onto its surface. Beth jumped back and stared incredulously at them, an involuntary gasp escaping her lips.

"Do you recognize those scissors, Mrs. Conor?"

For what seemed a long time, all she saw was the blood on the scissors. Was it Eamonn's blood that streaked its gleaming blades? She fought off the black spots trying to cloud her sight while she held on to the arm of her chair. Finally, Beth let out the breath she had been holding since the scissors clattered onto the table.

"Mrs. Conor?"

"I don't know. They look similar to a pair I own, but those are pretty common."

"Perhaps, but these came from the shed behind your cottage."

"What? That's impossible! Mine have been missing for days." Then realization dawned and she scrunched her eyes suspiciously. "Someone must have taken them and planted them afterwards."

"Missing, you say? Well, that's very convenient for you, isn't it? Except we lifted your fingerprints from these." O'Neill picked them up and held them like a dagger, keeping them in front of her eyes as he continued. "Now, normally I'd say a woman wouldn't have the strength to plunge these repeatedly into her husband's back."

He emphasized the point by striking downwards towards the table. She winced when the blade struck with enough force to imbed itself in the wood. When the inspector grabbed her left hand, she reacted by making a tight fist. He was looking at her curiously as he continued to hold her hand.

"But, I'd say you have the strength to do it, and a strong reason too," the inspector said.

Beth angrily pulled her hand back and pushed out of her chair. Away from the scissors that seemed to be glistening with fresh blood. "I didn't do it."

The inspector invited her to resume her seat and then asked, "Are you left-handed Mrs. Conor?"

Now she realized why he had grabbed her hand, but she smiled through her reply. "I'm ambidextrous as it happens."

"And where were you last Sunday night?"

"Home, with my son."

"Can anyone else vouch for your whereabouts that night?"

"No. I put him to bed about ten, and went soon after myself." Pressing her hands together she continued. "What time did he...?"

"Die? Early Sunday morning, according to the preliminary coroner's report. Do you maintain that you were in bed the entire night?"

"Yes."

"Then how did this fresh mud get on the boots?" O'Neill help up a pair of hiking boots that were covered in mud which had dried and caked most of the soles and sides. "I suppose these we found in the shed aren't yours either."

Beth pressed her hand to her forehead. She felt very tired, drained. The clock on the wall had to be lying to her. It had to be hours, not minutes, since she had entered the room. "I went out for a walk around the pond by the cottage, and I slipped on the edge and got them muddy, so I left them in the shed."

"When? Before you put your son to bed, or later?" The inspector voice held suspicion.

"I don't know," Beth said. "After."

"Just about the time someone was putting your husband in

the bay. What a coincidence, hmm?"

Beth crossed her arms and looked indignantly at him. "The bay couldn't possibly have the same kind of earth as around my pond. You should check that out first."

"Don't worry, we are. Tell me, do you recognize this glove?"

He handed it to Beth. She recognized it instantly, the blood on the thumb and webbing was hers from the crash. But how did they get it? Did they take it from her home? And the blood? What did they think? She decided to let them work for it.

"It's a cycling glove."

"Yes, a fancy one, and of American manufacture. How many people around here do you think use these things, and have an American-made pair?"

Beth had to concede the point. There were not many that took to the sport the way she had. She was well known in the area because of her bicycle clothing and equipment. "Probably not many."

"Probably only you. What do you suppose it was doing in Conor's car, under the driver's seat? Very careless, don't you think."

"I don't understand. His car wasn't where his body was found? Where was the car?"

"About two miles from your house. Not a bad distance to walk home."

"Then why would I wear my gloves? I only use them when I'm cycling, not driving or walking."

"They could come in handy for transporting the body without getting any fingerprints over the car."

"Inspector, did you notice that my special gloves are cut out for the fingers?" Beth permitted herself to gloat for a moment. "What bloody good would they be for that?"

"Then you admit this is your glove?"

Beth had to admit, he was good. "Yes. But surely I wouldn't have forgotten them when I left the car. I think someone planted them, just as they stole my scissors." Another thought occurred to her, an important one. "You said the body was transported. Does that mean he was killed somewhere else?"

"We're still examining all the evidence," O'Neill said.

"Are you... are you going to charge me?" She felt her heart seize while watching the slow motion tableau before her. O'Neill got off the table and looked at each of his colleagues. She tried to read behind each blank face, what their collective decision was. Finally the inspector turned to her.

"Not at this time. However, you are not to leave the vicinity of Cork County. There is a lot of evidence yet to sift through, and I'll be talking to you again. That is all for now. Thank you."

Beth felt light-headed as she stood up. She hoped they wouldn't notice her steadying herself before turning. She was almost to the door when the inspector asked one final question.

"By the way, Mrs. Conor, what does your son think of his father?"

"What do you mean?"

"Did he hate him enough to help you? His prints are on the scissors as well."

Michael Fitzsimmons paced across the rug as many times as he thought his wife would tolerate. She had been trying to concentrate on a worn tarot deck when he had come in. He noticed it was laid out in the traditional Celtic cross on the coffee table. He wished he could concentrate on the way the brown twill outfit she wore accented her pale skin and slim figure. Instead, his gaze kept falling to the cards, ominous thoughts rising to the surface.

She lifted up the significator card and sighed heavily. "Really, Michael, I think you've quite well put a hole in the rug. Do stop pacing."

He stopped and stood in front of her. "This whole incident has got me on edge. First this Williams fellow comes by and demands I sever my maintenance contract with Deagan and use the company Conor Shipping employs. Highly irregular, I'd say." He threw up his hands as he began pacing again. "Then Conor's son turns up dead, and the police are swarming all over the campus. Who in God's name do they suspect, anyway?"

"I'm sure I don't know," she said, barely looking up from her cards. "What was his justification for changing the service contract?"

"He said both our costs and his at the shipyard would be reduced and, of course, that meant more support for the university." He ran a nervous hand through his graying hair, and then patted his acidic stomach for relief. "He knows how much we depend on sponsors."

"Well?"

"But I got the distinct impression he really wanted to see Deagan thrown out. I think he would have pushed it to economic blackmail if I hadn't agreed."

He began pacing again, "I hate bloody lawyers!"

He finally stopped pacing and went to the table, leaning over it. "And now this Inspector O'Neill is asking delicate questions about Deagan's background. Do you think he's suspected of killing Conor over this?"

Finally she looked up, giving him her full attention. "I don't know, but Deagan does have a violent temper. You said so yourself after that little incident at the party." A look of distaste wrinkled her face. "Perhaps it was just as well you fired him. Besides," she said, her hands embracing the spread in front of her, "the cards had already indicated there would be a problem with him."

Michael looked again at the cards she had laid on the table. It had taken him some time to get used to her preoccupation with them. On the other hand, her accuracy was chilling. Try as he might to rationally explain it, her predictions, not to mention the naming of forces and issues that influenced the outcome, were often bang on. Unable to resist, he eyed the cards carefully. "What was your query for this spread?"

"Oh, nothing really," she said as she scooped them up. "You

shouldn't worry."

"But I am worrying," he said grumbling. "Two of my professors are at the Garda headquarters right now. For all we know, they may be charged."

"I don't think so. At least, not yet."

Michael wondered what made her so sure. He watched as she placed the last card, the Judgment card, back into the Chinese lacquer box. He didn't mention his fears about Patrick McElheny to her. Patrick's long association with Sinn Fein, the political arm of the IRA, was becoming an issue again. There was plenty to worry about. Plenty.

CHAPTER 25

GARDAI HQ

Brendan O'Neill was gazing down the corridor, still reflecting on Mrs. Conor's look of horror, before following his officers into his private office. He debated whether his last question had been proper. In murder, was there ever an improper question? He pointed to two scarred office chairs on rollers in front of his desk. The life had been beaten out of them by countless treks across the floor, transporting bodies that abused them on the journey. Regis's chair was particularly vocal in its squealing protest as the sergeant's bulk settled into it.

"Well, what do you think?" Brendan slipped into his own plush leather rocker, adjusting it to look down at them over his desk. He wanted their input before deciding which direction to take with the case.

"She has a very forceful personality, doesn't she?" Regis cleared his throat before continuing. "For a minute, I thought she was the interrogator. I'd say she had the motive and the will to carry it out."

"There's nothing wrong with a forceful personality," Jenny interjected.

Regis swiveled his chair to face her, a look of astonishment on his face. "Jasus, and the saints preserve us! I didn't mean that was bad, just that it would help her carry it out and appear so much in control here. Although, in your case, lass..."

"Enough." Brendan said to stave off any impending argu-

219

ments. "Do you think she acted alone? Assuming she did do it."

"I don't believe she could have done the damage to his face," Regis said, absently stroking his own. "And the coroner said he was probably killed soon after the beating. She'd have had trouble moving the body by herself, and her point about planting evidence was a good one." He shook his head, lips pursed, a gesture familiar to Brendan. "Too many damaging clues for a very intelligent woman to slip up on."

"I agree," Jenny said, much to Regis's surprise. "Too many clues. But I do think she's strong enough to handle the body. At least enough to leverage it into the trunk. I could do it, and she's bigger than me."

Brendan folded his arms, and tried to visualize Jenny wrestling with Conor's dead body while stuffing it into the boot. He was distracted by Regis shifting in his chair, eliciting more pathetic cries of protest from it. Brendan wondered if the seat had chosen this moment to finally give up the ghost and collapse under his sergeant's weight.

Regis said, "What about the beating, though?"

Regis and Jenny exchanged looks before she responded. "Maybe she used a blunt object on him when he attacked her, and then resorted to the scissors while he was dazed," she said. "Mind you, I think he bloody well deserved it."

Brendan turned toward her, surprised at her show of emotion. "But in no way could this be considered self-defense."

Contrite, Jenny replied, "I know that, but I also know that everyone seems to look the other way when a wife is beaten."

"Not on my watch, Jenny."

Jenny sighed, "You know I don't mean you, Inspector." With more feeling she added, "You're the best."

Wishing to get the meeting back on track, Brendan waived the thought away. "Regarding the marks on the body, we haven't been able to identify anything that could leave the same bruising as fists." Brendan leaned back in his chair, his eyes flicking from face to face. Then he added, "And if it was fists they were most likely from a male."

"You mean she had an accomplice? I agree, I think more than one person was involved. But why would she leave the other incriminating evidence behind when she left for her parents' house?" Regis pulled on his nose, making it redden. Then, looking square at Brendan, he concluded, "And why drop off the body so close to where she lives?"

"If she was planning to kill him, it makes no sense," Brendan said. "But what if Conor precipitated the whole thing with the attempt on her life at Healy's Pass?" He paused until he had their full attention. "Mind you, we don't know this for sure, but the damage to the left wing of Conor's Audi is consistent with his trying to run her over. I have forensics trying to match the paint scratching from her bike with the damage to the car. So, assuming that, what if he came to the cottage late that Sunday night."

Looking up from the forensic reports, Regis interjected, "And we do have tire tracks that match his car near her cottage, although we can't be sure how old they are. And he still had a key, although I'm told it no longer fits the lock. Just the same, two of those interviewed suggested that he visited Beth every few months."

"Most places aren't locked around her, anyway," Jenny said, and then added, "but I think she'd keep the place locked up tight with him around and changing the locks certainly suggests it."

"True," Brendan said. "But this time he came to kill her and a lock might not stop him. Still stabbing him when he broke in, if she was alerted, makes sense. O'Hara's son could have helped her while she fought him off. The wound he'd inflict wouldn't be deep, but then if she picked the scissors up afterwards and finished him off, that would account for both their prints being on the murder weapon."

Jenny went over to Brendan's desk and picked up the scissors. "By the way, where did you get the blood to put on this duplicate pair of scissors? That was quite theatrical of you inspector."

Brendan laughed before replying. "As it happens I own a similar pair and cut myself while I was considering how the things would have been used. It seemed too providential not to employ them to shake her up."

Regis chuckled, "Well it certainly startled me when you slammed them into the wood."

Jenny held the scissors by the twin handles in front of her, blades pointing outwards "Could the boy have held them up like this, and Conor backed or fallen into them with enough force?"

"I don't think so, Jenny." Regis said, an involuntary shudder coursing through his body.

Brendan wondered how his sergeant was coping with being on a real case instead of reading from a computer data sheet. Regis began shuffling some papers, and then looked up.

"Inspector, the coroner's report did say that the boy's prints on the scissors suggested that he had held it like a dagger, didn't it?"

"That's right."

"Then I don't think he could have held it in one hand with enough strength if Conor fell back onto it," Regis said.

"Until we see the boy, we can only theorize about it, but it doesn't seem likely," Brendan said. He waited for a moment to see if they were both following him. "Then her motive to visit her parents, and leave her son behind when she came back, makes sense. The boy might still be in shock from what he witnessed. After killing her husband, Mrs. Conor would have been panicked and not been in full control of her faculties. She would have made mistakes."

"But when she returned and found that her place had been searched," Jenny said, "wouldn't she know the weapon had been found?" She placed the scissors back on the desk. "She certainly looked surprised when it almost dropped in her lap."

"She could be a good actress, or she could have been taken by surprise by the dramatic way the inspector presented it," Regis said to Jenny's back, then turned to Brendan. "I agree with Jenny, it was a bit theatrical."

Brendan gave Jenny a sly wink, which she returned, an elfish grin on her face. It was not the first time he and Jenny had exchanged such knowing winks, but then he straightened up in his chair when he remembered where he was.

"But if it was self-defense," Jenny said, going along with his change of mood. "Why not just call in the police?"

"'Tis true, but there are a couple of other things to consider," Brendan said. "First, her arrangement with her husband was strictly between them, and not common knowledge. Many people, including her friends, might view her deception as proof of guilt. Now add to that having her son witness it, and maybe even participate in it. The emotional trauma of killing anyone, especially a spouse, can unhinge even the most logical mind."

Jenny moved closer to Brendan's desk, leaning her hands onto its polished surface. Her hazel eyes held sparks of gold, her face animated as she followed his reasoning, looking for an opening. A flash of delight flitting across her face told Brendan she had found one. "But now that she has had time to think about it, why not confess?"

"Well, Jenny, don't forget there is still obstruction of justice, covering up a homicide. She could be charged with involuntary manslaughter, based on additional evidence we find. The notoriety would surely cost her her job, and she wouldn't want her son testifying at the inquest. There are reasons why she might not be ready yet."

Regis said, "So you want her to think about it a little more?"

"I want us to think about it a little more," Brendan said. "I'm not convinced she did it. But if she did, this fellow Carey might have helped. That would account for the beating. This Carey fellow looks like he can handle himself. And then it could be murder we're talking about; premeditated murder." He gave them a moment to consider this before continuing.

"After rendering Conor unconscious, either one of them could have used the scissors. Or Carey might have done it himself, then, realizing what he had done, tried to shift the blame to her. But just having Mrs. Conor to himself may not have been enough. I wonder if he had another motive."

The room was becoming very stuffy. Brendan could smell his own cologne, combined with the emotional strain of the morning's work, giving off a less attractive scent. He went to the lone window that looked out onto Quay Street and opened it, trading the clammy chill for the stale air engulfing his office. He rested his hands on the stone sill, looking down at the sluggish traffic and more swiftly-moving pedestrians. The air held the sharp tang of the sea, mingled with the smells from O'Toole's pub as it geared up for the lunch crowd. Temporarily refreshed, he moved away from the window.

Jenny was looking at him with some concern. She formed a soundless question with her raised eyebrows and he tilted his head and shrugged in reply.

Assured, she asked aloud, "Do we have time to take a break before we bring in Mr. Carey?"

"Yes. Why don't you tell him we'll be ready in about twenty minutes? And check with the sergeant's desk to see if Patrick McElheny has arrived yet."

"Right."

His sigh was heavy as she left the room.

Jenny was halfway down the corridor when she heard the explosion. The window next to her rattled in its casement just as she heard glass shatter downstairs. She scuttled down the stairs, removing her baton while staying close to the wall. She cursed herself for leaving the automatic in her locker, and prayed that no one was rushing up the stairs, gun in hand, to meet her. A roaring sound came from below and she gripped the baton tighter. When she got to the first floor, she slid over to the shattered window and cautiously looked out, her eyes widening.

A dark sedan in the car park behind the station was in flames, its top nearly blown off. The flames roiled out of the car like an untended blast furnace. A quick look around confirmed that no other cars were in the lot. She pushed open the rear emergency exit, sounding the alarm, and started towards the vehicle.

As she came closer, she detected a strange but familiar smell, and looked down to discover that the fine hairs of her forearms had blackened and singed. A few more steps and her skin would begin to blister. She dared go no closer. Hand raised, she tried to squint into the waves of heat emanating from the sedan. The overpowering stench of burning rubber and electrical wiring was poisonous to breathe.

Did she pick up the smell of burning human flesh in this conflagration? She turned as someone was rushing up behind her. "Don't go any closer!"

It was the Inspector, out of breath. He held her arm as if she would have plunged into the blaze. She patted his arm. "There is no way I'm going closer to that, Brendan."

They stood side-by-side gazing out the inferno in astonishment. Then he said, "I've got the fire brigade on the way. The building's been secured. Do you know what happened? Was there anyone in that car?"

"I saw a silhouette for a brief instant on the driver's side, before the flames got so bad. I don't know what started it, but I think it was a car bomb." She looked significantly at Brendan, who had turned very grim.

"Christ, that's all we need. I'm going to the main entrance. Check on everyone here. Don't let any leave, understand?" He gripped her shoulder and gave it a reassuring squeeze before running back inside. She placed her own hand where Brendan had touched her and sighed while looking around.

Once inside herself she noted that the corridor looked deserted. She didn't see Sean Carey in the waiting room. The click of a door opening caused her to spin, clutching her baton more tightly. She spotted Carey coming out of the loo carrying a briefcase. He stopped for a moment before coming over to an undamaged window and looking out. Jenny moved towards him as he gazed open-mouthed at the car, now completely enveloped in flames.

"Jesus, what happened?"

"My guess is a car bomb," she said, watching him closely. "Why did you bring that into the loo?" Jenny pointed to the briefcase.

"Huh? Oh, I have my final exam in it. Don't want that falling into the wrong hands."

"In a police station?"

"Eh, I suppose I am a bit anal about that."

"Mind if I see what you've got?" Seeing his look of puzzlement, she added, "In the briefcase." She kept one eye on him while peering inside. He seemed momentarily confused until she held up his pocket computer and gave it the once over.

"Hey, you don't think I set the bomb off, do you?"

"Can't be too careful. Looks all right. Thanks. Where is Mrs. Conor?"

She followed his gaze as he turned towards the row of chairs, and then scanned the long corridor. She didn't like the panicked look on his face, and followed him down the corridor. A door opened suddenly at the far end of the hall and Beth entered, breaking into a run when she spotted Sean. Jenny turned away as they embraced.

"Sean, what happened? I just went outside for a breath of fresh air and heard that terrible sound." Beth followed their gaze. "Oh, dear God." She stared out the window at the burning car.

All three watched the activity as the fire brigade arrived, and quickly set up their equipment. Two nozzles pumped thick foam over the car, covering it in a white blanket. Some of the foam lifted sluggishly into the air, rising like a departing spirit. Jenny felt the heat lessen as the fire, cheated of its oxygen, slowly died. Some of the foam dripped off the front grill, exposing the number plate.

From behind her, Jenny heard a sharp intake of breath.

"My God," Sean said, "that's Patrick's car!"

Peter slipped quietly back into bed. The late morning sun spilled through the partially opened curtains, casting a white bar across the bedspread. Soon he felt Shannon begin to stir, then nuzzle closer, rubbing her breasts against his back. He could feel her nipples harden, and he turned over to give them the proper attention. While he cupped her breasts, she drew closer, rocking her hips against him until he was hard. She had just slipped her hand down to stroke him when the phone rang.

"Damn! Peter, I thought you took the phone off the hook."

"Not while the police are having a field day around here." He reached over her and picked it up after the fourth ring. "Yeah? What! Are you sure? Anyone else hurt? Shite!" He slammed down the phone and jumped out of bed. Swearing under his breath, he grabbed his trousers off the chair and climbed into them, almost catching himself in the zipper.

"Have a care, love," said Shannon. "I may want that later; still on you."

"Come on, get dressed. I have to meet a friend."

"In that case, leave your willy here."

"Christ, but you're a jealous bitch. And you snogging Patrick, too."

She looked hurt. "It was your suggestion I find out more of what he knew about Conor."

"But not in your bed!"

"It didn't go that far!"

Peter wasn't sure he believed her, but with McElheny dead it seemed pointless to argue now. "Listen, there was an explosion in old Cork. Car bomb. And I know who they'll be pointing the finger at. Just remember we were here all morning."

"Oh, that alibi I can easily give."

Peter watched her move gracefully over to the dresser for her clothes, her milky skin in sharp contrast to the dusky browns and yellows of his bedroom. Time seemed to slow to a more languorous pace, as she glided to the window. A bar of sunlight squeezed through the heavy curtains and roamed over her naked flesh.

Peter saw it touch shoulder, breast, and inner thigh as she drew closer to its source. She stretched her arms out, pulling back the edge of the curtain and he watched the play of light as it thrust through to search the gentle curve of her belly. Shannon moaned as the heat of the sun probed lower on her body. Dropping her clothes beside her, she flashed him a lusty smile.

"Whatever you say, love," she said. "I'll tell them you were here making love to me all morning. But shouldn't I look as though that were true?"

Peter crossed the room, her eyes drawing him to her. Was she going to tease him again as penance for returning late? When she lowered her eyelashes and turned to gather up her clothes, he knew he'd been suckered again.

Time sped up as she dressed. When Shannon put her hair up, exposing her neck, he hungrily kissed it, turning her slowly and searching for her mouth. Her lips brushed his cheek, stopping at his ear to whisper words that stirred his blood. Then he felt her pull away.

"But not whenever you say, love. You were in a hurry, right?"

"You could get yourself in a lot of trouble with your mouth, Shannon, my love. But we do have to leave." The look on her face told him she wanted the game to go on a lot longer. Too bad.

They went out to his car, the engine still warm from its earlier drive. Shannon paused to look at him over the top of the car, and he waited for her comment.

"And where did you just come back from?"

"Just an errand I had to do."

"It wasn't anything illegal, was it?"

Chagrined, Peter said, "Not this time, love."

She continued to look at him curiously for a moment, and he

feared she'd change her mind about providing him with an alibi, but she merely shrugged and got into the car. They were both silent on the drive back to the Bay Mist Pub.

CHAPTER 26
GARDAI HQ

The constant buzz of wagging tongues was getting on Inspector O'Neill's nerves. He could scarcely believe that this many people could cram themselves into the narrow alleys that abutted the Garda station. Both the left side and rear entrances to the car park were filled with the curious. Some elbowed for space to get a closer look, others stood on tiptoe to see over similarly bobbing heads. He turned to the officer closest to the barricade. "Flanagan, would you keep the gawkers back a bit. I can't hear myself think."

"Right, Inspector." The man turned back to the throng pressing against the wooden barrier. "All right. Get back there now. This isn't a circus."

Out of the corner of his eye, Brendan noticed someone trying to get his attention. The worn and smudged trench coat was a clearer identifier than the press pass.

"Inspector? Inspector O'Neill?"

"I don't have time right now, O'Toole." He tried waving him off with a dismissive backhand, but the man came closer, hunched over a notepad.

"It was a bomb, wasn't it, Inspector?"

Soft murmurs passed through the crowd at the mention of a bomb. Brendan served up a discouraging look, but the reporter continued, unperturbed.

"Was it IRA handiwork?"

"Who suggested that?" The inspector tried to pin him to earth with a fierce stare, but was greeted by the look of innocence only a hungry reporter could pull off.

"Just speculating, that's all, Brendan."

"Well take your speculation somewhere else. We don't need anyone starting wild rumors around here, O'Toole. Officially, this is just an explosion. Nothing more."

"Can I get your attention on this later, after you've looked it over?" said O'Toole, gesturing toward the blackened heap of metal.

The snap of a flashbulb punctuated the silence, and Brendan blinked in irritation. "Tell your man to keep his camera out of my face, would you. Later, O'Toole, not now." The inspector turned on his heel and headed over to the remains of the vehicle just as its door was snapped open with a shriek of tortured metal. He paused several meters away and looked on.

Brendan could feel Regis's eyes on him as the charred body was removed from the blackened car. The bombing had awakened old memories and his sergeant sensed it. His jaw quivered from clenching his pipe too tightly in his teeth. The sweat beading his forehead was not from the dissipated heat of the charred car.

At the sound of men approaching, conversing in hushed voices, he turned. The bigger of the two men he recognized as Captain Donohue of the Cork Volunteers, in full uniform. The man beside him he did not know.

"Inspector O'Neill?"

"Yes. What can I do for you, Captain?"

"This is Liam Pearse, our expert on arson. He's ready to go over the car now, with your assistance."

Pearse gave him an appraising look. "I'm told you're an expert in explosives."

"Well, actually my trainer at the Brest Academy, Richard Draper, is the expert on bombings, but I've seen my share." Brendan shook hands with the Captain, who returned to his men. Brendan turned his attention to Liam, a short wiry man whom he estimated to be in his forties. He had intense, nervous eyes that never stopped moving. He rubbed his hands together and shuffled from foot to foot as though dancing on live coals. Brendan thought the man had the perfect disposition for an arson expert, or maybe, he mused to himself, his job had made him like that.

"I've heard of Draper, Inspector." He wiped a rag across his face and stared at it for a moment. "If you've picked up a scrap of what he knows, I can use your help."

"I'll do my best," Brendan said, "but I've also put in a call to Bill O'Boyle. He took over Draper's position at the academy. I'd like to keep any bomb and device fragments here for him to look at later." He motioned for the man to follow him.

"No problem. So Draper doesn't teach in Dublin anymore."

Brendan paused before replying, taking the pipe out of his mouth and tapping ashes out on his shoe. "He was killed disarming a bomb in London last month."

The man stopped in his tracks. "Oh. Well..."

"Come along, Liam, this one's already done its damage. Let's see if we can piece together what it was."

Two men with a stretcher approached. The charred body had one black arm covering the remains of a face. "You'll need dental records to get an ID on this one, Inspector," said the taller of the two. "Where do you want the body?"

"Go and see Sergeant Muldoon, the large fellow rubbing his nose over there. We've got someone on the way to do an autopsy." Brendan looked once again at the corpse and shuddered. "I don't envy Bridget this job."

They waited for Regis to join them after directing the men with the stretcher, and then all three walked over to the remains of the car. The men in the brigade had removed the door to get the body out, and jacked up the driver's side of the car to expose the undercarriage.

Regis handed him a photograph taken while the body was still in the vehicle. Brendan glanced into the driver's seat, checking the location of the body and comparing it with the photo. Nodding, he exchanged the photo for a dark smock that he used to cover his suit. He and Regis exchanged grim looks.

Humming to himself, he grabbed a torch and scooted under the engine compartment. The sound of scrapping and tapping joined his off-tune air, and soon a discordant symphony of sound rose from under the car.

Liam Pearse looked questioningly at Regis. "I think it's the inspector's way of dealing with a nasty job, Liam."

"Pity since he can't carry a tune." Then the humming stopped and both men bent down to see why.

"Liam, have a look at this."

As Liam joined him, Brendan pointed the beam on the remains of the bomb, identified more by the locus of its destructive path than anything recognizable to any but a practiced eye. There were some fragments fused to the chassis, and he identified them to Liam for removal and analysis.

They were under the car for twenty minutes before coming up for air. Brendan directed Liam and Regis to his offices while he took off the filthy smock and shook debris out of his hair. Back in his office, he turned on the electric kettle for tea, and pulled out a tin of Danish cookies that he kept far away from Regis. Then Brendan turned his full attention to Liam.

"From the position of the body and blast site, the main force of the explosion was up through the engine compartment. Driver's side. There are just enough remnants to identify a receiver." He fired up his pipe and waited for the fact to sink in. "An inductive coil and other pieces were almost intact."

"What about the explosive?"

"If we're lucky, the explosive will have a chemical signature we can trace to the manufacturer. But there may be no record of the final sale, and it can be time-consuming." Brendan glanced over at Regis who was taking notes. "And we may not have the luxury of time on this one."

Liam looked alarmed. "Why do you say that, Inspector?"

"Call it a policeman's hunch, Liam." Brendan set his pipe down. "But if it was terrorist-inspired instead of done to kill my key witness, we'll have to move fast."

"What's your plan, then?"

"I think we'll have better luck analyzing the parts of the triggering device. From my first look, I'd say this was the handiwork of Crenshaw's trainees, but I'll want O'Boyle's opinion on this as well."

"Crenshaw?"

"He was a captain in the army; an expert on bombings and incendiaries. After the war, he went to the six counties, and worked with IRA recruits. He specialized in remotely-triggered bombs. Claimed they were safer for the bomber, and reduced the chance of innocents being caught in a blast."

"IRA!" Liam's mouth stayed open for seconds before he continued. "But what makes you think one of Crenshaw's people was involved in this?"

"He hand-built a number of coils set to an unused frequency band to prevent false triggering, and they all looked like this one." The inspector turned the coil in his hand as he continued. "Though not usually in such good shape. I'll need more information, but it is a possibility I'm pursuing,"

The whistling of the kettle seemed to put Liam and Regis on edge. Brendan waited a moment before moving his eyes meaningfully from his sergeant to the offending instrument, and Regis leaped up to silence it.

"Inspector," Regis said as he poured boiling water into the cups, "would Deagan have trained with this Crenshaw do you think?"

The inspector studied the coil once more and then sighed. "Most likely. And he is our prime suspect. But he and Patrick were associates, not enemies."

"Well then could it been done to look like an IRA bombing to shift suspicion away from the real culprit?"

"It could, particularly since they're usually careful about militant activity in the Republic. But if it wasn't one of Crenshaw's trainees, then it was someone who studied his work." Brendan rubbed his pipe along his jaw, pondering his last reply, and then tilted his head towards a thoughtful Pearse. "Any ideas, Liam?"

"Well, I agree with you about the way the blast happened. I've seen fragments similar to what we found here. But the handiwork..." His head dropped to his chest then he looked up again. "I just don't want to see another one like that."

"Aye, nor do I." Brendan nodded briskly, causing his pipe to drop ashes. Frowning, he set down the pipe and wiped his lap.

Noticing that Regis seemed down, he picked up the tin of biscuits and set them near him. Staring at his sergeant happily munching away was better than looking out the window. He needed little reminder of what might be in store for them if the madman was not found. And quickly.

"There is one other thing," he added. "It looks like the receiver was placed far enough away from the bomb that it would be recoverable after the blast. Almost like the killer wanted us to find it."

Beth and Sean came back after lunch to answer more of Inspector O'Neill's questions. The female constable met them, looking much calmer than when they had left. Streaks of soot on her arms betrayed the fact she had been working around the demolished car. Beth shivered at the sight.

"Mrs. Conor, Mr. Carey. The inspector will be ready for you in a moment. I'll tell him you're back."

Beth nodded dully, her mouth dry. The walk back through the dispersing crowd of onlookers had unsettled her. Snatches of conversation had broken through her resolve of emotional detachment. Words of death, bombs, and murder had struck her like casually thrown stones. There were tears in her eyes by the time they had run the gauntlet of curious glances.

After the constable had left, Beth turned to Sean. The grim set of his mouth softened, and the smile that followed warmed her heart. She hoped it would give her all the courage she would need to get through the next few hours. "Did Seamus say when he'd be here?"

"He should be here any time," Sean said. "We could both use his support and his brains. There's no doubt you're being set up. Maybe he has some ideas about who and why."

"God, I hope so. I've never felt this helpless before. And I don't like it."

"It's hard to think of you as helpless, Beth. That's one of the things I love about you." Sean paused for a moment and placed his hand over hers. "But anytime you need someone to lean on, anytime at all, you can count on me."

Beth bit back a sob at the back of her throat. She tried to form an encouraging smile in reply, but her chin trembled and refused the weight of her leaden cheeks. She gazed up at the patterned ceiling and took a deep breath to drown the despair filling her chest. "Oh, Sean. This is so crazy. Here we are just getting to know each other, and all bloody hell has broken loose."

"We'll weather it, darling. We're both pretty tough, you know."

She felt his strong hands on her shoulders, caressing her and strengthening her at the same time. She marveled at the power flowing through her at his touch. This time she did manage a smile. He was helping her in ways he could not know. Or perhaps he did, she corrected herself.

Footsteps down the hall caused her to turn apprehensively. She recognized the Inspector's measured tread. The young constable was close at his heels as he came over to them.

"Mrs. Conor. I'd like to talk to you a bit more. But first, I have some questions for Mr. Carey." Turning to Jenny he said, "Constable Magruder, when we finish up here, go to Bantry and get Constable O'Reilly to assist you on that search."

Sean and Beth exchanged questioning looks before Sean said, "I'm ready, Inspector. Lead the way."

Beth watched them both go up the stairs. The sounds of the final clean-up outside came in through the shattered window. She couldn't resist one last look, as the ruined car was moved.

"It's being moved over to our warehouse, impounded as evidence," Jenny said.

Startled, Beth turned to find the constable behind her. Beth managed a brief smile, then headed for the loo. Once inside, she splashed water from the wash basin on her face. Why was Sean so worried? Was it just the bombing, and the loss of his friend, Patrick? Was there more she needed to learn about him? "Oh, God, what a mess."

Her reflection did not offer any solace. The image blurred as tears filled her eyes.

Brendan closed the door after motioning Carey to a seat. He went back to his desk, many thoughts competing for attention. He waited a moment to calm himself, then opened up a notepad and began.

"Mr. Carey, how well did you know the deceased?"

"Which one, Inspector?"

"Sorry, I meant Eamonn Conor." Brendan suppressed the irritation of being caught off-balance. The man was self-assured and clever. He would have to give this his full attention.

"Eamonn and I were classmates in college. I knew him pretty well then, but I hadn't seen him again until..."

"Yes?" Brendan noted the hesitation and the flash of guilt that momentarily moved over his face. This Carey seemed to be hiding something. Was he protecting the woman?

"Until just before he was killed. Friday, that is."

"And what was the purpose of that meeting?"

"Oh, he just stopped by when I was at lunch to say hello."

"And this was after how many years?" The nonchalant wave of

the hand did not throw the inspector off.

"Eh, about eight."

"And he just stopped by to say hello?"

"Well, we talked about old times, you know, that sort of thing."

"He didn't warn you to stay away from his wife?"

"Certainly not."

"And you didn't hold any animosity towards him?"

"No, why would I?"

Brendan pulled some sheets out of his desk. It was material he knew would be useful for this interview, but he knew that bringing out fresh documents after asking a key question had a very unsettling effect on his subject.

"According to three witnesses, you stated you would, to quote them, 'see him in hell if you had to do it yourself.' You know where this happened, don't you?"

"Yes."

The dispirited answer confirmed Brendan's suspicion that the man was not telling him everything. Not by a long shot.

"Now, Mr. Carey, would you be so kind as to tell me where you were this past Sunday night." And I hope to God you don't tell me you were with Shannon Ryan, he silently prayed.

"Well, I was out with Seamus Dunoon, pub crawling. He's a prof..."

"Yes, yes, I know who he is. And how late were you at it?"

"Until about half past eleven. I had an early class."

"And then?"

"I turned in at about midnight."

"And why did you make that remark at the Bantry House, assuming you didn't plan to actually kill him?"

Beth was relieved to see Seamus coming down the corridor. His hound's-tooth jacket was clenched in one hand, and his white shirt was open at the collar, exposing fine blonde hairs on his massive chest. His expression was grave as he hugged her fiercely; his tone betraying his concern.

"Beth, lass, how are you? I just got the word about Patrick. Christ, what a mess. Where's Sean?"

"Seamus, I'm so glad to see you. Sean is with the inspector now." She kept her voice low and gestured to Jenny, sitting at the far side of the line of chairs. Then she turned him slightly to introduce him to Jenny, who was looking at him with what Beth perceived as reverence.

"How do you do, Professor Dunoon," Jenny said. "You don't remember me, but I took a class in particle physics from you a few years ago."

"Really. Was this for police work, then?"

"No. I was considering your field at the time before deciding that police work was what I really wanted. I love being out in the field, interrogating suspects, searching for clues." Now a big smile spread across her face. "Sorry, I have a search to do now. I'll let them know you're here."

When the constable was at the top of the stairs, Beth said, "They've been in there a long time. You don't think he suspects Sean, do you?"

"I think the good inspector's job is to suspect everyone, so I wouldn't worry unnecessarily over that. He seems to be a very competent man, though. And not unkind, despite an impenetrable suit of armor."

They both turned as footsteps sounded on the stairs. When Sean came into view, he was troubled and he seemed startled by the flood of light on his face. O'Neill's face was composed and unreadable when he spoke.

"Ah, there you are, Professor Dunoon. I had a couple of follow-up questions for you first, Mrs. Conor. And then I need to see you professor, if you don't mind."

"Not at all, Inspector," Seamus said. "Glad to help out."

"I'll wait for you here, Beth. But first, I'm getting some fresh air," Sean said.

Beth looked after him with some concern before following the inspector back up the steps. She saw Seamus conferring with him before they both disappeared from view.

CHAPTER 27
DEAGAN'S HOME, BANTRY BAY

Garda Jenny Magruder pulled her car in front of the weathered sign that proclaimed Deagan's Bantry Garage. The office to the right had a big picture window facing the street and a man of considerable size sat behind the desk. His hand was pressed to his forehead as though pondering something he was reviewing.

Jenny nodded to Constable Dennis O'Reilly and his fellow officer Aidan Reynolds to follow her in. The screen door screeched as if it hadn't been lubed in several years, but it served the purpose of jerking the man upright as they entered.

Whatever question the man was going to ask was never spoken as he noted the uniforms. Jenny showed the search warrant to the man who had been filling out forms on Peter Deagan's desk. An employee, no doubt, she assumed. He looked it over with growing alarm and then back at her.

"Here, what's this for? Why you searching here?"

"I'll ask the questions if you don't mind. What is your name?"

The man was taken back and looked at Jenny with ill-disguised anger."What the fook, er, sorry, sorry." Apparently the man realized swearing at an officer was not a good idea. "I'm Bill, I keep the books for Peter. He's not here now."

"Not a problem if you have keys to give me entry to the garage, the upstairs and the basement."

Slowly getting up Bill shook his head gravely. "Peter isn't going to like this."

"I certainly hope so if we find something of interest. Let's go." Jenny motioned for the constables to follow her.

Mumbling to himself, Bill grabbed a handful of keys from the top desk drawer and headed into the garage. The smell of petrol and oil hung heavy in the empty bays. They walked through saw-dust scattered over the floor that had absorbed all the oil it could and now seemed to be part of it.

All three officers looked around them for any signs of con-cealment, but it did not seem to be a likely place to hide incrim-inating evidence and Jenny quickly steered Bill to the basement while the two constables probed and poked in the garage.

When Bill unlocked the door, Jenny placed her hand over her baton as if an assailant waited on the other side. This door was well oiled, opening soundlessly. Jenny concluded that Deagan must use the space often. The musty smell alone would suggest this was the basement as the handrail-less wooden stairs continued into dark-ness.

"Where's the light switch?" she said.

"Don't know, never been down here myself. You want me to find it?"

Jenny looked at the tall broad shouldered man and decided she didn't want him at her back. "No, I've got a torch, thanks."

Snapping on her light she went cautiously down the stairs. Basements had bothered Jenny ever since she was trapped in one as a child. She had sneaked into the basement because she knew there was cool stuff down there. But she didn't realize that the door would lock behind her. Then when the single light bulb swinging on its power cord had burned out she was left in darkness and frightened. Her screams for help had gone unanswered. And then there were the rats.

She cleared her mind of those thoughts just as the basement door closed behind her and she froze near the bottom stairs; wait-ing. She listened for the sounds of footsteps coming down but only silence filled the stairwell. After a moment she took the final stairs and swept her beam around trying to assess the room's size.

It was a generous room with high ceilings and cardboard boxes stacked neatly along the walls and on the many shelves. In the far corner there was a separate room built out from the wall with a locked door. Jenny was glad she'd taken the keys before going downstairs.

Locating the key that went with the lock she slowly opened the door, not sure what she would find inside, but her senses told her she'd find something. The room was small, about three meters square. In the corner was an old steamer trunk and she went to it immediately.

The trunk was locked, but there wasn't a key on the ring that matched it. She would not be defeated so easily, however, as she pulled out a set of lock picks her locksmith father had given her as a gift. This was after the incident with the locked cellar door. He had told her that now that she was a trained locksmith she could open any door with only a hair pin.

The lock opened easily under her talented fingers. Inside she removed the top pullout drawer and flashed her torch along the bottom. There were old tools, rags, a pair of muddy boots and a big knife and scabbard. Reaching down inside, bent at the waist and off-balanced she tried to reach the knife. Her hand closed on the scabbard, but the knife slipped out, dropping to the bottom, hilt first. The lip of the trunk bit into her stomach as she leaned in further, trying to reach the knife. Then she heard a shoe scrape behind her.

Suddenly she was shoved forward and as she began tumbling into the trunk rude hands grabbed her legs and jammed her in the rest of the way. Before she could react the lid was shut and she heard the padlock click. Then she heard footsteps retreating and a door closing. Jenny reached around for her torch and realized she dropped it outside the trunk. Damn!

Dennis and Aidan cleared the garage and offices and went looking for Jenny. Dennis went to the basement door, but found it was locked. He called out to her but got no response. Dennis, a fan of horror movies, recalled the old admonition, "don't split up or you'll all die" and became uneasy. Going back to the office he found Bill once again hunched over his work.

"Where is Garda Magruder?"

Bill looked up at him, puzzled. "I let her into the basement and then came back here." Amused he added, "Lost her already? You lads are pretty careless."

Dennis was not amused. "Come on, open the door. It's locked again."

"I gave her the keys. Maybe she went upstairs." He nodded above him where Deagan's apartment was located. Swearing under his breath Dennis headed for the stairs.

In total darkness, Jenny tried to turn over in the tight space. She was on her knees, her back pressed against the unyielding trunk lid and not much room side to side. She was furious that someone had gotten the drop on her, but tried to calm down. While she was not by nature claustrophobic, her cramped position was sending bolts of fear into her and her legs already felt numb. A sob escaped her clenched teeth and she almost gave in to despair.

Remembering her training, she took long, deep breaths to calm herself and then slowly began turning her body to the right against the back of the trunk. At one point she became stuck, unable to move up or down and almost panicked. Pressing against the sides she finally broke free, but a sharp pain lanced into her upper thigh.

Feeling along her leg her hand grasped the blade of the combat knife, the tip had pierced her pants and was stuck in her thigh. The wetness her fingers detected told her she was bleeding. If she continued turning, the blade would penetrate deeper, hitting an artery and she'd bleed to death stuck in this ungainly position.

Straining with all her strength she was able to back up enough for the blade to come free. Cautiously she resumed turning until she was on her side facing front. She stopped to draw in ragged breaths and then drew in her legs enough to turn onto her back.

Once she was on her back she used her legs to push on the trunk lid, but it wouldn't budge. Then something bit her bloodied hand and she jerked it back. Oh God, don't let it be rats, she thought. Something scurried over her leg, and she felt a weight on her bleeding thigh. It squealed loathsomely. It was a rat!

Before it could take a bite out of her leg she grabbed the animal and tossed it down by her feet. Then she brought her boot down hard on the animal. Her stomach churned as she hit it again and again until it made no further sound. If there was one rat . . . but she left that thought unfinished.

When her breathing was under control she heard a faint banging coming from a distance. Dennis would find her, but did she want to wait that long? And how badly was she cut? Then she remembered the knife; that big, nasty looking knife. Reaching tentatively around her, afraid of another bite, her hand contacted the blade, still slick with her blood.

Holding the knife in two hands she swung it against the trunk's wicker side below the latch and felt it slice through. Twisting and hacking she enlarged the hole enough to get her hand through and reach up to the lock.

Now came the tricky part. Selecting one of her picks, she reached through the hole and blindly felt around the lock for the keyhole. Angling the pick into the slot she slowly turned it, feeling for the release. Just as it was about to come free she lost her grip and dropped the pick. "Shite!" She pounded the side of the trunk and cursed again.

Concentrating hard she worked a second pick into the lock and imagined its mechanism and where the release would be. After a few more tries and curses she finally heard the click. She pulled the body of the lock down, turned the lock and lifted up the shackle, praying she had enough leverage to free it from the hasp's staple. When it cleared, she heard the lock hit the floor and she pried the hasp free. Finally Jenny slammed the lid back, the knife in her left hand in case someone was still in the room with her. There was no one.

Jenny could tell the knife had not cut deeply into her thigh, but it still hurt like hell. She needed something to serve as a tourniquet. Sifting through the dirty rags she spotted a metal box at the very bottom and removed it. It looked like a gun box and she opened it. There was only one magazine and no gun inside. Checking the load she noted it held 9mm rounds. Taking the knife and box with her she left the room and headed toward the stairs as the sounds of pounding grew louder.

"I'm coming," she shouted. There was no way she'd let Dennis know how frightened she was, but if she discovered who had jumped her she'd have another use for this knife.

Beth O'Hara squeezed into the booth between Seamus and Sean, feeling as if she were being protected by two massive book-ends. Her leg, pressed tightly beside Sean's, felt as if it belonged there. She played with a lock of his dark, curly hair, enjoying the embarrassed grin he tried to cover by studying the menu. The four or five items Delaney listed on it each day hardly warranted a detailed analysis, so she decided to hurry him up. "If you need more time to study that bill of fare Sean, I can ask himself to come over and explain it to you."

"I was only trying to decide what to drink," Sean said. "You don't think it's too early for a Guinness, do you, Seamus?"

"Too early? When is it ever too early?"

"You're right, I forgot myself. I think I'm for the fish and chips."

"That sounds grand," Beth said. "I could certainly use a drink now after those interviews. But I'm for Delaney's salmon and a pint of shandy." She watched Seamus and Sean make sour faces and laughed. "You two. Come on now, it isn't that bad. It'll go well with the fish."

"Dreadful waste of a good ale," said Sean.

"Disgusting use of lemonade," said Seamus.

When the drinks came, she made a point of smacking her lips, then running her tongue over them. Seamus laughed and shook his head before tasting his pint. Sean meanwhile had turned serious again and her smile quickly faded. As Delaney came over to take their order, she patted his arm.

"Well, well, me favorite faculty members. Anything strange?"

"The usual," said Seamus. "Yourself?"

Delaney sighed and then dropped his voice so only they could hear. "My boy is working for me, now. But he's like a thorny wire, he is. Spilled two drinks just this morning. And me with a light crowd." Shaking his head he added, "Do you want this one on the slate?"

"As long as we don't have to raid a bank to pay it off later," said Seamus.

"Get away outta that! You don't get a better meal for the money and you know it, Seamus."

After the barman had left, they settled down to compare what each had learned from their interviews with the inspector. Heads close together and voices hushed, they had the look of fellow conspirators. Beth was glad they had a comfortable, high-backed bench in the lounge, away from the clatter and chatter of the bar. Sean and Beth summarized their interrogations while Seamus listened and took an occasional note.

"Well, he hasn't brought us up on charges," Sean said, "but there's no joy in that."

"I'm inclined to think he has other fish to fry on this one."

"Why do you say that, Seamus?" Beth silently prayed it was true.

"Well, neither of you has a solid alibi for Sunday night, but he can't place you at the scene of the crime. In fact, he isn't sure what the scene of the crime is."

"What do you mean?" Beth toyed with her drink, absently erasing wet circles on the yellow placemat before taking another sip.

"He wasn't killed where the body was dumped. Who would meet in a place like that, or take a chance of being seen? More likely it was done somewhere else. What do you think his habits would be late on a Sunday night, Beth?"

Beth was thoughtful for a moment. "He hated to drive in Cork, I can tell you that. Waiting behind a line of cars crossing the bridges used to set him to howling at the other drivers. He'd find the nearest car park and leave his car there. If he stayed at the Imperial, that's where he'd leave it."

Seamus asked, "Did he usually stay at the Imperial"

Smiling Beth said, "He always had to have the best so yes, that's where he stayed." Another thought occurred to her. "He didn't like to drive at night, either. Claimed it was bad luck."

She didn't notice Sean wince at her last comment before she added, "He was usually on his third scotch by then. No, I think he'd prefer to meet someone at the hotel, or walk a short distance."

Sean said, "Could someone have picked him up?"

"He generally didn't like someone else driving, but it's possible," Beth said.

"I'd think he'd expect to be picked up at the hotel, and sure someone would have remembered seeing a car there that late," Seamus said. "I think we can rule out his being killed in the hotel; the Gardai would've checked out obvious possibilities first. No, I think he was lured out of the hotel, and walked to some pre-arranged meeting place."

"Or was picked up close to the hotel," Sean said.

Seamus stroked his beard for the tenth time and then said, "What would be your guess, lass?"

"I think he'd walk to a meeting place if it was confidential or if he couldn't chance being seen with the person in the hotel," Beth said. "Eamonn was not one to put himself out unless it was very important."

Just then, Delaney's son, Jack, came back with their food. He almost spilled the contents of his tray as the plates slid dangerously close to the edge. Sean stood up and hastily took hold of the tray. Seamus steadied the lad, who appeared to be swaying unsteadily.

The boy's voice seemed equally unsteady when he asked, "Is that the lot?"

"God, I hope so," Seamus said, as he patted the lad away.

Beth looked over at Sean, her face impassive for a moment then a suppressed snort of laughter escaped before she could clamp her hand over her mouth. For the lad's sake, she tried to muffle her laughter, until she turned to see him career off yet another table. At that point all three exchanged eye rolls as Delaney grabbed his son by the ear and led him off.

"I don't think his son is working out too well, Beth." Sean was still shaking his head in disbelief.

When Beth had caught her breath, she replied. "Lord, I think we needed that diversion. Where were we, anyway?"

"I was wondering," Sean said. "You mentioned earlier that the inspector identified the abandoned car as Eamonn's." He continued after she nodded. "Well, then, somehow the killer would have known something of his habits, to locate and identify the car at the hotel. If the car was left close to your cottage, deliberately, then the killer must have known something about you, as well."

"Could be whoever was following me. Wait! The green Honda. There was one at Coomhola Roost, and that's also close to where the car was left." Beth's face was animated as she considered the possibilities.

"That's right." Sean said. "The green Honda. One followed me from Gougane Barra, Beth. The same one that followed you up, I bet."

"Hold on a minute," said Seamus. "What green Honda? I thought you said a black sedan ran you off the road?"

"Yes, it did. But that was Eamonn's car. The Honda I noticed first on Friday, but it could have been tailing me the whole week."

"You're sure it was Eamonn who drove you off the road, then?"

"Yes, Seamus, I'm almost positive. I remember a similar car the last time he came up to see Julian about three months ago. It was an Audi, I think. I didn't make the connection until Sean told me he was in town and up to something. Hmmm."

"What?"

"What is it?"

Beth continued to ponder. Finally, she said, "In the second interview, Inspector O'Neill all but said the car they found was the same one that ran me off the road. He indicated that if Eamonn was making another attempt on my life, I might have a claim to self-defense."

"So he confirmed your suspicions," Sean said. "Could Eamonn have been the prowler you suspected the night of the party?"

"I did consider that possibility," she said. "But what was he after?"

"If he was trying to kill you..." Seamus paused and stroked his beard before continuing. "No, surely not with your son there. Spying on you, maybe. You brought a strange man up to your cottage and..."

Confused, Beth interjected, "A strange man?"

"Well, that's how it would appear to the locals. And not just to a bog-trotter, either."

"Maybe he wanted to catch me in an illicit act," she said. "Have a reason to make me look bad to..." Her mind raced ahead, fitting pieces together and tearing them apart, looking for the key that would link them all. Then she had it.

"Early this week, my father-in-law called and mentioned that Ian Williams, his solicitor, would be out to see me. A later call from Ian stressed our getting together, but then I didn't hear from him again. What if John was thinking of writing his son out of the will?"

Seamus paused in his note taking. "That's true. You did say that was the sword of Damocles he held over his head. If Eamonn could discredit you, and make it look as if you were the unfaithful one, he'd be back in his father's good graces."

Sean said, "But why try to kill you later, then?"

"If he had to manufacture evidence that I could refute, it'd be easier if I could never challenge him. And he'd be free to do whatever he wanted. He'd already presented his father with an heir. John does dearly love his grandson, you know."

"It's easy to see why," Sean said.

"I can't see how he could plan that attack so well," Seamus said. "How would he have known?"

She recalled the actions of her assailant on Healy Pass. "I have the feeling it was more coincidence than anything else. The driver took his time before trying to run me off the road; almost as if debating if it were the thing to do. The attack seemed half-hearted, too, as if he never fully committed himself to it. And he was going the other way when I first encountered him."

"So the opportunity was there. He wanted his inheritance intact, so he turned killer," Sean said.

"I can't think of anything else that would impel Eamonn to take the chance of killing me himself. He could be violent, but he never took chances. Besides, he really liked our arrangement. He had the money and all his chippies to play with. Why else would he come after me?"

"And how do you know Mr. Conor was aware of Eamonn's infidelity?"

"That, Sean, is the piece I was missing. It was the same thing nagging at the back of my mind after John's call last week. He wasn't surprised that Eamonn wasn't there, and that I didn't know where he was."

Then another thought came to her. "If he knew what was going on, what if John hired someone to check up on me?"

"Fair enough," Seamus said. "But who did kill him, then, and what should we do about it?"

"Whoever it is tried to throw suspicion on Beth," Sean said. "That could also mean he wanted her out of the way. Maybe more so, now."

"I agree," Beth said. "My instincts are still flashing danger signals at me. But what can we do? The inspector still has us as prime suspects."

"I'd say we try to find some clues ourselves to present to him," Sean said. "Point him in the right direction, instead of at us."

Beth looked from one to the other. "Alright detectives, where first?"

"The Imperial Hotel," said Seamus. "We might find someone who saw Eamonn Conor just before he was killed, and verify if he was on foot. We can also find out just what your father-in-law knows about this."

Sean looked apprehensive about this and Beth asked, "What is it, Sean?"

"This is a heck of a time to meet your father-in-law. What will he think when he sees his son's old friend is now courting his wife!"

The green Honda was parked far down the street from Delaney's pub. The figure inside brought his binoculars up when he saw the trio leave. He scribbled something in his notebook before getting out of his car to follow them. The big burly man had to be that physics professor his boss had told him about.

The transmitter lay under a shirt in the back seat. Later he'd plant it at the O'Hara woman's shed. But now he needed to see where the three of them were going and whether it spelled trouble for his employer. There might be some more wet work for him. Fattening his bank account would please him enormously and then he'd get the hell away from this progressively dangerous situation and his increasingly dangerous boss.

CHAPTER 29
IMPERIAL HOTEL, CORK

"John? We have company," said Dr. Tommy Mansfield.

John waited expectantly as the door opened wider to allow Beth, Sean, and Seamus to enter. He immediately went over to Beth and hugged her, like a drowning man to a life preserver. "Beth, thank God you're safe. I just heard the news of the bombing on the wireless." As he released her, he saw Sean behind her. "Sean Carey? My goodness, I didn't know you were here."

"It's good to see you again Mr. Conor, I -- "

"Oh, please call me John. Tommy, did I tell you about Sean? He was one of Eamonn's best..." He paused for a moment, his usual tight control all but gone. "I'm sorry; I don't quite have myself together. Forgive an old man his silliness."

"There's nothing to forgive," Beth said. "I know it's been a terrible shock, but I'm safe, and so is Julian. Sean and my good friend, Seamus Dunoon, have been a rock of support to me."

"Ah, that's who this fellow is. I never would have believed someone could make Sean appear small, but you certainly do," said John.

"A Scotsman, I should have guessed. And as big as the highlands themselves," said Tommy, leaning against the door.

Seamus turned towards him. "And who might you be, Sir?"

"Dr Mansfield, John's physician. But please call me Tommy."

"I don't think I've ever heard of a doctor called Tommy." Seamus scratched his head in recollection.

"You have no idea how long it took me to call him that!"

John found himself enjoying the camaraderie, regretting he had not learned to demonstrate love as he had discipline. Perhaps his son would not be on a slab now if he had been a real father. A more pressing thought occurred to him. "Beth, does the inspector suspect you of all this? Surely not."

"He wants Sean and me to stay in the Cork area, but we haven't been formally charged. We actually came here for two reasons. One, of course, was to see how you were getting on. I'd have been by sooner, but I only returned from Galway late last night."

"Yes, I'm sure they had many unpleasant questions for you." The thought of his daughter-in-law being abused by cruel interrogations was very upsetting. "They should be finding my son's murderer, not harassing you and Sean."

"John! Don't do this to yourself. You've done what you can. Now leave it to the police," said Tommy.

John sighed. Tommy was right. He was letting the guilt hook him into another tailspin. It occurred to him that something had changed, that this doctor had also become a good friend and confident. It amused him greatly. His good friend, a doctor no less, and healing John in ways no doctor ever did before.

He felt a laugh, liberated from deep inside him, bubble out, filling the room with a sound still alien to his ears. Had he really just laughed? "Well, you can see what I've been reduced to, Beth. I now have a nursemaid named Tommy looking after me." The thought nudged another deep laugh, amplified by Tommy's perplexed look.

"John?"

"Oh, quiet, I'm enjoying my first good laugh in years. Let me savor it."

"Perhaps we can all begin healing." Beth came over to John. "Father," she added softly.

"Bless you, Beth. Bless you," John said as he held her to his heart.

"Then there was the second reason," said Beth.

"That's right," said John, "you did mention two reasons."

Beth related what the three of them had discussed at Delaney's pub. Seeing the pain on her father-in-law's face, she presented the facts gently and swiftly.

"Yes," John said, "I did ask Ian to check up on him. I've suspected for some time that things were not good between you. But I didn't ask him to follow you."

Sean sat next to Beth as he asked. "Is it possible that Ian was overzealous in his investigation?"

"Ian, overzealous? Well, normally I wouldn't think so. But my son's murder has affected him. His idea of changing the will was such a good one, too."

Beth gasped at this, but John hurried on.

"Now, it's not like it sounds. I was trying to find a way to bring Eamonn back in line, and Ian wanted to help. His idea was to have you and Julian holding a larger interest in the company than Eamonn. We hoped he would behave himself to get your cooperation. Besides, you would have done a much better job."

"Probably so," Beth said, "but why didn't he try to reach me, then?"

"About the will change? He told me he missed you at the Fitzsimmons home, and then you disappeared." John said.

"Oh, yes. Sean and I did leave early." Seeing the confused look at John's face she added, "Julian was sick so Sean drove me home."

John looked from Beth to Sean. "Is something going on between you two?"

Sean reached out for Beth's hand and they smiled in answer. "I would not have been able to get through this without Sean." She placed her free hand over his. "He's been my rock."

John looked from Beth to Sean with a look of concern, but said nothing more.

Into the silence, Seamus said, "How long have you known this Ian fellow, anyway?"

"I helped him get his degree. Before that, he worked in my Belfast offices. He was obviously too smart to stay a lowly clerk so, when he resumed his studies, I offered to pay his tuition on the condition that he come to work for me in England. He seemed very eager to leave Belfast, anyway. Can't say I blame him."

"So you wouldn't question his loyalty," said Seamus.

John shook his head firmly. Then it was Sean's turn.

"Did Eamonn know about the changes to the will?"

"No. Ian and his partner prepared the new will. I've signed it, of course. I wasn't going to tell Eamonn until Beth knew. That's when Ian tried to reach you at the faculty party, but received no answer to his calls. I think he even went to your cottage on Saturday, but you were out."

"Yes, we were in and out most of the weekend."

"Wait a minute," said Seamus. "You say Williams had Eamonn followed? Who was that?"

"Mike Mac-something," John said, "a private investigator out of Belfast. Why? Do you think it was he who followed Beth?"

"I don't know," Seamus said. "Perhaps we'd be better served trying to retrace your son's steps Sunday night. If we know where he was killed, we might know better who had the opportunity."

"A good idea, as long as you include motive to narrow the possibilities." They all turned to Tommy, who had been silent until now. "Who'd benefit from his death."

"And what about Patrick's death?" Sean said. "Somehow the two are related, but I'm at a loss as to how."

Beth searched her mind, trying to recall Eamonn's complaints about the Conor Shipping Belfast operation. Unions? IRA threats? "John, do you think this could be business-related? You mentioned that union problems were bad this past year, and I know Eamonn had a number of death threats because of his hiring practices in Belfast."

"The union has been a sore point for some time. MacFarlane, the union boss, and I have been at each other's throats many times. They wouldn't stoop to using violence, busting a few heads, but a car bomb would be out of his line."

Beth said, "What about the IRA threats?"

"That's something else altogether," John said. "I warned my son countless times about taking them on. He disliked anyone telling him what to do. I tried to maintain a fair ratio of Catholics and Protestants when I ran the Belfast operation. It's just good business."

Seamus said, "But Eamonn didn't follow that line?"

"He was firing the Catholics and replacing them with his Protestant friends. It was idiotic. I don't know a better way to ask for trouble."

"Let's see what we have here, then," Seamus said. "We have Peter Deagan, who, rumor has it, is in the IRA. We have Patrick, who was Sinn Fein, the IRA political arm, and we have this Mike fellow from Belfast. That sounds like the link you were talking about, Sean."

"I know," Sean said. "And that's only the ones we know. There could be others."

"Others?" That made Beth decidedly uncomfortable. "But they wouldn't operate like that down here, would they?"

"Not officially," Seamus said. "Both sides in the six counties have so many splinter groups that total control of them is impossible. And don't forget, some of these groups could also be in it for private gain."

"That's grand," Sean said. "We've narrowed it down to about ten thousand suspects."

Seamus said. "Well, you didn't want the Inspector's job anyway, did you, Sean?"

Sean slowly shook his head. "No, I find subatomic particles much more predictable."

CHAPTER 30
COOMHOLA ROOST
THURSDAY

The somnambulant hum of the engine and the heady aromas of late spring put Brendan at ease. Sitting in the back seat he passively observed the view as Regis piloted the car up Coomhola Mountain for the interview with Kitty Doyle. He looked guiltily over at Garda Jenny Magruder to his left and placed a firm hand on her right leg. She winced slightly. "Does it still hurt, Jenny?"

"Only when I see Deagan's smirking face. I want in on the collar."

"And so you shall."

Regis peered at them from the rearview mirror. "How did you do that Houdini act, then Jenny?"

There was a broad smile on her face, "It's a trade secret, Regis."

Brendan examined her hand. "Did you get shots for this?"

"Yes, I hate shots more than anything," she shuddered.

Regis had to laugh at that. "Jasus, trapped in a steamer trunk with rats and it's shots you be worryin' about. You're one tough constable, Jenny."

Jenny just smiled as she lay back in the seat and Brendan draped a protective arm around her shoulder. He was damned proud of her resourcefulness and her courage.

Earlier, he and his two officers had poured over topography

maps of the Bantry Bay area, focusing on the area where Conor's ditched car had been located. Since Kitty's Coomhola Roost and the O'Hara cottage were both within walking distance, either could be the focal point of the murders and a further talk might uncover additional clues. He would welcome any clues, right now.

Leaning into him, Jenny asked, "Inspector, what makes you think we'll learn more from this woman?"

"For one thing, Jenny, we know more now, so we can pose new questions. For another, she's a friend of Mrs. Conor, and could be unconsciously covering for her. And, finally, a lot of witnesses remember more after the first questioning because they've been thrashing it about in their minds. The Doyle woman also sounds like a keen observer."

"And it was my first time in a while interrogating someone," said Regis. "I could easily have missed something the inspector would latch onto with all fours."

Brendan smiled wistfully and wound down the window as they slowed to turn into the driveway. Getting out of the car, he was overwhelmed by the scents and colors of flowers of all description lining the entrance. He stood in admiration.

The owner had a sure hand at gardening, from what he could see. And the lovely red vines covering the front, now why couldn't he have that kind of luck? All he ever saw was a dead pansy's folded face before it shriveled and lay prostrate at his feet. Maybe he'd find the secret after walking the grounds.

Brendan let Regis and Jenny take the lead as he made a close inspection of the garden. He stopped to sniff the heady scent of a tea rose here and fondle a petunia's delicate petal there. When he stood up again, he found them at the door looking curiously at him.

"Hadn't seen this variety before; just wanted to catch the scent." And now he was explaining things to them. That was not good. What was wrong?

"Inspector?"

"I'll be right along. Just go in without me." Brendan waved them ahead and walked along the garden. He still felt guilty sending Jenny into Deagan's lair and he strolled the garden for solace.

He drew a measure of nurture from the familiar scents and colors. The floral display reminded him of his mother's garden in Belfast. On a visit last summer, the neighborhood had put up a concrete barricade across from her house. The dark shadows it cast seemed to make his mother's butterworts wilt. She tended the garden listlessly now, going through a routine that once gave her joy, but now only purpose.

His thoughts were interrupted by movement from his left, and he turned rapidly. An older man wearing coveralls and a straw hat was moving through the rows. His face was weather-worn, with eyes a brilliant blue under the unruly blonde hair that crept out from his hat. Though slightly built, he worked a trenching tool with considerable authority. Seeing Brendan, he set it down and came over with quick steps that hardly disturbed the soil.

"Good day to you, Sir. I see you're enjoying the garden." The man stopped a few paces from Brendan, placing hands on hips and tilting his head for the reply.

"Aye that I am. The name is Inspector O'Neill." The man's blue eyes brightened with interest. "And who might you be?"

"Sandy Doyle, the proud proprietor and the gardener." He extended a slim hand that was lost in the inspector's large paw. He looked fearful he might never see it again.

"Ah, then this is your work, is it?"

"It is, indeed." Sandy swung his head from left to right as if to say, all this is my doing. Then he bent to pull an offending weed from the flowerbed before casting an appraising look at Brendan. "Is there something I can help you with, Inspector?"

"Well, I was going in to talk to your wife about the recent murder."

"Oh, terrible thing." His face creased in sadness at the remembrance. "And poor Beth, such a lovely girl."

"Really? Some of the townspeople think she's rather stuck up, from what I can gather." Brendan had noted it was a common theme of his interrogations with the townspeople and he wanted other viewpoints. The surprise on Doyle's face seemed to be contradicting that assumption.

"Probably just jealous. Or they can't deal with an intelligent, headstrong woman. She is that, and it took me a little while to adjust to it." His eyes sparkled again as he continued. "But she's as kind and generous as anyone I've met. Mark my words, Inspector." He wagged a soil-tipped finger at the inspector for emphasis. "If you're suspecting her of having anything to do with this, disabuse yourself of it. She's innocent."

"You may be right, Mr. Doyle. I don't think she's guilty either, but a number of the locals think her capable of it."

"Such as?"

Brendan thought of his list of names and the most memorable came to the top. "Well, there was Shannon Ryan, and..."

"Shannon Ryan, is it! Well considering her own history, I'm not surprised."

The inspector followed Doyle's show of emotion with interest. "What sort of history might that be?"

"Well, I have to rely on me own wife's experiences for this, now." He held his hands up in front of him as if physically distancing himself.

Brendan was learning that it was a bad idea for a married man to claim any personal knowledge of the woman and gestured for him to continue.

"It seems Shannon and the deceased were spending a bit of time together just before Eamonn met Beth working at his Belfast office. The talk had it that Shannon was packing her bags for a trip to the altar at one point. Now, d'ye think she'd be a wee bit put out by Beth taking over, Inspector?"

"That's very interesting." Brendan yanked a notebook out of a bulging jacket pocket and made some notes in it. "There's something else you might be able to help me with."

"You have only to ask, Inspector."

"Have you noticed anything odd about one of your guests of the last week?"

"Odd? Out of the ordinary, like?"

"Yes."

The man absently stroked his jaw, leaving behind streaks of dirt that he quickly brushed off. "Well, there was this one fella. Stayed the week with us. Mike Martin, but that wasn't his real name."

"How do you know that, Mr. Doyle?"

"Please, Inspector, call me Sandy. My Da gave me a friendly name just so people would use it."

Brendan smiled, his professional demeanor compromised by the man's friendly manner. He couldn't remember having an easier time conversing with anyone. "As you will, Sandy."

"Well, he's from the six counties, for one thing, and Catholic. How many of those do you know called Martin?" Here he held up his hand to forestall Brendan's next question, "I spent my youth up there, so I know the dialects and the attitudes."

"Fair enough. So what was he up to?"

"Well, it was hard to get a straight answer out of him, for one thing. As you can appreciate, I enjoy conversation. Hardly a soul that won't have a few words with me. But this fella was the most closemouthed, unresponsive Irishman I'd ever met. And I don't think it was in his nature. I caught him more than once wanting to have a chat and biting his tongue."

"What else did you notice?"

"He kept the oddest hours I've ever known for a salesman. Now take Sunday, for example."

"Yes, do take Sunday." Brendan saw its significance slowly dawn on Sandy.

"Right, that's the night of the murder. Do you think he had a hand in it, then?"

"It's possible. What can you tell me, Sandy."

"When he was on the phone that morning, I noticed he had this strange device over the mouthpiece, and was looking around as if somebody might be eavesdropping." Sandy's voice dropped to a conspiratorial whisper, as if to emphasize his lodger's secrecy. "At lunch here, he meets a fella that drove up to see him. And he's the travelling salesman. Well," he amended, "the man didn't appear to be a client. After lunch, they both left in Martin's Honda. I do know that make. Lots of 'em around."

Brendan interrupted him. "This fella he met. Can you describe him?"

"Didn't get a good look. Tall and slim was all I noticed. I was trimming the roses back here and just saw them in the dining room. Perhaps herself can fill you in on that."

"Fine, and the tall man... He left his car?"

"Yes, a new sedan, dark, expensive looking. I'm sorry, I'm not up on the models."

"Did you see him pick up his car?"

"No, I didn't, but the car was gone the following morning."

"What time would that have been?"

"About 5am. That's when our day starts."

"Could he have returned for it that night?"

"I don't see how. One of our guests complained about not finding a spot when he returned about midnight. So it would have to have been after that, I'd think. It is rather curious, isn't it?"

"Very. And what time did this fellow, Martin, return?"

"He was back the next morning to collect his things. Claimed he had to go into Waterford late to get something, and decided to spend the night there."

"One final thing. How did he settle his bill?"

"With travelers' cheques, I believe."

Brendan suppressed a curse. Hard to trace, unless the bank was unique. But maybe his luck was changing. Who knows? "Thank you Sandy, you've been a big help."

"My pleasure, Inspector."

They shook hands like old friends departing. Brendan looked back while retracing his steps to the main entrance to see Sandy once again tending to his garden. As he approached the front door, he spotted Regis through the bay window, his back to Brendan, speaking to a big woman in a gaily-colored apron.

As he opened the door, all three looked in his direction. "Is there anything you'd like to ask her, Inspector?" Regis nodded over his shoulder at the proprietress.

She was a big-boned woman, like his Ma, sturdy, a commanding presence but with a welcoming smile he rather liked.

"Yes, there is," Brendan said. "What can you tell me about Mike Martin, Mrs. Doyle?"

"Mike Martin." She kneaded her apron while contemplating the question. "I'm not sure there is much I can say about him. He kept pretty much to himself. Kept odd hours too."

"Yes, I got some of that from Sandy."

"You called him Sandy; everyone calls him that," she was all smiles now.

Brendan already knew why, but he plunged ahead. "How much of his comings and goings can you recall?"

She looked confused. "My husband? He's always here."

"I'm sorry, I meant Martin." Brendan nodded his head. One could not assume anything. He knew that!

"Oh, of course!" She had a hearty laugh and it rebounded off the beams above their heads while her round body shook. Brendan suppressed the laugh building in his chest. He had to be professional here, but he was finding it difficult. Regis was staring off in another direction and Jenny had an enormous grin on her face. So much for being professional. He cleared his throat.

"I'd like to see the guest register and any of his travelers' cheques if you have them."

"Certainly, right this way."

They followed Kitty to the registry. Regis moved beside Brendan and whispered, "What's this about, then, Inspector?"

"I just talked to Sandy Doyle. He had some interesting things to say about our Mr. Martin. And another man he met here. Perhaps, she can fill us in." He related the gist of what he'd learned while Mrs. Doyle produced a travelers' cheque and registry card.

"Here you are, Inspector."

"So he identified his residence as Dublin. Yet his travelers' cheque is from a bank in Belfast. Very interesting, indeed!" Brendan was getting the scent, and like a bloodhound, was ready to follow its elusive trail.

Jenny interjected, "Do you think he's involved in this, then?"

Brendan waved off the question to ask one of his own. "Mrs. Doyle, do you recall the gentleman who dined with this Mr. Martin on Sunday?"

"Why, yes. He was English, I think. Very well spoken. No flies on him, I can tell you." She stared at the ceiling as she elaborated. "Um, quite tall and thin he was. It seemed like Mr. Martin was working for him. At least, he deferred to him now and again."

"Did Mr. Martin call him by name?"

"Well, I suppose he must have. Now, what was it? Sorry, I can't remember."

"How did he pay the bill?"

"It was put on Mr. Martin's account."

"Well, thank you, Mrs. Doyle. If you do recall anything else, don't hesitate to ring us up. Come on, let's go!"

"Where to, Inspector?"

Regis barely got his question out before Brendan was pulling him along and out the door. Once outside, he issued his commands. "Jenny, when we get back, I'd like you to have another talk with John Conor and his physician. Get any information you can on Ian Williams, his solicitor. And see if he can check his records for names and descriptions of anyone this Williams might have hired or worked with over the last two years." He paused while she wrote it down.

"Also anything he's got on business partners, competitors, unions, threats against him or his son. Anything to give us a motive." When he was sure she had it all down, he turned to Regis. "We're going to find the actual crime scene, Sergeant."

"The crime scene?" Regis glanced around him. "But where do we start looking?"

"Right on our own doorstep. We'll start at the Imperial Hotel and take it from there."

"But we know he wasn't murdered there." Regis looked very confused.

Brendan pulled out his fat notebook and turned to a folded down page. "New information. One of our constables talked to the bell captain that was on duty Sunday night and provided some very interesting information on Conor and possibly one or two men following him that night."

"He didn't take his car?"

"No, he was on foot. Someone else took his car to dump the body."

Jenny interjected, "Someone lured him out of the hotel? On what pretext?"

"That I don't know, Jenny, but the spare descriptions I have at least suggests one of the men was Peter Deagan."

"That bastard!" Jenny spat and Regis jumped out of her way.

"Come on Sergeant, we'll use our brains to discover where they went."

"I hope you use them to stay out of the rain, Inspector," Jenny said, staring at the sky. "It looks like we're in for some."

They all looked up at the sky, darkening ominously as thick low clouds quickly rolled in.

CHAPTER 31

The wind had picked up, sending sheets of rain against the stone buildings. The light from an occasional car made them glisten, and the droplets seemed to move with each car's passage. The sad wail of a ship's horn sounded in the distance. Overlaying that was the hiss of tires on rain-slick streets. One car found a virgin pool of water to invade that kicked up a fine spray that nearly drenched Brendan before he could sidestep the unwanted shower. He looked around, momentarily disoriented.

"Well, that's what I get for daydreaming. Christ, what a night."

In a hushed voice, Regis said, "It does feel spooky in this part of Cork tonight, Inspector."

Because Regis was not one to be easily spooked, Brendan was surprised by the comment. He watched his sergeant pull the hood of his slicker tighter over his rain-soaked face, his eyes shifting restlessly. Brendan would never admit to having a sixth sense when he came to detecting, but on this dark night he realized he was going almost solely on instinct. Perhaps his sergeant was experiencing the same thing.

The inspector leaned into the rain, pulling the brim of his fishing hat lower. He kept his pipe turned down to protect the bowl, occasionally drawing through it like a snorkel, as if to filter out the heavy mist that surrounded him. They walked together to the far side of the bridge as sheets of rain flowed past them in shallow waves.

Turning behind him he said, "You don't mind the walk, now, do you, Regis?"

Regis came up beside him and they huddled together for comfort. "No. If this is what it takes to get some new ideas brewing on this case, we'll walk."

Brendan looked around just to make sure no one was within earshot, and then smiled warmly at his companion. "I do believe we're making a full-fledged detective out of you, me boyo."

It was the fourth bridge they'd crossed that night. Like the others, it was deserted, its single working streetlight weakly probing the night. The street lamp on their side of the road was dark. When Brendan directed the beam of his torch to the glass enclosure atop the lamp he noted that the bulb was missing.

He pulled his overcoat more tightly around him. Then he realized it wasn't the weather that was making him cold. Even late April rain didn't make things this chilly. But, unmistakably, he did feel a chill. He stopped and rested against the bridge cornerstone, his hand unconsciously tracing the brass plate. He felt his fingers tingle on the cold metal and suddenly turned to look down at the plaque. His pencil torch picked up the dates and dedication.

"Of course," he whispered, "Eamonn's namesake." His thoughts raced ahead, forming hypotheses and drawing conclusions, rejecting them only to come up with others. Words came out, but not linked to any rational discourse; they tumbled apart and were lost in the mist. Finally he reined in the ideas spilling over him, took a deep breath, and logically put the pieces together again. He turned to Regis, who was gazing at him in puzzled, open-mouthed wonder. It was a moment before Regis dared to speak.

"Is this the revelation you were speaking about, then, Brendan?"

Brendan looked at him oddly for a moment, and then a broad smile lit his face as he looked into his sergeant's earnest, but confused look. He gave Regis a fatherly pat on the shoulder.

"I'm sorry, Regis. I haven't warned you about my brainstorming sessions when some new information hits me, have I?"

"No, and it would have kept me from worrying about you now, if you had. Was any of that supposed to make sense?"

"No, but think about this. Who is this bridge dedicated to?"

Regis glanced down as Brendan had and, using his own torch, illuminated the plaque. "It's in honor of Eamonn De Valera. One of my personal heroes, in fact."

"Right, and a good president he was. But, not exactly a hero to many Protestants, considering his background, wouldn't you say?" Acknowledging Regis's head shake, he continued. "And isn't it coincidental that our Eamonn probably died somewhere around here. Would it not be ironic if it was right here?"

"What?"

"Hear me out. We know Conor was not out for a stroll that night. He came down here to meet someone; maybe Peter Deagan. Or possibly Deagan was following him to the assignation. Then a tall man following after them could have been Sean Carey or even this Williams fellow."

Regis considered this before replying. "Williams was having Conor followed so he'd know he'd be staying at the Imperial."

"Right, although considering Conor's penchant for all things expensive, he'd have guessed it anyway." Brendan was pleased his sergeant was tracking his thought processes.

"The coroner's revised report placed his death at between midnight and two. He was last seen leaving the hotel's lobby at half past eleven. That's about a fifteen minute walk from there. Then he meets someone and is beaten senseless. Then, and we don't know how long this was, he was stabbed and killed, at least another fifteen minutes, or longer. That would fit the time of death."

"Right, but then what, inspector."

Brendan noted that the rain had stopped before he continued. "Whoever killed him was also on foot and would have to go back to the hotel to get Conor's car, then drive it here and load his body into it." Brendan turned to look over the railing. "My guess is it was under this bridge. Less chance of someone turning up at the wrong time. That and the light being out on this side of the bridge make it the one ideal location"

Regis nodded in agreement. "Right, and this time of night an hour, hour and a quarter to get to Bantry Bay if he didn't chance speeding."

Brendan added up the time. "So he'd have gotten the body in the water, tied Conor's belt around that pipe and left around two in the morning."

Then Brendan had another thought, "Wait a minute! What if Patrick spotted the car leaving the bay? And knew it was Eamonn's car?"

"Shannon did say he left her around that time." Regis shrugged his shoulders. "But why keep it from us?"

Brendan smiled broadly. "I always thought his excuse for stopping was thin, but seeing a familiar car leaving the lay-by? That would surely inspire him to stop."

When Regis nodded his understanding the inspector continued. "And that could mean Patrick had some idea who might have killed Conor. He and Deagan were conferring at the scene. Maybe Patrick knew it was Deagan and tried to blackmail him."

"That would be a very foolish thing to do with a bomb maker," Regis replied, and then the realization struck him. "Shite!"

"Indeed it would, but then Deagan must have had another accomplice doing the killing. Maybe this Belfast detective.

Regis pondered this for a moment. "But what about this Williams. Where does he fit in?"

"That was one of the things I had not considered before and I hope Jenny will bring us that information later." Brendan shook the remaining drop off his hat before replacing it on his head. "Maybe he needed the son out of the way and saw his chance when Deagan beat him up."

Regis looked over the railing where Brendan had just stood,

then added, "So Conor was heading towards a meeting place he and the killer agreed to, and it would have had to be close, quiet..." He looked down below him, "...and dark."

"Right! The bridges that connect the old town offer the best seclusion, and each is an easy landmark to find. And this bridge is the darkest and most secluded we've found. If they met under the bridge, or he was induced to go under the bridge, what better place to beat him up and kill him. The irony of the bridge's dedication would appeal to a certain type of person; certainly someone in the IRA, don't you think?"

They both looked at each other for a moment, the idea taking root. When Brendan started down the steps to the river, Regis was right behind him.

They came to a long chain-link fence that was anchored to the truss of the bridge at one end and a stout metal pole at the other. There was a chain and padlock on the gate. Brendan yanked it, making sure it was secure, and then shone his torch on it.

"Notice that the lock is new, but the chain is rusty, Regis. What do you make of that?"

"It could have been just recently replaced. Maybe broken...or forced open?"

"Right. Now look at the chain closely."

"It looks all nicked up. Here, this looks like the teeth of a bolt cutter."

"Right again. But the chain is heavier than the lock. If someone did break in, they might have failed to snap the chain and went for the lock instead. Shine your torch on that sign over there while I take down the number."

Regis complied and Brendan recorded the property owner's number on the 'No Trespassing' sign. "Come on, then. We'll call in the morning and ask how the lock was broken. If it was as I suspect, we'll have 'em open the place for us. I'll bring O'Boyle in on this, too. He's damn good at forensics."

"The fella from Dublin?"

"Right. I think we're getting close on this one, Regis. I can feel it in my bones."

"I'm only feeling cold in mine. D'ye think we could stop in at O'Toole's for a nip o' Jamesons?"

"Regis, my friend, we shall indeed. I'll even buy the first round."

Knowing that a first round suggested more, Regis eagerly followed the inspector back over the bridge.

CHAPTER 32

The city sparkled in the morning light. The sun, with no clouds for company, sent bright shafts of light down every alley-way. Countless flowers, spilling from window boxes, stretched to reach the sun's embrace. The old stone steps of the Cork Gardai HQ held on to the last of the rain in shoe-worn cavities. Regis sat on the bottom step, oblivious to the dampness. Brendan was trying unsuccessfully to get him into his car, parked at the side of the road.

"Come on, Sergeant. God, you're slow this morning. Are you going to use your arse as a blotter, now?"

"Have a care, Inspector. Me head is still not sitting right on my shoulders."

"Well, you were the one who insisted on joining Colm on 'Gil-garra Mountain,' and then taking over the fiddle. I didn't know you played that well, Regis."

"I don't usually, but I think I was in me cups."

"Swimming in your cups is more like it, but you were still on key, I'll say that for you. You've met Bill O'Boyle, haven't you?"

The two men exchanged greetings as Regis joined them at the car. O'Boyle's haggard, red face was a perfect complement to Regis's mournful mug. The first time Brendan had met the man in a Dublin coffee shop, he had looked at O'Boyle appraisingly, and wondered about that abused face. O'Boyle had volunteered, "You know, O'Neill, I don't need to spend the nights on my elbows downing jars of whiskey. I come by this look naturally." The men had laughed, shaken hands, and become fast friends.

Regis worked his way into the car, shoving Brendan's detritus out of the way. O'Boyle got into the back and crushed an empty packing box. He jumped back as though something valuable had come to harm.

Regis turned at the sound and then gave O'Boyle a wicked smile. "Don't worry, Bill, if it was worth anything, he wouldn't keep it in here."

Brendan merely scowled as he put the car in gear and drove to the bridge.

"Inspector, has Cowell got back to you?"

Brendan glanced over at Regis as he replied. "Yes, he lost track of Deagan last night. He's not in Bantry now and staying low, but Duncan is sure he'll pick up his trail again and then we will bring him in."

Brendan took the turn off Lapp's Quay, heading to the De Valera Bridge. "He did overhear part of a conversation between Deagan and Shannon Ryan."

"So what kind of arrangement do those two have, anyway?"

"Beats me," Brendan chuckled. "They're both users. Probably know they're using each other and don't care. Or it could be deeper than that." He stared wistfully out the window as they came to a stop behind a line of cars leaving the city for work. He would have preferred to walk, but the equipment they had to bring would have weighed them down. Finally, traffic moved sluggishly forward and Brendan continued.

"Seems Ryan has been keeping Deagan informed of how our investigation is going. Now where d'ye suppose she's getting that information?" The inspector was not finished, but he wanted to get his sergeant thinking about it. "I just learned she's been working part time in Cork at O'Toole's pub." Regis eyebrows shot up at that. "I think, for the time being, we'll have our men using a different pub."

Regis leaned forward. "Did he ever show up to have that blood work done?"

"No he didn't, but Constable Magruder found an undershirt of his with blood stains on it behind the washing machine. Seems he didn't get rid of all the evidence. Although I'm sure she'd have preferred to draw the blood herself."

"Is this Deagan a suspect, Inspector?" O'Boyle looked confused.

"Sorry, Bill. Deagan is one of my main suspects, but he is not the mastermind. He may even have been forced to help out, but at least we have his blood type and our lab found another blood smear from the car that might be the assailant."

Regis added, "And we have his muddy boots in that trunk Constable Magruder was trapped in."

O'Boyle asked, "Trapped in a trunk? How did that happen?"

Brendan shook his head, "Don't ask." Then he looked away

"What about that DNA stuff?"

Regis responded, "It's still a pretty new science, Bill, and we don't have a lab close by. I understand the FBI is working up a database for it, but we're a bit behind the curve here." Then Regis added to Brendan's surprise, "We still need to do the footwork in this investigation. Can't do it all with computers."

He winked at Brendan

Pulling into the gateway below the bridge, the inspector showed his badge to the attendant. They stopped at a weathered log used to keep vehicles from rolling into the river, and headed for the office. Inside, an old wizened man squinted up at them as if they were from another planet, fixing them with a cold stare. The office mimicked the man: spare, old, dusty, and unkempt. Little light came in through the grimy window, and even less heat. He pulled his shawl around his shoulders, and cast them an accusatory glare as thought the draft that had followed them inside was their fault.

"Well, what is it?"

"Morning, the name is Inspector O'Neill. I just talked to you about the break-in."

"Eh, who broke it?"

"No, the break-in."

"I certainly didn't break wind, did you?"

Regis and Brendan exchanged looks of disbelief. Brendan was girding himself to try once again when a burly, hard-looking man in a gray uniform came through the door.

"You must be the Gardai. Name's Flanagan, Tom Flanagan. It's all right, Phil, I'll take care of it." He said the last loudly to the clerk, who appeared startled by someone speaking loud enough for him to understand. He mumbled under his breath and turned his back on them. Flanagan and the three policemen walked over to where the sun's rays failed to reach under the bridge.

"Like I was say'n, we don't go under the bridge." Flanagan pointed down. "This orange line is as far as we can stack our containers. No light under there, anyway." Turning back to the gate, he said, "And about the lock. We just thought some kids had done it to raise a ruckus, or maybe for a tryst." He gave Regis a knowing wink. "Know what I mean?"

"You saw nothing amiss out here in the parking area close to the bridge?"

"Not a thing. Oh, some tire tracks, but none leading over to the building. None of our stuff was tampered with, so we didn't bother checking any further."

"So, as far as you know, no one has been under here for the last few days?"

"That's right, Inspector. No reason to, like I said."

"Fine. We're going to set up some tape to keep people out while we work the area. You have no problem with keeping your men out?"

"No, have at it." Flanagan saluted the inspector and then walked away.

O'Boyle set his case down on the ground and went to work. After surveying the entire area, he suggested confining their exploration to under the bridge. The torches picked up red-stained earth in a number of places, and they marked it off while O'Boyle took samples and did preliminary blood spatter analysis. Regis and Brendan helped with the tape measure, and assisted in the pouring of the plaster for the tire tracks. The quiet darkness was disturbed by countless bulb flashes and the reeling in and out of the tape measure.

"Here's a good footprint impression. Regis, another box, please."

After O'Boyle had spent some time looking over the area, he made a preliminary sketch, and then beckoned the other officers to join him back in the warm sunshine.

"So, Brendan, what do you and Regis make of this?"

"Well," Brendan said, "it looks like a struggle took place here, no doubt about that. Heavy traffic obliterated most of the footprints except under the bridge, but here it does look like two, maybe three, sets of prints."

"Three sets. The third set goes right to where most of the blood pooled and then away."

"Where the body fell, you mean," Regis said.

"Right. Someone came by to take the body away, or issued the killing blows. Or both. See here, where this set of heel marks are dug in sharply, and the obvious drag marks of the corpse."

"So the killer had help." Brendan said, while kneeling over the spot O'Boyle had identified.

"Yes, but there are a lot of footprints around this area, many covering each other. So it isn't clear which one actually did the stabbing."

"Do you have enough clear prints to determine if one set belongs to Deagan and one set to Conor?"

"Yes, I do, Inspector, since you have Deagan's boots and the deceased's shoes. And a good match for the third set whenever you get a suspect to do a comparison. I just need to make some cross checks on this and we're done."

"Excellent." Brendan turned to his sergeant. "Regis, you can tell the foreman we're almost finished here."

It was late morning before they had completed an exhaustive survey of the crime scene, and had taken all the molds, measurements, and photos they would need. Brendan was still writing in his notebook when Regis tapped him on the shoulder and gestured that they were ready to go.

CHAPTER 33
COOMHOLA

Sean felt something tug incessantly on his arm and roused himself from deep slumber. He looked up at the oak crossbeams on the ceiling, trying to remember where he had seen them before. For that matter, where was he?

"Wake up, Sean!"

"Mmph! What...?" He cast about, slowly registering shapes, then details, finally recognizing Julian's face.

"Sean, are you awake?"

"I think so. Where am I? What time is it?"

"We've got trouble here, Sean."

"Huh? What kind of trouble, Julian?" When he raised up to look around, the boy was gone. Or was this just a figment of a dream? He rubbed his eyes to clear them while looking around. His mouth tasted like stale scotch, and smacking his lips did little to relieve the sensation of having just consumed a pound of earth. He slowly unfolded his long body from the couch and tottered in the direction of what he hoped was the bathroom.

The water he splashed on his face was cold and it revived his dulled senses. Where was he? He wasn't in his own bathroom. Was it a hotel? Then a familiar scent tickled his nostrils. Beth's scent! He glanced down at an array of feminine toiletries and saw the cologne bottle. Definitely her cologne. He stared at his reflection in the mirror for a long time, his eyes unfocused, before he realized he was naked.

And here he was, puttering around Beth's cottage in the buff. That would not do. At least not yet, he told himself happily. He grabbed a towel off the rack and went back to the living room. He couldn't find Julian anywhere. Didn't Julian talk to him only minutes ago? Then it hit him. Julian was in Ennis with his grandparents. What would he be doing here? He must have dreamed it. He went back down the hallway, heading for Beth's bedroom. Maybe she knew if her son was back.

Beth leapt out of bed, swaying on unsteady legs, and then sat back on the edge as her brain raced to catch up. What was that sound? Was that Eamonn moving down her hallway? "My God, it can't be!" Then she remembered the previous night in the hotel.

She and Sean had left together. He had not been fit to drive, and she had brought him back here. Why hadn't she just dropped him off at his place? Anyway, that had to be Sean, careening off the walls like a bear in the woods. The jolt of fear melted away, and she felt her life resume an ordered beat. He did say he took some time to wake up. She hoped he wouldn't damage anything in the process. She got back under the covers, arranging the bed more neatly than was her custom, and waited.

His knock on her door started a tingling of anticipation, and she was a little surprised at her own boldness. Was it proper to welcome him into her bedroom? And what was proper anymore? "Come in, Sean."

"Are you decent, then?" He said through the half-opened door.

"Yes, but I'd like to change that in a hurry." The door opened wide. Sean's head peered around it. His eyes were wide as well.

"Did I hear you right?"

She beckoned him into the room. She sat up slightly, holding the covers high on her chest. She liked the sleepy, warm innocence of his smile as he entered and closed the door. He stayed there for a moment, a towel round his slim waist, lean hard muscles in his arms and shoulders flexing as he twisted the ends of the towel more tightly around him. Then he walked slowly over while she held her breath, afraid of breaking the mood. When he stood next to the bed, she lowered the cover, exposing her breasts. Following her cue, he let the towel drop to the floor. He looked down at it absently before speaking.

"I couldn't have hidden this behind it any longer, darling."

"No, indeed, it would take a much larger towel." She raised the covers up so he could slide in next to her. The sensation of his hard body next to hers sent a thousand stabs of pleasure through her. Each point of contact held its own small caress. She moved over him, greedily coveting more. Her breasts flattened on his chest, her belly filling in the hollow of his flat stomach.

She felt heat and pressure, his arms around her, surrounding her, pulling her down to a warm dark place. They called each other's name. Then, as the intensity doubled, only moans and cries filled the air. His face floated inches from hers. Was she above or below now, and did she care? Her toes pressed against the limits of damp sheets as rings of pleasure sweep through her. She had no weight, floating with him for a moment, before coming to rest once again on the bed.

"Beth, this is so good, I can hardly believe it. Where did you...?"

She placed a hand over his mouth. "No talk. Let's just hold each other, please." She felt him smile behind her cupped hand. They held each other tight, afraid that such pleasure might be too fleeting.

Beth had drifted off to sleep when Sean shook her awake, his voice insistent.

"Beth, is Julian back?"

She bolted upright and rubbed her eyes. What he had said slowly registered. "What? Julian's with my parents."

"But he came over and woke me up this morning and then disappeared. At least, I thought he did."

"It was a dream, darling," Beth said. "We were up late. Maybe you brain was working overtime."

"Right enough," Sean said. "Playing amateur detective and drinking single malt scotch. Did we solve anything?"

"Well, you and Seamus did get to the bottom of the bottle."

"I suppose I did imagine seeing Julian, but it certainly felt real. He was even wearing that green jacket he likes so much." Sean watched Beth's eyes open wide in alarm. "What is it, Beth?!"

Beth hugged herself to control the trembling. Not another dream! Julian had asked specifically to bring the green jacket. What did this one mean? Was it another premonition? Maybe it was time to let Sean in on her nightmarish visions. "Sean, do you put much stock in dreams?"

"You mean besides you?"

"Be serious. I mean dream analysis, premonitions, that sort of thing."

"I did take a course covering things like that at Stanford. It's the done thing back there. I tried some personal experiments, even learned to do a tarot spread."

"You did? Did it help you at all?"

"Definitely. The gal I was dating there was real big on tarot."

"Oh, you!" She pounced on him and wrestled him down beside her. Soon her passion ignited again and she found Sean an eager partner once more. They made love more slowly this time as Sean's tongue roamed places that curled Beth's toes and drew soft moans. How could she be so shameless and wanton?

Finally, still in each other's arms, they resumed the conversation. Beth told him about her dream and Julian's on the Cliffs of Moher, and the readings Kathryn Fitzsimmons had given her over the last two months.

"Well, I can't vouch for the accuracy of dreams and tarot spreads," Sean said as he sat up. "Their very nature makes it impossible to duplicate, which is fundamental to scientific validation. Maybe tarot is just a manipulation of symbols, as Jung suggested.

But as many warnings as we seem to be getting, I think we should treat them seriously. Do you think we should call your parents, just to make sure Julian is all right?"

They were interrupted by the phone, which sounded abnormally loud to Beth. She looked over to Sean for reassurance, and he nodded at her to pick it up.

"Yes?" She waited a moment as static cleared and then heard her mother's voice. "Mum! We were just going to call."

"Dear, I'm calling about your father," Mairin said.

Her mother's voice sounded lost, and far away. Beth's mind raced over countless possible catastrophes before her mother continued.

"He went fishing around the Aran Islands, and there was a storm."

She paused again, and Beth reached blindly for Sean. He caught her hand and moved beside her.

"They don't know where he is, child. They found the Hags Head broken up on the rocks of Foul Sound."

"Oh, God. Are they looking for him? Is he...?" Beth didn't try to finish the thought.

"They're scouring the coastline between Cora Point and Taunabruff. I just got a message from his friend, Padraic. The seas are still too rough to venture out far. There was no sign of him around the wreck. It was about a mile off shore, but they couldn't get close enough to see if he jumped off before it struck. I pray he did."

Beth turned to Sean, tears already filling her eyes before speaking into the phone again. "Mum, how are you? Who's there with you?"

"Just Julian. Mrs. Clancy said she'd come by and spend a while. I...I'm managing. I just wish I knew more. The waiting is desperate."

"We'll be there as soon as..." She stopped for a second as she remembered Inspector O'Neill's instructions to stay in the area.

What could she do? "Mum, I'll head up there as soon as I can."

"Are you all right, dear? I know this news is hitting you hard too."

"Yes it is, but I still have some things to settle with the Gardai."

"You're in trouble, aren't you?"

"Just a little red tape is all, dear," Beth said. "You know how these things can tie you up. I'll be there quickly."

"Come when you can, then. I'll let you know as soon as I hear anything."

"Let me speak to Julian for a minute, Mum. Does he know?"

"Only that his grandfather ran into a bit of trouble out there. I couldn't have him worrying too."

"No, of course not." She took her first deep breath of the conversation, and then chewed on her lower lip. When she lowered the phone, Sean reached over to kiss the worry from her mouth. She pressed the phone to her ear again when she heard her son's voice.

"Mum? Are you there?"

"Yes, my darling. How are you?"

"I'm fine, but Granny's very upset," Julian said. "Are you coming soon? I miss you."

"I miss you too, love. I'll be there very soon."

"Is Sean coming with you?"

"Yes. Is that all right with you?"

"Yeah, I suppose so."

It wasn't a wholehearted endorsement, but it would take him time to adjust. How would she explain to him all the changes that had occurred over the past few days? She looked over at Sean, who seemed to read the concern in her eyes.

"We'll be fine, Beth."

She nodded before resuming her conversation. After a few more exchanges, she hung up. She felt like a cork, bobbing on a wind-swept sea, tossed by malignant forces she could feel but not see. Even Sean's tight clasp could not dispel the feeling of death extending skeletal hands into her chest.

Casey O'Hara had been shocked at the suddenness and violence of the storm. Whitecaps became angry waves and the fishing boat was tossed about roughly. Casey had to grab every handhold he could find as he headed toward the stern. He remembered that he'd forgotten to re-secure the engine housing when he'd adjusted the idle earlier. Served him right for thinking he had everything under control.

Just before he reached the wheel a rogue wave smashed against the boat and he was tossed on the deck. The huge volume of water nearly drowned him as he slid along the deck. He slammed against the gunwale and was momentarily dazed. He heard the bilge pump turn on as the bilges choked on the incoming water.

Casey watched in fear as another wave drove massive water into the engine compartment before he could re-secure the housing. He half crawled over to it just as the engine sputtered and died. Casey pressed the starter button and prayed it would kick over. The engine nearly started, but then gave one last shudder and died just as another wave struck, driving the powerless boat toward the rocks.

Smoke and steam hissed out of the engine compartment, but he tried once more to start the engine even though he knew it might explode. He hit the switch but even the starter was silent. Now the only sound came from the endless waves driving the boat ever closer to the jagged rocks near Dun Aonghasa off the big island of Inishmore.

The dark outline of the coastline hid the deadly rocks he knew extended out from this part of the shore. The waves and current were driving him toward it and his 24-foot craft would not stand a chance once the underside was ripped out. The sea winds whistled and moaned their remorse, but the sound only chilled his spine and numbed his legs.

He had little rudder control now that he'd lost power and crashing against the rocks was inevitable. He moved forward from the wheelhouse, grabbing handholds on the cabin's deck, half-blinded by driving rain, until he reached the yellow inflatable raft lashed to the cabin deck.

As the boat rocked from starboard to port, he steadied himself and began unlashing his rubber raft while holding tightly to the cabin's rail. He knew if the wind took the small lifeboat he was as good as dead, so he moved his left hand to hold the rope that encircled its sides while he freed the last line with his right. The wind tried to tear the small craft from his hands and he felt his grip loosening.

As he released the last tie-down the raft began to lift up and he had to reach up with both hands to keep it from going over the side without him. Just as he was recovering his balance another wave broke over the boat and Casey and the raft were thrown into the turgid sea.

CHAPTER 34

GARDA HQ

Jenny Magruder was fuming when Brendan and Regis returned. Regis saw the look first and excused himself, pleading a full bladder. Brendan took the stack of printouts with the analysis of the crime scene over to his desk and motioned Jenny over. She came over reluctantly, and stood with hands on hips.

"I thought I was on this case, too."

"You are, Jenny, but I can't spare all my people at one crime scene."

"Well, it would have been nice if you had at least told me what was going on."

"I am now," Brendan said, patting her shoulder. "I'm going to update you on what we found. Then I want you to fill me in on what happened with the good doctor."

"Are you still trying to protect me, Brendan?"

Brendan saw Regis peek his head around the door. "Not now, Jenny," he said, softly enough so Regis wouldn't hear. He watched Regis tiptoe over with exaggerated caution. Then he glanced at Jenny. She had hers arms crossed, and was beating a tattoo with her shoe. Brendan raised a forbidding hand toward Regis.

"Don't you two start in again."

"I wouldn't dream of it, Inspector. By the way, do you not think Jenny would be the perfect one to draw out Phil? Sort of loosen him up so we could learn his secrets."

"Phil?" Jenny and Brendan said in unison.

"Yes, you know the clerk at the bridge."

"Oh, Phil." Brendan appeared to ponder it for a moment, conjuring up the sight. He had to pass a hand in front of his face to keep the smile from spreading any further across it. "I don't think so, Regis. Lord knows he certainly didn't hear anything that night."

"All right, what are you two going on about, now?"

"It's just been a long morning, that's all," Brendan said. "Let's go over this first, and then Jenny can tell us what she learned from Dr. Mansfield."

Brendan covered the substance of the reports made at the bridge and the preliminary blood analysis that O'Boyle had just completed. Jenny occasionally looked up from her note-taking, eyebrows raised at the significance of what they had found.

Finally she said, "So the footprints and the blood match those of the deceased, and one other set of footprints belong to Deagan." Jenny paused before looking at the inspector, "Did you use those muddy boots I had Dennis retrieve from Deagan's trunk?"

"We did. Good thinking on your part and the mud could be from the bridge, although it could be from anywhere along the river.

"Deagan's boot was the right size but it could belong to anyone of Deagan's weight and size. The other footprints are from rather expensive English shoes, however. Those prints are probably from a tall, lightly-built man. Again, we can only generalize here. You know, averages being what they are."

"O'Boyle got all that from footprints?"

"The shoe size and depth of the footprints in muddy soil gave him some idea of a man's size and weight. We got one good heel imprint in fine muddy soil from very new shoes. The stylized letters on the crest centered in the heel allowed O'Boyle to make a positive ID on them. It was a bit of luck and, Lord knows, we could use some."

"Do you think they could belong to Carey?" Jenny said.

"It is possible, although I've only seen him wearing walking shoes. Besides, he and Deagan don't seem to get along very well. I'm not sure they'd work together. What do you think, Regis?"

"I agree. I can see him helping out the Conor woman, but not Deagan. The killing could be IRA-related, but the hired detective's physical description doesn't match up."

Jenny added, "We know that Conor was making loose talk about exposing Deagan. A Margaret Fitzgerald overheard Conor's end of a conversation at a Bantry coin box on Saturday last. They don't take kindly to that sort of thing."

"No they don't but attacking and killing someone here would be a bold move," Brendan said. "And sure they'd hate a Protestant that didn't hire Catholics at the shipyard, but more likely they'd wait until he was back in Northern Ireland. Then in the constant violence going on there one more death would get far less notice. They don't want everyone against them. It wouldn't be smart."

Jenny said, "So? They never made any mistakes?"

"Point noted," Brendan said, "and we still don't have conclusive evidence on the perpetrator of the bombing of McElheny's car. What did you find out?"

Both men now focused on her as she flipped through her notes.

"Well, the doctor is a keen observer, I'll give him that. He agrees that Williams has a lot of influence over John Conor. In fact, he said a strange thing to me, almost an aside."

"What was that?"

"He said Mr. Conor had treated him like the son he never had."

"Interesting way of putting it. What else?"

"He said Williams was very concerned about Conor's health, asking detailed medical questions including what medication he took. He has been very cool towards the doctor, but the doctor thinks that's because Conor relies on him as much as Williams."

"And what did Mr. Conor have to say about Mike Martin?"

"He said the description could fit the man Williams hired out of Belfast."

Brendan turned to Regis with a knowing smile. "Does he have a name?"

"No, but he is checking it out with his Newbury office."

"And did Conor have any suspicions as to who might have had a motive to kill his son?"

"He mentioned unions, competitors, the IRA, and others. Too broad to be of much use, I'm afraid. Oh, and I asked him about his will. We know money is always a big motive. He was hesitant to provide details and referred me to Williams."

"And?"

"I had the devil's own time trying to reach him until Mr. Conor gave me his private beeper number. I'm more confused about the will's changes now that Williams has explained them." She let out a sigh of exasperation.

Brendan sat up abruptly. "Changes to the will?"

"Or maybe he unexplained them. He's very condescending, and he threw more lawyer jargon at me than I could possibly understand. I don't like him."

"I've had my suspicions about Northern Ireland involvement, but I agree with Jenny." Brendan nodded in her direction. "I think we should follow the money as they always say on those cop shows."

Pulling another report from the stack on his desk, Brendan continued. "However, O'Boyle confirms my assessment of a Crenshaw-style bombing. Deagan was certainly IRA, and could have made the bomb, but I have a feeling he's lost his taste for that sort of thing."

"Really, Inspector? I thought you were hot to get him in here," Regis said.

"And I still am. I'm sure he's involved in this, but I see him more as a pawn. He certainly isn't the mastermind."

"So who is your Moriarity then, Inspector?"

"Well I don't see myself as Sherlock, Jenny, but I sense we have a very cunning and cruel mind behind all this.

Jenny said. "But how is Williams mixed up in this? Seems like he'd only be out for financial gain."

Brendan smiled and leaned back in his chair. "Only financial gain? Conor Shipping is more than just financial gain to a certain type of person."

"You're working on something, Inspector," Regis said. "What is it?"

Brendan allowed a satisfied smile to hint that the chase was on. "Here's what we do next."

CHAPTER 35
IMPERIAL HOTEL

The sun, at its zenith, dispelled the chill of the morning. The Imperial's high windows were open to the muted strains of traffic, and the occasional hail of loud Corkmen. The delicate lace curtains moved gracefully, dancing in the arms of a freshening breeze. John Conor half reclined on the settee, sipping tea and breaking his fifth biscuit in two, promising himself four-and-a-half would be his limit. He put his book down just as the phone rang.

"Conor here."

"John, it's Beth. I need your help. Are you free?"

"Always, for you, my dear. What is it? You sound upset."

"Mum called a while ago. Dad's boat was smashed and he's missing."

"What! When...where? Galway Bay?" He listened intently as she related the sketchy details while nervously crumbling the other half of his biscuit. When she paused for breath, he jumped in. "I'll put my resources at your disposal. I've got the company helicopter here in Cork. I'll dispatch it immediately."

"Oh, I wasn't even thinking about that, but that's a grand idea. Could it drop Sean and me off at my parents' house? There's a large field behind it that would do."

"Right, no bother. Ralph's on duty. Good man."

"There's one other thing, the most important really. I need Inspector O'Neill's approval to leave the Cork area. I could use your support in assuring him that I won't run."

"As it happens, he's on his way here to talk to me about something. Important, he said. There was a female constable, Mac-something, here last night asking us a slew of questions about the will, and that detective Ian employed. I get the feeling they suspect someone else, now."

"Constable Magruder, John. You're terrible with names! Then you think he'd let us go?"

"I don't see why not. If they object, I'll put on the pressure."

"Just don't overexert yourself."

"Over exert myself? Ha! I feel better now than I have in years. I don't know..." John paused to absently wipe the crumbs from his hand, while he grasped the next thought. "Maybe being able to help you and Julian has made me feel like part of a family again. It could even be the Irish weather. Tommy was right; I found I actually missed it. Mornings like today, with the rain cleaning the streets, and now the sun warming things up. It feels good." He leaned back in his chair. "But I am worried about Casey now. And you. And your dear mother, Mairin, isn't it? How is she doing?"

"You remembered her name. I'm so glad," Beth said with more warmth back in her voice. "I think you were too hard on yourself before."

"I deserved it, but now...now I think I'm earning my keep again. Ah, that must be the inspector. We will find Casey. We'll talk later, love."

"Thanks again."

John's step was lighter as he crossed to the door and opened it for Inspector O'Neill and his sergeant.

"Come in, Inspector. I'll call down for tea. And more biscuits. I've devoured them all, I'm afraid."

"Regis can sympathize with you there."

"Right, Mr. Conor," Regis said. "Sure and I'd be glad to take temptation out of your way."

John smiled broadly. "I see I have a fellow-addict. It's a terrible cross we bear."

After phoning room service for more tea, John gestured towards the chairs on the other side of his coffee table.

"I have one request before we start, Inspector. My daughter-in-law just called to say her father was lost at sea and his boat sunk. Her mother is very distraught and Beth implored me to ask you if she could go up there to be with her. I'll vouch for her character."

"There's no need, Sir. I think we can allow it. I'm convinced she had no hand in it." Brendan paused a moment after glancing at his sergeant. "However, technically, she hasn't been exonerated, and could be called upon to answer more questions. So I will need a phone number where she can be reached day and night."

The tea service arrived on a trolley. The bellhop handed a roll of faxes to John and seemed surprised to be receiving a tip. While the two officers plunged in, John unrolled the fax paper and scanned the contents before handing it to the inspector. "I think this may interest you." He watched Brendan read with growing excitement before handing it to his sergeant.

"McAfee from Belfast," Brendan said between sips of the Earl Grey tea. "I've heard that name before, and I'll bet it's related to the bombings."

"It does say he was pulled in a few times in connection with local bombings, but no convictions," Regis said as he returned the fax. "You have good resources, Mr. Conor."

"I took the liberty of asking my office to send me everything they had on this detective Ian hired when your Constable Magruder asked about him. Her description fit Mike McAfee well enough that I had them make inquiries in Belfast, Dublin and Portsmouth. This is the result."

Brendan said, "Do you think your solicitor could be working with McAfee?"

"Impossible! Ian has strong loyalist sympathies. That was evident when he worked for me in Belfast. I hadn't mentioned that he was in the 1st Battalion Parachute Regiment before joining my company."

Brendan looked up sharply at the mention of 1 Para. "No, you hadn't. Where was he stationed?"

"He was stationed in Londonderry. That's where he was born. He didn't like it too much though; that's why he went into a different area of the law. He told me that 'bloody Sunday' was the last straw. Had a rough time of it."

"So did everyone else there." Brendan said. "And his regiment was heavily involved in the slaughter."

Regis said, "Then you don't think he knew that McAfee was in the IRA?"

"I don't think he'd tolerate a republican, violent or not, working for him," John said. He poured tea for himself and handed the cream to Regis.

"We believe that two men killed your son," Brendan said. "Peter Deagan is the one who most likely beat him up. Casts made of footprints at the crime scene matched a pair of his boots. We have evidence to place Deagan there, and he had plenty of motive. We have a warrant for his arrest, but he's disappeared."

"Disappeared!" John half rose from his chair before the inspector stopped him.

"I have a man that's been keeping an eye on Deagan. I don't think he'll get very far. This McAfee could be an accomplice who perhaps drove your son's car when it was ditched. There could be others, of course, but those two and the mastermind are the key figures, in my opinion.

"Mastermind, you say?" John sat up and placed his tea on the sideboard; his interest quickening.

"Yes, at least the one with the most to gain and the one most in the background. I need a bit more evidence to prove my suspicions are correct. If you can answer a few more questions, some of a sensitive nature, I believe we can nab him."

"Anything to find those responsible, Inspector." John rubbed his hands together, spoiling for a fight and primed to help in any way he could.

Brendan signaled to Regis to take notes before turning to Conor. "Now could you just go over the changes in your will with me, and their significance to Beth and Julian, and anyone else?"

"Didn't Ian explain them to your officer?"

"I think he was less than forthcoming."

"I see." John again went through the details of his will and their implications as well as he could without Ian being there to explain the fine points. He had almost finished when the inspector interrupted him.

"Excuse me, Sir. What would happen if Beth, as well as Eamonn, had died?"

"Well, then, Julian stands to inherit everything."

"But he's rather young to make those kinds of decisions."

"Of course. Ian Williams and his partner, as executors, would see to that until Julian came of age."

"I see. Both of them?"

"Well, I suppose, technically, it'd be Ian. Why, what are you driving at?"

Brendan and Regis exchanged knowing looks that troubled John.

"One other question. If your daughter had been convicted of killing her husband, how would the will be executed?"

"Hmm, well...I'm not sure. I could call my office and ask Joshua, Ian's partner, to give me an interpretation."

"Fair enough. Where is Williams, by the way?"

"Finishing up a business deal around here."

Regis said, "Would that be in Bantry Bay?"

"Why, no. What makes you say that?"

"We had some information that both he and Eamonn were seen together there," Brendan said.

"What? Ian told me they met in Cork so he could inform Eamonn in person of the changes to the will. I wanted Ian to record my son's reaction to the news. I was not aware of any other contact between them." John rubbed his chin, lost in thought for a moment. "Are you sure he wasn't there to see Beth about the will?"

"This was days before Mrs. Conor said she was informed of the will changes," Brendan said.

John Conor was stunned by this information and looked deeply puzzled and concerned.

CHAPTER 36
ARAN ISLANDS

Casey O'Hara and his raft splashed into the sea. Casey had a death grip on the tow line as the raft bounced along the waves. He took in mouthfuls of water as he pulled the raft toward him in the roiling sea. Just as he was alongside the raft another wave drove him under. Only his grip on the tow line, now a life line, kept him from being pulled under the waters and away from the boat.

When he surfaced he saw that he and the raft were heading inexorably toward the jagged shore. He managed to hold onto the raft and scrambled into it even as another wave pushed the raft ever closer. Casey hugged himself, shivering as the wind picked up, dropping his body temperature. How he wished he'd had time to grab a coat before being tossed into the sea.

But he had no time for that now as he bobbed on the angry sea. He unsnapped the oars and set them into the holding brackets and began rowing for all he was worth. His forward momentum slowed even as the dark outline of the stony coast became clear and the sound of booming surf filled his ears. If he had needed any more motivation to row harder that surely did it.

There was sharp pain in his shoulders but he ignored it, gritted his teeth and silently prayed as he rowed. Finally he began making forward progress against the tide and slowly made his way back out to sea. Better to battle the sea further from the coast, he thought.

He watched forlornly as his pilotless boat finally struck the rocks. The sound of splintering wood and shrieking metal reached his ears as the waves repeatedly bashed the hull against unyielding rock. As he sat mesmerized another wave struck him from behind and he lost one of his oars. "Shite!" His curse was devoured by the wind, which howled back his answer.

He grasped his last paddle in a death-grip and continued rowing out to sea, his craft turning back and forth as he constantly made corrections. Casey turned on the raft's bright flasher in hopes someone would spot his small craft. Now he was at the mercy of the sea, with one oar to stave off the storm.

The sound of the helicopter lifting off from the Conor Shipping helipad was deafening. Beth, Sean, and Seamus waited until it had leveled off and Cork had disappeared from view before resuming their conversation.

"Thanks for coming along, Seamus," Beth said.

"No bother," Seamus said. "When Sean called to have someone cover his class, I thought you could use another hand. After we drop you and Sean off, I'll take over as spotter for the pilot. The seas are very calm now, with excellent visibility. We'll find him if the Aran Islanders don't first."

"Just be careful out there," Sean said, grasping his friend's shoulder.

They watched Killarney's lakes sweep past. It was only a moment until they were over Tralee Bay, then the mouth of the mighty Shannon that separated County Clare from Kerry and Limerick Counties. Ralph, the pilot, followed the coast to Liscannor Bay and moved inland towards Ennistimon. Beth pointed out the landmarks to him. He touched down in a green pasture, the grass flattened to the ground by the whirlwind from the chopper's blades.

Sean and Beth crouched down as they exited and then turned to watch Seamus take off again, before running partway to the house. Mairin came out onto the porch and waved as they approached, her arms opening in greeting. Mother and daughter clung tightly to each other, each afraid to say a word, until they had given each other solace.

"Mum, how are you? Any word?"

"I'll tell you inside, dear. Julian is over at Mrs. Clancy's. I came back here when I got your call." Almost out of breath, she looked up at the tall man blotting out the sun. "And this must be Sean."

"It's good to meet you, Mrs. O'Hara, although I'd wish for better circumstances."

"Yes. Now you will be calling me Mairin, after this? Come inside, the two of you. A cup of tea will stand us all." The roar of the blades had finally receded, and the helicopter was now a small speck in the cloudy sky.

Mairin led them into the sun-filled breakfast room, setting them by the large bay window and poured tea.

"This was my favorite spot as a child, sitting on the window seat with the curtains drawn," Beth said.

"Her own private world," Mairin said. "We always knew where to find her, curled up with a book for a pillow."

Beth asked her question again. "What's the latest news, Mum?"

"Encouraging, so far. Padraic and some of his friends went over what was left of the Hags Head and found the raft missing. The lashings were untied, so Casey had time to get it ready, is what they guess. The raft is smallish, but fairly new." She paused as concern spread across her face again. "I'm afraid they found a paddle broken nearby washed up on shore, so he had no way to maneuver it. His friends are covering the area in the direction of the wind and currents. Galway Coastal Rescue also has a couple of planes and helicopters scouring the area."

"Seamus is spotting for the chopper that brought us here," Beth said.

"Bless him, such a wonderful gentleman. And Mr. Conor's help is greatly appreciated. Now, what was that police business all about? I heard about a murder down there on the wireless. Do you know who it was?"

Beth clasped her hands together and leaned forward to tell her mother the story. She watched Mairin float fingers to her face before they settled nervously on her chest. It was long moments after Beth finished before her mother spoke again.

"Beth, child, it's all so horrible. To think you and Julian had to put up with that..." Mairin used her apron to blot her eyes. "...that man all these years, and then the police accuse you of murder. Why, they should have given you a medal."

Beth glanced over at Sean who seemed distinctly uncomfortable. What was it that Eamonn held over him? Even now?

"Poor Eamonn, he only knew pain, and that's all he could give," Beth said. "Maybe he'll rest easier now." Beth looked at both of them for a moment. "I'll feel better when Inspector O'Neill finds the killers. I'm still uneasy about them running loose."

"Killers, is it?" Her mother's eyes opened wide. "Are you safe here, d'ye think?"

"The inspector did tell us to be careful, after filling us in on what he'd found. Well, he did after he checked out Sean's shoe size, anyway." She smiled at Sean, but got no answering smile. Instead he turned away and looked out the window at lowering clouds. Then with a sigh he turned back and finally managed a smile.

"I felt like Cinderella, except I prayed the shoe wouldn't fit," Sean added.

Mairin looked from one to the other, detecting a line of tension she thought the murders had produced. "You two have been through a lot in the last few days," Mairin said.

"You have enough room for everyone here, Mum?"

"Oh, yes, plenty of room here for Sean and Seamus. Now, did you say Mr. Conor is coming up himself, Beth?"

"He's driving up with his doctor," Beth said.

"Has his own private doctor, does he?"

"He hasn't been in the best of health, Mum. But I think our fine Irish weather is putting him right."

"Well, we've room for them, too."

When the phone rang, all three went over to the table where it sat. Sean stood behind Beth with his hands on her shoulders, and she leaned back into him.

"Yes?" She waited through the static. "Yes, this is she." Mairin frowned into the receiver. "A lot of static is what I'm getting." After futile moments trying to hear, she replaced the phone in its cradle and turned. "It's a bad connection. They're working on a patch from ship-to-shore. It sounded like... like he was really lost ...gone."

Beth moved from Sean's embrace and went to her, holding her tight; willing her own strength to flow into Mairin. Her mother clutched Beth's shoulders, and buried her face in Beth's blouse, her sobs quietly muffled. Beth watched Sean helplessly spread out his hands at his side, palms towards her. Then to her surprise, he spoke.

"He's going to be fine Mrs... Mairin. After all, he has me to meet yet... and I him."

Mairin rewarded Sean with a weak smile while she and Beth held each other, and waited out the long minutes together. They were riveted by the sound of the next ring. Beth felt each ring send chills up her spine. Mairin picked up the receiver and held her breath before speaking.

"Yes?"

"Is this Mrs. O'Hara? Hello, can you hear me?"

"Yes, this is she. Who is it?"

"This is Padraic O'Brien of Inishmore."

"Of course, Padraic, what news have you got?"

"We're still searching. I know Casey. This storm wouldn't stop him. Probably floating in his raft, bored waiting, wondering when I'll fetch him. We have a couple of them noisy eggbeaters up there using lights now, but we have to stop until morning. Our curraghs can't be out any longer, much as the lads want to stay with it."

"I understand," said Mairin. "My prayers and blessings to you all."

Beth knew the grave look that went with her mother's sigh, seeing her slumped shoulders, weighed down by concerns real and imagined.

CHAPTER 37
CASTLE O'HARA

Beth sat up in bed, the last remnants of her dream fading even as she tried to remember it. She was sure it was about her father, images of churning seas still playing in her mind, but the outcome of the dream was lost. She turned to face Julian, curled next to her. He was warm to her touch, and she felt his forehead.

"Umerug. Leave her 'lone...don't."

"Julian, wake up."

"Huh? Wha?"

"You have a bad dream, Jules?"

Beth knew it was the same bad dream. She stroked his cheek as his eyes opened wide and he looked around. Propping up some pillows behind her son, she waited for a response.

"It was the same one, Mum." Julian frowned as he tried to describe it to her. "Except now he had really long, bony fingers. Like that Halloween skeleton. Really creepy."

Beth held him tight as he trembled. "You are a little feverish, darling. Why don't you stay in bed? I'll make you some toast and tea."

"With lots of milk?"

"Of course." Kissing his forehead, she threw on a dressing gown, and went downstairs to the kitchen. Her mother was sitting at the table looking out the window, her eyes puffy, but her jaw firm. She looked up when Beth came in and put on a brave smile.

"How did you sleep, dear?"

"Fine, Mum. Did you manage to get some sleep?"

"I think so," Mairin said. "I remember punching the pillow a lot, though."

"Julian has a little fever. He had that same dream again. It's strange; both times he was feverish, too."

"The Tuatha De Danann often had prophetic visions when they had a fever."

"The Druids?"

"Indeed, the Druids. Some of our own descendants carried those traditions forward. Sadly, none for centuries."

Beth watched her mother reach for the telephone just before it rang.

"Hello? This is Mairin O'Hara."

"Mairin, it's Padraic again. We found him! He's fine. Well, spittin' mad, actually, since he lost his boat, but he'll be glad to hear your dear voice again, I'll wager."

"That's wonderful news! Bless you, Padraic. Bring him home safe to me, please."

"It'll be my very own pleasure, Mairin. He'll be on the Ballyvaughan docks in jig time." He filled her in on the details and then hung up.

Beth came over to her mother's side just as Sean entered the room, followed by John and his doctor.

"What is it? Good news?"

"The best, Sean! They found Dad, and he's all right!" Beth moved behind her mother and placed her arms around her neck. Mairin tilted her head back into Beth's chest before reaching up with her free hand to gently touch her face. They stayed like that, eyes closed for a moment in silent communion. When Beth opened her eyes, Sean was holding hankies out to both of them. Her mother replaced the phone and addressed them all.

"They're bringing him in to Ballyvaughan on Padraic's fishing boat. Then John's helicopter will bring him to the hospital in Ennis. He's in poor shape, but more upset at losing his boat."

"Tell him I'll buy him ten new boats," John said. "Just so he gets back safe and sound."

"Is Granddad back?"

They turned to see Julian come in, his hair still pressed to his scalp. Sean picked him up, and was hugged fiercely in return.

Beth felt fresh tears form as she watched them together. "Yes, love, you'll see him very soon, now."

The women hugged and the men clapped each other on the back. Then they all danced an improvised jig while Julian sat on a chair, clapping them on. Finally, tears dried and feet tired, they all piled into chairs and couches.

"I'll have breakfast ready soon. I hope you all brought your appetites. I know mine is getting sharp," Mairin said.

Mike McAfee hated to be kept waiting, particularly in an exposed hotel room. Its square dimensions offered little relief from its commonplace furniture, or the bleak morning view of Shannon airport which the lone window provided. Still, after dropping off the rented car, he was almost home. He had tried to keep the IRA out of the mess that grew around Conor's murder, but he feared he had not been too successful. He felt as if he were in a foreign country, even though it was only a short flight to Belfast. He would not breathe easier until he was home.

At the agreed-upon knock, he moved swiftly to the door, checked the peephole and unlocked it. "About time," he said. "What kept you?" He looked down at the rustling of a paper bag.

"Traffic in Limerick was nasty. Here, I got you this for your headache."

A chill went through him as he looked up into the black cylinder of a silencer. It hissed once at him and his head jerked back. He tried to step back to recover his balance, but found himself falling. There was something hot on his forehead and he tried to reach it, but his body refused to work. His last sensation was the insubstantial feel of the floor as it came up to meet him.

Regis took the call from John Conor. He began making notes, finding his scrawl becoming jerky and unreadable as the significance of the information hit him. As soon as Conor rang off, Regis tore the page off the pad and raced to Brendan's office. He entered without knocking.

"Are we not observing the social conventions, now, Regis?"

"Sorry, sir, but this is really important." He started to drop it on the inspector's desk, then realized only he could decipher it. "Mr. Conor got an interpretation of the will. Apparently, the phrase 'if she cannot carry out the duties of protector' would apply if she was in jail and unable to take care of her son. In that case, Williams would manage the estate and the company on Julian's behalf, upon Mr. Conor's death."

"So heads, Williams is in charge if O'Hara dies, and tails, he's in charge if she goes to jail. That's a very definite motive."

"Conor didn't comment on it, but he sounded worried." Regis turned as the door burst open again and Jenny came in waving a notepad.

"We found it!"

"I take it you don't mean a new way to break into my office, Jenny."

"Oh, sorry. But I got back a positive response on the trench coat belt from Hampstead Clothiers on Wellington Road. They sold two in the past week. One to a local doctor, but the other one was sold to a Mr. Williams of Newbury, England."

"That's our man." Brendan said as he pounded his fist on the desk. "I'd say he took a real personal involvement in this murder. I'm going to request a warrant that he be detained while we search his car and person. Also his rooms at the Nevermore House, and anywhere else he's checked in. Regis, see to it."

Regis went out the door right behind Jenny, passing her as he said, "Good work, Jenny. You know, I think you're starting to think like the inspector."

"Regis, a compliment? You must be slipping."

"I'm glad you think so."

As the phone rang, Brendan reached for it with one hand, while jotting notes with the other. He was looking at his notes, only half intent on the conversation, until the mention of IRA got his attention.

"What was that again, Pat?"

"The request you put out yesterday about your suspects. I think we found one of them. Our boys are just getting there to check out the corpse, so if you're here in the next couple of hours, we'd be glad to wait before removing it."

"Have you got an ID yet?"

"His wallet's missing, but he was about the right size for McAfee. He was knee-capped, both knees, then one shot right between the eyes. Nasty business! Close enough for powder burns on his forehead. No one heard a thing and we suspect it was a silenced weapon."

"That sounds like an IRA assassination." Brendan considered the other facts just uncovered. "Or it could have been the removal of an accomplice that was now a liability."

"So this is related to the case you're on then?"

"Right, and our suspect could well be still in the area. I'll take the helicopter. Where should I put down?"

"It's close to Shannon Airport, just use our pad there. I'll be by to pick you up."

"Thanks, Pat. I owe you." As soon as he put the phone down, he was yelling for his officers, giving them his orders as soon as they arrived. "Jenny, what did you find out about Williams?"

"He's checked out of the Nevermore House. He wasn't there this weekend past."

"Blast. Well, check the phone records. No, better still, ask Conor what numbers Williams gave him before Conor arrived in

Cork. When you find the place he stayed at on Sunday, here's a list of what I want you and Regis to look for. I'm taking a little ride up to Shannon Airport. Looks like one of our suspects was killed in a hotel close by."

Regis said, "Should we consider Williams armed and dangerous?"

"Assume he is."

Jenny took the lead entering the Nevermore House. She walked over to a black walnut desk. It took up most of the space on the right side of the wide stairway to the second-floor rooms. The desk's green-domed lamp cast harsh light onto a worn ledger. Under its light, a woman in a teal business suit was running her finger down a column. She peered up at them through octagonal glasses resting low on her nose.

"Yes, can I help you?"

Jenny flashed her ID, and the clerk's eyebrows rose as her eyeglasses dropped lower on her nose. "Constable Magruder of the Cork police. Wanted to inquire about one of your guests."

"Which of our guests do you wish to know about?"

"Ian Williams." Jenny watched her flip back the pages, quickly coming to the entry.

"Yes, Mr. Williams did stay with us for a week. He checked out Tuesday, this week."

"Has his room been booked since?"

"Yes, but they won't check in until later today. Would you like to see the room?"

"Yes, and we'd like to talk to the maid who cleaned it. Is that possible?"

"Surely. That would be Mary. She's still on duty. Oh, there she is."

Jenny followed her gaze towards a rear entrance from which a red-cheeked, plump young woman emerged. She looked at Jenny apprehensively as she drew close. "Constable Magruder of the

Cork Garda, Mary. I'd like to speak to you about one of the guests."

"Yes, Sir, I mean Constable."

Jenny looked behind her to see what devilment Regis was up to. He was wearing the most angelic look she'd ever seen. "How am I doing?"

"Grand, Jenny. Just grand," Regis said.

"Mary, what can you tell us about the gentleman that was in 4A last week? Mr. Williams."

"That would be the tall Englishman?" After Jenny nodded, she continued. "Well, he acted a little odd. But he was English, after all."

Jenny and Regis exchanged amused looks before she continued. "Yes, but what in particular did you notice? Did he entertain visitors? Keep strange hours?"

"I only remember one visitor. A man about forty or so, burly, short."

"Did you catch his name?"

When the maid shook her head, Jenny tried to think what direction Brendan would want to take with the questioning. "What kind of hours did he keep? Did he ever go out late and return in the early morning, say?"

"Oh, I think someone would notice that! The main door is locked after ten. I turn in then, myself."

Jenny felt Regis's hand on her shoulder, and knew he wanted to ask questions, which was just as well. She was getting nowhere.

Regis turned to the maid and rubbed his jaw, something Jenny had seen Brendan do countless times before asking a question. "Mary, how would someone leave the hotel late at night without rousing anyone?"

"You mean sneak out?"

"Exactly. Is that the back door?"

"Yes. He could get out that way, but it locks as soon as you close it."

"And to get back in?"

"You need a special key. Only Mrs. Finch has the key." Regis glanced back at Jenny and looked a question at her.

"I think we should take a look at this door, don't you, Regis?"

The maid took the lead with Jenny and Regis following in her wake. The door appeared quite substantial, painted a functional black with a modern door handle and latch that gleamed in the low light. Regis opened it and squatted to look at the locking mechanism end plate. He rubbed his hand over it and then invited Jenny to inspect it. She wasn't sure what to look for until she noticed pieces of debris that were sticky to the touch. Then she had it. "This is some kind of tape here. This door was taped over recently, wasn't it Regis?"

"That would be my guess," he said. "Williams could have made his exit and entrance through here. Let's check the room and call this in. Do you want to see if the rest of the staff knows anything?"

"Yes," Jenny said. "We should also attend to the other item on this list."

Brendan saw the patrol car pulling up just as they touched down at Shannon Airport, near an Aer Lingus Cargo warehouse. He clapped the pilot on the back and ran, head lowered, over to the vehicle displaying a Limerick Garda emblem on the door. The door swung open and a thin, stooped man with sad eyes exited and offered his hand. It was his friend Sergeant Patrick O'Shea.

"Pat, good to see you again. Thanks for waiting."

"No bother," Pat said. "My own forensic expert is out sick. I could use your expertise. It's a bad business, this."

"You don't know the half of it."

When they were underway, Brendan filled Pat in on the highlights of the case, including descriptions of the other two suspects.

"I'm confused about something, Brendan. Why did this Williams help out the IRA?"

"Who said he did? I have no evidence that anything they did was official IRA business. I think Williams is just using these poor bastards to serve his own ends."

"Using the IRA? How?"

"You mean you've never heard of Special Air Services agents posing as provos? Feeding them information about a barracks they can assault for guns, only to run into an ambush."

"Like those three lads killed in Gibraltar in '88, you mean." Pat said. "I'm glad I don't have to work up there. Probably have joined the Ra like my Uncle John if I had. Hip deep in me own piss in the H block by now."

"Is he finally out?"

"What's left of him," Pat said. "He still worries about loyalist death squads. Wouldn't want any of that going on here."

"Some of it still filters down," Brendan said. "There's been a lot of talk about a loyalist backlash, with sectarian violence moving this way. That was one the things that bothered me about this Williams fellow."

"How's that?"

"He's a loyalist and influential. If he gets his hands on Conor Shipping, there's no telling how much money he could funnel into the six counties. I mean shipping, for Christ's sake. He could even bring the munitions to them."

"That's a damned unpleasant thought," Pat said. "I hope we catch him fast."

"I've alerted John Conor, but he still doesn't believe Williams would do this. I need hard evidence to persuade Conor to change his will . . . again. And to watch his back, for that matter."

The car pulled up to a neutral-looking airport hotel. Brendan was sure he'd seen the same one in every airport he landed at. So far, he didn't see any reporters, which was a blessing this close to the airport. They took the outside stairs to the second floor where the officer guarding the door recognized Pat and opened it.

"No sign of forced entry," Pat said. "This is where we found him, poor chap."

Brendan looked at the body, stretched out on a blood-soaked rug. Dark stains covered each knee, and the head was thrown back. He checked the small entrance wound in the center of the forehead, noted the powder burns, and checked the exit wound. "This could be McAfee. Looks like the fellow whose picture came over the wire."

"Christ! The shot took off most of the back of his skull," Pat said as he backed up. He turned to a man taking scrapings off the rug. "Did you locate the bullets yet?"

"All except the head shot, Inspector," the officer said. "Is this our Corkman?"

"Inspector Brendan O'Neill, this is Johnny O'Grady," Pat said. "He's taking over for Frank."

Brendan shook hands with the bright-faced muscular man. "What have you got, Johnny?"

"As far as I can tell from the entrance wound in the head, the bullets all came from the same weapon. Looks like a 9mm round," Johnny said. "Shot at close range in both knees and the head. Someone wanted him to suffer, I'd say."

"You recovered the bullets shot in the knees, I see," said Brendan.

"Right. One, almost intact, penetrated pretty far into the floor; the other shattered the right kneecap, and pieces of that bullet were all over the place," Johnny said.

"So he was definitely on the rug when he was shot in the knees."

"I think so. I'm just learning blood spatter analysis, mind you, but that's what these patterns around both knees would suggest, and the one bullet in the floor was at the correct angle."

"What about the head?"

"The rug behind his head was too heavily soaked to make out a clear pattern," Johnny said. "And the damage suggests that that bullet should be in the floor, too. Haven't been able to verify that." He looked directly at Brendan. "I was told not to move the body until you saw it."

"Notice anything else odd about the rug?"

"No, except it's a bad color for this room."

Brendan smiled before continuing; remembering how vital a sense of humor was to staying sane in their work. "Right. Actually, I was surprised it wasn't twisted underneath him. If I was shot in the knee, I think I'd move around a lot in pain before the head shot. And both knees?"

"Right enough." Johnny's face brightened. "That's what was bothering me about this, and I didn't see it."

Brendan went over to the back wall. "You have some fine flecks here at about the height of his head. My guess is he was standing, perhaps having just opened the door, when he was shot." Brendan mimicked the motion of opening a door, being shot and moving backwards.

"He could have fallen over here, landing on his back. Then the shot in each knee would produce these spatter characteristics. That's the other thing. Someone wouldn't be so cooperative about positioning the knee for an accurate shot, yet both of these shots were bang on." After Pat flinched he added, "Sorry, poor choice of words." He watched O'Grady scratch his head as he turned, trying to visualize what Brendan was describing.

"And where would that bullet end up, then, do you think?"

"As luck would have it," Brendan said, "I think it went out the open window. We can't be positive of the angle until an autopsy, but it looks about right." Using a pen as a visualization tool he explained the path of the bullet.

"The shot went through soft brain matter, but there might be some bullet particles from hitting the skull cap. Lift up his head and search for any signs of a bullet. I'm betting you won't find any." Brendan looked on as O'Grady made a thorough check of the rug and floor.

"You're right, Inspector. If he was done on the floor, it was a magic bullet."

"I've never been one for magic bullet theories, anyway. You, Johnny?" The officer looked up at Brendan confused for a moment, and then smiled his reply.

Pat said, "You're saying this was made to look like an IRA execution?"

"Yes, and I think the fella who did it is still in the area. I'm going to ring up my men and see what they've found."

"Good work, Brendan," Pat said. We'll give you a full coroner's report on this as well."

"Fine," Brendan reached inside his coat and pulled out some paperwork. "Pat, put out a bulletin to detain either of these men if they try to board a plane. Here's a fact sheet on them."

"This one looks like a mean bastard," Pat said pointing to Peter Deagan's image.

"He is, but Williams is the real dangerous one," Brendan said pointing to the other sheet. "Assume they are armed as well."

"Fair enough."

Brendan went out to the landing and watched the planes take off. He hoped his suspects were not trying to escape that way, not when he was breathing down their necks.

CHAPTER 39
CASTLE O'HARA

Sean Carey lay back on the pillows on the couch, his eyes focused on the rain drops collecting on the bay window. He was mesmerized by nature's frenetic painting on its many panes. He blinked, and then focused beyond the glass barrier at the wind-throttled trees in the middle distance. They were trying vainly to keep their leafy garments intact. Then the wind seemed to turn its attention on the house, its attenuated howl curling through unseen cracks, and spilling chilly reminders of its displeasure around him.

Now that he and Beth were in the clear, it was time for him to tell her about his drunken ride to hell. He needed to be completely truthful with Beth or they could have no life together and he wanted one desperately. And while they were both alone with Julian asleep upstairs, this might be his best chance.

Beth came into the room with a tray of tea with scones and jam, which was always a welcoming sight to Sean. But now he steeled himself for what he had to say; finally. His hand shook as he took a sip of tea and then set it on the end table.

"What is it Sean? You look very troubled."

Sean thought of what he had to say knowing he could lose this glorious woman that had brought him back to life. "I need to t-tell you something else about Eamonn and me." He took a deep breath as if diving into a dark sea from which he feared he would never breech the surface.

Beth sat still, her knees pressed together, her arms hugging her shoulders as if awaiting a killing blow. "Is this about the girl you might have gotten into trouble?"

Sean smiled grimly. "No, I lied about that. It was Eamonn that had gotten her into trouble and then later he had bought off her family."

He leaned closer to her as he continued. "This was sometime later. We had been drinking at the Sea Mist. We downed the better part of a bottle of single malt scotch and Eamonn as always said he was okay to drive. So we headed back to your cottage, but Eamonn took a wrong turn and we ended up on Drumdubh East."

Beth nodded, "I know the road."

"By then I had dozed off, since I was no help with the roads around there. I was awakened by a squeal of brakes and a jarring impact. It was good I had my seatbelt on since I was thrown forward violently. I was a little dazed, but Eamonn got out of the car swearing."

Sean gulped some tea and then continued. "He got back in the car, his face grim. He said we hit a drunk that had staggered onto the roadway. I was going to get out of the car, but he held me back. He told me it was too late; the man was dead."

"Oh, Sean! What did you do then?"

Sean wished he had a scotch now, and swallowed hard before responding.

"Eamonn said no one had seen the accident. It was the dead of night, he said." Sean paused a moment and drew in a nervous breath. "He said we should just leave the scene."

"Oh no. What did you do?"

"I told him we had to report it, but he said no and then drove off. I pleaded with him, but then he said if I didn't go along he'd convince the girl to say it was me that had gotten her pregnant." He looked up at her and saw the look of horror on her face and could barely go on.

"I would have been thrown out of school and I'd worked so

hard. So hard!" Sean lowered his face into his hands and his hands into fists. "I'm so sorry. You must think I'm weak for giving in."

"As I'd given in to Eamonn," Beth said a catch in her voice.

Sean looked intently at her. There was sadness there, but not disgust as he'd feared. He breathed in hope.

"I did try to find out who it was later. To see if there was something I could do for the family. I knew Eamonn would do nothing, but I couldn't let it go. I checked all the papers, but found nothing. There were no funerals around that time and no one was reported missing. I thought, surely someone would have missed the poor fellow."

Beth was suddenly alert. "Sean, you said you never got out of the car, right?"

Puzzled, Sean nodded.

"So you never saw a body. It was just Eamonn's word." Angrily, she continued, "And now he had your solemn pledge to never speak about it or the girl he got in trouble."

"But we hit something! That I know."

Beth nodded then continued, "Did you know there's a big sheep farm where you were driving? And the Clancy brothers let them graze all over the place. I've almost hit one more than once. In broad daylight."

Suddenly Sean was back on that road. He could almost feel the heater blowing hot air on him, making him drowsy. The contour seat molded to his body, the subtle vibration of the luxury car's powerful engine, all lulling him into a dream-like state. Then there was a squeal of brakes and the heavy impact of a body. It was a substantial weight, but it could have been a sheep.

Now he focused on the sounds he had heard. Could it have been a sheep's mournful bleat and death throes? The cry didn't seem human, the more he thought about it. But the cries still tore at his heart as any animal's death would for him.

"Jesus, Beth, I think you're right!" He jumped out of his chair, unable to contain himself. "It finally makes sense." Then full realization took hold. "That bastard set me up."

Beth gave him a sad smile, "Yes, always the bastard. Do you realize how he's manipulated both of us?"

Beth got up and began pacing, breath puffing from the sides of her mouth as if emitting steam. Then she began muttering.

Sean watched in amazement, but finally said, "It doesn't make a lot sense to be mad at him now. We have better places to focus our energy."

Beth stopped pacing and then looked down at him. She finally smiled, "Oh yes, we do." Her smile became lustful. "And soon."

Sean was at first bemused, then a smile he could not hold back, spread to the tips of his ears.

"I see that look," Beth said.

Peter Deagan hated taking orders. But now he had no choice if he wanted to stay out of jail. The stories he'd heard of his mates locked up, bullied by the guards, making hell all the more brutish was more than he could tolerate.

But could he really kidnap a child? He'd never sunk that low. No, on second thought, he had sunk even lower. It was his bomb that had caused the fiery death of a small boy and his mother. He wouldn't have pressed the remote, knowing the target's family was in the car, but it wasn't his choice; only making the bomb.

He looked down at his hands and thought about how good it was to send his fists crashing into Eamonn's smug face. Luring him to the bridge was easy. The fool thought Peter would actually kill his wife. Against all logic, Peter still thought he could win Beth over, but he wanted something he could never have.

Still, Patrick had said it was Eamonn that had gotten Peter's contract terminated and that was enough to stoke his anger. But the man never admitted it, even after repeated blows and now Peter realized someone else was pulling the strings at Conor Shipping and he was being played for a fool.

The peat fire came alive as zephyr fingers spun it to a higher pitch, pushing the earthy scent out into the room. Beth moved closer to Sean, a self-satisfied sigh full on her lips. She rested her chin on his knee, and the weave of her hair draped his leg in reddish gold. He enjoyed the way it piled over her cheek, exposing the nape of her neck. He let his fingers roam through the curls in the hope that they would become ensnared. Sean felt her weight shift as she lifted her head to speak.

"Why haven't we heard from them?"

"I don't know." Sean said and again looked out the window. "It could take a while yet. Your Mum will know when to contact us." They both started when the phone rang. Beth lunged over him to pick it up.

"Yes...What!" Beth waved Sean away when he tried to ask who was on the phone. She was listening intently, and then she smiled.

"He is! Oh, thank God. What? Broke down? I'll be right there."

Sean stood by her impatient to get the news. "Well, who was it?"

"Mairin. They're at the hospital. The doctor says Dad is going to be fine. He's weak from exposure, and clinging to that battered raft all night didn't help, but he's a fighter."

"Your whole family are fighters; especially you." She acknowledged his compliment with an engaging smile that held his attention for a moment before he resumed. "What was the problem, then?"

"Her car broke down, and she and Seamus are stuck in town. I'm taking the van to pick them all up."

"Your Mum seems to have the same luck with cars that you do,"

Beth stuck her tongue out before replying. "Will you be all right here with Julian? I know he wants to come, but he's still a little sick. I don't want him out in this weather."

"Of course. I'll see if I can win a few hands and get some of my money back."

"Don't let him get the upper hand, Sean. He's pretty good at rummy."

"So I've noticed. Hurry back."

Inspector O'Neill nervously cleaned his pipe while Jenny Magruder drove. His first thought had been Regis, but his sergeant wasn't about to set foot in a helicopter and he needed someone to join him fast at Shannon Airport. He knew Williams was making his final move after eliminating McAfee, and Beth and Julian were in grave danger. This mother and son he'd protect with his life if necessary.

On the other hand, Jenny had been more than eager to join him. What he had observed over the last week confirmed that she was a brave, highly competent officer. Not that it should surprise him. He'd been over her personnel file many times looking for any signs of weakness. He wanted to spare her any unnecessary pain. Was he being too protective? Old habits. Sometimes she seemed like a daughter he never had.

"I should have figured it out sooner, Jenny. If Williams had not been so meticulous about getting the right trench coat, I might never have been on to him. The first hint was learning he'd been in the constabulary, though. I remember when our unit was called in to support the Derry RUC, how hard the feelings were towards the people in the Bogside. I knew trouble was brewing."

"William's unit and yours were involved in 'Bloody Sunday,' Inspector?"

Brendan sadly shook his head. "That was the final straw for me. My job was to protect the people in the Bogside, not harm them. When I saw what some of the other constables were doing during the riots... I heaved my guts up. I wanted to turn in my badge then and there."

"Why didn't you?"

"Because there was a lot of blame to pass around, and I wasn't going to set myself up for playing scapegoat. Now, Bill Ealey, as he called himself then, had been given a chance to retire, or get mustered out for his actions. Not hard to see where some of his hatred came from, is it?"

"So William Ealey becomes Ian Williams. What arrogance! We got a quick reply to our query, once we sent his photo up to the Derry barracks," Jenny said. "They still remembered him."

"That was good detecting, figuring out he'd rented two cars," Brendan said. He was very pleased, only a father could have been more so.

"It was Beth who gave me the idea," Jenny said. "She called to tell me about the green Honda, and her guess that Williams had used it to shadow her. He rented it when he arrived at the airport."

"Right, the kind of car that suited his frugal personality. The black BMW he rented for the weekend, on the other hand, suited his murderous side."

"Regis and I asked if anyone saw that car around the Nevermore House," Jenny said. "A neighbor a block away identified a similar car parked on his street on Monday morning. It stuck out like a sore thumb. It was gone when the neighbor returned from work that evening. It fit the description of the sedan Williams rented in Cork."

"So Williams shared the Honda with McAfee," Brendan said, "Letting McAfee use it to follow both Conors. He was at Doyle's place on Sunday for dinner where he dropped off the BMW. Then he had McAfee drive him back to Cork in the Honda."

"So, back in Cork, he taped the rear door of the Nevermore House on his way out on Sunday night. What did he do next, Inspector?"

"He waited outside the Imperial for Conor to walk out, and trailed him to where Deagan was waiting to beat him up. When he saw Deagan leave the bridge, he went in and used the scissors on Conor that he stole from O'Hara's cottage on Saturday. Conor probably never regained consciousness. Deagan pounded him pretty hard."

"But, Inspector, couldn't he have just waited by the bridge with Deagan?"

"Only if Williams wanted Deagan involved in homicide, and could convince him to do it. He's too clever for that. See, he never let on to McAfee or Deagan what he was doing. And he knew they were both IRA, even if they denied it. That was the reason for the two cars."

They had just left Shannon in a rental and headed north on the M18 headed toward Ennis. Brendan adjusted his seat back to get more comfortable in the compact. It was fine for Jenny but he had to keep shifting his body to ease the pain in his back. Sighing, he resumed their conversation.

"After he ditched Conor's car and walked to Doyle's place, he had plenty of time to drive back to Cork. No, all he had to do was pay Deagan to beat him up, and then follow Conor to the assignation that Deagan set up. Deagan might have had suspicions later, and McAfee too, particularly if they compared notes. They still couldn't meet, though, because that would have blown their cover."

"Why did Deagan agree to beat up Conor, then?"

"Money, for starters. He must have been desperate when his contract was dropped. That was almost half his yearly gross. And he thought Conor was the one that instructed the university to drop his contract. That was another reason. Now we know it was Williams that had the contract cancelled. He set up Deagan perfectly and Peter had nowhere else to turn."

"Do you think Deagan is still active in the IRA?"

"Could be; we may never know," Brendan said. "But McAfee certainly was. He may have been trying to recruit Deagan again, or spy on Williams."

Jenny got off on the N85, heading west to come in below Ennis and then sped up before turning to Brendan. "Spy on him?"

"I had a long talk with an old crony in the constabulary. He wouldn't give me much information on loyalist activity, but he did mention that there was a lot of provo surveillance of Conor's Belfast offices. At first, I thought it was preparation for a hit. Now, I wonder if Williams hadn't been feeding money to the loyalists all along, and they were trying to get a fix on their supplier."

"How much money are we talking about, then?"

"Maybe not too much at first, but you remember Williams took over most of Conor's duties late last year?"

On her nod, he shifted position again before continuing. "And I told you about the munitions in that warehouse the IRA tried to bomb?"

"You think it was Williams that financed them, Inspector?"

"Ironic, wouldn't you say?" He softly chuckled. "Well, another contact said that a quarter of a million pounds dropped in the Ulster Freedom Fighters laps, and no one can figure out where it came from."

"Jesus, Mary," Jenny said. "Do you know how many guns and bombs that would buy?"

"I don't even like to think about it, Jenny."

Jenny hunched forward in her seat, willing the car to go faster. "We have to stop that son of a bitch, Inspector."

"We will, but please have a little regard for an old-fashioned Irishman, and go easy on the cursing, would you?"

"Why, Inspector? In America, a lot of women curse."

"Probably with good reason, too, but not here, please."

Her smile was wide as she looked over at him. "All right, seeing as how you're a proper gentleman, I'll hold my tongue."

As they rounded a tight corner there was a loud explosion and the car swerved dangerously out of control. Jenny swore as she tried to correct the partial spin they were in. Brendan braced himself on the passenger console. He also swore under his breath.

Sean and Julian sat by the fire, their stocking-clad feet curling close to the grate. Both made loud slurping sounds with their tea, each trying to outdo the other. Finally, Julian had to stop as he choked on the liquid. Giggling, he wiped his face. The house seemed suddenly quiet, too quiet. Both pricked their ears, turning in every direction to pick up a sound. After a moment, they heard a low shuffling noise coming from the back of the house.

"Was that sound coming from the porch, do you think?"

Julian shrugged his shoulders. "I don't know Sean, but it sounded kinda creepy."

"Well, don't worry lad, I'll go and see what it is."

Sean slipped into his shoes and moved into the hallway leading to the glassed-in porch. The storm-darkened sky made mirrors of the porch windows, and he saw only his image reflected. "I'm on the wrong side of this one-way glass," he muttered. Sean pressed his forehead against the cool pane and peered out, blocking the reflected light with his hands like binoculars to see into the distance.

His eyes were just beginning to adjust to the low light level when he jumped back startled. Had he just seen a dark presence flit past the driveway? His heart raced, and he worked at keeping his breathing steady. When he looked again, he saw nothing, heard nothing. He snapped on the outside light and it cast feeble light on the driveway. Only shadows remained, the branches of sheltering trees moving to the swirling wind's changing directions. He checked the lock and then went back into the living room and stopped. Julian was gone!

"Julian. Where are you?"

No answer.

"Julian!"

Looking around, he suddenly wondered why the storm was louder in this room. Then it hit him. The front door! He raced over to it and found it wide open. Rushing out the door, he spotted a figure moving down the driveway to a distant car. He had Julian. Sean ran after him, fear spreading in his chest like cold acid. His feet felt heavy, his shoes concrete slabs. When he was almost on him, the man turned and shoved Julian to the ground. Sean stared into eyes black as pitch.

"Peter! What the hell do you think you're doing?"

"Oh, just taking the lad for a little walk, is all." Peter's tone spoke of darker things.

"Get out of here."

"Not without my charge."

Peter lunged at Sean and pinned his arms, wrestling him to the ground. Sean was surprised at the suddenness of the attack. He squirmed on the ground trying to get free, but Peter's strength was almost overpowering. He finally leveraged his long legs, twisting from side to side, and broke free. He swung wildly, striking a glancing blow that Peter hardly noticed.

Sean had just started to get up again when Peter struck him in the chest with both hands clasped together, knocking the wind out of him. He gasped for breath, trying to maintain his balance. He had almost succeeded when he was struck hard by Peter's boot to his head. He felt his head snap back, impossibly far back, and then only blackness.

"Sean!"

His senses reeled. He could hear Julian but from a distance. His vision slid in and out of focus. Sounds roared in his ears. The smell and feel of earth assaulted his nose and he realized he was face down on the ground. He pressed upwards with his arms and a wave of nausea almost caused him to throw up. Gagging he tried once more to rise but only succeeded in tottered over onto his back. His senses swam, unable to distinguish up from down.

"Sean."

The sound was much fainter now. He could not tell if Julian was farther away, or if he was slipping away to another place. It seemed too cold in that place, too hard. He had to rest, just for a little while. Then he would get up again.

Sean opened his eyes and watched two orbs of light come closer. They shimmered and danced up and down, like fuzzy moons, gliding in concert to some unknown beat. As he desperately tried to focus, they turned into head lamps. A car was coming directly towards him.

He lurched up and staggered on rubber legs toward the porch, which seemed impossibly far away. He weaved in place, unable to move from the spot as the sound of the engine grew louder. He tried moving to his left but the lights followed him, relentlessly pinning him in their ghostly beams. He waited for the impact, his legs refusing to move any longer.

He barely reacted to the squeal of brakes. Looking down, he saw the bumper inches from his legs, and placed his hands on the vehicle's hood to maintain his balance. Then he heard a door slam. The sound of steps coming closer dimly registered as a large figure came at him, and he steeled himself for another blow.

"Sean! Sean, what happened to you?"

He recognized Seamus's form silhouetted in the head lamps. He came over and held Sean up in his huge arms. They both turned as another car came up the drive. It was Mairin's battered Rover.

"What happened to you, Sean? Where's Julian?"

Seamus was gently shaking him as he repeated his last question. His eyes were still adrift in their sockets, tracking objects haphazardly. The van's passenger door opened, but he barely recognized Beth as she got out. Her face looked terribly white. When she was closer, she put a fist in her mouth to stifle a scream. The same scream he felt in his throat.

"Peter. It was Peter." He spit blood out of the side of his mouth, forming the words around a numbed jaw, and continued. "He came in the front door when I was checking the back." He slumped fully into Seamus's arms, his legs like jelly. Seamus held him tighter. Sean looked at Beth over his friend's shoulder. "I chased after him and tried to stop him, but he was too bloody strong."

"Oh, God. Oh, Sean." Beth opened the door as Seamus helped

Sean into the house. "What did he say? What does he want?"

The anguish in Beth's voice brought on a wave of guilt. How could he have let this happen? When Mairin entered and saw Sean's face she gasped and then went to fetch a first aid kit.

When he slumped into a chair, he got his mouth working somewhat better. "He didn't say what he wanted." He tried a sickly smile. "He said he was taking Julian for a little walk." Then anger took hold. "The bastard!"

Then another thought occurred to him. "How's Casey?"

Mairin used a disinfectant sheet to clean the blood from Sean's face, clucking her tongue as she went. Then she replied, "Casey wants out of the hospital. It's all the doctors can do to hold him there. And sure, he'll be all right; a few exposure problems, but cross as a bear. We jumped my car with the van and Seamus drove Beth back ahead of us." She looked at him, full of concern and worry.

The sound of a phone ringing somewhere in the house struck a discordant note. Beth leaped from her chair to answer it,

Seamus made sure Sean was settled in the chair before asking, "D'ye feel up to relating exactly what happened here?"

Sean felt his head begin to clear, but his tongue still felt too thick to fit inside his mouth. "I think he was alone. He must have tried to get in the back way, and then went around to the front when I came out on the porch. He ..." His voice trailed off as Beth came into the room, her expression unreadable.

Solemn-faced and pale, she sat down next to him, her eyes restlessly roaming his bruised face. After a long moment, she said, "Are you all right, darling? You look awful."

"Thanks. It's not the tie, is it?"

Beth didn't smile at his attempt at humor. His own throat was tight and he wanted nothing more than anything to cry out his anguish. But he couldn't. He didn't dare. She needed him desperately, even if she would not voice it.

Seamus turned to Beth. "Was that someone from the hospital, then?"

Beth paused before replying. "No, that was John's doctor; they missed the turning and are a bit lost." She shrugged, but her voice sounded distant and shaky to Sean, but it must have been seeing him banged up and Julian taken. God what a mess this day had become.

Beth touched the unbruised side of his face. "How are you feeling, Sean?

Lousy, but OK I guess."

She straightened up and fixed him with a determined look, and then turned to her mother. "I'll take the Rover and have them follow me back here." Mairin looked up at her, puzzled.

Beth moved over to the cloakroom and took down a slicker. She mumbled under her breath, but Sean registered what she said. "The dream; it's the dream become real." Then she was gone, only thin tendrils of water spread against the floor to mark her passage. Moments later they heard the Rover's engine start and the car turning around in the driveway.

It was not long after Beth departed that another car drove up to the house. Sean and Mairin exchanged puzzled looks and she went to the door.

"Oh, it's John and the doctor," she said turning, a confused look on her face.

Seamus signaled Sean to stay put and got up to greet them. To his retreating back Sean said, "How did they get back so soon?"

When John Conor and Dr. Mansfield entered they were quickly apprised of the situation. The look of horror and concern on John's face was obvious as he approached Sean. "How are you doing, son?" He put a hand on Sean's shoulder and he found it very reassuring somehow.

"I'll be much better when we get Julian back. But I'm OK."

John's face took on a dark cast. "It's that devil Deagan again. Why the hell didn't the inspector have him locked up already?"

He sat down heavily in a chair, his face contorted in thought. "It's ransom he wants and he knows I can provide it, the bastard. Has he called with his demands?"

Sean finally reacted to the word ransom. His mind was still in a bit of a fog but now he recalled Beth's words as she departed and he jolted upright. Reaching out a hand, he firmly grasped Seamus's arm. "Jesus, I know what she meant."

"Beth? Meant about what, Sean?"

"She said it was the dream become real. Did you hear her?"

"I heard something about a dream, but it made no sense," Seamus said. Behind him Mairin had a look of fright on her face. "Oh, Jesus, her dream about Julian in danger." She looked over to Sean. "And herself in danger, too!"

"It was her dream on the Cliffs of Moher she was talking about," Sean was out of his chair now. His friend looked warily at Sean, but Mairin nodded her head. She knew, too.

"What does it mean then?"

"In her dream, the wind carried Julian off the cliff. It could be a metaphor for a powerful force trying to harm him."

"Like Peter, you mean?" Seamus still looked confused and Sean could hardly blame him.

"Exactly. What if it was he who called, telling her to meet him there alone, if she wanted to see her son again?"

Seamus suddenly understood. "And then what?"

John and Tommy were still very confused. John asked, "Are you saying there was a phone call and you sent her out there by herself?"

Sean went over to John and now it was he placing a hand on John's shoulder. "Beth said the call was from you asking for help getting back here."

Tommy said, "No we just needed more petrol. That's what delayed us."

Sean nodded at that. "That was her excuse to get to the meeting place alone. I know that's what Deagan wanted." Another thought occurred to him. "He may be planning to return to the six counties and take Beth and Julian with him."

"That's crazy!" John was fully alarmed now.

"So is he." Sean said to him and then went over to the fireplace and hefted the poker. "But he won't get the better of me a second time, I promise you."

"You can't go out there," Seamus said. "You could have a concussion."

"There's no time, Seamus."

Tommy immediately went over to Sean. "Let me at least check you out first. Seamus is right, you know." He took out a pocket torch and passed it across Sean's eyes. After he turned it off there was concern in his face. "It could be dangerous to leave now."

"It will be dangerous for Beth and Julian if I don't! We're isolated here, too long for the police to respond in time."

Sean paused as other possibilities raced through his mind. What if he was wrong and they were out on a wild goose chase when the kidnapper called? What if it wasn't the cliffs, but some place in the Burren that reminded her of the dream? No, he'd trust his instincts this time.

As he straightened up he fought off another wave of nausea, but smiled at Seamus as if everything was fine. "I'm going."

"Well, you aren't going without me." Seamus then turned to John Conor. "You have the Cork Garda number for the inspector?" On John's nod, he added, "Call him and the local Garda, but caution them we might have a hostage situation and to proceed carefully."

John seemed relieved to have something to do. "You two be right careful out there. Remember O'Neill said there was also the mastermind and that might well be Williams." His face turned bitter. "And I trusted him like . . ." He looked at Sean, "Like a son."

Sean turned to Mairin, "Stay by the phone. In case I'm wrong."

"Be careful, Sean" Mairin hugged herself." This is a very dangerous man you're takin' on."

Sean nodded and then turned to Seamus. "Let's go, she has nearly a half-hour start on us." He concentrated on walking a straight line to the door, feeling a bit ridiculous holding a poker. "Uh, maybe you should drive, Seamus."

"You can bet on it, laddie," he said, shaking his head in disbelief.

"Thanks."

"For what?"

"For being there for us, Seamus." He gave John a warm look. "And you, John. Your help has been tremendous."

John Conor waved it off and said, "No bother." Then he gave Tommy a sheepish look.

Seamus took the lead as they went out. The light breeze picked up as they headed to the van, which sat there rocking gently in the wind.

CHAPTER 40
THE BURREN

Beth had never driven the Burren's back roads so recklessly. For the third time, she almost lost control going around a sharp bend. Coming out along the coast above Lahinch, she took the R478 that skirted Liscannor Bay, its grand sweep blunted by the rain. The road turned north and when she passed St Bridget's Well it was less than three kilometers to the Cliffs.

She slowed only long enough to catch sight of a tourist sign that pointed to the visitor's center. Above it she connected with Burren Way off the main road and drove slowly north. The instructions had been vague about the ruins where they would meet

Finally, she was at the Cliffs of Moher, her headlights pointing uselessly over the precipice and out to sea. The presence of the sea was like a heavy force pressing in on her. She killed the engine and lights and darkness surrounded her. The sound of her car door closing was swallowed up by the pounding of waves rising up the cliff's steep sides. The constant drumming seemed to surround and penetrate her.

She grabbed the slicker out of the back seat to protect her from the wind and rain that swept the clifftops. Her blouse and skirt would not offer much warmth. And the black slicker would make her a less conspicuous target against the lowering sky and cloud-obscured sun.

Beth's footsteps on the unyielding earth were muffled as

she turned her back on the sea and walked up the rise towards the ruins were she would meet her son's kidnapper. The rain had slackened, and a feeble sun peeked through cracks in the heavens, bleeding red on the horizon. There was enough light to discern a dim shape in the distance, which became a ruined wall as she got closer. Beyond it, she could make out the outline of an old church.

Whose voice had it been on the phone? It really didn't sound like Peter's, but it had been disguised, of that she was sure. She came up on the left side of the ruins where the waning light would reveal anyone hiding, waiting to catch her unawares. The topless casement windows cast twisted shadows in her path. The sea's muffled voice countered her labored breathing. No other sounds intruded. She held her breath while crossing the last few steps out of the ruin's shadow, wary of any sound or movement.

Beth stopped at the sound of stones rolling down an incline, and she spotted a shadow emerging from a doorway in the ruins. The indistinct shape took form as it came closer, but the face was still hidden in shadow. Then the apparition spoke.

"Beth, how very good to see you again."

"Who is it? Show yourself, you bastard!"

"Now, now, is that any way to talk?" The figure came closer. "How's this, can you see me well enough now?" A glimmer of light etched dark shadows down a long thin face, making the grin appear like a death mask. Bone-like fingers fluttered outwards in advance of the parody of a courtly bow.

"Ian!"

"Precisely."

"Where is my son?"

"Oh, did I say I had your son? My, my, what an oversight on my part. No, actually, I believe Deagan has your son. But taking good care of him, I'm sure. We do need him healthy after all, since he stands to inherit Conor's estate." All the while, his face held mocking innocence.

"The will. Somehow you set it up to benefit you."

"Of course. I must say, you're cleverer than I thought. If Glynnis hadn't told me about the inquiries made about the will," he placed his arms akimbo, "I might never have guessed how close the inspector really was."

"Did she tell you where we were, too?"

"Yes. Someone in love does very strange things sometimes." He stepped closer. "Don't you agree?"

"But why? That's what I don't understand. John trusted you. You wouldn't have lost your job." There was disbelief in his face. "We would have kept you on."

"Kept me on?" Lips pulled back from his teeth, he continued. "Like some insignificant lackey? Only there to do your bidding and lap up the table scraps? Oh, no, I wanted more, much more."

He was very close to her now and his eyes blazed. "I was practically running the company when John was ill. Do you think Eamonn could have done that? Eamonn in charge of the company would have been the worst possible choice! He didn't even pretend to respect me. He only saw me as a tool and a dirty one at that, to protect him from his – how should I say – indiscretions?" His chuckle sounded foul and sinister. "Your father-in-law I could stomach, at least."

"So you killed Eamonn, with my scissors. It wouldn't be hard to slip in unnoticed."

"No, indeed. You are so trusting here in the Republic; hardly a locked door in the south."

"Of course, you knew about the arrangement between Eamonn and me. And Sean, you followed him too." His self-satisfied smile was her answer. "And John was to be your next victim, wasn't he?"

"Perhaps," Ian said. "It depends on his health, after all, and his medication. Such a tricky thing and so easy to overdose."

"You played everyone against everyone with Machiavellian skill."

"Thank you." He produced another of his grisly bows. "And

with Eamonn dead and you in jail, who else do you think John could turn to?" Ian's cool delivery turned heated as he continued. "I treated him like a father. I should have been his son. Eamonn only knew how to spend money, not create it. And with both of you gone, I would be in complete control again."

"But why kill Patrick? What did he have on you?" Beth was desperately trying to buy time but for what, she didn't know.

"He saw Eamonn's car when I dumped the body. And he knew it was me that followed Deagan. Thought he could make a little extra on the side. But I don't accept blackmail from republican scum. The bastard would have used it to free some of his comrades, no doubt. I'm just sorry I didn't get to see Brendan's face when that bomb went off, but I only had a view of the back of the parking lot. But come, I have much to show you."

"Show me what? I'm not moving from this spot until you tell me."

Ian smiled his mirthless smile and then grabbed her arm in a vice-like grip. She struck out with her other hand but he seized it as well. She continued to resist, freeing one hand to rake his face. He struck her hard on the jaw. She heard her teeth click hard together, and then saw nothing but spinning blackness.

Jenny Magruder was able to get the car back under control, but the wobble up front told her they had a blowout. Brendan had the same thought. "A blowout now? Just what we need."

Before he was out of the car, Jenny already had the trunk open and was pulling out a spare. He reached in for the jack and lug wrench. Just then a Garda car, blue light flashing came up behind them and the driver got out. It was Sergeant O'Shea.

He came up to the inspector out of breath. "Brendan, we just got a call in from John Conor." He caught his breath as he came up to the car. "His grandson was kidnapped and they suspect Peter Deagan was the culprit."

Brendan slammed his fist on the hood. "Damn!"

The sergeant stepped back before he added. "And he said Sean Carey and someone named Seamus were going after him."

Brendan sighed, "Oh that's just grand." Nursing his sore fist he asked, "Did Mr. Conor say where they were heading?"

The sergeant nodded and said, "The Cliffs of Moher."

In the background Brendan heard the jack grinding and the car began to rise on its side. "Anything else?"

"Yes, and it might be related. A call was passed to me from Cork that a Duncan Cowell was trying to reach you." He pulled a message sheet out of his pocket and gave it to Brendan.

He turned to Jenny. "How does it look?"

Jenny stood up and brushed dust off her uniform. "It's pretty bad, Inspector. The wheel rim is badly dented."

"Pat, can we borrow your car? "You can call your HQ to come pick you up and bring reinforcements."

Turning back to Jenny, Brendan said, "Duncan wants us to meet him at the Cliffs of Moher visitor center."

Alongside the inspector, Jenny raised both eyebrows. "Then it's definitely related."

After contacting his office, Pat came back to them. "I have some of my men heading this way. We'll meet you at the cliffs, right?"

"Yes, rendezvous at the visitor center. We've no time to lose."

Jenny got into the driver's seat and Brendan jacked the passenger seat back before getting in and slamming the door. Blue light flashing, they sped off.

Beth's first sensation as she slowly regained consciousness was a rocking motion. Was she on a ship? She felt hands on her, moving over her. Groggy still, she swayed in a dream-like state until she heard the fabric of her blouse rip. Then fingers reached inside her bra and tugged on it until the straps broke. She shook her head, fighting off the effects of the blow. What was it? Where was she? Then she became aware of Ian's hard breathing as he reached under her skirt, searching for the top of her panties.

"No! Stop it, damn you."

"Now, don't get so excited, my dear." He was using that hatefully reasonable tone a parent uses with a child. "I only have to make this look like a rape. It's not to my taste, you know. You see, when they find you at the base of the cliff, it has to look as though Peter tried to assault you. You, of course, had to shoot him before he could have his way with you. But he didn't die until he pushed you off the cliff. Tragic really, don't you think?"

Ian didn't wait for Beth's answer. Her panties separated and came off, and then she felt Ian's icy fingers on her. Her head still throbbed, but now it was starting to clear. Pretend rape or not, she'd stop him somehow. Even if all she had was her teeth. Her hand swept the ground, feeling for a rock she could dislodge to smash the smile off his grinning face. Suddenly, she felt his weight lift off her, the hand clutching her breast grabbing a last strand of cloth.

As she looked up, she saw two figures struggling in a ghostly light, both grunting and swearing. The sun was now only a slash of red low in the sky, and the combatants were in dark profile. At first she thought her rescuer was Sean. How had he guessed where she had gone? Then, as they turned, she saw Peter's unmistakable profile. He shoved Ian to the ground and stood over him, daring him to stand again.

"So it was you all along, you slimy bastard! I think I'll toss you off the cliff now. We'll see if the fish like you as company." Peter had just grabbed his shirt when Ian spoke.

"Before you do, perhaps you'd like to hear how your mother died that day in Londonderry."

"What? What do you know about that, you bastard?"

Peter hesitated, his fist poised and ready to strike. It was then that Ian pulled a gun out of his pocket. Beth could see the glint of steel from a snub-nosed barrel.

"Peter, watch out! He has a gun"

Her voice was drowned out by the roar of the pistol. Peter clutched his chest and sank to his knees, then with a groan, toppled sideways. Ian struggled to his feet and began dusting himself off. He stood over Peter, breathing hard.

As Ian got his breath back, he said, "Now who'll be food for the fishes, Peter?"

With his hand clutching his chest, Peter tried uselessly to stem the crimson flow. He coughed up blood and spat it out as he tried to speak. "What...do you know...about it?"

"About your mother? A last request, Peter? Why not. You've helped me. But where's the boy?"

Beth's legs felt like jelly. Only her arms seemed able to prop her up as she strained to hear what Peter said.

"After you... Ian," Peter said in a pain-filled voice.

"All right. Let me see. Londonderry. There were a lot of Catholic heads cracked that day in the Bogside. We really thought it would end the damned civil rights marches, you know. Turned out just the opposite. Now, I didn't intend to harm your mother, it just started getting really insane. Stones and bottles flying, clubs swinging. We just got carried away. Before we knew it, we were cracking every skull within reach of our batons."

Peter coughed up more blood. Beth could only look on as she desperately tried to get control of her aching body. She wrapped her slicker over her torn clothing. She looked up at Ian, who seemed to enjoy Peter's pain as much as she was saddened by it.

Ian continued, "I saw her go down, but then the crowd surged forward. I didn't find out until later that she had died. Of course, we covered it up. Couldn't have a bad image for our boys, after all. But you and your IRA buddies put a price on our heads, and I had to get out."

Ian slipped the pistol in his pocket and wiped blood off his face. "Turned out better for me, though, didn't it, Peter? I'll have control of Conor Shipping, and you'll just be a dead murderer. Revenge is sweet."

As Ian laughed indulgently, Beth's stomach tightened. Anger worked its way up from her belly, infusing her limbs with new life, and she went into a crouch.

Unawares, Ian leaned over Peter again. "So, what can you tell me about the boy?"

"Bugger all...is what you...get. Bastard!" Peter's head slumped to the side, a hollow rasping in throat.

Ian reached down and shook him. "Peter! Where's the boy?" When he received no reply, Ian straightened up and looked in her direction. "No matter. His car has to be around here, and I'm sure he brought Julian. But it was very naughty of Peter showing up twenty minutes early for out little tryst. You'd think he didn't trust... "

Ian looked down to find Peter grabbing his leg, his bloody hands staining Ian's trouser leg. As Ian tried to break free of the iron-like grip, he lost his balance and cursed as he fell. Ian's gun slipped out of his pocket as he reached out to break his fall. Momentarily stunned, his face buried in the wet grass, he slowly rolled unto his back. When he did he felt the weapon against the small of his back.

Peter struggled to get up, but only succeeded in getting to his knees. He crawled towards Ian, his eyes murderous black holes. His hands found Ian's neck and began squeezing, thumbs pressing down on his windpipe. Ian tried to pry the fingers off, but Peter's grip was like iron. Unrelenting pressure caused his tongue to protrude from his mouth. His eyes bulged. Desperately, he reached under his body for the gun, but Peter's weight on him prevented his pulling it free. Blood vessels swelled to the bursting point. Ian felt his bladder go.

Then, as Peter shifted position, Ian freed the gun and he pointed the muzzle into Peter's stomach and fired twice. Peter screamed in pain but held his death grip for another few seconds while Ian tried to maneuver the gun for another shot. Then his grip relaxed and he fell across Ian.

Ian had to work hard to roll Peter's dead weight off him. Grunting he finally freed himself and crawled away, gasping for breath. His eyes never left the body, as though it might spring to life once again. Ian's smile was gone. Fear was etched into his face now. He crawled off a few paces and sank on the ground shaking.

Ian didn't react when Beth got up. She walked stiffly over to Peter, who lay face up, staring at the clouds pulling across the darkened sky. Her hands on his chest were sticky.

"Oh, Peter. I'm so sorry."

"Beth?" His voice was a whisper, and she could only guess what energy it took for him to talk. She leaned closer.

"Yes, I'm here."

"Julian's fine. I wanted to... hurt you. But not when... I saw you... in his face. He's in my car...below the cross...Get away! I'm sorry... I wanted you... and I only...hurt you.

"Don't. It's all right. I forgive you Peter. I know you tried to make it right again."

"I can't make... people right. Only machines... only ma..."

When she looked into his eyes again, they were dull, no longer bottomless black pools that saw only pain. She closed his eyes with trembling fingers, and then she sensed that Ian was behind her.

"Leave him be! Time to finish this. Get up!"

Beth was pulled up by her hair. Startled at first, she turned and kicked Ian savagely in the crotch. She watched with satisfaction as he screamed and went to his knees.

"And here I didn't think you had any, you bastard."

From his crouched position, Ian shakily raised the pistol and pointed it at her face.

"Bitch! How would you like your face blown off."

"That would mess up your plans, Ian. How would you explain both of us dying by the same gun?"

Beth turned her back on Ian and started out across the plain, unsure of her directions. Her back tingled as if the killing shot would quickly find her, but there was no shot. She felt life come back into her legs as she broke into a run.

The full moon had come up during her struggles and now ghostly light painted the cliffs. Trying to get her bearings, she hoped it was away from where Peter left his car, and Julian. Her face still hurt from her struggle with Ian, and she made poor time. With trembling hands, she tied her tattered clothing together against the chill and pulled the slicker tighter. Soon she heard running feet. Ian was closing in on her fast.

Where was she? Her sense of direction had deserted her, and she searched in vain for familiar landmarks. She scrambled over rocks and tufts of grass that cast a chiaroscuro pattern in the moonlight until she saw a familiar building. It was O'Brien's Tower.

She was at the same spot as in her dream! Why hadn't she recognized it sooner? The sound of Ian's labored breathing was getting closer. She whirled to find him slowly advancing, not sure of his prey, but daring her to run past him. She feinted to the right, then dodged left and headed for the tower. Its dark shape suddenly loomed in front of her, and she circled it looking for the entrance.

Half-way around, she spotted an even darker spot in the moss-covered stone; a black portal. She ran her hands over the doorway, feeling for a handle. Strong odors assaulted her nostrils, and the door was cold and damp. She found the latch and pulled, hoping it was unlocked, but the door held firm against her furious shaking.

She knew Ian was slowly approaching, and turned to find him only meters away, gloating. She tried another feint, first to the left and then ran to her right, but this time he was ready for her. He stuck out his leg and tripped her. She fell face down, rolled quickly, and had just started to rise when he pushed her back down with a foot to her chest. He stared down at her in triumph.

"Well, this is an even better spot than I picked, Beth. And the blood, that was a nice touch. I'm so glad you dipped your hands in Peter's blood. It will seem so much more realistic, don't you think?"

"You'll never win. Julian will know what a bastard you are. John will see to it someone else is appointed to take care of Julian if I'm dead."

"Oh? John has nowhere else to turn. Julian already knows me and trusts me. You know that, too, from your many visits to see John. I made a special point of entertaining the lad, don't you remember?"

Beth's rage built. She didn't know how to stop him, but she was determined that he wouldn't get away with it. When she tried to get up, he pressed down harder with his foot. The pain in her chest became almost unbearable. Suddenly, he removed his foot and grabbed the hood of her slicker. She reached behind her, trying to break his hold.

A crack of thunder drowned out her curses. The storm moved closer just as Ian began dragging her towards the wind-swept precipice. The howling intensified and the strident call of the gulls was harsh on her ears. Her body was half-dragged, half-lifted over the ground. The slicker made it easy for Ian to tow her, as her fingers reached out desperately for any handholds to stop her forward progress. Her head hanging down, she saw eternity loom closer.

"This is where we part company, my dear, "Ian said.

He began shoving her over the slope of the cliff, and Beth clutched his jacket. "I'll take you with me!"

His fist smashed into the side of her face, and her body went limp. He yanked her hands off him, and slowly rolled her over the edge. Only half conscious, she felt she was falling in slow motion, as if in a dream. The world was filled with space, and no landmarks. How long did it take to fall? Would it be over quickly, her skull crushed on the rocks below before she felt the contact? Or slowly, her body broken, waiting for the incoming tide to take her out to sea?

CHAPTER 41
CLIFFS OF MOHER

In the passenger seat, Sean pressed his right foot hard against the floorboards, willing the car to go faster. Seamus drove expertly through Liscannor, the lights spreading over winding road and grassy culverts. He prayed they would not be too late.

Seamus broke the grim silence. "Where should we start looking?"

"I'm not sure," Sean said. "We can pull off at the top and look down along the cliffs."

"Awful dark even with a full moon." Seamus looked out his window. "And now wrapped in clouds."

Sean's chest burned from fear but he would not relent. Impatiently, he asked, "You have a better idea?"

When Seamus shook his head, Sean pointed out a spot to pull over. The dust was still settling around them when Seamus slapped his forehead.

"Jesus! Why didn't I think of it before?"

Sean looked over at him."What?"

"I just remembered I still have the binoculars I used when we searched for Casey," Seamus said. "I threw them back here to take back to John."

"Are they good for night use?"

"They're infrared." Finally he saw a smile from Seamus. "Perfect for use at night."

"Great. Get them out."

Seamus rummaged in the back seat and pulled out a large set of binoculars that he hung around his neck. They raced out to the highest point above the cliffs. Sean anxiously scanned the horizon for any movement. He didn't expect to see a thing, but then a light winked on, far down the coast, just in from the cliffs. Seamus spotted it too and trained the binoculars on it.

"It's a car," Seamus said. "Must be the dome light. I think I see movement inside."

"Let's get a little closer."

Beth struck the ground hard, and the air slammed out of her lungs in a grunting cry. An umbrella of darkness began to close over her eyes, and she fought to stay conscious. Senses swimming, she was in a falling dream, fearful an eternity would elapse before she touched firm ground again. Was the earth still moving beneath her? And was she sliding slowly and inexorably towards some unseen abyss?

Instinctively, she reached out for something to arrest her slide, her right hand grasping a tuft of hardy grass. She gasped for air, but her lungs would not fill up. Was she still alive, or was she dying now, slowly? Her brain felt as if it was swimming in a pool of mercury, light and free of gravity. Images of her life drifted in and out.

She must be caught in her nightmare on the cliff! She had to wake up. Wake up! She had to get up and go to the loft to see if Julian was all right. At last, air rushed back into her lungs. Daggers of pain shot through her body, the first message that she was still alive.

Tentatively opening her eyes, she saw the sloping top of the cliffs against a clearing star-dotted sky. Moving her head towards her left, she saw black space. Then she focused on a beacon of light in the distance, surrounded by a sprinkling of dimmer ones. Tilting her head down, she began to make out more lights along what she realized was the south coast of Galway Bay. Looking straight ahead, she focused on a rotating beacon of light. That had to be the Fardurris Point lighthouse on the Aran island of Inisheer.

The lights oriented her to the horizon. Finally, she looked down, and saw the phosphorescent glow of the surf pounding the cliff base. She had only fallen three or four meters to another ledge. Her right hand tentatively roamed over the slim ledge and found a solid rock outcropping to anchor herself. As she gently rolled to her right, her outside foot slipped off the ledge, dislodging soil and loose rock.

The sensation of falling made her stomach lurch, but she kept a death grip on her rocky handhold. Then her left foot found better purchase on the ledge to anchor it, stabilizing her position on the slightly sloping ledge. She knew her perch was tenuous, and fought to clear her mind.

She looked up when she heard Ian's curses foul the air. Would he come down to finish the job? She had to move. But to where? The ledge she was on ended only a meter beyond her legs. Tilting her head back and looking behind her, Beth noticed that the ledge went around a curve in the cliff face. Did that lead up, or down the steep face of the cliff?

Fear motivated her to try to get up slowly, but her body wouldn't respond. Her heart slammed against her chest. Was her back broken? If she was paralyzed she was as good as dead. She used her left hand to feel along her lower back and pinched the flesh of her buttock hard. Blessed pain and energy flowed up through her lower body and she was able to rock slowly from side to side.

When she tried again to raise to a sitting position her stomach muscles cramped and burning heat spread down to her lower abdomen. Beth moved her free hand over her stomach, stopping when her fingers touched torn flesh. It wasn't a deep cut, but it seemed to be the source of pain.

Pain or not, she needed to move from this spot before Ian found a way to get down to her. She listened intently, and heard him moving along the cliff, testing one insubstantial foothold after another. Each time, earth broke free, some landing on her. What if he began dropping rocks on her?

"Hold on, dear girl. I'll be down to put you out of your misery."

Ian's derisive promise impelled her to greater effort. More feeling returned to her legs and back. Holding her left hand over her stomach she slowly began to rise. Her stomach muscles tightened and sharp pain almost made her stop. Gritting her teeth and tears filling her eyes, Beth braced herself and slowly rose to a sitting position.

Gasping from the effort she used her left arm to resist the downward pull of her sloping ledge. From her new position, she could see how close she had come to falling off, and she shuddered involuntarily. She had to fight to maintain her position as small stones and dirt trickled down around her. This was not the sort of place she would choose for a picnic.

Above her, there was a cracking sound, and a large rock landed where her head had been only moments ago. It was Ian, trying to knock her off her slim perch. She had no choice but to move to a more protected spot. Feeling along each leg, her free hand came away with streaks of blood, but no broken bones. She slowly turned and went into a crouch, using both hands to feel for handholds in the cliff face.

When she was sure her legs would hold her, she gingerly got to her feet, using the cliff wall to maintain her balance. She stood painfully; her legs were bruised and stung from a dozen small cuts, but the shakiness mercifully subsided. Leaning against the cliff wall she felt around her for any cracks, chinks or exposed roots that offered support.

When she was sure her legs would hold her, she crept along the ledge, her back pressed against the cliff face, jagged outcroppings scrapping her slicker as she went. Her fingers searched for every handhold or protrusion as she made slow progress. A sudden gust of wind tried to tear her off the cliff, clutching at her blouse and flurrying her skirt. She stopped and waited for the wind to subside. Soon the ledge smoothed out to a steep up slope, ending in a sharp drop-off. Which way could she go? The cliff walls looked unassailable in every direction. The only good thing was that Ian could not get down to her

She closed her eyes and concentrated on every sound. If Ian was still there, he was being very quiet. She looked up, fighting vertigo, to see if he appeared, but no movement caught her eye. Was he looking for larger objects to rain down upon her? She rounded the corner of the ledge, balanced precariously, just as she heard the telltale crumbling of loose rock behind her.

Ian looked down, trying to find where Beth had gone. It was just his luck, picking a spot with a ledge to break her fall. How was he going to get her off that ledge? He had been unable to find another rock big enough to do the job. His eyes, adjusted to the light, picked out a dark shape that could only be Beth. He was almost certain there was no safe way down.

Moving around from point to point, he was stymied by the forbidding slide each cliff face presented. He would need a rope to get down if he couldn't locate a large enough object to dislodge her. Swearing under his breath, he started back towards his car. Maybe he could roll a tire down on her, or hit her with the jack.

Time was running out for him and he feared how much O'Neill knew. He'd covered his tracks well, tossing blame on countless lackeys. He surely wasn't under suspicion. Not really. Only this stubborn woman stood between him and salvation for his brothers-in-arms. He thought of last Boxing Day, when he'd flown into Belfast to present his comrades with the money he'd skimmed from a dozen contracts. If they were impressed then, just wait.

The Libyans had been the toughest negotiators, but in the end he'd come up with the perfect deal. Conor Shipping lent legitimacy, and would create new markets for their oil. The tankers would carry weapons in sealed containers, covered by tons of oil. A perfect marriage of the container shipping technology Conor had perfected.

And what weapons! Nothing as puny as an AK-47. No, he would have missiles, laser-sighted machine pistols, bombs. In the not-too-distant future, maybe even a neutron bomb. That would be grand. He'd only have to set off one in Dublin and they'd think better of trying to annex the six counties. They were worried about a loyalist backlash? He'd show them a real backlash, one that would end any republican dreams of conquest in the north.

He looked around, disoriented in the darkness. Where the hell did he leave his car?

The patrol car Inspector O'Neill had commandeered came off the N85 at Lahinch and took the turning that led to the cliffs. Brendan thought about how fortunate it was he'd had Deagan followed. Duncan Cowell and he had been friends when they'd worked together in Belfast. Duncan had been the best tail he'd ever seen; north or south. Now it was paying off when he needed it most.

CHAPTER 42

THE CLIFFS OF MOHER

Sean lost sight of the light as they drove down the coast. One minute it became brighter and larger. The next it was gone.

"Could be they turned off the light," Sean said.

"Or there could be an obstruction since our angle is constantly changing."

Sean spotted an old battlement first and pointed it out to Seamus. They drove slowly past it, leaving the lights off as they got close. Both listened carefully for any abnormal sounds which might be heard above the constantly pounding surf. Nothing.

"Sean! Up ahead. I saw the light again."

Sean barely caught the wink of a light before it went out, but he had a fix on its location. Beyond a low hill, they spotted a good place to leave the car and quietly got out. The smell and sound of the sea filled the air, all else was still.

"I'll bring a torch, but we should use those binoculars," Sean said. "We don't want to announce our presence."

Seamus scanned the field, looking for anomalies. Then, coming on the west wind, they heard the sound of muffled pounding. Moving in that direction, they crested a rise and discovered the phantom car. The weak dome light revealed small feet striking the window and when they were closer; Julian's frightened eyes. He stopped pounding as they approached, cringing until Sean softly called his name.

"Julian, it's me, Sean. Open the door."

"Sean, is that you? I'm tied to the seat. Help!"

"Thank God, he's all right," Sean said, as he came alongside the car. He found the door partially opened. "How did you get the door open, Julian?"

"With my feet. I couldn't get out of the seat, though." He looked frustrated. "The wind kept closing the door on me."

"Who was it, Julian?" Seamus asked, while cutting through Julian's bonds.

"It was Peter, but he didn't hurt me. Not really."

Freed, Julian rushed into Sean's arms. Sean held him tightly, and choked back tears. He had little time for tears now.

"Sean, I knew you'd find me!"

"Where's Beth, lad?"

Julian looked around, disoriented. He clearly did not know, so Sean asked another question. "How many of them are there?"

"I only saw Peter. But he told me he'd be back after meeting someone," Julian said.

Seamus was sweeping the grounds when his glasses paused at the top of a rise. "Sean, why don't you take him back to our van to wait. I'm going to that rise over there. I think I saw something."

Sean looked where Seamus pointed, but saw nothing. "Right. But be careful, and don't go far. I'll be back in a second."

When Sean left Julian at the car, he cautioned him to stay put. "But I want to help you find Mum," he protested. His fingers brushed Julian's face. "It's too dangerous son, but we'll bring her back to you safe and sound." Julian seemed to beam at Sean calling him son and he made what he hoped was an encouraging smile.

Then he made his way back to where he had left Seamus. He wanted to use the torch, but feared giving away his position. The rain began lightly again, and visibility worsened. What if he took a wrong turn? Or blundered into Peter's path, and himself without a poker? He saw the dim outline of O'Brien's Tower off to his left, but little else as he headed north.

He started up a rise, his shoes providing little traction on the wet grass. He hoped he was following his friend's trail. Why had he let Seamus go out there alone? He had only thought about getting Julian to safety. Swearing under his breath, he topped the rise and looked around him. Nothing, until a hand reached out and grabbed his leg.

"Keep down," Seamus whispered. "You want them to spot you up here?"

"Jesus, don't scare me like that." Sean squatted down next to Seamus, who was kneeling over someone. The thought that it might be Beth caused his heart to stop for a moment. Looking closer, he could see that the figure was too large.

"Who is it?"

"It's Peter," Seamus said. "He's dead. Shot a number of times. It looks like he put up quite a fight, though, poor bastard."

Seamus looked from the body to him. "It seems we were both wrong about his role," Sean said.

"Yes," Seamus said, as he wiped the rain from his beard. "Come on, the real bastard is still in front of us.

They raced along the ground, keeping low, their breath coming in gasps. Up ahead, the dim shape of O'Brien's tower served as a reference point. They headed directly for it.

Brendan spotted Duncan's truck and directed Jenny to a spot just off the road. Duncan got out of the truck as they approached.

"He got here about twenty minutes ago, Brendan. I couldn't chance getting any closer. There'd be nothing but the sea behind me."

"Good work, Duncan," Brendan said. "Still have the old touch, I see."

"Thanks. I lost him for a while outside Ennis. Must have slipped onto a back road. But he came back down the road and I picked him up again. He seemed to be alone." Duncan paused for a moment and looked hard at Jenny. "I also saw a van heading over that rise farther out. Too far to identify who was in it. There could be a few people attending this party. Is this all you've got?" He nodded towards Jenny.

"I'm plenty," Jenny said.

"She is that, Duncan. How many in the other car?"

"At least two."

Brendan sighed, then went to the boot and found two 9mm Berettas that he had hoped Pat still kept in his car. He gave one to Jenny. She ejected the magazine and checked the load. "An extended magazine, 15 load, very nice." She hefted the weapon while Duncan looked on dubiously.

Brendan checked his as well before pocketing the gun. To Duncan, he said, "This could get very dangerous. Maybe you should stay here."

"Not with the bastard you're tracking," Duncan said. "From what you've told me, his money has already caused blood to flow in the six counties. I brought my shotgun."

"Duncan, I appreciate you want to help, but I need you here to direct the police when they arrive." Seeing his friend's disappointment he added," I should also mention that I was alerted that Sean Carey and Seamus Dunoon were headed this way. That could have been them you spotted earlier. We don't want to be shooting civilians."

"Should we split up, Inspector?" Jenny looked from one man to the other. "There's still a lot of terrain to cover on the cliffs. Maybe we should come in from both sides."

"I agree," Brendan said. "Take your wireless and head down the coast. Go about three kilometers. Then walk back here, but stay low. If I encounter Williams or Deagan first, I'll call on the wireless and wait for you to get there. I want you to do the same."

"What about the van? What if it's more of Williams' men?"

"I don't know," Brendan said. "Williams could have backup, but I think he's doing this solo. Just be ready in any case."

Ian was on his way back to Beth, using the tower as a guide.

THE BURREN WEEPS

He thought he had heard a car stop close by, and moved cautiously. Just as he came into view of the tower, he spotted two tall figures outlined against the cliff. Beth had told someone where she was going! Lying bitch! He set down the heavy jack and the tool box. Unable to find a long enough rope, he had no recourse but to use the jack or the heavy box. Now, things were getting more complicated.

Sean felt the chill in his bones even though the rain had stopped. His shoes leaked buckets. He was sure the squishing sounds they made could be heard for miles. The wind howled angrily in his ears. He could almost believe it was the voice of a banshee wailing a warning: Beware!

"I can't see much in this weather," Seamus said over the voice of the sea pressing against the cliff's base. "Could we have missed her?"

"Somehow, I think this is the spot," Sean replied. But where is... Did you hear something?"

They both listened, trying to pick out other sounds over the whistle and roar of the storm.

"Sean, is th.... ou?" The sound was whipped around by the wind, and lost in its swirling gusts.

"I did hear it," Sean shouted. "Beth! Beth! Where are you?"

"Down here!" The voice was weak and strained.

Good God is she clinging to the cliff! Stoked by fear he ran to the precipice and looked down, sweeping left and right. At first, he saw nothing. Then when Beth spoke again, he saw her, less than four meters below, on a ledge that looked impossibly narrow. How did she manage to hold on in this storm?

"Beth, we're here. We'll get you out of there. Just hold on!"

"Watch out for...Will...s. He's up...." The wind whipped part of her words away, but Sean couldn't miss the sob that followed it.

"What?" Sean swore at the wind. What was she saying?

"Williams!" The word rose up from the ledge before the wind

buffeted it and tore it away.

"Seamus, I think she means Williams, the lawyer. My God, he must be the killer!"

"Williams, of course! He may still be around here, then."

The two looked back towards the tower. The storm had diminished, and the cloud-wreathed moon traced pearly fingers on its stones. Sean imagined a hundred ghostly men lying in wait behind the tower. "Seamus, do you remember if there was any rope in the van?"

Seamus pondered the question before sadly shaking his head. "There was a pile of stuff in the back, but I don't recall any rope." He rubbed his beard. "But it's worth a try as long as Beth can hang on down there."

"All right, but be careful. Stay low."

"You present me with quite a challenge, Sean. I haven't been low since I was two."

Sean managed a half smile before Seamus disappeared in the gloom. He went back to cliff face and then looked down, searching for Beth. Her face, pale white in the moonlight, seemed to hover in space, just out of reach.

Brendan used the tower as a reference point. Gun drawn, he was close when he saw a figure near the cliff's edge. The man fit Williams' description, but he had to be sure. His wireless squawked at him and he turned the volume down, praying the sound hadn't carried.

"Inspector, where are you?" It was Jenny's voice.

"I'm almost at the tower," he whispered. "There's a man close by. Could be Williams." Brendan released the transmit key and put the radio to his ear.

"We found a van, engine still warm, no one inside." There was static for a moment, and then Jenny's excited voice came back on. "Someone is coming this way. Christ, he's big!"

"Don't shoot until you're sure who it is." Then there was more static.

"Well, well. Isn't this a pretty picture," Ian said.

Sean didn't hear Ian until he was almost on top of him.

"This is how you kill two birds with one stone," Ian said. "And you're the stone, Carey. Over you go!" Ian lunged at him.

Sean felt himself beginning to roll over the precipice and braced himself with one arm while grabbing onto Ian's leg with the other. When he was balanced, he scissored his legs around Ian's, and twisted his legs until Ian fell backwards. They rolled along the cliff, alternately pinning each other to the ground. Sean felt Ian reaching for something in his pocket and held onto his arm.

"Sean! What's happening?" Beth's voice held terror.

When Ian shifted position, Sean found an opening, and brought his knee up sharply into Ian's chest, knocking the wind out of him. Then, using both hands, he yanked hard on Ian's arm, just as he was pulling the pistol out of his pocket. The weapon spun out of Ian's hand landing in the grass.

On their knees, they grappled over it but Ian was closer and snatched it up. Just as Ian was bringing the pistol around Sean seized his gun hand in a vise-like grip. The gun neutralized he pulled Ian toward him and struck a glancing blow to the jaw, snapping his head back. Then he twisted Ian's arm until he cried out in pain and dropped the gun once again. This time Sean kicked the gun and it landed three meters away.

While Sean was off-balanced Ian surprised him with a head butt coming up under his jaw. His head snapped back and he lost his footing and his hold on Williams. He shook his head to clear while Ian ran for his pistol, slipping on the sodden earth. Sean crouched, ready to sprint after him when he felt a powerful hand on his shoulder. I'm dead, he thought. He watched numbly as Ian picked up the gun, and then glanced to his left, wondering from which direction the killing shot would come.

"Drop it, Williams!"

The inspector, half in a crouch, removed his hand from Sean's shoulder to hold his gun in a two-handed grip. He was bringing the weapon up to train on Sean's assailant when Ian ducked and ran for the tower. Brendan fired a warning shot, kicking up earth in front of Ian, who, heedless, ran on. Brendan brought his gun up and fired just before Ian made it to the tower. Brendan wasn't sure he'd hit the man before he half fell, half dived behind the stone building.

Jenny took in a ragged breath and let it out before lowering her weapon. "Seamus, you gave me a fright!"

"That was nothing compared with staring down the barrel of your gun," Seamus said.

"I'm sorry, Professor. I couldn't be sure if you were friend or foe."

Seamus quickly filled Jenny in on the situation. When he got to the part about Julian, Jenny stopped him.

"He wasn't in the van!"

Seamus groaned. "We have to find him. That maniac is still out there, somewhere."

They all heard the two shots. Jenny hit the button on her unit. "Inspector? What happened? Are you alright?"

"I think I winged him. He's behind O'Brien's tower. Carey is here, and Mrs. Conor is stuck on a ledge. We need to get her out. She's weakening fast. I've got the tower covered. Come quick!"

Seamus was already looking for rope in the van and came up empty. Someone else was coming up fast and Jenny spun, her gun trained on the figure. "Duncan, I told you to stay at the visitor center."

"I heard gunshots and came anyway."

Seamus came back from behind the van. "Duncan, we found Julian and put him in the van, but he's not here. See if you can locate him."

"And see if you can follow orders better while I assist the inspector!" Jenny rolled her eyes before heading up the hill.

Seamus cautiously followed her after placing the binoculars in Duncan's hand.

Beth could only guess at what was happening above her. When she saw Sean pushed partly over the edge, she instinctively moved to catch him if he fell. She ignored her brain's message, which screamed at her that they would both plunge to their deaths. She be damned if she'd lose the man she wanted to spend the rest of her life with.

As she edged along the narrowing ledge, her next footfall ended in space. She held to her slim hold, a cry escaping her lips. How much longer? How much more could she endure? She took one step back so both feet were firmly on the ledge, and looked up to see where he was. She heard their struggles and looked desperately for a place to climb. The moonlight revealed few places of purchase, but she had to try. She stripped out of her slicker, which kept bellowing with wind and holding her back. She watched it float on the wind like a gull.

Then Beth thought she heard someone cry out. Then, as she placed her first foot into a split in the rock, she heard gunshots.

She slowly and painfully pulled herself up. Her knees were raked by the rocky surface, but she ignored it. She rested a minute before taking her next step. Her free foot probed the cliff, feeling for another opening to anchor herself.

"Beth!"

She looked up for the last time, hoping to see his face, and was startled when she did see it. His arms reached out for her. But how was that possible?

Above her Seamus grunted while holding Sean's ankles. He still wondered if this would work, but he knew he could take Sean's weight and Beth's for a while. His grip was firm on Sean's bare ankles; flesh against flesh. His shoulders ached, feeling the strain. His arms were over the precipice and Sean dangled in space, so near to Beth, but she would need to reach up to him.

"Sean, pull yourself up, you'll be killed, too!" She had only to reach up and he'd grab her hands, but how could he pull her up? This was insane. Then a strong gust of wind threatened to push her off the cliff face and she raised her arms and closed her eyes. Then she felt strong hands grab her wrists and her body swayed like a pendulum in the fierce wind.

"Let me go, Sean. We can't both die."

Through gritted teeth Sean said, "You are my life, Beth. I'll never let you go now!" She looked into his eyes and knew the truth of that. So be it.

"We're pulling you up!"

She felt herself lifted slowly up and used her feet to gain purchase and ease some of her weight. The sounds of two grunting men told her they were giving it all they had. She sobbed put kept finding footholds as she was slowly leveraged up.

Seamus's arms were like lead weights, but his grip was still firm. He slowly rocked his body backwards until he was clear of the ledge and Sean's feet were visible. Another heave and Sean's legs came over the sloping ledge.

Seamus breathed hard from the effort, but now he could raise half way up and pull steadily until it was Sean's arms over the side holding onto Beth. "Hold on, Beth we've almost got you," he shouted as encouragement.

Beth did not look down, only up at Sean. He held her forearms and she was able to grasp his as well. Miraculously she found herself pulled up until her head cleared the cliff and her body was dragged on the grassy slope. All three of them gasped and struggled for breath before Sean took her into his arms and she felt his hot tears on her face.

She felt his arms around her, his lips on her cheek, his words in her ear. Now she could give vent to her own tears. He pulled her away from the edge, and took her in his arms. Her body shook with the release of tension. Her muscles burned as Sean held her tight, telling her over and over again that he loved her, and that everything was all right. The knowledge slowly worked its way past the layers of control she had used to survive. She was safe!

Brendan had waited until Beth was clear before attempting to take on Williams. He had held on to Seamus' legs until the man was able to leverage himself up. But he was still amazed at the power of the man. Jenny had covered their rescue, sweeping her gun back and forth restlessly.

Even if Williams was wounded he was still very dangerous and could be hiding with a gun in his hand. He made sure all three of them were safe before going after Williams.

"Jenny, you move to the right, I'm circling to the left." Brendan had not yet taken up his position when Williams came out from behind the tower, holding a gun in one hand, and a squirming Julian in the other.

"Just stay where you are! I want a car and safe passage, or the boy dies," Ian screamed at them.

Brendan knew that sound. A desperate man who would do anything. He had to try to reason with him. He looked at Julian, and saw the shattered body of the MPs son in Belfast. No, he would not let it happen here. "Take it easy, Williams. We can work this out."

He watched the man nervously swing his gun from him to Jenny. From the corner of his eye, he estimated that she had a clean shot at him. The child was a poor shield. His struggles were also making Williams a moving target. How good a shot was she?

Brendan noticed the blood on Ian's right shoulder, the one that held the gun. He had to use his good arm to control the boy. He would not be able to aim and fire effectively. Did Jenny notice?

Suddenly the squirming boy broke free, and rolled away. A

gun fired twice. Two slugs tore into Ian as he tried to bring the gun around. He staggered back, a look of supreme surprise on his face. He turned, as if to escape, and pitched face first off the cliff. Brendan got to the edge in time to see the body strike the jagged rocks, the arms and legs at impossible angles. A wave came in, lifting Ian's lifeless body before relinquishing it. Jenny came up beside Brendan and helped him to his feet. "That was close enough, Jenny."

Beth was still weak but she opened her arms and her son ran into them. They hugged and cried while Sean and Seamus leaned over them protectively. Through her tears, she saw Duncan move into view, then Inspector O'Neill and Constable Magruder.

Sean said, "How badly are you hurt?"

Beth took a deep breath, and exhaled in shaky jerks.

"Oh, just a few dings," Beth said. "No worse than a nasty bike crash, that's all. How did you all get here?"

"We'll fill you in later," Sean said. "God, I thought I'd lost you. "

"Not any more, Sean." Beth embraced Sean again as he gently lifted her up. She touched Seamus on the cheek, knowing the moisture her fingers felt wasn't from the rain. She stood tall, with her two men flanking her and her son pressed close, clutching the front of her skirt. She had persevered and, despite the ache of her body; she felt better than she had in a long time, a very long time.

Brendan came over to her and held her offered hand, clearly delighted to see her safe. "Thank the good Lord you're safe. And in good hands."

"Thank you, Inspector. And Jenny, Duncan. I can't tell you how much."

"You and the boy are safe," Brendan said. "That's thanks enough."

Brendan shook hands with Duncan. He watched him catch up with the rest of the troupe, strolling arm in arm off the Cliffs of Moher.

"Good shooting, Jenny," Brendan said. "How do you feel?"

She had tears in her eyes as she looked out to sea, and then blinked them away as she turned to Brendan.

"I've never... had to kill anyone, Inspector." She wrapped her hands around her stomach and looked up to Brendan expectantly.

"It's hard. It will be for a while. It's healthy to feel pain in your gut. Killing should always be our last choice. Healing is better. D'ye need some of that, Jenny?"

"Yes."

"Then come here," he said. He opened his arms, and she went into them.

"I think my sister was right. You have become a damn fine officer. You even managed to not call me Uncle Brendan."

"It wasn't easy," she said. After all, you are my favorite uncle."

Down the hill the sound of sirens signaled the arrival of the Garda. The sirens became louder as they climbed the hill and soon blue lights and headlamps illuminated the scene. As doors opened and men shouted, Brendan turned to Jenny.

"Let's get out of here, Jenny. Regis will be worried sick until he hears from us."

Arm in arm, they laughed into the teeth of the wind. It swept the sound down to cavort along the cliffs. And the sea enfolded the ebullient sound to its breast.

THE END

THE BURREN WEEPS

BY JIM HAMMOND

The evening rain falls heavy on barren plain
The parched earth opens its many mouths
To lap hungrily 'til no drop remain
Unquenched, the Burren thirsts for more

The incessant sea crowds cliffs of dissolution
And forages up each earthen break
Seeking wounds to salve with liquid absolution
But sea returns to sea unclaimed

Now man revisits each treeless spot
Where bounty once was his
And raises his abode on a cheerless plot
And covers the land in blood

After touching so much coiled hate,
Cross blasted plain and rolling hillock,
With no end the blindness to his fate
From its shriven bowels, the Burren weeps

If men see the waste of paths ill-trod
Of brother's hand lifted 'gainst his kin
And return the Burren's tears chill-shod
It will taste long of his remorse

For the sea skirts wide Eire's sad shore
While the Burren faithfully waits,
For the tears to reach its tender core
And still its weeping heart.

ACKNOWLEGMENTS

A novel like this is written in solidarity with the land that has captivated me for most of my life. Writers write alone, but we are never truly alone in our imaginations as we write. This seed of the idea for this novel came in the 1990s, when I toured Ireland on bicycle several times—once, across the entire island from Shannon Airport to Rosslare Harbor in County Wexford. And indeed the road did rise to meet me with the wind always at my back. So many people I met, so many stories told in such rich language I had no choice but to write it down.

I would like to thank several people specifically: To Carolyn Flynn my bonny editor, who for some reason stuck with me even when I was late with a reply, and without whom this novel might never have seen the light of day. To my first editor Ms. McPhee for helping with Irish terms and slogans of my original draft. To all the Irish I met on the way who touched my life in countless ways and to the Emerald Isle that took me to her very heart.

And finally, thank you to Barbara Kline-Hammond, who accompanied me on many of my Irish treks and for being my support throughout. This book is for you.

THE PHOENIX SOCIETY

BY JIM HAMMOND

Jason Richards is a gifted research chemist seeking a cure for Alzheimer's disease. His first mistake is isolating himself from his wife and brother in his quest. His second, injecting himself with his experimental drug that almost kills him. Almost. When

he wakes up on an operating table with an unknown substance pumping into his arm he has to ask himself if he really is alive. Welcome to the Phoenix Society, a crematorium with a difference. Their plans for Jason don't include incinerating him, but transforming him into a mindless creature from whom they can harvest organs. The Society's head, Dr. Curt Wagner, is a gifted but unscrupulous doctor who may have a cure for organ rejection, the bane of all organ transplant operations, but is the cost too high? The Society is unaware that their drug cocktail, mixed with Jason's own experimental drug results in an entirely new kind of human being; one that will prove hard to kill. To make matters worse, one of the doctor's transplant patients goes berserk and kills several people. The doctor soon finds Lieutenant Brinkley, a tenacious detective from San Francisco, on his trail, even as Jason escapes the crematorium. Jason must come to grips with what he has become, and elude the Society's security forces, as well as a phantom presence that shadows his every move. As the bodies stack up, Jason becomes a suspect and must elude the police. The odds become higher when Dr. Wagner kidnaps his wife. Jason must return to the crematorium to confront the evil doctor, save his wife, and restore his sanity.

Made in the USA
Monee, IL
26 June 2021

72348807R10225